THE CHRONICLES: DARK HORIZONS

EMMA LOVE

The Chronicles: Dark Horizons

Copyright © 2019 by Emma Love

All rights reserved.

Cover design by Evan Cakamurenssen

Editing, proofreading, and formatting by Three Point Author Services

This book is dedicated to Grandma Suzy for teaching me how to reach for the stars.

PROLOGUE

October 11

Entry #1

I think around a year ago I lost my memories. I don't know how I can do the things I can do. I don't even know my own birth name. All I've known is how to move from one place to another in a hurry because of the people chasing me.

Whoever is reading this journal, keep in mind I have no clue where I came from, who the hell I was, or why I'm here. I only know I can read, write, and fight. Everything else I do turns into a mess if I touch it. I'm not sure why, but it does.

One day I hope I can remember why I make a mess of things. For now though, I can only search for the truth of my past.

In order to find the truth, I have to keep things straight, which is where the journal comes into play. My journal is dedicated to making sense of everything my friends and I experience; it will tell you who to trust and who to hate. It will explore the past and explain who I am. Please take time to read each entry. I will not leave out a single detail. I promise there are no lies in this writing. And I never break my promises.

I promised my friends we would find out what happened to us, together. I've trusted them for a long time. They can do what I can do, and I know they're good people because…well, I'm always right about people. It's something I'm able to do whether I like it or not.

My friends' names are self-given: Hawk, Strike, and Viper.

They are my family. Not by blood, but by life. I'm not sure what happened to my blood family. Honestly, they're probably dead anyway. But I'm happy with the family I've built. They make everything worth it, and I'll do anything to make sure they'll never get hurt again. That's why I need the truth. The issue is that I can't figure out *how* to find the truth. Hopefully something changes soon, but for some reason, it's like trying to grab onto smoke. I can smell it, but not grasp it.

Before I go on too much, I should tell you what I call myself. I don't want to forget. I have given myself the name of…

ONE

THE LAST APPLE

STORM

I trace out the next letter, but the ink fails me; nothing is marked. Sighing, I toss the hollow pen behind me. I put down my journal and sit in the static of my shared room.

The only source of light is a sliver of window above me that reflects the constant motion of vehicles and feet moving about the street. Light beams onto the other bodies in the room, who are asleep on their own mats. The faint drowsy breaths of my roommates, the occasional scuffle of feet, and the creaking of the wind pushing the structure above whistle in my ears. I take in a deep breath, trying to block out the fumes of the city, and exhale. The warmth of my breath appears in the crisp air. I throw off my blanket and lay it on Hawk. The only thing visible on her is a wavy bundle of blonde hair.

I stand from the mat on the floor. I'm brushing the dust-bunnies from my shorts as I tiptoe and zigzag to avoid waking the others. I hop over Viper into a narrow hallway that leads to a sagging staircase. As I trek up the stairs, my bare feet become colder with each step on the molding wood. Grazing my hand across the rough bricks, I clamber up the spiraling staircase, away from the basement. The stairway continues to spiral up to the second floor and another hallway dripping with shadows greets me. The light coming from the kitchen beckons me. I'm filled with relief when I reach the hazy room. I approach the boarded windows and stand close to the slits of sunlight, attempting to avoid the frozen air by embracing the morning rays.

The kitchen is dimly lit due to the boarded-up windows. It contains a musty table with two rusting chairs. On one of the chairs is a wilting cardboard box that holds all the food. The room is made up of eroding red bricks and a rough concrete floor stained by unknown causes. Scattered around the room are the remains of pictures, cloth, and various scraps. This room and the basement are the only safe parts of the building. Everywhere else is too unstable to walk on. The house is two stories, but the second floor is filled with dangerous paths on paper-thin floors.

My stomach growls. My moment in the sun comes to an end as I peek into the box on the chair. A perfect maroon apple surrounded by dust shines back at me. My stomach howls, begging for the fruit as I snatch the apple from its resting place. I bring it up to my lips.

"Boo!"

I scream and my fingers release their grip on the apple to cover my mouth. My cheeks start to burn.

"Strike!" I turn to her. "Don't do that! You probably woke up the whole neighborhood!"

"I didn't, but your scream did," Strike says and picks up my apple from the floor. "Looks like someone is a bit grumpy today."

She grabs a part of her maroon shirt and brushes it off. When she holds up the apple, the broken light from the windows paints her grey eyes, transforming the irises into a glimmering silver. She bats her eyelashes at me in an attempt to break my frown. I grin and pluck the apple out of her hands, taking the first bite out of it. I hop up onto the table behind me as Strike opens the box and frowns. My eyes widen.

Shit. I took the last piece of food we had.

"So, uh, how'd you sleep?" I ask.

Strike yawns. "Pretty good."

"Pretty good, huh? You mean nightmarish?" I bite into the apple. "I heard you mumbling and rolling around last night."

Strike closes the rotten box. She turns her head to me and flips her hair, the fading golden strands catch in the sun. The light creates a white outline around her head all the way down to her shoulders, but the shadows consume her features.

"It's not like you didn't do the same."

She straightens while looking around with her hands on her hips. I tense up.

"Well, at least you're not dreaming about dead...dead...flowers," I reply. "Honestly, it can't get any worse than that."

"Did you seriously just compare my nightmares with dead flowers?"

"I was just givin' you a more positive take."

"Yeah, sure," Strike pauses in thought. "Hey."

I flinch. "Yeah..."

"Did you just ta—"

Strike is cut off by a scream. "*Viperrr!*"

Fast footsteps sound from the hallway. Viper sprints in while cackling. Hawk stomps in after her, in a cloud of grainy white powder. It has completely caked her hair, turning it into a clumpy nest, and is stuck between the grey feathers of her wings.

"She botched the hair brush!"

Viper goes into a laughing fit. I hold my hand up to my mouth.

"This isn't funny!"

"It's the funniest thing I've seen in months!" Viper exclaims.

Hawk shoots Viper a glare. Her blue eyes ignite as if an inferno has erupted inside her small frame.

"I'm gonna kill you!"

Hawk lunges at Viper. With a toothy grin, Viper steps to the side. Hawk slams her head into the wall next to Strike and me. The building shakes as Viper backs up to my other side. She roars with laughter.

"This is payback for takin' my puddin'!" Viper exclaims.

"Does it look like I care about your stupid pudding? I was hungry! It was the only thing we had that day!" Hawk charges Viper again.

I jump between the two. Hawk screeches to a stop. I take a large bite of my apple.

"How about we just calm down?" I say. "So I don't have to bury Viper tonight."

"I swear, Storm, you better not give me some speech about bad karma or voodoo horse-shit you learned at your job," Hawk says.

I raise my brows. "Sorry that I want a quiet morning for once. Besides, it's stupid to kill someone this early over hair or food. So, how about Viper helps Hawk clean whatever that is in her hair out, and Hawk doesn't kill Viper?"

Hawk breathes in. "What about the brush?"

"Viper will get us a new one."

"Qué? No!"

I turn to Viper and try to contain my smile. "We're all girls with long hair. We gotta brush our hair too."

"First, she gets me a new puddin'." Viper crosses her arms, trying to contain a grin.

"Okay, I see what's happening here. I'm gonna go out today after work for more food. I'll get your stupid pudding, *Viper*, and then I'll wrestle up another precious brush, *Hawk*. Everyone happy?" I ask, looking between the two.

"No." Hawk stomps out of the room.

"Please go help her, V."

"That was a good one, right?" Viper giggles.

"Yeah, it was."

"I heard that!" Hawk shouts, from down the hall.

Viper laughs and disappears into the hallway. I look to Strike, but she only shakes her head at me.

"What?"

"You took that last piece of food without sharing, didn't you?" Strike asks.

I sigh. "Yeah. Yeah, I did."

"Well." Strike grabs the apple. "Good luck—you'll need it today, Goldie." She disappears into the narrow hallway.

Frowning, I walk to where the cracks between the boards are widest. As I lean against the wall, the striped sunlight drapes over my face. I watch the slow movements of people walking along the cold streets and sidewalks. An unlimited number of minds, with unknown motivations, swell around the city blocks and alleyways. I can only guess what each person has in mind, but I never know whether I should fight or fly, at first glance.

Shaking off the thoughts, I wander down the hall and then down the stairs into my room. The bickering between Viper and Hawk echoes from the basement's murky second hall as they try to wash out the white concoction. Strike leans against the wall across from them and watches in a quiet laughter. I slip into my room as I try to figure out how the hell I'm going to afford pudding.

When I walk in, an old mirror that's leaning against the wall glints in the low light. A deep crack splits it in half. One side reflects and the other is obscured by the shadows. Staring at the sliced reflection, I can't help but wonder what happened to that mirror. We found it when we got here but haven't touched it since.

Breaking my gaze from the mirror, I step over my mat and bend to open the box that holds my clothes. A grey long sleeve and a pair of black jeans are layered over my shorts. My dark wings slide through the slits in the shirt. I fold them tightly against my body before putting on a black parka to help conceal them. Rummaging through the jacket pockets, I find a hair tie and swing my hair up into a pony-tail. My feet slip into a pair of muddy, purple boots and I slide a pair of cracked sunglasses over my eyes. A discarded pen catches my eye when I reach for my backpack, so I toss it in before I head upstairs.

The thought that I need to get more ink crosses my mind. That same thought reminds me I need to get gloves for everyone after some asshole stole our last collection. My coworkers mentioned they heard winter was going to be a biter this year. So, I guess that also means I need to scrap for blankets and jackets, along with regular food and water, for when those winter months come.

Turning right past the kitchen, I approach the three boarded windows in the next room. Kicking the bottom board out into the alleyway below allows me to crawl through the narrow gap and leap out onto the pavement. Grunting with effort, I reposition the loose board back in the hole, aka our door, and head out to leave Bricktown.

A scuttle of dead leaves travels with the wind along the sidewalk. The unaligned bushes have all died; they are now bundles of ratty branches. As I take in a breath, the sting of the autumn air cools my senses. My fingers tighten from the cold. I raise my hood over my head and stick my hands deep in my pockets. Bricks surrounding the streets dwindle away, morphing into smooth concrete that imprisons the ground all the way to the skyline. The buildings block out the sunlight, and I dwell among their crowded shadows. The crowds are hustling through their own lives, thankfully unaware of my presence.

At first glance, I look like any other person. But, a closer look underneath my sunglasses and jacket would say otherwise. The people who know that they're human would run or attack at the sight of me. At the sight of my eyes, teeth, and scars. I know why they do it now; they think I'm a monster. I'm not a monster, but I know I'm not entirely human, either. I don't really know what I am. But at least I know how to blend in.

Ahead of me is the old tower where my boss keeps her business. She insists she's a *businesswoman of the natural illusions*, but I know she's a con woman. I honestly don't care what she is, as long as I'm paid.

I shoulder past a bustle of people and stop at an intersection, waiting for the signal to walk again. My senses expand. Burning gasoline, scabbing manure, and moist litter swell in the breeze. There is a mismatch of constant motion ranging from a bicycle, the occasional vehicle, and horse-pulled carriages. As always, there's the shouting and the beeping of cars and the whinnying of each horse. My head throbs as I swivel it to the right, but the piercing pitches prevent me from hearing any tiny sounds. I have to rely on my eyes to pick out any officers in the crowd. They are always sniffing the air for anything out of the ordinary. Once they're onto my scent, the pack appears. If that happens, my only hope is to outrun them.

The crosswalk light goes green, but I wait thirty seconds for the stragglers who tried to make the light. I walk across the street along with a group of indifferent people, careful to stay on the outside near the carriages. I'll gladly take the terrible smell of horse breath rather than the morning-breath of strangers.

The old tower looms, blocking out part of the sun. Its top looks as if someone took a bite out of the side. I've heard from my coworkers that its damage was caused by the war years ago, but somehow it never fell. It has been abandoned for longer than anyone remembers. Its only function now is to exist as a reminder of the past.

My eyes scan down the tower to its narrow base. Even from this distance of about two blocks away, I can sense the boss will get a crowd today. Hopefully, I won't have to stick around for too long. Work is tedious but has its perks—mainly getting paid to run errands and pick pockets. And if I do quick work, I get more money. Somehow, my performance has been above average lately. It should be enough to get what everyone needs today, if I 'borrow' a few things.

I twist through another crowd mesmerized by phone calls and reading tablets. Each person wears grey or black trench coats. White is a rarity, like any other bright color. The crowd's greyness spreads like ink, even making the red stop lights dull.

I'll never understand why these people work six days a week. Hell, I can only manage four without keeling over. I couldn't care less about the work or money; the only reason I need either is to buy food. Some days I couldn't care less about the food, even though I need it to survive, because sometimes I couldn't care less about—

I fall to the concrete with a thud. A groan escapes my throat. Waves of people drown me, and I struggle to catch my breath from the jolt of the fall.

A shadow leans over me with an outstretched hand.

"Sorry, miss!"

They haul me up and the shadows fall away. Light blue eyes, dark brows, tailored black hair, and a relaxed smile appear.

"Don't worry about it," I say.

He's well-built and towers above me in his sky-blue tracksuit and white tennis shoes.

"I'm really sorry, again. I got distracted there. I was trying to figure out who you did your hair."

"My hair?"

He points at my head. "Yeah, the grey streak there. I've never seen someone pull that off before. It looks really good!"

"Thanks." I start walking past him. "Well...have a good day."

"I can walk with you, if you want."

"Sorry, in a rush. Gotta get to work." Jeez, can't this guy see I'm busy?

I'm one turn away from work when I notice the sun has gotten too high—I'm late. I weave through the shopkeepers setting up their tents in rows that stretch as far as the center of the square. My work, also in a tent, is at the base of the faded blue tower.

"Hey! You're late, Niña!" my boss yells from her tent.

"Sorry." I jog faster. "Ran into some traffic."

"That's what they all say." She waves me off and steps out of the tent. "I gotta run and get somethin' real fast. Hold down the fort for me."

Her arm holds the curtain open as she pushes me in. I stumble, trying not to trip on the props scattered about, on my way to the desk that holds my work for the day. Curly, the assistant, sits there counting his tips.

"Hey Curly, what's my lucky numbers for today?" I ask, as I always do, while reaching for the list.

"They're ten, eighteen, and twenty." He puts his hand over the list. "And, hold on a sec."

I raise a brow. "What is it now?"

"Um...will you please wait and lace up Boss's corset? Help her with the hard to reach places?"

"Why can't you?"

He runs his fingers through his thick hair. "I don't know how."

"Don't know how! Curly, you've been the assistant for how many years now?"

Curly mutters something before placing the money down. He scratches the black scrub growing on his face. As he slowly stands, he stares down at me with his doe eyes.

"And where's everyone else? I thought we were all supposed to be here today?" I ask.

Curly walks to the back of the tent, unbuttoning his white shirt. "Boss said they all went to the base. Some were hoping to become trainees or guards. Apparently, the forces are giving out a pretty good deal," he explains. "I'm surprised you didn't go with them. Boss was worried we wouldn't have anyone left."

"I'm not ever gonna go near that base."

"I told Boss that. I said if you weren't ever gonna tell us your real name, why the heck would you go to the base?" He snickers.

"What about you? Fixin' to join? Get some hair on your chest?"

"Me? No, I'm...I'm just trying to learn how to be like Boss. But anyway, I have a job for you." He takes off his button-up, revealing a white tank top underneath. "I need you to get me something. In return, I'll get anything you want."

I groan. "Not this again. I already got you that crystal ball thing."

"Please! I need you to get me this. It'll be the last thing, I swear."

"I don't know. Since everyone isn't here, I'll be doing three times the work." My brain is already working through a new plan. Maybe I can get him to get me the hard things like the pudding, the blankets, the hairbrush, or the matches.

"Listen, I can cover for you. I can get what is on Boss's list easily. Please, I need this. I'll do anything. It doesn't matter how much. I'll get it for you," Curly says.

"I don't know. Last time you got me something..." I could get a backpack, gloves, and even a pen out of this! I'll only have to get food and water today. I might even get to bed early tonight and with a full stomach.

He clasps his hands together. "Please."

"Fine," I say. "I'll get what you need, if you get everything I want."

I grab a receipt and a pencil from the desk to scribble everything down, before handing it to Curly. He scans it. A look of disgust spreads across his face.

"This is it?"

I narrow my eyes. "I can add to it, if you're up to the challenge."

"No, please. No."

"What's the problem then?"

Curly points to the list. "It's just that...I didn't expect it to be so simple. I thought I was gonna be spending a fortune, but I have all these things at my house." His dark eyes flick up to mine.

"You must be rich then."

Curly laughs. "Not really. Don't worry about it. Can you please get me these things called tarot cards? You can find them at Bub's. He promised to save some for me. They should be there by now. I can get your stuff by noon after my lunch break."

"Yeah, sure. They're called tah—rot cards, right?" I ask.

"Sure," Curly says. "Now, please turn around."

"Why?"

"I'm about to change shirts."

I roll my eyes but comply. "Buddy, I've known you for how many months now?"

"I don't know, four? Doesn't matter, I don't even know your real name."

Ha, I don't either.

"And I'm not a stripper, kiddo," he chuckles.

I cross my arms. "Are you done yet?"

"Not yet, kiddie. That's what I'll call you today, kiddie. Perfect, isn't it?"

I hide my smile. "Beautiful and even better than the one from yesterday. What was it? *Sunnies*? No, that was from a week ago. Yeah, I remember now. It was *Pipsqueak*."

"Please, the name suits you. You're like what? Five foot three, four?" He zips something up. "Finished."

When I turn around, I'm blinded by his tight, glittery costume.

"Ravishing, isn't it?"

"Sure," I snort.

Curly walks over to the desk and begins to search through the drawers.

"Anyway, what's put you in such a good mood today?" I slide up on the desk.

"Well, it's two days until the weekend and—" Curly grabs onto something in the drawer. "—I have a hot date tonight."

"Ew." I scrunch up my nose. "Who has time for that sort of thing?"

"You'll understand when you're older."

Curly puts on a headband, pushing back his thick hair. I pocket the money he leaves for me on the desk, a witty, charming comment on the tip of my tongue.

"Hey! Curly! Hurry up and lace up this damn corset. Show's in ten!" Boss yells.

"Kiddie's got you."

I'd rather die.

"Sorry! Gotta run! Curly's got ya!" I say.

"Hey, wait!"

"See you at noon!" I sprint out of the tent.

I run away and maneuver along the sidewalks toward my destination. Bub's is an antique stand at the end of one of the long rows of useless stands. Ones that sell simple crafts, like birdhouses or wind chimes. Last week, I got the crystal ball from Bub's for Curly. I almost had to pound someone's skull in for it. I got my journal from there too, along with a book I read to the girls.

Curly's forty dollars burns a hole in my pocket. It's so much money for something so useless.

Vendors screech as I pass. The crowds are dwindling, allowing my footsteps to echo between the closely-packed buildings. Further down the row, the booths become sparse and the shouting of bargains lessens due to the lack of prey.

Eventually I find myself in a maze of worn dressers, chipped benches, broken mirrors, and cracked statues. The clutter could be seen from a thousand miles up. Each time I visit, I get lost in the artifacts hidden here. Bub tells me the items are pre-war—valuable to us, but not the dead owners. It's surprising to me that people didn't think they were important in the past. Bub says maybe it's because they thought the present was permanent and inconsequential. I'm not sure if I agree with him.

I weave through the clutter, past a few statues and decaying somethings; Bub is nowhere to be found. A new statue stops me. It's a little girl sitting on a stone bench. She's reading a hefty book, her stone eyes keen on the words. At her side sits a basket of food with an apple on top. She's smiling, frozen in time.

"Interesting piece, ain't it?"

I jump. When I twist around, Bub is smiling at me.

"I found it in one of those abandoned buildings in Bricktown. Pretty neat right?" Bub asks.

"Sure is."

"Anyway, kid, what can I do for you today?" Bub asks.

"Curly sent me for the cards."

"Ah. Came just in time. There's a fellow here wantin' 'em, I told him I had to wait and see if a regular wanted 'em or not." Bub leads me deeper into the maze.

"Thanks. Curly would have been upset."

"That boy is way too sensitive for my likin'," Bub replies. "Needs to man up."

I roll my eyes behind his retreating back. Bub turns a corner, before heading to his seat. I follow as a stranger appears in the haze of forgotten value. He's wearing a black trench coat, hints of black slacks, and a grey button-up. A pair of shiny, oak-colored shoes are visible along with short, brunette hair that looks wavy. I can tell he's around my age, fourteen or fifteen.

He's skimming through a red and white book. Golden letters adorn the cover. When his brown eyes meet my gaze, a chill runs down my spine. Shadowy circles appear under his hollow, graying eyes. A faint scar runs down the right side of his lip. His eyes squint a fraction as his jaw tenses and his breathing changes.

I realize I've been holding my own breath just as he looks away. The brown-eyed boy pulls out a leather wallet from his trench coat. I eye his silver rings as his tan fingers sort through the wallet.

"How much for the cards?" I ask, not taking my gaze off him.

"Forty."

Exactly what I have. Let's bring down the price.

"All Curly gave me was twenty."

"Not good enough. How about you? You got it?"

The stranger places the money on the table. "How much for the book?"

"Ten."

Another slip of money is put down, fifty in total. His gaze moves up his sleeve, checking a diamond-encrusted watch.

"Damn, kid, you got a nice watch for a fifteen-year-old. Where did you manage to get that?" Bub asks.

"I'm fourteen. And I—"

"Listen, Bub, can we barter here?" I cut him off. "Curly has always been loyal to you. So why not give him some slack? You know, maybe just focus on his hard-earned money a little more."

"Sorry kid, no can-do. I got a mouth to feed. Tell Curly he should send more money next time."

I groan as Bub pulls out the deck of cards from a drawer. It's an intricately-designed black box with golden letters. They read: *Tarot*. The stranger examines the box.

I huff. What have I done? I won't get my stuff now. Waving off Bub, with tight lips I march out of the maze.

Footsteps echo behind me. Glancing over my shoulder, I stop when I see the stranger nearing. He fumbles with his purchase upon his approach, his gaze searching for mine. The sunlight hits his eyes, turning them a gold that nearly matches my own.

"It sounds like you need this more than I do. I honestly don't know anything about it. I just saw the box and was interested, but I'm not really into cards." He holds out the fancy black box.

"Thank you."

The stranger nods with a shy smile before he turns around to walk back to the stand. I trace the lines of the box with my index finger. Now I have enough money for food for months. Even enough to have three meals a day. Enough money to support everyone. All thanks to one stranger.

TWO
IN THE IRISES
STORM

The screams of a thousand beings roar in my ears. Endless arrays of red fill my whirling vision. My feet fly over arrays of bodies glued to the earth by the blood flowing from their veins. The metal blades in my arms are on edge, ready for a thrill. I'm unable to control my movements, controlled by the whims of another as I chase a pair of targets.

As I corner the two in an alley, they claw at the brick wall until their hands drip with their own blood. I slink toward them, my footsteps clicking on the cracked concrete. Both targets whip around. They have peculiar glowing eyes, long canines, and layer of fur on their skin. Each one is humanoid, but their true nature is animalistic. They are monsters.

Shallow hisses slither past their fangs into the tense air. Their dark claws unsheathe and twitch in anticipation of my next move. One is more masculine, with bright blue eyes and white fur coating its skin. The other is feminine, with piercing green eyes and grey fur dappled in black spots. Both wear tattered clothing in an attempt to look human. I see the truth.

The white-furred monster charges me. Its crystal eyes flash

across my vision to the side. I see the glint of its claws out of the corner of my eye. I lurch backward. The feline beast slashes only air. I unleash the knife from its hiding place at the top of my forearm, slicing across the monster's chest. It screeches and tumbles to my feet, completely paralyzed in shock. Slitted pupils expand as it stares up at me when I block the sky from its view. Scarlet drizzles out of its chest. The monster holds its hand out, but my blade rises. It strikes clean through the monster's neck. Blood splatters onto my black armor.

Stepping away from the lolling head, I wipe the mess from my helmet. The second monster is quaking in the corner, shrouded in shadows. It stares at me with bulging eyes. I march toward it. My fingers flick, ready for a new challenge. The metal claws in my fingers unsheathe.

An unrecognizable force rams into my back, sending me flying off my feet to the ground. I snap my gaze to the attacker. An unwelcome chill slithers down my spine. I freeze at the sight of their irises that are glowing two different colors. It's as if the gold and silver hues grip my spine and twist it into submission. The attacker towers over me, casting me in its shadow.

The monster howls as it slams something against the right side of my helmet, instantly shattering the transparent coating. Power blasts me onto my back. My right eye burns. All at once, the vision before me vanishes like dust spiraling away in a breeze and I'm swept away into nothingness. The breath is knocked out of me as I lie suspended in total darkness. Something surrounding my body sways with the caress of a light breeze.

"*Storm!*" A distant voice urges.

The dark sky far above is filled to the brim with tiny but radiant stars. The chilling breeze cools my exposed skin.

The voice returns. "Storm!"

When I close my eyes, the swaying disappears and I'm met with the jolting sensation of my chest moving up and down. My eyes snap open, the right one still burning.

"Storm! Oh my god! Oh my—are you okay?" Hawk stops shaking me.

I blink. Stray tears roll down the left side of my face.

That's never happened before. Has it?

"Storm? Can you hear me?" Hawk cups my face to study my eyes. She wipes the tears away.

"I'm..." My metallic blades and claws are glistening in the small rays of light. I've scratched my thighs and chest; blood drips from them. "I'm fine."

Hawk finally releases my face. "Sorry I shook you so much. I thought it was your program..."

My claws project out of my nail beds, and the blades protrude out both of my arms, two per arm. I retract the claws and blades. It's a slow process that makes me shiver with effort. Once complete, I search Hawk's arms for wounds, but she pulls away.

"I'm fine. Don't worry about it," I say. My hands are shaking.

"Do you want to talk about it?" Hawk asks.

Two colors penetrate the thoughts swirling in my mind. I take a breath that doesn't help. "It was a memory. I'm not sure when it happened but..." I take a deep breath before continuing. "It's the one y'all always talk about. The one with the monsters being killed."

"And your program was in control, wasn't it? Were you wearing that armor?"

"Yeah. Does this mean..."

"I doubt it." She stops in thought. "I doubt it'll start talking to you like it talks to us. It would have started by now. And I doubt it'll attack you. When you woke up, you were you, and that's all that matters. Those wounds are bound to get infected, though. I'm gonna get you something to cover everything. Stay put."

Hawk leaves before I can object. I scan the room, but Strike and Viper are nowhere to be found. The mirror glints out of my periphery, and I turn to it. The same crack still shows my reflection split into two. My face is pale, and my gold eyes are bloodshot. With shaking hands, I grab my journal and pen to finish entry one, from yesterday.

. . .

I HAVE GIVEN myself the name of Storm. There are a
few things you need to know about me. The day I
woke up with no memories, I was in the middle of
nowhere with three strangers lying next to me.
Cold and confused, I woke each of them, hoping at
least one could tell me what had happened. No one
knew. The only clue was a note Strike had in her
jumpsuit pocket that said to go north and trust
no one. We had no memory, no food or water, and
no money. We had nothing.

The only reason we made it to Kansas was
because Hawk and I figured out how to fly. Even
so, it took a few weeks. At the time, I didn't
trust them but after being in Kansas for a month
or so, I grew closer to them. It was around that
time that we gave ourselves names. Also, we
figured out we're around fourteen or fifteen. To
be on the safe side, we say we're fourteen.

We planned to stay in Kansas until we understood our own individual abilities, but the girls
quickly started getting confusing dreams that we
eventually figured out were mainly memories. I
was the last to get the flashbacks.

Aside from the dreams, our time in Kansas City
brought something much darker to our doorsteps.
We realized we are being hunted. We realized that
people—called officers—are trying to revert all
of us back to the program's control and force us
into our darkest places.

It happened one night when we weren't paying
attention. Officers attacked us out of nowhere.
Viper was collared with one of their machines,

allowing her program to take over. I blame myself. My first thought should have been to protect Viper, instead of fighting the officers off.

Fortunately, we escaped and discovered that the collar doesn't reactivate the program permanently. Once we were able to cut the collar off, its hold on Viper faded. Now it's my job to make sure we aren't collared again. I have to: Viper hasn't been the same since, and even Hawk and Strike have changed. All of their programs have worsened over the past few months. My friends fight its control over them the best they can, but sometimes their programs are too much for them to handle. They need me to help them when it becomes too much.

Aside from the collars, we don't know what the officers want with us. We assume it has to do with our abilities, but their goals are unknown. To be safe, we pack lightly and only stay in one place for a short time, six months or less. We've been in Oklahoma City trying to uncover more information, but we'll need to move on soon.

As for our abilities, we train together to better understand what we are capable of. The following is a list of the abilities we currently know of:

- Flight: by wings. Be sure to cover them in public with a long jacket that goes past the waist for good measure.
- Night vision and super senses: not controllable. Viper and I can't figure out where the abilities come from or how

they work. The abilities are constantly active. There isn't really a "shut off" for them.

- Metal claws: work just like a muscle. Claws extend out of nail beds and have a metal coating. Type of metal unknown.
- Extendable blades in arms: two sets on each arm (one top, one bottom). They are the length of the forearm and are controlled like the claws are. Appear to be the same metal as the claws. Use caution; they are razor sharp. Cover any wounds sustained during use.
- Shapeshifting: extent of ability is unknown. Can be painful. Need more practice.
- Take care not to hurt anyone or reveal our abilities to others.

The others remember the past when we train. but I don't. They refuse to tell me of the visions they see, saying they want to spare me the horrors. They know from the memories that we were taught to fight a certain way, and were intended to be deadly. While we all know fighting is a strength of ours, with more training, we learn to control ourselves more and uncover new abilities. It hasn't been enough to provide all the answers, but every day we learn something.

The other issue we face is the program. Each of us has a program inside of our mind, and it has the power to control us against our will. The program is more deadly than all of us combined. Its origin is unknown. Its motive is unknown. The little information we've pieced together about the program has come from brief flashbacks. Strike told us she thinks the program is there to force us to fight for something or for someone. It makes sense, but the only thing I know for sure is that the program is evil and has done terrible things. And, I refuse to believe the program's actions are my own. The program has killed people. The extent is unknown. But I know we are not murderers—the program is. It's one more mystery we must solve.

Sometimes the program can take partial control of my friends, causing their bodies to shake uncontrollably or stiffen. We call it a program attack, and it happens from time to time. When this happens, I don't let them out of my sight. I don't trust anything they say, and I make sure to isolate them. Then we wait. I study their eyes. If their pupils are normal, they should be fine. If their pupils are nearly invisible, I knock them out, because the program is in control. Each time the program takes them, I see cracks form in their minds. I'm worried if this continues, they'll one day shatter right in front of me. I can't let that happen, but I don't know how to protect them yet. I'm hoping the answers we find will repair the damage done to them.

A few more tips to my future self before I end this entry: always keep your sunglasses on to conceal your eyes, wear a coat at all times to cover your wings, and use something cleanish to cover cuts from the blades. Don't smile too much. People get anxious when they see your canines are slightly extended. Make sure to remind the others of these rules.

This journal will be a record of my dreams as well. If you can figure out the meaning in them when I couldn't, it may lead us closer to knowing what happened.

I JOT down a few notes about my dream: the monsters, dead bodies, the city, the armor, and the wound on my eye, noting the wound must be the origin of the scar that cuts into my right eyebrow.

That's another thing I should write down—where I think all my scars came from.

I raise the trembling pen.

"Found some!"

The voice causes me to jump in response. I slip the journal back into my pack while Hawk leans over me, gently taking hold of my left arm. Rolling up my sleeve, she wraps my wrist with a bandana where the two knives slid out. To the side of the injury, on the underside of my forearm, is my tattoo. The small letters read, *WDXX12*. Hawk tightens the bandana and moves on to my right arm.

"Where are the others?" I ask.

"They bolted upstairs to fight over the food you brought in last night. Both of them wanted the canned peaches," Hawk scoffs, throwing her hands into her lap. "They're such animals."

I grin. "With no restraint whatsoever."

"For sure." Hawk knots the last bandana. "Sadly, we don't have any more cloth." She sighs. "I can maybe get something while I'm at work."

"Don't worry about it. I can handle a few scratches."

"Liar. You always whine, even more than Strike."

I laugh. Hawk returns my smile before sliding next to me and placing her head on my shoulder. Her blonde hair drapes into my brunette locks. Her warmth stops the shaking in my hands and the stiffness of my muscles. I close my eyes and lean my head on hers. Hawk's wing curls around me. The feathers keep me warm.

"Are you headed out today for that new job you were complainin' about last week?" I whisper.

"Don't remind me. Viper and I are both going this afternoon. We're washing horses."

"How about Strike? What's she doin' this afternoon?"

"Trying to sell the art she was making yesterday. I'm not sure what it is, but some sap may buy it. It's pretty good, though. It kinda reminds me of an oak tree but from really far away." She reaches up and twirls my hair. "Do you want me to braid this today? It shouldn't take too much time."

"What time is it?" I ask.

"Close to midday."

My eyes snap open. I'm supposed to meet Curly soon! I rip away from Hawk, dive to my box, and grab my parka. Saying goodbye to Hawk, I rush out the door while throwing on my jacket. I'm up the stairs and I nearly flatten Strike on my way out. I apologize in a blur as I kick out the third board and slide through the gap feet first. Landing on the concrete, I snatch the board and slam it on the window. I take off down the sidewalk at lighting speed.

Yesterday after work, Curly promised to give me his extra food today if I did him a solid. I need to get there as quick as possible or the deal is off.

Zigzagging through a crowd, I'm slowed at almost every turn. I stop at the red light on the crosswalk as the whirling traffic barely grazes my nose. I let out a few heaving breaths.

What are my options? Flying? Should I fly? No, don't be stupid. I'll be seen instantly. I've already learned that even as fast as I am, the crowds will prevent me from getting there in time. What else can I do?

I glance toward the temporarily-stopped traffic beside me. The stoplight is only a few feet away, and it's the only one for miles. At the front of the line is a carriage drawn by four horses and three drivers. The back of the carriage has no grips, but the top does. The carriage will soon be moving fast—not as fast as a car, but faster than running through crowds. It might give me a chance to make it in time.

The light turns green. One driver lashes the leather whips onto the horses' backs, and they take off. I launch forward past a military car and behind the carriage. As the carriage begins to pick up speed in the center of the intersection, I leap onto the back of it. My grip holds on the top bars. I look around to confirm I've gone unnoticed.

The carriage soars across the tar road. I'm completely weightless but the wind drags at me. I refuse to let go as the carriage barrels past the first block—two more to go. My heart stops when one of the wheels sinks into a pothole, causing one hand to slide off the bar. I swing my hand back up and readjust my grip. My heartbeat returns.

I turn my head and notice the military car behind me. If I fall, its bumper, with the word *Aurex* carved into it, would bulldoze me. I squint and can see the men inside laughing their asses off at me. Rolling my eyes, I face forward.

The jagged tower looms closer from where it sits on the frontline of the incoming dark horizon. The end of the third block rushes past. My stop is almost here. I release my right hand from the bar, grasping only with my left now. With all my might, I swing from the moving carriage onto the sidewalk. I roll. I'm quick to plant my feet before I take off in a sprint, dodging merchants and shoppers along the way. My feet soar across the concrete. A crowd has gathered at the base of the tower, no doubt watching Boss's show. Not slowing my momentum, I brace myself for impact with the crowd and the incoming insults from those pushed. As I dive through, an array of pinks, oranges, reds, blues, and purples lift overhead. The hues combine, strands swirling in the gray air, as a voice carves through the chatter of the crowd.

"Thank you! Thank you all for witnessing the Ambient Ambrosia!" Curly yells.

I reach the front as Curly holds out Boss's magician hat to the crowd. The glittering colors float around him, wrapping themselves across his shoulders and between his ankles. His suit sparkles in the last rays of pale light, and the vibrant colors frame his typically reserved features, which have morphed into the practiced grin of a showman. My eyes widen. It doesn't matter how many times I witness this show; I'll never get used to its color.

"Please! Feel free to tip! It will recharge the Ambient Ambrosia's power!" Curly places the hat down.

The smoke begins to fade and the patrons step up, one by one, placing their tips into the hat while Curly smiles. There is a sparkle in his eyes that is not seen often. His gaze meets mine. He motions with a bend of his chin in the direction of the tent, and I nod back.

After hugging the outside of the crowd, I manage to slip inside and beeline for the desk where I sit on its corner to wait. Looking down, I notice the cards from yesterday have been laid out. Each card has a little work of art on it, and is titled to match. I swivel to the other side of the desk. The images of The Magician, The High Priestess, The Fool, and The Chariot catch my eye.

What is their purpose? Who created them?

I scan to the second row to find The Hermit, The Sun, Strength, and The Hanged Man.

What do they mean? How do they work?

I study the third row that contains The Hierophant, The Emperor, and—

"Hey kiddie!" Curly cuts in. "Aren't they cool? I tested them out on Boss so I don't need your help anymore."

I sigh, not looking up at him. "Sorry, I overslept. Is there still a way I could get the food?"

"Well, I can read your palms. Maybe tell your future. I need more practice if I wanna make money off it. I've almost got it down."

"Can you really tell my future?" Now I look up at him. "Or are you just going to make up random things that I wanna hear?"

Curly's eyes widen, his mouth unhinges, and he drops the hat full of tips. His entire body tenses before he takes a step back. He slides a hand over his mouth and looks like he's about to run. Run and let the world know of his shock. I think I know why.

I reach up for my sunglasses, but there's nothing to grab. My heart sinks. I left them at home. I calculate the time it would take Curly to get away; about three seconds. Twelve to alert the population.

"Curly..." I don't stand, in fear he'll run. "I can explain."

"You're one of...of them."

"I'm not..."

"W-why should I-I trust you?" Curly takes another step back. Now, he needs only one second.

"If I were, you would already be dead," I whisper. "Curly, please. I'm your co-worker and your friend. Please don't run."

"You're...a monster. But how are you not rabid? How—"

"I'm not one of those monsters, I promise. I...I know it looks bad, but please don't run away." I shake a bit. "Please. If you do, they'll find me. They'll take me away."

Curly keeps his distance. "I don't understand. You look like one. Your eyes—"

"I don't know, Curly, okay? I don't why I look like one of the monsters," I blurt out. "I need you to understand though, I'm not here to hurt anyone. I'm just trying to get by like anyone else." Tears are on the rims of my eyes. If he runs, the officers will be on me in a second.

Curly's gaze softens. "Okay...I believe you. But I think you have more explaining to do."

I sigh as his arms fall to their sides. His eyes suddenly glaze over in thought while his eyebrows scale his forehead. His expression pales before he rests his hands on his head.

"You have to get out of the city," he says.

"Wait, what?"

Curly rushes over to the desk and snatches a backpack from underneath it.

"Yesterday, two people came by looking for you right after you ran out. They told me they were employers and you said you'd be here to meet them. I told them...I told them you were going to Bub's. Jeez, why am I so stupid? One of them was in a trench coat. He had a scar." Curly draws a line on the right side of his lip with his finger. "He seemed pretty serious. His friend was in a blue tracksuit, and described you perfectly. They were really anxious, seemed desperate to find you as fast as possible. I just thought it was business, you know? Time is money sort of thing."

My veins turn to ice.

"I saw something on the trench coat's watch; it had that emblem from the Safe Zone. I think...I think he's from there. I think he and his friend are here to track you down. They could be the higher-ups from there. They sure looked the part—the type of *seekers* you hear about but never wanna meet. You gotta get outta here. Get out as fast as you can." Sweat has collected on his forehead. "Get outta here before Boss comes back. She's still waiting for the crowds to disappear. I'll tell her you went to the base; she won't know a damn thing. I won't say a damn thing to no one. I promise."

Curly unzips the top of his backpack, whips out a pair of silver sunglasses, and forces them onto my face. He takes out his clothes from the backpack and zips it back up.

He shoves the backpack into my lap. "Take it. It has all the food I promised, and my paycheck. It's about thirty bucks in cash. It should get you far enough."

"Why are you doing this? I can't take this, I—"

"I'm sorry I acted that way before. I'm not that kind of person— the kind that screws over people who are different. Human or monster, I know I shouldn't be afraid of you. No matter what you are, you're still my friend. And don't worry about it, just get out of here." He brings his face eye level with mine. "I'll be okay, don't worry. I'll be okay. Listen, you're a good person. A really good person. You've been one of the only people that has tried to become my friend. You try to be a friend to everyone. That's so rare. And you don't deserve anything that those men want to do to you. You have to get outta here. Please go. Please live. Not just for me, but for all those people in life that need a friend like you."

Curly grabs my hands, staring at my palms. "You...you'll face too many trials, betrayals, and deaths. But despite it all, you'll prevail, just as you did in the past. You'll protect the ones you love, and you'll find what you're looking for. Listen to your instincts. Stick with your family and the light will find you."

My mouth gapes. Curly pulls me up to my feet from the chair and leads me out from behind the desk. He puts his hand on my shoulder as we walk to the doorway overflowing with grey light.

"You did what I wanted. You paid me. We're even now. Now take the pack and go, while the crowds are still around. Make sure you're not being followed," Curly whispers, releasing his grip on my shoulder.

I take a partial step out of the tent while sliding the pack on. My mind reels as I stop to look back at Curly. I may not see his colorfulness ever again in this life.

"Curly."

"Yeah?"

"The people I trust, my friends, they call me Storm."

"Storm...I'll never forget it."

And I will never forget his brilliance.

I nod, holding a frail smile, and rush out of the tent. I put my hood up. Focusing on my surroundings, I slink across the square. The clouds above limit both the light and the shadows.

The crowds swarm the concrete jungle with a constant buzzing. With my head low, I keep to the denser areas, despite my dislike for them. I expand my hearing to listen to the mixture of conversations consuming the space.

"How much for it? Why that? Is there a bathroom here? Honey! Get away from there! Yeah, I'll be home for lunch. Shut up! How have you been? What's that? Why are you this way?"

The conversations are jumbled, lacking a clear end, and each one is like a power drill to my eardrums. My breath is strained. I turn the corner, back to the sidewalk that leads to my home, sinking deeper into the swell of moving bodies. The pace is slow. Too slow.

They could already be at the house. I could be too late. They probably already trailed me to work because of my carriage idea. Shit. They could be following me right now.

I glance over my shoulder, scanning for any familiar faces in the crowd and praying I don't lock eyes with one of them. The wind pulls at my hood, but I yank it back on. My heartbeat overpowers my hearing, preventing me from noticing any signs of danger. I close my eyes, then take in a deep breath, holding it for a bit.

Keep your cool. Keep your cool.

Breathing out, I open my eyes. With my head still low, I tighten the straps on the backpack and keep pace with the crowd. Clouds have marbleized above, and the whistling wind blows between the cracks of the buildings.

I approach the end of the second block—only one more to go. A large crowd merges with mine, pushing me to the center of the bustle, and the walkers begin to pull out their umbrellas. Moments later, the first rainfall appears. It's now difficult to scan any face due to the sheets of mist.

In my head, I'm planning the next steps. I'll grab my other bag, stuff our food in it, and the others can pack whatever fits best. We'll take the alleyways to the edge of town. From there, Hawk and I can fly us down to our old home in the woods. We should be safe for a while there, at least long enough to figure out where to go next. Maybe we can head for Texas. I hear the outskirts of Dallas are in ruin but hidden from civilization.

The rain intensifies. A black wave of umbrellas ripples through the crowd. I can no longer see the sky, only the cracks of grey between the blacks, but it's worth not being seen. The swell of umbrellas halts, waiting to cross the intersection, and I swim through the sea closer to the front. I flick my fingers together, staring down the red light glowing through the misty rain. It turns green. My heart skips a beat. The crowd resumes its flooding of the sidewalk. Once past the vehicles, the crowd veers to the right. I continue straight, in the direction of my home. Rain pounds my jacket, dripping down my hood right onto my nose. Wind tears at me and tries to pull me away from my path. I listen for sounds of stray footsteps, but I can't hear much because of the raindrops shattering my senses.

After another gulping breath, I reach the abandoned building—my home, now former home. Bolting for the entrance, I almost run into the brick wall as I pound on the board.

"Basta! I hear ya!" Viper shouts.

I take a step back, my breathing fast, waiting for the board to come loose. Finally, the board is kicked out and I snatch it in midair. I slide it through the hole and scramble through the gap. Viper grabs my wrist to help me through. Once inside, I fly to my feet, grabbing Viper's shoulders.

"Pack everything. We have to leave now. Tell the others."

Viper drops the board and sprints for the basement. She calls out to Hawk and Strike, relaying the message, while I hastily pile the cans of food into Curly's backpack. I sling it over my shoulder, walking back to the window to wait for the others. As I turn the corner, I see a hand with silver rings reach through the gap.

THREE

THE INTRUDERS

STORM

I bolt to the entrance of the hallway and flatten myself against the wall. The board falls on the pavement below with a sickening thud. The other boards are torn to pieces as a foot slams into the building. The stranger pulls himself through the torn away window. I cup my hand over my mouth.

Suddenly the original, bolted door slams relentlessly. A group of people grunt from the outside, trying to tear it down. I slide sideways across the wall to the next staircase. The door splits apart, forcing my retreat into the hallway as the stranger turns the corner into the kitchen.

Bam!

The loading of guns follows.

"Make sure only one tranquilizer hits each target. We don't want any overdosing," a familiar voice commands. It's the man in the blue tracksuit who knocked me down yesterday.

A group of footsteps cautiously click on the concrete. I estimate that there are five intruders total. Tiptoeing to the stairway I meet Hawk, Strike, and Viper with our bags. Viper hands me my belongings as sweat drips off her forehead. I point up to the second floor, the others nod, and we creep up the stairs with Strike at the lead.

"Turn over this place! They're here! I can hear the heartbeats still!" the blue tracksuit yells.

The clicking turns into a deafening drumming dispersing throughout the building. As they enter the hallway, we reach the top of the stairs, out of sight. We all freeze where the floor turns into aged wood. One step on the thin wood could mean capture.

"What now?" Strike asks, eying the floor. "They'll hear us if we go into the next room."

"Or we could fall through," Viper whispers.

"Let's lure them up here," Hawk whispers. "They'll hear us come up, and we'll ambush them in that room when they break down the door."

"Then what?" Strike counters. "How will we get away?"

"We'll do it as we go," I whisper. "C'mon, we need to get out of sight."

We scurry across the hallway to a room filled with junk, and I barge through the wooden door. The intruders have fallen silent. They are following our footsteps to the stairs now. I let everyone inside and hastily lock the door. Turning around, my eyes snap to the boarded windows.

That's our escape.

"How many are there?" Strike asks.

"About five," I whisper. I strain my hearing to pinpoint the location of the intruders. They're still on the first floor.

"This will be easy then," Viper says.

"No, they have tranquilizers and probably collars." I say while throwing off my bags. "We need to remove the boards from those windows. I'll keep guard at the entrance while y'all get rid of them. Once the intruders get up close to the door, we can jump out before they even realize we're gone." I take off my jacket and tie it around my waist, exposing my wings. Footsteps stomp up the stairs.

Hawk follows my lead with her own wings. "They'll be able to shoot us in the air with those guns. We need to slow them down somehow. Storm and Strike should lure them into the center, where the floor is the weakest. Hopefully, it will collapse on them." Hawk hands her bag to Strike. "Then Storm and I will fly us out after they fall."

"We're cutting it close, but what the hell." Viper takes my bag. "Same partners as usual then?"

Hawk and I nod. More footsteps creak on the wooden floor. Whispers bounce between the intruders. We fall silent and split into two groups. Hawk and Viper go to the windows, tearing the boards off like pieces of tape. Strike and I take our positions behind a fallen wardrobe on the other side of the room. We squat but keep eyes on the door.

Strike holds up one finger, a sign that she will take the first man if necessary. I nod while unsheathing my bottom blades.

Slam.

The door jolts forward. My shoulders tense and my fists clench. Hawk and Viper finish ripping off the boards. They flip a table over and duck behind it.

Slam. Slam.

A blow to the center of the door sends wood-chunks flying. Strike and I pull back further behind the wardrobe. My heart pounds in my ears.

Bam!

The door splits in half with a boom. Ears ringing, senses expanding...The deafening footsteps almost make me almost throw up. But on cue, I grind my blades against each other, creating a sound that could split eardrums if it were any louder. I continue the motion as the footsteps approach us, the floor groaning with the sudden increase of weight, and I hold my breath. I pray for the floor to collapse as I grind the blades together one last time.

Strike unsheathes her own pair of top blades. My eyes are on the empty space to my side, every inch of me ready. Suddenly the harmony of wood splintering slices the air, with shouting as its melody. Strike and I look out from our cover. Three of the intruders still stand around two gaping holes in the center of the floor. A few portions of floor are stable. The remaining officer wears a collar on his belt, gun drawn at us. The blue tracksuit and the trench coat stand there as well.

Strike sprints across the walkway toward the officer. She pierces one blade through his shoulder, causing his grip on the gun to falter. Strike tears the blade away from his heart through his armpit. He screams. Strike twists to the other side of him as he collapses onto his knees and she plants her sneaker on his spine and forces his body over the edge. Strike whips her head toward the next two targets—the tracksuit and the trench coat. She raises both blades and attacks the tracksuit, nearly severing his shoulder, but leaves the trench coat to me.

Darting from behind cover, I jump while digging my heel into the wall. I catapult myself in the direction of trench coat. Soaring past the gaping hole, I lash my blade across his chest. He doesn't flinch. I land next to him. Unsheathing my top blade, I swing it at his thigh but a flash of silver blocks it. I follow his top blade, protruding from his right arm, up to his eyes which are wide and wild from adrenaline. Our arms shake from the pressure of the contact. His brows raise and his mouth gapes like he's never seen blades before. I slash my free blade across his shoulder, causing him to retreat closer to the hole in the floor.

He uncovers an additional lower blade on his left arm. "You're probably wondering who I am. Why I'm here."

I'm not.

He jabs at me with an upper blade. I parry his blow, causing him to take another step back.

"I'm here to put you in your place!"

He's a Brute. I'm not going to waste my air trying to reason with him.

I jab to the right, but dart abruptly to the left. My blade tears across the Brute's chest. A flicker appears in the corner of my eye—his blade. I move to the opposite side. The knife flies near my left cheek, slicing it. Blood sprays into the air. I grit my teeth. The Brute now stands on the edge of the hole. I plant my foot, preparing to charge him. He widens his stance.

Suddenly something whirls over my head and slams into the Brute's chest. The force causes him to stagger into the hole and disappear. I glance back where Viper motions for me to get going. I nod, turning to the hole where the Brute's silver rings clutch the edges. He dangles above the rubble while attempting to scramble back up into our space. When I lean over the hole, I remove my sunglasses. Staring him down, I raise my foot into the air while my blood drips onto his face.

I will always win the fight.

The Brute gazes at me with wide eyes. His mouth opens as if he's read my mind. Every inch of me would love to say something out loud, but I'm running out of time. I pound my foot on his silver rings and watch as he falls.

I run to the window, hurdling the table, with my hand outstretched, reaching for Viper. She grasps it. We leap out of the window together.

I spread my wings, allowing them to catch in the wind. We descend closer and closer to the street. I rear back and swoop above the city's buildings. As I lock my arms around Viper's waist, she straightens her body out. My wings beat, taking us further away from the buildings.

The city becomes more alien by the second, a miniature world where I could never have enough room to roam. I stop flapping my wings and glide through the sky. Hawk and Strike fly closer to us.

"To the old house?" Hawk asks.

I nod. We graze a patch of clouds, heading toward the dark horizons, away from the misty city. The freezing rain rushes in my ears. It surrounds my entire body. My teeth chatter, but I embrace the coldness. I'd rather be cold than captured.

* * *

My hair is a frizzy nest framing my face, tangled from the whipping of the high winds. It'll take days to brush out. I settle my head on the comfort of Hawk's stomach and take in the crisp air. Hawk and I lie on a patch of underbrush at the edge of the tree line. The tender swaying of the field and the fluttering of fallen leaves beckons me to sleep. A breeze brushes over my skin, and the cold rays of a setting sun strike through the dying branches. The wind carries an undertone of rain and the branches constantly drip with dew.

Flying for the better part of a day can drain a girl. Narrowly avoiding capture can drain a girl. Dealing with the fact it's all my fault can drain a girl. How could I not see the signs? How could I lead them straight to us? I'm supposed to protect the others. How could I fail again?

I sit up. Strike stands a few feet away with her head leaning back against a tree; her clouded eyes study only the sky. Above her, Viper sits at the intersection of two branches; her drooping eyes study the endless tangle of trees.

We've been silent for hours.

We sit on the edge of the wilderness, where a field of green fades to gold. The dying grass shimmers in the sun's fading rays, the field more radiant than it ever could have been when it was alive. As the yellow rays fall across my skin, a twinge hits me in my chest and a soreness pulses from my blood-encrusted cheek. I place my hand to my chest, but the twinge only festers.

"I'm sick of this," Viper whispers. "I'm sick of all of this."

Hawk sits up. "What do you mean?"

"I'm so tired. So tired of not knowing a damn thing. I'm tired of havin' this damn voice in my head that I know nothing about."

"I'm sick of the nightmares," Strike says.

"I'm done with running all the time. Having to be paranoid to survive," Hawk replies.

I feel the same way. I'm tired of losing connections with good people. I'm done with the pain. I'm sick of being out of control.

"Then we can't sit and wait anymore to get what we want," I say.

"What do we do?" Hawk asks.

"We make our own starting point. No more waiting for it to come to us. Next time, we follow the officers after they attack."

"That's insane. And how can you even be sure it would help?" Strike asks. "They may not have any of the answers we need."

"Even if they don't, those people know something about us," I say. "They have information. Information we want, and they're gettin' it from somewhere. That somewhere is our source. I know it."

"I like where this is going," Viper remarks.

My mind races. "First, we just have to track them down and find where they work. Once we reach the cabin, we can figure out the details. But how? Just look at us! I mean, we were built for this. We were built to fight. It's obvious. Why else would we be hunted by officers and seekers? The people hunting us obviously see us as a threat."

"Hold on. Hold on. Let's slow down for a second," Hawk says. "We're talking about jumping into an unknown here. An unknown that has guns and collars."

"C'mon, Hawk," Viper replies. "They—"

"No, listen. We don't know what we can handle yet. How could we follow them, most likely end up fighting, knowing something worse that we don't know anything about could push back? It's suicide. It'll make things worse. We can't—"

"Nothing they throw at us could be worse than what we've been through," Viper snaps. "They have nothing on us. I'm with Storm on this. I wanna find the truth and I wanna life."

"Think about it this way—the more knowledge we have, the more dangerous we are. We can get dangerous enough to the point where they'll finally leave us alone. And at that point, hopefully, we'll know what happened to us," I say. "The only way to do that is to track down the source, you know? It's just a starting place. We won't have to do it forever."

Hawk breathes in. "The truth does sound nice. A life too. But we have to be careful. Those officers are smart. We can't make stupid mistakes like in Kansas, or we'll be captured."

"Exactly, so this is a bad idea," Strike says. "I'm sure there's another way. Maybe if we wait long enough, our memories will come back."

"Strike, we don't know how much time we have left. If we wait, we could get collars on our necks or worse. The program could overpower us one by one. It's been getting stronger, you know that. There's no time to waste anymore," Hawk says. "I can get behind this. I'm in."

Strike crosses her arms and fixes her gaze on the ground. After a while, she says, "I have one condition. You all have to promise that nobody gets killed. That includes us and the people we have to fight, even if it's the only way out of getting caught. Nobody gets killed. I'll only be in if you guys promise to be careful. Following the officers will be dangerous."

"And we'll think things through from every angle when we make our plans. Nobody will be killed, and we won't die on you. But you gotta understand it's either fight or flight right now," I say. "I don't know about you, but I'm tired of flying off with my tail between my legs. All of us are. The best thing we can do for ourselves is to face the fight head-on."

Strike doesn't respond.

"Don't worry too much. It's not like we're planning on jumping out of exploding buildings or dive-bombing into skylights," Hawk says. "We're starting out easy by following a few officers around, seeing what they're up to, and figuring out who their boss is. We'll figure out the simplest next step from there."

"Yeah, we won't be raisin' rebellions or shit like that. Just raisin' hell. It'll be fun, a bonding experience," Viper says.

Strike looks up. "All of you promise."

"I promise," Hawk says.

"I do too," Viper adds.

I nod to her. "I promise."

Finally, she says, "I'm in."

After an eternity, the sun sinks below the skyline. Yellow, orange, and red rays blanket each of us. They're one of a kind, but the colors fade into a natural darkness. I'm struck by both awe and the loss of the now invisible sun for what it provided.

FOUR
PURPLE TIE
STORM

With a quick click, the tip of the pen disappears back into its home. Leaning my head against the tree trunk, I hug the journal to my chest. I unwillingly close my eyes. My mind spins as I think about entry three.

I keep a page or profile on each person I meet. My flow stopped when I reached the pages for the Brute and his partner. I know that the Brute only has two blades and can barely use them. Other than that, they are both mysteries. I know nothing about their weaknesses, their strengths, or their motivations.

I urge my eyes open and sit upright. Grabbing the branch above, I pull myself to my feet. I survey the area from the treetop, searching for any movement and checking for any signs of mortal danger. The wound on my cheek pulses. I'm sure there's a bruise at this point. After rubbing my dry eyes, I lower my gaze to the bottom of my makeshift watchtower.

Hawk, Strike, and Viper are asleep at the tree's base. Hawk's grey wings, splattered with white, fan out around the three of them. Viper stirs, and her eyes meet mine. She frowns and shakes her head at me. Viper slips out from underneath Hawk's wing before standing with her hands on her hips. I sigh as I sit back onto the branch. The sound of her claws as they cut through bark murmurs throughout the brush. After a few moments, Viper has hoisted herself up and is at my side. Her eyes record every detail of me.

"I'll take next watch. You need to go to sleep," she whispers.

"I don't need to."

"Oh no, not this again." Viper moves her face closer to mine. "You don't just need to sleep, you have to. It's basic life shit."

I shake my head. "I'm staying here. As long as I—"

"Fine, fine. I get it. I don't wanna speech." Viper rubs her eyes. "If you wanna stay awake, I can keep you up all night."

"Thank you."

"I could keep you up three nights if you wanna?" Viper elbows my side. "C'mon, it'll be fun. No sleep is the new...*la manía*. Sounds good, right?"

"I would do it in a heartbeat if it would keep us safe."

"Don't be hard on yourself. This isn't your fault."

"I should have been more careful."

Viper's finger passes gently over my cheek before she turns my face to hers. The glowing of her green eyes coats my skin in rare warmth.

"Don't say things like that. Stop thinkin' about this. It's not healthy to try to control uncontrollable stuff. This is something we have to deal with. It's our life."

"They wouldn't have found—"

"You've already done more than enough." She traces her finger down the scab on my cheek. "You ran all the way from work to warn us and you helped with our escape, even adding a new scar along the way." She leans her head onto my shoulder. "Now, let's talk about something else."

"Like what?"

"This night. It's so quiet, so clear. It's like there's no darkness in it."

"It's clear because we have night vision."

"Not in that way," she murmurs. "Look around you. Take it in and live in the moment. It'll do you some good."

I push my hair back and raise my chin to the sky. Branches twist around the stars, concealing many, but framing the remainder. The gusts of wind rustle the branches. The occasional shuffling sound of an animal bounces between the tree trunks, and the faint breathing of my friends echo below. The air is scented by the rich underbrush, vibrant leaves, and fresh water. Focusing on the hints of vegetation touched by the previous rain quiets my mind and drugs my thoughts, making my eyes flutter and my muscles loosen.

"You have a point," I mutter.

"I always do."

"What are you supposed to think about during nights like these?"

"Anything. Or nothing at all."

My eyes begin to fail me. I yawn. Viper snakes her fingers around my hands and gently holds them. I glance at her hand and up her arm where her tattoo is still visible. It reads, $WSXX45$.

I lean my head on hers. "I won't fall asleep."

She snuggles closer to me without a word. She always has a point, derived from the knowledge she has. Or should I say experience? I don't know where she comes up with her advice or how she has the ability to show me a new way of thinking. I mean, none of us remember the past to its fullest. Things aren't always what they seem; our dreams aren't always reality. It's up to us to decide that. So, since her memories are so faded...how can she know all these things? How does she have the wisdom she has? Because she doesn't always show it. Maybe Viper was born with her wisdom. Viper was born with the ability to find new outlooks. I've found that she can alter perspectives...She can alter beliefs too, I bet. That's a strength more powerful than the threat of a bullet. But Viper doesn't use it enough. She may second guess it. It's a strange paradox.

My eyelids relax further. I allow the weight of my head to rest fully on Viper. Can someone like me, who wasn't born with too much wisdom or at least doesn't remember it, have wisdom like hers? Has my lack of wisdom caused all these problems? Maybe if I had taken a different path, we wouldn't be in this mess all over again.

My breathing slows, my senses dull, and I start to slip away from Viper's side. My arms jerk in an attempt to catch myself, but they are stuck in place by something cold and uncomfortably nostalgic. My eyes burn and blur from the artificial light. Something is strapped around my mouth, forcing my teeth to bite on rough material. At my temples, something squeezes, applying pressure. I'm in a dully lit room with grey concrete walls and a stained concrete floor. I try to move, but I'm chained to a metal chair. My arms and legs are locked in place by silver cuffs.

"Doctor, Number Twelve is awake," a voice says from behind me.

"Excellent. Turn it on."

A few small clicks sound, and the humming of anxious electricity vibrates throughout the hazy room. Another pair of footsteps click closer to me and a man settles into my field of vision. His slender build is showcased in a glossy black suit. A purple tie is strung around his neck and clear glasses cast a reflection from the streams of buzzing lights above. The Doctor bends over, slipping his hand into a pocket as his blue eyes analyze my own. His dark irises are filled to the brim with a paralyzing curiosity.

"Hey, Twelve. Ready for today's session?" he asks. He pulls out a small, grey machine, his eyes now glimmering, and clicks the red button. With the machine at his lips, he begins to speak.

"Subject *WDXX12*. Day ten. Still completing respondent conditioning." The Doctor pulls out a silver whistle from his pocket and holds it out in front of his lips. "Just tell me when to stop." He sticks the whistle in his mouth.

He blows into it and a shrill sound expands in the air, causing my chest to tighten. I clench my fists. My body tenses. I bite down on the material. My fingers snap, waiting. The Doctor points to the person behind me.

It's as if thousands of needles shoot into my bones. I flinch, the pain radiating from my temples down to my toes. The whistling sound grows louder. I close my eyes when the needles turn into exploding bullets. Shrieking, my jaw locks up and I beg for him to stop by shaking my head side to side.

The whistling intensifies. The bullets transform into a newly discovered agony. My screaming stops even though I would gladly allow it to continue. With quickening breath, it feels like my heart is about to tear open my rib cage. My body shakes uncontrollably.

The shrill sound stops along with the buzz of the electricity. I slump in the chair, my head hanging from the weight of the crown attached to my skull. My limbs jolt at random. My jaw remains locked and my breath is still fast. The Doctor's curious gaze meets mine, his eyes a swirling abyss.

The whistle sounds again, getting louder and louder until it's deafening, like moving machinery that pulses electricity through each vein in my body. Everything goes black. The piercing sound multiplies in volume by a thousand. The thundering frequency forces my eyes open and I sit up with a jolt. Viper grabs my waist before I lose my balance on the branch. I grab onto her, panting, the electricity still rushing through my body.

"W-what was that?"

"A damn heli," she mutters. "Are you okay? You woke up with a start there."

"Just a nightmare." My head is throbbing. "Don't worry about it."

Viper nods slowly. "Do you think that heli was the officers from before?"

"I honestly have no idea, but I don't think those things come out this far on the regular though."

"C'mon. It looks like those two are awake now."

Viper and I lower ourselves from the branch to crawl down the tree. I tuck my journal at my side.

"Did you guys see that?" Hawk exclaims.

"Um, yeah. We were just in the tree, not on another planet." Viper jumps down next to Strike.

I leap from the tree, landing next to Viper, and grab my pack from the tree's roots. I slip the journal back into the safety of a side pocket.

"Do you think—"

"Most likely it's those officers," I cut Strike off. "I'm pretty sure those helis don't travel this far from the city's base."

I take a knee, grabbing Curly's pack, spilling its contents out. I slip the food and bottled water into my pack along with Curly's cash.

"I think we shouldn't fly. It sounds too risky if those helis are around," Viper says.

"Wait, we should be okay. If a helicopter is coming, we'll hear it. Storm and I can just dive down to the trees," Hawk says.

I stand up, slinging a much heavier pack over my shoulders. "Do you think I'm ready for that though?"

"I mean, you're decent enough at it. It'll be good practice for your uncoordinated ass."

I sigh and cross my arms. "Fine, but Viper will go with you; she'll listen for any danger since your hearing is...average."

"Below average," Viper says as she sneers at Hawk.

Hawk elbows Viper and mutters something in her direction. The girls begin to pack up their things. I place my sunglasses over my eyes and tie my jacket around my waist. As I rub my pulsing temples, I walk to the golden field and stop at the edge. Strike and Viper make their way to the center of the dry field.

The sky is pale; dawn has broken. The field is lifeless. The leaves are stagnant, and even the birds are mute. Everything feels washed out.

Hawk joins my side. "Storm? Are you ready?"

I blink. "Yeah, sorry."

Hawk's gaze stays on me, just for a moment, before I see Strike give me a thumbs-up. She raises both arms over her head and turns around. Hawk and I take several paces back, preparing our wings for takeoff. I launch forward. All my energy, strength, and momentum carry me across the earth, and with a flap of my wings I'm airborne. I soar across the field, causing the fading gold to ripple beneath me.

With my arms extended, I lock onto Strike's wrists, pulling her into the sky with me on rapidly beating wings. We skim the treetops as I find my balance and allow my wings to glide through the air. I pull Strike to me. When I wrap my hands around her waist, she sighs with relief. Shrieking and a chorus of laughter filters in from the side. I glance over to Hawk and Viper—who is dangling from one of Hawk's arms and flailing her legs, her mouth twisted into a scream.

"This is what you get! This is what you get!" Hawk exclaims. "Next time you think about botching the hairbrush, you better remember who your pilot is!"

"Hawk, let me up!"

I laugh with Strike as Hawk pulls her up. Once my laughter dies, the whistling wind buzzes around my temples and I turn to Strike for some relief.

"How'd you sleep last night?"

"Not very well. I had a bad memory," Strike replies.

"You can talk to me about it if you'd like to."

"Oh, it wasn't that bad."

"No, shoot away."

She takes a breath. "It started off with a man standing over me. I think he was wearing a black suit and glasses. The two women surrounding him kept calling him *Doctor*. My arms felt so heavy...hot and numb. The Doctor was talking to me, but I couldn't make out what he was saying really, only bits and pieces that I can't really remember now..."

"What do you think the memory was?"

"My arms were wrapped," Strike says in a darker tone. "I think that the memory was after they put the blades in my arms. It's hard to explain, but when I woke up this morning it was like they were new. Their weight was so apparent; it was so weird. The memory ended when they started to take me somewhere."

I'll have to add this to my journal.

"Interesting," I mutter.

"Why?"

"There was a man like that in my dream too. Have you seen him in any other dreams before?"

"Um...I have from time to time."

This could be a lead. "Maybe those two have seen him. We can ask at the cabin tonight."

"We need to talk about one of the officers too, the one in the blue tracksuit, the Blue-eyed Goon," Strike says.

"What about him?" I ask.

"I picked up on a few things about him that all of us need to talk about. He's interesting."

"How so?"

"He has some sort of super speed and senses. He was able to dodge almost all of my attacks. I could barely dodge his. He was talkative, but passive in his attacks. Focused more on defense, I should say," Strike replies. "He's strong and trained to fight someone with blades. Although he did seem surprised by a few of my blows. And he had a revolver sticking out of his pocket, but he never used it. Never even reached for it."

"What else?"

"He was smart, but I was able to trick him into falling into the hole. So, not all that clever."

"A common trend with those guys."

"Where do you think they came from?" Strike asks.

"The Safe Zone, I guess. A buddy from work tipped me off to them being on our trail; he thought that's where they came from."

"That buddy of yours sure was helpful. Isn't he the one who got us all those supplies?"

I smile a bit. "Yeah, he did."

"He could help us out in the future, don't you think?"

"For sure."

Strike and I grow quiet. We take in the rippling forest below, the pale sky, and the wonder that comes from staring at the expanse the horizon has to offer. It's without end, an unknown filled with new experiences waiting to happen. Hopefully it's filled with the type of experiences that won't cause a headache.

* * *

SOARING TOWARD THE EARTH, I pass through the branches and my speed picks up. I angle myself vertically—too vertically—and Strike yells at me, but I manage to lift away from the approaching ground. Dropping Strike, I catapult away. *Shit.* I spread my wings and flap them desperately to slow myself down, but my feet hit the ground with so much force, I have to roll through a pile of dead tree limbs and leaves. When I pop up, Viper's hysterical laugh bursts out behind me.

"And she sticks the landing!" Hawk yells.

I take a bow. Strike groans while getting to her feet. She glares and shakes her head.

I shrug. "Better than last time."

Strike raises a brow. "Let's just get inside. I need to lie down for a few weeks."

I turn to the house and I barely recognize it. The old house is a log cabin with a pointed roof, smothered in ivy and moss, and always sits in the shade of the trees. It's surrounded by fallen leaves and snapped branches. There's a set of stairs leading up to a wooden porch with dirt as its carpet. A busted window is featured at the front. To the side of the window is a broken screen door, the outer door leaning against a nearby wall.

"Home sweet home," I mutter.

"Looks worse than before," Hawk says before walking to the stairs.

I clamber up the stairs behind her with Viper on my tail. Hawk slowly opens the screen door; it creaks in response and I peer in over her shoulder. Dirt and leaves swirl over the wooden floors. A mouse scurries across the hallway from the living room into a bedroom, and a faint dripping echoes through the cracking walls.

Viper scoots in. "I mean, it's fixable."

Hawk steps in and the floor groans underneath her blue sneakers. The breeze that fills the house makes us all shiver and brings the biting aroma of a molding ceiling. Hawk takes off her backpack and flips her jacket over her wings.

"Looks like we're going to town tomorrow, Storm. For sure," Hawk says.

I step into the hallway next to her. "Do either of you remember where the brooms are?"

"Follow me." Strike pushes past the three of us.

She takes a right with me at her heels, walking into the kitchen connected to the living room. Tattered cloth, hanging from the window, flows in the breeze and fragments the afternoon light. Beneath it a rusting sink, connected to a long counter that spreads the length of the wall, drips brown water. In front of me are the remains of a second window and a wilting stove.

I stroll deeper into the kitchen and set my pack on the wooden island in the center of the space. Walking to the dusty counter, I lean against it with my forearms. Hawk sets her pack next to me. She walks past the counter and through a gap leading into the empty living room. There's an open door—thanks to Strike—at the back of the room. The skylight above is blocked by the swarm of ivy and moss and more leaves. The right side of the room has a brick fireplace, its hearth stained with black, and to the left is a bare wall.

Hawk's hands land on her hips. "Looks to me like we only need to sweep, dust, and fix a few things."

"Let's make a list of supplies tonight then," I say. "In town, we can start checking off the supplies we need and find some work."

Hawk nods. "I say we start off by fixing the front door. I'll check if the back needs work too."

She walks in the direction of the back door just as Strike appears with two brooms. When I ask about the shed, Strike says everything is still there. She throws me one of the brooms and I catch it with ease. Grasping the hastily duct-taped handle, its damage caused by one of Viper's antics, I balance the broom against the counter. Viper sits on top of the island, rummaging through my bag. When I ask her what she's doing, she pulls out a can labeled peaches and unsheathes a claw.

"A late lunch."

"Good idea! Throw me a can," Strike says.

Viper passes out black beans to Strike and sweet corn to me. She opens the cans for us with her metal claws. I munch on the corn, satisfied, as I shake more into my palm.

"What are you three doing?" Hawk asks, from behind me.

"Lunch. Want some?" Viper asks.

"Shouldn't you guys be cleaning?"

"We're on a lunch break," Strike says as she shoves a fistful of beans into her mouth.

Hawk opens her mouth, but before she can say a word, Viper tosses her a can. Hawk catches the airborne food, narrowing her eyes.

"Fine, let's eat."

"You're lettin' us 'cause I gave you the oranges, ain't you?"

"Damn right." Hawk slides the can to me. Viper giggles as I cut it open with a claw and slide the can back to Hawk.

Turning to Viper, I ask for my journal. She hands it over along with my pen. Whipping the journal open to the entry about the Brute, I scribble down the notes Strike told me about his partner, the Goon. Hawk asks me why I'm writing.

"Strike and I were talking about the officers. I'm calling the one in the trench coat the Scarred Brute. The other, in the blue tracksuit, Strike named him the Blue-eyed Goon. We think we've figured out their abilities, but we can't be sure unless we see them again." I pause, rereading the Brute's section. "The Brute only has two blades, a top on his right arm and a bottom on his left. He's slow with them. I think he only understands the basics. I don't know any weaknesses he has, or many of his strengths, but he tends to be more offensive. The Goon, on the other hand, he's defensive; he likes to dodge attacks. Strike says he has intense speed and he's able to dodge attacks like a maniac. We know he has super senses like Viper and me, since he could hear our heartbeats inside the house. Any other weaknesses and strengths are unknown."

"Does he see at night, too?" Viper asks.

"We aren't sure," I reply. "But he carries around a revolver in his pocket. He didn't use it in the fight, but if we see him again...keep that in mind."

"Anything else about the Brute?" Hawk asks.

I shake my head. "Both of them are mostly a mystery right now. I couldn't read any motivations the Brute had."

"Same goes for the Goon," Strike says. "He was talkative, but it was obviously an attempt to get under my skin."

I take note of that. "My friend from work was the one who tipped me off about them. He mentioned that he thought the two were from the Safe Zone. Possibly higher-ups, seekers, due to the Brute's attire. We can't know for sure."

"That's crazy," Hawk mutters. "They came all the way from the east, just for us?"

"Sounds like it."

The people after us must be getting desperate if they're willing to travel so far. I flip the page, dating the fourth entry *October 14*.

"We know where the people are coming from now," Viper points out.

"You're right. We know where to look now," I say.

"That's the start we need," Hawk says. "This is good. We should start figuring out a way into the Safe Zone. Maybe when we follow them, there will be some way around that wall."

I put my pen back to the thin paper to add information about the Safe Zone.

"We still need to be careful; we don't have all the information we need yet. Like the where and when," Strike replies.

"Yeah, you're right," Hawk says. "It'll take time, but we'll get to that point."

I finish writing the last sentence.

"Oh, and..." Strike pauses. "Before we forget, Storm and I were talking. We've both had a memory about a man, people called him Doctor, and we were wondering if either of you guys had a memory with him in it."

"What does he look like?" Hawk asks.

"Purple tie, black suit, dark hair, blue eyes, and glasses," Strike says.

"I've only heard the name and the voice," Viper says. "I heard it during a memory of me fighting against a large man. The man said I could take a break, but that changed when the Doctor came in. He told the man something along the lines of 'pain will only make her better.' So the man kept going because the Doctor told him he would lose his job if he didn't."

"I've heard him, too," Hawk says. "Never seen him though. I've heard the name 'Doctor' in a dream where I'm sitting in a classroom of some sort, surrounded by empty desks. I couldn't make out what was on the chalkboard, but a teacher was saying something to me, then he must've walked in. The Doctor asked how the lesson was going, and the memory ended after that."

"Tell us if you guys ever see him. This could be a lead," Strike says.

"What kind? Who do you think this is?"

"Storm said she saw him when he was conditioning her. I saw him...after what I think was my blade surgery." Strike trails off. "Viper saw him when she was training to fight. You saw him when you were in a classroom."

"And?" Viper asks.

"All those things have a common theme—they're developing us somehow. He was in charge in your memories. This man, this doctor, I think he was responsible for creating us."

The clarity brings silence to the room. It's another step, but it's also paralyzing.

"So, he's after us?" I ask.

"We can't know for sure, not until we learn more. There could be other doctors like him. If any of you guys have a memory of him, or any person like him, tell Storm so we can keep track of them all," Strike says.

"The Goon and the Brute must know him. If he developed us, what stopped him from developing them? How else would they know about us? How else would they be able to fight us? They have the same abilities as us. I mean, the Brute has blades and the Goon has super senses," I say, slowly.

"So, they could be our replacements..." Strike trails off.

"It's possible," I mutter. "I need to write all of this down."

"Go ahead. We'll start cleaning," Hawk says.

I put pen to paper, my thoughts racing, and scratch out everything in sloppy handwriting.

October 14
Entry #4

FIVE THINGS I Learned Today

#1: Since meeting the Scarred Brute and the Blue-eyed Goon, we know that the people after us are coming from the east coast, in the Safe Zone. The Safe Zone is basically the entire east coast, excluding the Floridian Isles; its borders are Tennessee, Kentucky, West Virginia, Pennsylvania, and Alabama. All sealed off from the rest of the world by a massive wall. We plan to move there next. Just need to figure out a way in. Most likely, the people who did this to us, and are hunting us are there.

#2: I experienced another memory in my dream. I was being electrocuted while a man, referred to as "Doctor," blew a whistle. It was painful. I had a headache for hours afterward. The purpose of the electrocuting is unknown. I'm not sure how I feel about that yet.

#3: "Doctor" (clear glasses, black suit with dark purple tie, dark brown hair, pale skin, and a rough voice) has been seen or heard by all of us. Strike saw him in a memory that she believes to be her recovery after blade surgery. Hawk heard him while learning something in a class-room, and Viper heard him while training to fight.

#4: We think the Doctor is one of the persons responsible for the creation of our abilities. It makes the most sense. His status and intentions are unknown. All we can guess is that he helped develop us.

#5: The Brute and the Goon may know the Doctor; it could be how they tracked us. The Doctor could have developed them, just as he may have developed us.

FIVE

IMPROVEMENTS

STORM

Is the best way to get information through the Brute and the Goon? Or through a random officer? What route should I take? Is there another way that I'm missing?

I write these questions out in entry five. Hopefully, I'll be able to answer these questions sooner rather than later.

A hand waves over my face. "Storm...earth to Storm?"

"Yeah?"

Hawk raises a brow. "You ready? Or do you need a sec?"

"I'm ready."

Closing the journal, I slide it into my backpack. I hop down from the kitchen counter, grab my backpack and parka, and slip into my purple boots. Hawk has already left the kitchen and is walking out the front door. I scurry after her while tying my parka around my waist. I reach the doorway and slide my sunglasses on. Jumping down the steps, I land next to Hawk.

"Where are the other two?"

"They're out back, still clearing out all the shit. We've been working on it since this morning," Hawk says.

"Oh." I frown. "Why didn't you wake me up? I could have helped."

Hawk shifts her gaze to me. "You looked like shit yesterday. We wanted to make sure you slept as long as you needed."

We pass the border of the tree line and slip into the shadows of the dense forest. I step over a log, pushing branches out of my way.

"I wasn't that tired. Y'all could—"

"Storm, you were so tired last night, you didn't even bother taking out my braiding work. And you hate sleeping in braids. Besides, when you're tired you make this face like you've been kicked in the stomach...It's not a good look."

"Thanks, I think?"

"I'm serious, hummingbird."

"Hummingbird? That's a new one."

"It's 'cause you're like, always trying to make the days and weeks twenty-five-eight. Hummingbird should be your name instead of Storm. It's much more fitting."

"Oh yeah? Well, your name should be ankle-biter. It's much more fitting."

"Why's that?"

"'Cause you're short and a pain in the ass."

"We. Are. The. Same. Size. If anything, I'm a bit taller."

"As if."

"But you're right, I am *the* pain in the ass."

I laugh just as we reach the clearing. It's a tiny strip, spilling over with thin grass and leaves, the sun fully blazing into it. The patch smells of fresh dirt and dewy undergrowth. It's so protected that the grass is still green, the white and yellow flowers are still blooming. The breeze catches the individual blades, making them shimmer and gently domino throughout the space like waves. Nothing has changed since I last saw it. It's like it is permanently frozen in time.

"I'm glad to see the clearing hasn't gone to hell." Hawk steps into the tangle of grass. "Nice and soft too, just like I remember. This will be perfect for our training today."

"I thought I had Viper today."

Hawk looks back to me with a small smile. "Not after yesterday's shitshow, you don't. I switched with her. I have something new to show you anyway."

"Should I be excited?" I walk to the center of the clearing.

"I mean, it seems pretty fun. I don't really know. I—"

I freeze. Hawk's eyes glaze over and her mouth gapes. Before I can say anything, she lets out a loud gasp. She holds her hand to her chest, breathing heavily. I put my hand on her shoulder.

She brushes off my hand. "I'm...I'm fine...Just a little flashback. I'm fine."

"Are you sure?"

"Yeah. It wasn't anything new...Anyway, are you ready?"

Her hands shake a bit.

Is she lying to me? I hesitate. "Yeah. No extra weight this time."

After a few moments, Hawk and I sprint. On my fourth step, I spread my wings completely. On my sixth step, I leap with all my strength. The trees rush past me, and I'm gliding in the open air. A shadow falls from above. I look up to see a pair of grey and white wings. Hawk gives me a grin. Her ocean eyes sparkle against the deep blue sky.

"Watch this!"

Hawk flaps her wings, pushing herself higher and faster into the air. She whirls ahead of me with intense control. Suddenly she flattens her wings and log-rolls so quickly she barely descends a centimeter. When the roll stops, she shoots her wings back out and balances herself into a normal position.

I smile. "Oh yeah? Watch this!"

I fly above Hawk, my wings beating. Once I reach the highest point, I tuck in my wings and lean backward, causing my body to flip over Hawk. I shoot downward. Engaging my wings, I sail beneath Hawk once again.

"Show-off!" Hawk coasts to my side, coming to my level. "Hey, do you remember how long this flight takes?"

"About five minutes, I think," I say. "We're almost there."

Hawk nods and looks away. Her blonde braids sway in the rushing wind. She squints due to the sunlight and her clothes ripple as we glide. She closes her eyes. A bright smile forms on her lips when she inhales the fresh air.

It's like Hawk gets a high from the open skies. It's the feeling of being weightless, untethered, and unburdened for that brief five minutes. I think it lets her recharge her strength. I wonder if her strength is natural, or if it's something she learned to survive. I doubt even she has the answer. I'm sure she doesn't want to know that answer. But I don't have a doubt in my mind about her willpower. It's terrifying, but also incredible at times. Unfortunately, Hawk will do anything to appear strong, even if that means she has to lie or be reckless.

I turn my eyes to the horizon. Will I ever amount to anything close to what she does? To what Viper and Strike do? I wonder what they see when they look at me. Maybe it's not my business to know the answer. Are any of my questions my business?

"Storm?"

"Yeah?"

"What are you thinking about?"

"Nothing...nothing at all. You?"

Hawk starts to chat me up, something about getting more sleep. I tune her out and turn my attention back to the horizon. A gap in the endless sea of branches approaches us quickly—the town.

"Hawk," I cut her off. "We better land."

Hawk nods and begins to descend. I follow her motions, making sure to keep my arms at my sides, and we aim for the tiny break in the trees. She directs herself to hit the red dirt road head-on. I mimic her as the ground rushes toward us. I flip my wings back while rapidly beating them. My body follows and my legs become vertical before I land on the ground a few feet behind Hawk. Hawk slips her backpack off and throws her jacket over her wings. Hawk tells me I've improved as I jog next to her.

I smile. "Thanks. It's easier when there's less weight." I take off my pack.

"Yeah, yesterday must've been an off day for you."

I put on my parka. "It was. I'm not used to carrying someone around during a flight yet."

"I wasn't talking about that. I meant something else."

"What do you mean?"

"I mean you seemed off. There was something bothering you."

"Oh." I zip the parka up. "I just had a headache."

Hawk raises a brow.

"Okay...I did have a memory before that, but it was just a memory. Nothing else."

"Just a memory doesn't cut it. I get if you don't want to talk about it, but don't avoid it and then call it *just* a memory. For you, a memory is a big deal. You haven't gotten as many as us. I just...want you to be careful. They can get pretty bad."

"I know. I have it handled, don't worry."

"I know you can handle it but...Never mind."

I sling my pack on. "C'mon, I figure we could shop for supplies first and then look for work."

"Sounds like a plan to me; here's the list."

"Perfect. It only looks like we'll need to go to two—actually maybe only one place. We obviously won't get everything on the list 'cause of money, but we should get enough to keep us busy for a while."

"Which shop?"

"The supply store near Viper's old work, the one near that music shop." I start leading us down the road. "I have a buddy there. If she's still around, we could get everything cheap. Hopefully that leftover money could go to replacing what we left in Oklahoma City."

"We didn't leave much, just the mats and blankets."

"That's good. We can use the remaining cash for backup then. Just in case somethin' goes wrong."

"For sure."

The rows of buildings remain at a distance as we approach the entrance to town; a sign on the side of the road marks its start. The painted letters are worn away, making the town's name unknown to outsiders, but it doesn't matter because nobody except us enters this way.

"Do you need any bandages for your face? That scab on your cheek looks pretty bad. I'm surprised it healed so fast," Hawk says.

"Eh. It'll probably scar over, but I don't mind it. That's a good idea though. We should buy, like, a first-aid kit."

"Are you sure we have enough money?"

"Thirty bucks, plus the discount we could get at the shop. Which we probably will, so I think we're in the clear."

We reach the first building: a patch of apartments. Horses, bikes, and old rusted cars dot the street. A few people walk around. Most of them are working or are out for a late lunch. At the end of the street, laughter and string music vibrate from a bustling bar and out into the eroding town.

The road turns from dirt to worn concrete. Cracks in the street have been neglected, never to be fixed by its citizens. Yet somehow, the cracks provide new life. They allow the natural order to grow. In the springtime, flowers bloom between the cracks. In the fall, there's only dying grass. Whichever season it may be, nature finds a way to flourish in the face of neglect. The buildings are blanketed with ivy, moss, and vines. There are bundles of tree branches extending over each building as if the branches are protecting them from the sun. It's a town camouflaged without resistance, a place where nature can live among men—a shadow of what it used to be.

I stop outside a wooden building with faded white paint. It has two windows in the front, both still dusty as always, and a welcome sign hanging on the wooden door. The sign's W is missing. I walk up to the door, which is missing its knob, and push it open carefully. The door creaks. With measured steps, I walk into the tiny space that's overflowing with different supplies hanging on racks and walls. Rust and mildew lace the air, making me scrunch up my nose. The store has only the natural light coming from the crusty windows; nothing electrical works. In the back of the room sits a small counter with someone's socks resting on top. The socks' owner is reading a coffee-stained newspaper, their face hidden behind the pages, and they don't look up to acknowledge their new customers. I approach the counter, Hawk right behind me, and clear my throat. They don't look up.

I clear my throat again. "Where's Miss Joe?"

"Dunno, who's askin'?"

"A buddy of hers."

The man folds his newspaper, revealing a fading hairline. He's wearing a slightly unbuttoned flannel with more coffee stains on it.

"Oh. You must be that Scarface gal then, right?"

I cross my arms. "Dunno, who's askin'?"

"Must be then. She told me about you." He puts the newspaper on the counter, leaning deeper into the chair. He stretches his feet inside his brown socks. "I see why you have the nickname."

"So, is Miss Joe in today or not? You're wasting our time," Hawk says.

"Did someone say my name?"

I look over my shoulder. Miss Joe stands in the entranceway with two plastic bags of fresh food. My stomach growls.

"Scarface? Is that you? Of course it is! Who else would wear sunglasses inside?" Miss Joe laughs. She walks over, sets the food on the counter, and gives me a bear hug.

"I'm glad to see y'all are still here," I reply, slipping out of her grip.

"It's been rough lately. Barely any business comin' in, but we manage. So, what can I do for you today, girlies?"

"We're just here to get some supplies for the house. It's still a fixer-upper."

"Perfect! I'm glad to see the city didn't change ya! I was worried when ya told me you were movin' there. Most people become selfish and rude up there," she scoffs. "How about this? You get a discount as a welcome home present, since you're still such a sweetheart."

My eyes widen. "Thanks!"

"Miss Joe!" The man jumps out of his chair. "You don't even know these kids!"

"Oh, hush up. Scarface here has been more useful than you've ever been, and she doesn't even work here!"

"Yeah! Hush up," Hawk sneers.

Miss Joe bursts out laughing. I giggle a bit as the clerk slumps back into his chair with his arms crossed. I hand Hawk the list.

"We won't take much. I don't wanna take all of your stock," I say.

Miss Joe pinches my cheek. "Always such a sweetheart. It's perfect to see you again."

I lean against the counter. "So, how's everything been? Anything exciting happen while I was gone?"

"Let's see...A few horses got stolen last month. There was a small flash flood last week and there's someone runnin' 'round stealin' all of the W's on the welcome signs."

I open my mouth to ask a question.

"Don't you have two other members of ya clan? How 'bout y'all stop by tomorrow? I have some work that needs to be done and that lazy bum behind ya never does it right. I'm sure you could use the cash, since y'all just made it back to town."

"Oh, it's—"

"No, baby. I insist," Miss Joe hastily cuts me off. "Come in tomorrow, with the other two."

Hawk approaches the counter, dropping our supplies and a first-aid kit.

"Yes, thank you, ma'am," I reply. How did she know about the other two? Did I ever mention them to her?

"Yeah, thanks!" Hawk replies.

Hawk slides over ten dollars. The clerk takes it and counts it, as Miss Joe packs the supplies into plastic bags and hands me the planks to carry. We thank her, not the man, and Hawk leads the way out of the store. As we step outside, Hawk beelines for the bar.

"Hawk? Where are you going?"

"Riddle me this, I'm pretty hungry. I know you are too, looked like you were about to rush Miss Joe in there. So, how about we get some hot food from the bar?"

"We have food at home."

"C'mooon. We can pop into the bar really fast, get some hot food for everyone, then go and train back home."

I hesitate. "Okay, we'll get the cheapest thing."

"Perfect."

We go to the bar, which is overflowing with drunken laughter. People hang out outside, chatting among themselves, with fistfuls of glass mugs. They sit on wooden stools and puff out campfire smoke from thick cigarettes.

The bar is slightly bigger than the supply shop, but it has actual lights. There's a long, stained counter, and tables are scattered over a trash-ridden floor. People are eating at the tables, throwing darts, or having too much of a good time. The air stings with sweat and puke. There's a subtle stale perfume scent as well, and the place has a climate all of its own—drunken humidity. It sticks to the skin and burns every crevice of the eye. I gag. Hawk somehow doesn't. She squeezes her way through the crowd toward the bar; I fall behind due to my luggage. I can only see her blonde head, bobbing through the swamp of laughing giants. Hawk reaches the bar, calling over the bartender. A burly woman leans close to Hawk, who attempts to sweet-talk her, and the woman smiles. I trudge through the swamp and make it to the bar; Hawk points to me and explains to the woman I'm a friend of hers. Hawk asks about the food options. The bartender leaves, with the promise of returning with the cheapest option. Hawk turns to me, but a large man flops between us with an empty glass in his hand.

"Excuse me, buddy, but we're trying to have a conversation here," Hawk snaps.

The sweaty man sluggishly looks at Hawk, a brow raised. He pauses and swallows. "Hoow old are you?" He leans in closer.

Hawk smirks. "Pretty sure I'm fourteen, or maybe thirty-three, but I honestly can't remember, bud."

"You're kinda hawt."

The bartender returns and declares that he's cut off. As the man throws a small fit, the bartender hands Hawk a bag of steaming fries and apologizes for the man. Hawk slips away from the counter, leading me through the crowd. I make sure to stay close behind her. Once we make it out of the swarming bar, I can finally breathe again. We walk toward the town's exit.

"See, it wasn't that bad."

I smirk. "Yeah, except for that guy."

"He was hella annoying." Hawk turns to me and her eyes widen. "Watch out!"

She shoves me to the side—something whirls past my ear, causing me to drop all the planks. Hawk ducks and a glass shatters behind her. I whip around to see the man from the bar getting beaten up by a group of men. They grind his skull into the ground and kick him relentlessly with steel-toe boots. The patrons of the bar watch and slide dollar bills to the center of their tables, muttering wagers. Nobody is stepping in.

I take a step forward but stop myself. Hawk starts to sprint toward the fray, I grab her wrist quickly to keep her leashed. She tugs against me as the sound of cracking ribs slices through the air, followed by slurred cries for help. Hawk continues to attempt to pull away from me, even as the drunken man stops struggling.

"Next time, pay us!"

A man swings his foot into the drunk man's skull one last time. He's knocked out cold. A bit of blood gushes from the side of his grimy face. His nose is splintered for good. The men vanish into the buildings as the patrons collect bets. Hawk's hand shakes underneath mine. She rips it away but doesn't look me in the eyes.

"What the hell Storm... What the hell..."

I cross my arms. Waiting for the outburst to come, for the shit-storm to ensue, for another fight to break out.

"Why did you—?" Hawk's face gradually changes to red as she rubs her temples.

"He's a drunk. He obviously had it coming to him."

"That doesn't mean we shouldn't step in. He deserves a fair fight at least."

"He didn't deserve it and shit like that is never fair. You know that."

"Not if we all help each other," Hawk says through her teeth. "Everyone deserves to be helped. Wouldn't you like to be helped every once in a while?"

I grab a plank from the ground. "Sure. Whatever. Let's get going. Help me pick these up."

"You just don't get it, do you? People sometimes need help. Do you even realize how much help we could really use right now?"

"I know. I know."

"You don't."

"Okay, fine, I don't get it. But that doesn't mean you have to have such a short fuse about it. It's worse than normal today, you know that? Let's just agree to disagree, okay?"

Hawk lowers her eyes.

"You need to understand that we have to handle our own business right now. We have to pick our battles, not join any more."

Hawk picks up a plank. "Next time, don't stop me."

I sigh. "I won't. I promise. You can join the tussle next time, and I'll be there to back you up if you need it."

Hawk takes in a deep breath. "Truce?"

"Truce. Now let's go. I'm itching to know what you wanted to teach me."

We pick up all the supplies and rush out of town. Approaching the road, I messily prepare for takeoff. As I manage to tie my jacket around my waist and put my backpack on, I flip out my wings. Right as we're out of sight, we take off, flying away from that town.

The wind has gotten colder. My teeth chatter as we slice through the sky. My stomach suddenly twists, growling at me. I beat my wings powerfully to zip past Hawk. The wind is no match for the both of us. I fly quickly, despite my heavy haul of wood, and we reach the clearing within seven minutes. We drop off the supplies in the clearing and return to the open skies for training.

"What's on the agenda?" I ask.

Hawk smiles. "Divebombs."

I grin.

"We'll need to fly higher for this!"

I nod and we beat our wings to scale the clouds. Hawk explains how to position my wings and how to slow down after the dive. We climb further and further away from the forest, its details gradually dulling as we go. The air thins, causing my breath to burn.

"How will I know when to slow down?" I ask.

"A little after the halfway point, not for long though," Hawk says. "You can watch me first."

"Isn't this your first time doing it?"

"I did it in my memories, didn't I? It should be a piece of cake." She grins. "Okay, we should be high enough now."

I flap my wings rapidly to stay in one place. Then Hawk puts her hands to her sides, pointing her head for the trees. She positions her wings. They're bent slightly further back, and they allow her to cut through any resistance from the air. Hawk hurdles toward the earth, getting smaller and smaller by the second. I hold my breath as she builds speed. Suddenly Hawk fully extends her wings and swoops up. Hawk barely misses the tips of the trees and shoots away, faster than any bird of prey.

I take in a deep breath. I can do this. I put my arms close to my sides. Aiming my head for the unforgiving earth, I position my wings back.

The slicing of the wind whistles in my ears. My braids levitate behind my temples and my smile grows as my speed picks up. My heart stops, but my adrenaline has taken the reins, keeping every ounce of me alive. The wilderness looms ahead with open arms, telling me it's time to slow down. I expand my wings and arms, my speed instantly decreasing with every passing inch. I angle up, bouncing away from the tree line, and shoot horizontally toward Hawk. Hawk cheers me on as I zip past her. I slow myself by beating my wings. Hawk catches up to me, giving me a high-five in mid-air.

"Now let's go work on your landing!"

THE GOLDEN SETTING sun peeks through the balding branches as we jog back to the house. Our stomachs are howling. Racing up the steps, I throw the planks into a pile near the door. I yank the door open; it almost rips off its hinges. I run into the kitchen and throw the sack of food on the table, ripping through the bag for the container of fries. Hawk charges in as I open the container. We both snatch a handful of fries—such salty goodness.

Hawk grabs my wrist. "Hold on, let's wait for the other two."

"Strike! Viper! Time to eat!" I yell.

A few seconds later, the door to the backyard swings open. Viper and Strike walk in, both sweating bullets.

"What took you two so long?" Viper exclaims.

"We wanted to get you guys a treat, since you've been working all day," Hawk says.

Strike beams "Aw. How sweet."

"Hawk just wanted something besides canned food," I say.

Hawk elbows my side.

I wince, holding my ribs. "I'm just tellin' them the truth!"

Viper and Strike go to work on the fries. Strike asks how town was.

"It was all right. Nothing too crazy happened," Hawk says.

I raise a brow. "She's lying. We almost got into a bar fight."

"It was not a bar fight, more like a street fight, but it doesn't matter. Either way, I could have taken all those guys with my eyes closed."

I turn to her. "You had to push me out of the way of a flying bottle thrown by a guy who swigged way too much beer. It was definitely a bar fight."

Viper perks up. "You could say goin' into town was a *swig*-cess?"

In between her busts of hiccupping laughter, Hawk exclaims it was a terrible joke. We join in with her contagious wheezing until we have sore stomachs and swollen cheeks.

SIX

THE FOUR DEMONS

STORM

Trying to fall asleep is like holding a flame to a wick that refuses to light. My mind is the flame, heated and capable, but it cannot find the wick in the night. It causes my eyes to burn and my body to melt into the concrete. Everything burns as if thousands of matches were being held against my skin, but the wick still refuses to light. When I do rest, I fall in love with it. When I think of rest, I hate it. Six hours could mean only nothingness or everything I've forgotten; I never know what will come. This unknown is what coats the wick, preventing it from burning.

My eyes scan the ceiling, studying every minute line and shadow, every imperfection and each unnatural mark. I hold my arms in front of me, taking note of every scar and each permanent black line. All are a reminder of the past that I cannot decipher.

Since I cannot remember who I was before, it feels like my past self is a stranger. She's the one who inscribed these scars on my body. Scars that trace both sides of my forearms, my fingers, and my spine; the scar trailing over my heart and face. More scars overlap the others on my arms, and even more run from the side of my neck to my collar-bone. All of them are her doing. It's strange that girl gained so many scars, but then had her shell cemented over my skin. It's strange that I know nothing of her motivations and that I don't know if she deserved the pain that caused these scars.

I rub my fingers over my tattoo, *WDXX12*, staring at it until I have to remind myself to blink. Each line was drawn by an unknown hand. Its identity is clear: the program's true name. At least, that's what Strike thinks. It's another reminder that the program is still lurking in my mind, I think, but I don't know where it is. I hope it is dark though. I hope it is cold. I hope this program feels more pain than I feel, because it deserves it.

It's dangerous, but I wish I knew of more about it. Then I could know about the owner of the shell I wear, and I could have answers to so many awful questions. Was my past self, what I know today as the program? And am I a part of the program or is the program a part of me? Was the girl before me a monster? If she was, does that make me a monster?

I unstick my back from the ground, heaving my softened limbs into a sitting position. Criss-crossing my legs, I glue my palms to my knees and allow my wings to unfurl around me. I wince at the soreness in my back from flying. Arching my spine, I stretch my wings out all the way. The muscles tighten, burn, and urge me to relax. I noisily breathe out when my wings curl back in.

Hawk mumbles something and rolls over to her side. I hold my breath. I hope I didn't wake her. At my side, Strike sleeps with her back to the wall. Viper rests on the countertop in front of me, with her limbs sprawling over the sides.

Hawk mutters again, her fists clench, and she tenses up. She breathes heavily. Her head shakes side to side before her murmuring becomes frantic. I reach over to wake her from her nightmare, but she shoots up onto her knees before I get the chance. Hawk screams. Her own fists beat her head over and over and over again. Hawk tries to stand but falls over on her side, beating herself over and over again. I grab her wrists and stand above her, trying to control her spasms.

Hawk's eyes are wide, her pupils almost non-existent. She shrieks like a scalding knife is severing her vertebrae one by one.

"Wake up! Wake up! Hawk! Can you hear me!"

Instead of a response, she grinds her teeth together. Hawk tries to rip her wrists from my grasp to beat herself. I slide down next to her, pulling her into my lap, and cross her arms over her lap to restrain her. Hawk wildly kicks her legs and twists in my grip. Her screaming only rises. Strike rushes to Hawk's flailing legs and pins them down. Viper latches onto Hawk's curling stomach. Hawk digs her back into my torso, leaning her head into my collarbone and screaming until it sounds like her vocal cords tear at the seams. My ears ring as Hawk drowns in the black air, unable to get a breath between her screams and through her grinding teeth.

I bury my lips close to her ear. "We've got you...You're safe."

Hawk continuous to scream, jostling around even more violently.

"I hope you can hear me. Listen to me. You're safe with us. You're safe."

The screaming disappears and her breathing slows.

"We'll help you with anything."

Hawk goes limp but I keep my grip around her. A sweat has broken out on my forehead. Viper lets go of Hawk's wrists, cups Hawk's cheeks with her hands, and lifts Hawk's head to study her pupils. I hold my breath.

Viper sighs. "They're normal again."

Strike and I sigh with relief. Strike releases Hawk's shins, resting back on her heels, and pushes her hair out of her face. She stares at Hawk, breathing heavily with her brows furrowed. There are tears glistening on the rims of her eyes. We all exhale, unable to conjure any words.

Hawk intertwines her fingers with mine. She's shivering when she turns her shoulders toward me. I meet her bloodshot gaze. The drying tears on her face burn my eyes and her shaking fingers melt my skin at the slightest touch. I wipe away a tear sticking to her face.

Hawk closes her eyes, rests her head on my chest, and curls up into a ball. I hold her. Strike and Viper join us.

I slide my fingers onto her wrist, trying to comfort her. Hawk relaxes into my lap and I cradle her tightly. My teeth clench, and my chest burns as my fingers stroke her hair.

I've never had a conversation with the program. All three of the others, Hawk, Strike, and Viper have. They know what it's like to stare down a demon. Only Strike and Viper can truly comfort Hawk; I have nothing to say.

"It's gotten worse." Viper slips away from us. "Now it's only a matter of time—"

"Don't talk like that," Strike cuts her off and pushes herself away from me. "The program has no control over us, not anymore. It must have built up or something. Hawk has suppressed hers for so long. As long as we keep our guard up, everything should be fine..."

"No. You and I, and Hawk, know it's gotten worse. All of our programs have been speaking more, making us our worst selves. We're too emotional and violent. It's only a matter of time before we can't do it anymore. When we'll have to give up control."

"If you start thinking like that, that's exactly what will happen! We can—"

"You don't get it Strike! We're done for! We both know it! The only one here who has a chance of lasting longer is Storm! But us, we've been attacked before. We're spoken to on the daily now! When all of this first started, it was only once or twice a month! We see the memories. We've seen more; the pain, the monsters, the killings by our own hands, by its hands. We've all had memories from that day! What happens if we lose control and history repeats itself? More people will die because we couldn't control it!"

Viper holds her head in her hands, pushing her long hair back. "Now it talks to me almost every day. It tells me I'm a murderer and that I shouldn't be alive. It tells me that I don't deserve to have control. I don't even know what I am! What I was made for! We know nothing about this thing! We don't stand a chance!"

"We have a chance! When we get more information, like how we planned, we can figure this out. We can all get rid of this thing together. Don't give up now! Be patient! The truth will come. I'm not going to let this thing control my life! And I'm not letting you give up!"

"Why are you saying this? You don't know if we can do it! We don't have any more time!" Viper snarls. "How can you be so sure the truth is coming?"

I'm numb, their shouting voices whistle in my ears.

Strike hesitates. "You don't know that our time is getting close. We have time. I know it. I feel it. I'm sure it—"

"Shut up! You're the rational one here, right? Then why are you—"

"Don't you get it? I'm next! I'm next because that's what happens. First Hawk, then me, and then you. Always in that order. They know how to break us down one by one to make the others afraid. We can't let our programs walk all over us. I know it can be controlled. I just know it. We can buy ourselves time. That's what we're good at. We just did it against those officers. We just have to be smart about this." Strike approaches her. "Viper, please. We have a chance. Don't give—"

"I didn't say I wanted to give up, but I'm saying we're runnin' out of time. We have to find this information soon or we're done for," Viper murmurs.

I get to my feet, holding Hawk's limp body in my arms. "One day, all of you will be able to control the program. I promise that. But today we have to keep our heads. If we don't, the day will never come that all of us can remember our names and never hear the damn program ever again." I shift my eyes to their wide ones. "Stop worrying about the future or the past. Right now, let's just let each other breathe, and focus on helping Hawk. We can talk things out later, when she's ready." I lay Hawk on her mat, making sure a blanket is placed securely over her.

Viper nods. "I'll...I'll go out and get some water for her."

"I'll go with you," Strike says.

Both of them make their way to the front of the house and disappear. Once outside, their whispers are still clear as day.

"Why are you comin' with me?" Viper asks.

"I wanted to apologize...if I hurt you in any way."

"Oh, thanks. It was just...Some bad stuff boiled up, you know?"

Their voices are fading.

"Yeah, we're all afraid," Strike says. "Storm was right though. Keep our heads. You made a good point too. We need to be more alert."

"Yeah..."

Their voices vanish. I'm left with ringing silence and Hawk's struggling breath. From what the others have told me, the program attacks build over time. The program gradually gets stronger and stronger. They can feel its presence. So, why didn't Hawk say anything? Why her, why them, why now?

I run my fingers through my hair, trying to find answers, but I'm left with an emptiness that rejects any rationale. It confirms that I was never intended to understand the inner workings of another's mind. I was only made to analyze and investigate it. But I guess that's how everyone is wired.

I sit down a little way down from her. I listen to her heartbeat, her steady breathing. Any spike in either and I will do anything to keep her bruises at a minimum tonight. Holding my head in my hands, I close my eyes in an attempt to tune out my whirling thoughts.

I lie on my back and spread my arms at my sides. I graze my fingers over Hawk's palm just below her tattoo, which reads, WFXX33. A few rays of light drift into the room, moving methodically across the aging floor. Hawk's fingers close on my hand before her bruising blue eyes meet mine. Her face is still pale, dotted with growing purple spots, and the morning sun grazes over her face. Hawk remains stolid, as if nothing happened. She stares at me as if I'm the one who has been attacked. But hidden deep in her eyes are hints of an extreme need. This need is unknown to me, but my mind jumps to a single theory—the need to persevere to new heights.

She opens her mouth to say something.

"Don't say a word," I say. "Just rest."

"We have to go into town soon."

"We're not going anywhere, not for a while."

"I'm fine."

"Stop lying. Just go back to sleep. The three of us will be watching over you."

"You're sleeping too then."

I sigh. "Haw—"

"Sleep next to me, or we go into town."

I pause. "Fine." I roll over on my side, closer to Hawk. "Wake me up when you wake up."

Hawk's grey wing blankets me, and I allow my own to rest on the floor. She grips my hand tighter. Her eyes flutter as they close, and she finally relaxes. Her wing provides safety from the morning light and I find my own eyes drooping.

I'll wait for her to fall asleep; it won't take long. I struggle to keep my eyes open, and eventually I only see darkness. I float with only myself for company. I'm cold from the damp ground beneath me. Plants sway around me, leaves flutter, and a slow coo emerges. Following it, I can make out a distant hum.

"Despiértate!"

My eyes snap open and I spring into action. Holding my hand up to block the light, I see Viper standing above me.

"See, I told y'all that's the only way," Viper remarks.

"Huh. I guess you're right," Hawk says.

"What?"

"Don't worry about it. Hurry up and get dressed," Hawk replies.

"But you shouldn't—wait, how long was I asleep for? Why are you up? You were supposed to wake me up!"

Hawk holds out her hand. "It's afternoon, almost night. C'mon, let's get going."

"But—"

"I'm fine. We can talk about it later. I need some more time to... gather myself."

Nodding, I take her hand and Hawk hauls me to my feet. I walk to my mat, picking up my discarded jeans from the floor. I slip them and my other clothes on before I shove my feet into my boots.

"Are you ready yet?" Hawk calls to me. "The other two are waiting on us."

I turn to her as Hawk finishes her braids. "Have an extra hair tie?" I ask. "Do you think I need my pack? It has all the money in it."

Hawk throws my jacket to me. "I'm not taking mine and check the pocket. C'mon, let's get going."

I check the pocket, snatching a hair tie, and I tie my jacket around my waist as I follow Hawk out of the living room. Twisting my hair into a ponytail, I keep close to Hawk as we leave the cabin. We jog after Strike and Viper, who have passed the tree line. The afternoon sun barely dents the shadows. The hair on the back of my neck stands on end when we catch up to them. Winter is getting closer, faster than I anticipated. Good thing we already have a way to get money before it hits. I'm not sure what we would do without Miss Joe's generosity.

* * *

I OPEN the creaking door to Miss Joe's supply shop. We walk in together, and Viper closes the door behind us. This time Miss Joe sits at the desk. The clerk stands in the back doorway, reading his coffee-stained paper. Miss Joe looks up from her book and her eyes widen, but she soon smiles.

"Scarface! Good afternoon! I see you brought your friends with you; how lovely it is to have *all* of you here."

I smile. "Sorry we're late. We had some extra work to do this morning."

"No worries." Miss Joe abruptly stands up. "Hey! Go get...the list for these girls."

The clerk nods, folding his paper, before he disappears behind the door. Hawk steps to my side with a plastered grin.

"Miss Joe, I'd like you to meet these two." Hawk grabs Strike and Viper by the shoulders. "This is good ole' Kitty." She motions to Viper. "And this is Fox."

"Pleasure to meet you two." Miss Joe drums her desk with her long nails.

I narrow my eyes. Miss Joe drums her desk faster. Her eyes twitch over her shoulder to the door before she quickly looks back to us.

"So, what are we doing today?" I ask slowly.

"Oh, just some heavy liftin' here and there. Robert isn't the strongest man around."

"Really? What exactly are we liftin'?"

"Oh, you know. Wood and other things..."

Hawk slips her arms off Strike and Viper's shoulders, backing away from Miss Joe. "Is there anything else?"

I exchange a few glances with the others.

"Maybe we should get goin'." I put my hand on Viper's shoulder, pulling her behind me. "I just remembered that Kitty needs to take care a few things at the bar. We'll see you tomorrow. Sorry for—"

A pain plunges into my shoulder as I notice a shadow in the doorway. I stagger back. My mouth gapes and my fingers grasp the dart sticking out of my shoulder. The world slowly fades around me.

"*Storm!*" someone yells, forcing my eyes to stay open a moment longer.

I meet my attacker's hollow eyes as they fire another dart. I plant my foot, ready to charge him, but my knees give out. I hit the floor, my head bounces, and my reality falters. I'm met with darkness once again.

SEVEN
DEWY-EYED HUMS

STORM

The faint beating of powerful wings flutters in the distance. A breeze, produced by the fury of feathers, coaxes my eyes open and I'm met with its creator. An owl dressed in cosmic black with heated yellow eyes rests on a jagged branch. The owl hoots.

When I sit up, the owl flies into the forest before me, along a path created from eroding vegetation. It vanishes in the mist that manages to slip past the murky branches above. Unsteadily, I get to my feet. After a few steps they are coated in mud and wet grass. My hair sticks to my skin, my clothes no longer provide warmth, and my fingertips are purple. I shiver feverishly. The aroma of a sky full of water, striking the underbrush, swells around me. Grey light illuminates the dark green leaves and grass. Its weak shine disperses, leaving only fragments in the fog. I have no way of knowing what time of day it is or where the sun may lay. The forest is in a limbo between night and day. Its thickness suffocates my eyes, ears, and breath.

The patter of rain is faint. My heartbeat throbs in my throat. The dense forest is silent. Neither the mist, the rain, nor the underbrush provide hints of security or danger; there is no indication of reality or illusion. There's nothing to tie together. A soft hum travels past the endless fog. The hums swirl along the path, beckoning my curiosity but strengthening my unwillingness. Neither want to coexist. But curiosity moves my feet toward the path, and I travel deeper into the cold fog.

As I walk, the vegetation thickens. The humming thickens. The fog thickens. Branches mesh together into an archway that leads to the end of a tunnel filled with pale, shimmering light. My eyes adjust to the light as I travel past the archway and step into the next realm. The hums are near.

A clearing of grass beckons me forward. Rain drenches each blade, freezing their presence in time. In the center of the field are the remains of a brick house withering in the weight of the fog. Piles of bricks make up three walls. The crumbling structure has a tangle of crimson roses that coincide with the dying bricks. The top of a rogue tree provides shelter. There are no doors to provide privacy, and no windows to control the shadows. The wild grass is the floor, the untamed roses like cement, and the sky is the only source of light.

In the branches, the owl pecks at a perfect maroon apple. Below the branches a peculiar item lies resting in a hole in the trunk of the tree. I walk closer, peeking in to find the body of a ukulele decomposing before my eyes. The faded instrument's strings have snapped and are curled at the neck. Its carvings have vanished. A beautiful lily thrives in the ukulele's center. An unpolished silver chain without a speck of rust is wrapped around its base.

The humming bounces off each brick and branch. I follow the sound to the next torn wall. At the edge of the field, a figure stands in the last rays of grey light. Her dark brunette hair is untouched by the rain. She is wearing a black dress and her hair is pulled back in a single braid. I approach her, unable to make out more because of the shadows. Her warm hums bring tears to my eyes I reach a trembling hand out to meet the owner of these misty hums, but the humming stops.

EIGHT

FORMAL INTRODUCTIONS

STORM

The sound of a skull smashing into a solid floor snaps me back to reality. Before me are two shaking silhouettes of struggling souls. One, wearing dark clothes, pins down the other who's wearing yellow. The shouts, the pain in my shoulder, and my caged reality set in. The Scarred Brute shoves the blonde head deeper into the ground with a massive hand. The figure remains motionless. Veins throb on the Brute's forehead. He bares his teeth and raises a shaking fist.

The Blue-eyed Goon grabs the Brute by the shoulders and rips him away from his victim. They exchange a glance, for too long, and the Brute tears his arm from the Goon. He straightens out his grey jacket and takes a step closer to the figure, pointing a finger.

"You deserve everything you get from this day forward! Every. Damn. Thing!"

The blonde is conscious but doesn't respond.

"And if they don't punish you, I'll do it myself!"

The Goon shoves the Brute further away from the blonde, stepping between the two. "C'mon, keep your composure, will you? It looks like we have an audience now." The Goon motions his head.

The Brute looks over his shoulder, locking eyes with mine, and a chill runs down my spine.

"Listen, you're right. She's a bitch. She knows that. Just calm down, will ya? Glacia will get what she deserves. There's no use in fussing over the inevitable."

The Brute takes in a breath, lowers his gaze, and walks to the door. "Whatever, let's get set up."

The Brute walks out. The Goon follows and the door slams behind them. Now the only source of light comes from a sliver at the bottom of the door. It's synthetic white. The light drapes onto Glacia and highlights the bloodstains on her yellow jumpsuit.

I keep to the floor, watching Glacia from behind a glass prison. My shoulder aches. The dart used to knock me out has a persistent vengeance. My brain swells, my bones are rubber, and my eyes melt. Each breath I take is a furious fight against my own lungs. Each move I make causes the world to slide away from me.

I'm shackled by rough metal chains to the floor by my hands and feet. I'm wearing a worn yellow jumpsuit. Hawk, Strike, Viper, and I each have a cage lined up against one wall. I'm next to Viper on the end, followed by Strike, with Hawk at the other end. This Glacia person is the only one who doesn't have a glass container to keep her prisoner. Her neck, hands, feet, and torso have shackles on them, all bound to either the concrete wall or the floor. She keeps her head on the floor, almost as if she's hiding from the superficial light but cannot escape it. Her pale hair is barely visible, and her facial features are left to my imagination. She lies still, her heaving chest the one sign that she's alive, even if she'd rather not be.

"Storm? Are you awake?" Viper whispers.

"Yeah," I rasp.

"Are you okay?" Viper puts her hand on the glass between us.

"I could be better. Are you okay? Are the other two okay?"

"I'm fine, just a little sore. And they're still knocked out," Viper murmurs. "When did you wake up?"

"When the Brute nearly clobbered that girl. You?"

"Same here. How long do you think we've been here?"

"Not sure." I hold my hand to my forehead, hoping to ground myself from the spinning world. "How about you ask the girl, Glacia?"

"Hey...Glacia?"

Glacia doesn't move, nor does she make a sound.

"Are you okay? Are you hurt?"

Glacia turns her head to Viper, her strong features showing themselves. She opens her frost-infused eyes, taking my breath away, but keeps her cheek to the concrete. Her light hair is styled into a pixie cut. She has sharp brows and a natural scowl with hollowed out cheeks. Glacia' skin is drained of color, as if she was carved from winter's harshness. She looks both as fragile and as severe as ice. She's not someone I would imagine existing in a prison. I'm surprised that she's managed to survive the Brute's outrage, possibly for many months.

"Glacia," Viper urges.

"I'm fine," Glacia rasps, coldly.

"Sorry to bother you, but—"

"You four have been here for a few hours now." Glacia unsteadily pulls herself up and leans against the wall behind her.

Viper and I sigh with relief. It feels like I've been knocked out for days. I scoot to the corner closest to Viper, lean against it, and let my head rest on the glass wall behind me, hoping for the spinning to stop.

"If you don't mind me askin', how long have you been here?" Viper asks.

Glacia motions her bruised head to the wall behind her. Arrays of crooked white lines are highlighted in artificial rays. They illuminate and frame her, like she's glowing against the bleakness of the concrete.

"About three months."

"Damn. What are ya in for?"

Glacia doesn't respond, choosing instead to close her eyes. She pulls her knees to her chest, the chains shaking as she does so, and buries her face in her knees.

"Listen, Glacia. I have one more question," Viper whispers. "Then I'll leave you alone."

Glacia opens her eyes. The shimmering from the door hits a single eye, causing her blue iris to glow.

"Where the hell are we?"

"The base in Oklahoma City. It has the highest security around. It's where they keep the most dangerous people. If you're tryin' to figure out a way to escape, you're a fool. Only idiots try to escape hell," Glacia snaps, her heart rate increasing. "Now leave me alone. I don't want a beating for speaking to you." She flicks her eyes to the ceiling.

I follow her gaze. In the corner sits a camera with a faint green light, aimed right at her. Viper and I exchange a glance. The increase of Glacia's heart rate was heard by Viper as well. Two possible reasons as to why it had happened is because she was either nervous or she was lying. Glacia closes her eyes again, her face disappearing from view.

The door whips open and I cover my eyes with my palms to protect them from the light. I hear two pairs of footsteps enter the room. The sound of jingling keys bounces about the cold walls. I spread my fingers apart to see two women guards standing there. One of them approaches my cell. She methodically unlocks the glass door and steps to the side to let the second guard into my space. The second guard towers over me, seizing the chain from the ground and tightening it until my arms straighten. I don't budge. She grabs my wrists. The second guard heaves me up onto my feet, her glare meeting mine.

"You do as I say, girl. Is that understood?" The second, more hefty guard spits.

I don't answer her. The corner of the guard's mouth curls up. She palms my head in her massive hand and whips the side of my head against the glass. My vision blurs and I slump to my knees. My body collapses underneath my own weight.

"Hey!" Viper snarls. "Stop it!"

"Shut up or you're next!"

Viper opens her mouth, but I shake my head at her. She closes it and sits back down with smoke coming out of her ears. Blood drizzles down my brow, pooling into my eye. The guard grabs my hair before she cocks my head back, forcing me to meet her dark eyes. She's got bird-like eyes, dark like a pigeon's and completely focused on her next meal.

"I asked you a question, girl." The second guard tightens her grip on my hair. "Are you too stupid or somethin'? Too drugged-up to speak? Or do mutt-looking fuckers like you not talk?"

"Stop it. Just let me unchain her so we can get this over with," the first guard replies.

Bird-eyes shifts her gaze to the first guard. "Don't worry so much. Seeker Emil and that fussy trainee won't mind if we have some fun. It's not often that we get fresh meat."

"I'm doing my job. You should too. Besides, the Doctors will poach us if any of them are too hurt."

We get a small break then.

"You're a real buzzkill aren't you, Montana?" Bird-eyes forces me onto my feet by my hair. "Here. She's all yours."

"That's not my name."

Keys glint in the low light, swaying and clinking as they hit the cuffs, and then my feet are free from the chains. Montana picks up the chains attached to the handcuffs and passes them over to Bird-eyes. Bird-eyes grabs my neck and shoves me out of the glass cell. I follow behind Montana. Bird-eyes takes up the rear, and they lead me into the doorway of white light. I squint when we step into the hallway. Everything, including the six grey blobs that surround us, is a blur to me.

"This is your entourage!" Bird-eyes exclaims. "So don't you try anything gutsy, girl. Otherwise, you'll get another dart in your ass or a taser to the eye."

The grey guards aim their weapons directly at me. Bird-eyes and Montana have tasers on their belts. Bird-eyes once again forces me to walk right behind Montana, with three guards on each side of me. The tips of their guns are so close, I can smell the darts.

Polish shines on the walls. There's an endless sea of lights above us. Everything is made up of concrete—the floors, the walls, the ceilings, and even the vents. Each hallway is identical and leads into another. Our footsteps echo loudly. I can't identify what's on my right or left, above or below, due to my hazy vision. Before long, the hallway ends at a steel door.

The Goon leans against the door. The tapping of his shoe travels throughout the static walls. He's dressed in all black and his eyes slice through everything, causing the hair on the back of my neck to stand up just before we make it to him. He tells the guards to go on a smoke break as he tightens the slack on my chain, causing me to stumble forward past Montana. The Goon leads me through the door into a grey room with bright lights that would never dare to flicker. Polished mirrors engulf the tomb and reveal three reflections. I eye my own image to see bruises collecting around the side of my face. Fresh blood shines on my skin. The scab is still there from my last encounter with the Brute.

The Goon seats me in a metal chair at a table that's been bolted down. He attaches my chains to the legs of the table and allows some slack for my hands. There's a crisp sheet of paper in front of me with only three lines written out on it. Below the fine print, there's a furious piece of handwriting that's lopsided compared to the rest of the sheet. Whoever wrote it was either in a rush, or raging.

The Scarred Brute, the third reflection, is leaning against the mirrors. He side-eyes me from underneath furrowed brows. I lock eyes with him, not backing down. He's wearing his grey coat, plaid scarf, and protective leather gloves. Strangely, I cannot see any signs that we had fought before. He's bruiseless, woundless.

The Goon exchanges places with the Brute. The Brute stiffens and slides into the chair across from me. He scans me up and down. I mimic him.

"Those damn guards, they damaged her." The Brute reaches into his pocket.

"But isn't that the cut you gave her on the other cheek?" the Goon asks.

The Brute huffs. "They were supposed to heal all the wounds before we met her." He pulls out a petite rectangular case. "Good thing I keep these on me."

"Are you sure that—"

"The Doctors ordered that all of them must be in perfect condition, the less use of the pills the better. It's our orders. Now..." He opens the box, pulling out a tiny white capsule, and grabs onto my chains. "Don't make this harder than it needs to be. This will heal you."

The Brute contracts the chain, pulling my torso over the table until I'm nearly nose-to-nose with him. The white capsule hovers above my lips, held there by his leather-clad fingers. His hollow eyes shift from mine. He switches his grip from the chains to my cheeks and forces my jaw open. I jolt back, but another set of hands latches onto my shoulders. There's a snap, and a foul taste disperses in my mouth. The Brute releases my jaw. I retract back, coughing and sputtering like a horse as I try to spit out the substance, but I already know it's been absorbed. I grit my teeth and continue to cough as a tingling sensation spreads across my face.

"Now we'll go through the formalities," the Brute says. "My name is Trainee Josh West. This is my partner, Seeker Axl Emil. Today, you'll be answering questions the Doctors requested we ask you before they arrive."

I lean back but keep my eyes on him.

"You have to answer each question honestly. We'll know if you're lying and if you do, there will be a punishment. Is that clear?" Josh asks.

I raise a brow.

"My partner has the ability to hear heartbeats. One irregular beat, and he'll call you out."

You won't get a word out from me anyway.

Josh picks up the sheet of paper. "Firstly, what do you call yourself?"

I notice something flash underneath Josh's plaid scarf, and I strain to see what it is. It's a piece of silver; a necklace of some sort, but I can't tell what type.

"I assume you still call yourself Number Twelve. That's the most probable. Wouldn't you think the same?" Josh turns to his partner. The necklace dislodges from his scarf and I see it's an unpolished silver locket, which disappears back under the plaid fabric as gravity takes its toll.

Axl nods without looking up.

"Secondly, why did you and the others decide to settle in Oklahoma City?"

Why is he rushing through these questions?

"That's an obvious one. You were in the city because of the shelter, food, and job availability. It's the most rational thing to do."

He's not even letting me respond. He's not interested in what these Doctors want to know. There's something else.

"Lastly, what's—well, that must be a typo. What's your favorite color? Weird. The receptionist must have mistyped all of this. Maybe she misheard them on the phone." Josh crumples up the sheet of paper, shoving it into his pocket, and flicks his eyes back to mine. "Now, I have a few questions of my own."

Here we go.

Josh leans his forearms on the table, so close I can smell the fire in his breath. "In regard to the horrific actions you orchestrated a year ago."

What the hell? What is he talking about?

"I want to know three things. First, I want to know how you sleep at night."

I don't...

"I want to know how you did it," his voice rises.

Did what? What did I do?

"And I want to know why you would abandon your mission. How does someone like you use your abilities to hurt all of those innocent lives?"

The memory...That's what he's talking about. The bloody day... The monsters. How many people were hurt? What was the mission?

Josh slams his fist on the table. "Answer me, dammit!"

It's not like I hurt him. I would have remembered him if the program had... I think.

Axl puts his hand on Josh's quaking shoulder. "Calm down. You haven't even let her have time to speak."

Josh takes a breath.

"She may look calm." Axl snaps his eyes to mine. "But her heart rate is through the roof right now."

I grit my teeth.

"She's not gonna talk today. Maybe she's too drugged still. Let's send her away, give her some time to simmer. We can come back and talk to her when the Doctors arrive, maybe even before then. Besides, we can still question Thirty-Three, Twenty-Seven, and Forty-Five now, and come back to her next time we're here."

"That's three months from now!"

"Would you chill out? You're giving her information, you dildo."

Josh's face reddens. "I—"

"C'mon. We're going outside."

They shuffle outside and slam the door on the way out. I strain my hearing to listen in on their bickering.

"What the hell was that?" Axl asks.

"I—" Josh sighs. "I don't know. When I saw her again, face to face...I don't know."

"You know you flooded that damn interrogation with your temper. Dammit, Josh. We talked about this."

They're silent for a few moments, so quiet I can hear their breath.

"I get that this is your big day. You've been waiting for this like, what, three years or whatever."

"Four. It's almost been four since I last saw her. It's been one since she was murdered," Josh mutters. "Murdered by the hands of that...that—"

"Abomination?"

"No. A monstrosity. I need to know for sure it was Twelve. But how can I if she won't even bat an eye?"

"The others can give us answers. She's just one of four."

"Yeah, but she knows the most. She—"

"I'll rough her up a bit then. See if anything changes. This has gotten too personal for you."

He thinks I killed someone he knew—a girl. He separated from her three years ago and then found out she was dead a year ago. I'm assuming someone found her body on that bloody day. Did I do it? I don't remember the program killing a girl—a human.

I close my eyes, putting my forehead on the cold table. Josh asks Axl to tell him what I say. His footsteps gradually fade away as the door creaks back open.

"You're impressive, you know that, Twelve? Most people crack when they just see the two of us together, or even hear Joshua West's full name. But I guess you lived in a shithole for so long you're out of the loop?" Axl stops at my side. "Josh has been a dear friend of mine for quite some time, so—" He palms the back of my head and slams my cheek into the metal table, causing it to dent.

I gasp and my whole body tenses up, squirming underneath the weight of his hand. My face tightens, tingling even more, and making it difficult to breathe. Axl's blue eyes lower to my level. They strike me with a strange curiosity.

"I'd appreciate it if you answered at least one of our questions. Josh needs to know. He's a busy guy with loads of important things to do. And you, you're just a yellow-eyed abomination. So make yourself useful, Twelve. If that's what you go by."

I bare my teeth at him; he applies more pressure and I wince from the throbbing in my skull. Axl smiles so much, he glows.

"A tough nut, aren't you? Usually people crack when their adrenaline lies to them. You know better, don't you? I hope your friends do too."

The hell...?

"Your friend who was awake, she cares for you. It sure sounded like it. When you were shot, she screamed a name. Storm, was it? I bet you care for her too. Wouldn't it be terrible if you came back to her with a broken jaw? Or you know what would be worse? If she had her fingers and toes broken one by one with you watching from that little glass cage. Its transparency, along with your night vision, will let you see all her blood if your silence continues."

He can't hurt me. Neither of them can. They have to keep us healthy one way or another.

"So, what do you say? Will you bless me with the privilege of hearing your lovely voice for the first time? Or will you and I get to have some fun?"

The tingling stops. So, I smile just as he did. I finally compel my heart rate to rest, with the assurance that I'm near untouchable to him.

Axl breaks his unnerving smile. "Are you nuts? Don't know what's good for you, maybe your still drugged I guess." He takes his hand from my head "You'll crack soon enough; I'll make sure of it. And I'll be the first to watch you fall, Storm."

Axl leaves the room, slamming the door. Once on the other side, he stops. The flicking of a lighter, followed by the sound of burning paper, permeates through the concrete wall.

"She's nuts..." Axl mutters to himself as he begins to walk "What did he ever see in her?" Axl's footsteps fade.

I'm left to my own thoughts.

The memory of the dead bodies everywhere surrounds me. The white monster and the monster with two-colored eyes. There's more to it. Now I know for sure it happened a year ago, before I gained control again. The mission they talked about, maybe it has to do with the program? I'm not sure. Before, I could only go off of the knowledge the others had of what happened that day. But there's more to it. More death than I realized. Josh has presented a new source of information. He's who we need to follow. He's our starting point—a new key piece of information.

Josh's accusations could be true. It's clear he believes every word he's saying. His motivations are clear now—all too clear. He's not just doing his job. He's doing it for someone else. No wonder he was so angry, but I couldn't care less. All Joshua West is good for is information. He doesn't have a filter due to his rage, which gives me an advantage. I just have to push the right buttons. Axl, on the other hand...I should watch my back when he's around. He's more calculating than Josh. Not knowing his motivations will be an issue.

The door opens. "Hey piss-eyes, nap's over!" Bird-eyes grabs the back of my neck. She hauls me to my feet and unchains me from the table.

Bird-eyes pushes me out the door, back into the twisting hallways, and drags me through the maze with my entourage at my sides. Bird-eyes begins to talk, but I tune her out.

Josh brought up the Doctors. These Doctors are coming in three months, and it sounds like they're in charge of what happens to us. Whoever they are, I don't want to find out in person. All I know is that we have three months to escape. That's the perfect amount of time to gather more intel, figure out who the Doctors are, and execute a stress-free prison escape. Maybe I can figure out why we haven't been collared yet. It could be because the collar is temporary? Maybe the Doctors are coming to permanently activate the program? If so, we have to escape in three months.

We take a turn and Bird-eyes pushes me back into the darkness. The room is as silent as before, but the remains of a conversation are still in the air. Glacia puts her head between her knees as we enter. Viper has settled down and is pressed up against the glass. Hawk and Strike are still passed out.

"You're next, Forty-Five," Bird-eyes yells.

"Are you talkin' to me?" Viper asks.

Bird-eyes opens my cell door. "Of course I am, you twat!"

Bird-eyes throws me in, locks my chains to the floor, and pushes me onto my back with a quick jab of her boot. I let out an *oof*, and before I know it there are chains around my ankles once again. The door shuts with a click. Bird-eyes moves on to Viper's cage.

"You better not struggle. And if you do, I'll make sure one of those damn darts goes up your a—"

"Shut up already, we don't have time for your talk." Montana appears in the doorway.

I tune them out until their bickering becomes incoherent mumbles. I watch as Bird-eyes wraps her arms around Viper's waist, allowing Montana to unlock the ankle chains, and wrestles Viper out of the cell. All the while, Viper scraps and screams. Finally, they push her out of the prison room and close the door. On the other side, Bird-eyes gives Viper the dart speech just as she did to me. Their footsteps disappear down the maze of grey hallways.

I sigh and lean my head against the glass with my back to the wall. Tracing my finger over my cheek, where my scab once was, it appears I have gained a new scar. My eyes widen and I feel my forehead—the cut is gone. The white capsule worked.

"Hey, you. You're Storm, right?" Glacia asks.

I narrow my eyes.

"Viper and I were talkin'. About escaping."

I clench my fists. "I thought you said tryin' to escape was for fools."

"I only said that 'cause they were watching us." Glacia motions back to the corner with the camera. Its light is red instead of green. "Those two guards, they're the ones who run the camera in here. They're in charge of us. Whenever the light is green, it means the camera is being monitored and when it's red, it's not."

"Does that happen a lot?"

"No, this never happens. The only time the camera is red is every day around noon. It must be when those two guards are resetting the system. I'm trying to figure that out for sure. It lasts about three to five minutes. Listen, we don't have a ton of time right now. I don't know when they're coming back."

"Do you know how to escape this place then?"

"I've been working on a plan for three months now. Having you and your friends here will speed up the process, if you want to help."

I unsheathe one claw and scrape a mark on the floor. "We'll help for sure. I don't plan on stickin' around for the next ninety days. I hope you don't, either."

Glacia raises a brow. "I don't. This is what I have so far..."

NINE

CLASSMATES

"Red light," Glacia whispers, her eyes focused on the camera.

I perk up and stop doing push-ups.

"Finally!" Hawk whispers.

"Back to what we were talking about yesterday. We have an issue."

"Sure as hell do," Viper says.

I sigh. "We'll have to wait. How long do you think it'll take?"

Glacia runs her fingers through her hair. "Based on the pattern, I'd say at least fifteen days."

"Damn it," Strike mutters.

"I knew we should have just done it then and there," Glacia whispers. "It's my fault."

"Don't be an idiot. If we had, we could be dead or worse by now," Hawk says. "Fifteen more days won't kill us. We still have time before they come."

"Agreed," I say. "Now Viper will have to—"

"Green light," Glacia says.

The green camera light glares at us. We all sigh. There's never enough time.

I mark another tally, number thirty, with a claw. Closing my eyes, I rest my head against the glass wall as I wipe sweat from my brow.

The only indicator of a passing day is Glacia's green light and red light. The days have no sunrise or sunset. Days have no night. Days have nothing to look forward to, except for the guard's occasional visit to feed us, bathe us, or beat us. The beatings are rare. They only come if we spur them with taunts. Viper and Hawk have been struggling with that. Whenever it happens, those white capsules are handed out an hour later like candy.

I let out a small sigh, bringing my knees to my chest in an attempt to get comfortable. But the rough floor, the closed-in space, and the dense air keep me in a state of boredom. I want to run in circles, to sleep right here and now, and to scream all at the same time. My head throbs. My chest tightens from the exhaustion of it.

I'm losing my mind.

Suddenly, the lock to the prison room creaks, and the door unlocks. This isn't a part of the pattern. A person on the other side hesitates to open the door; they crack it just enough to let a ray of light in the isolating space. The figure holds an ember-tipped cigarette, and the synthetic light overwhelms them in unbreakable shadows. The figure blows out a puff of smoke, and when the smoke disperses, it reveals Axl. Smoke falls across the room and eventually disappears, leaving its foul scent behind. Axl steps into the room, leaving the door wide open, and his blue eyes glow in the low light. He walks to Glacia and stops as he inhales more smoke.

"I see you look like shit," Axl mutters with grey air slipping past his lips.

Glacia looks up, her scabs and bruises revealing themselves. "I see you want lung cancer."

"They'll give me new lungs whenever I need 'em. I don't have to worry about a thing." Axl takes in another hit and squats down to her level. There's not a sound between the two for a full three minutes.

"What do you want?" Glacia brings her knees to her chest. "Why are you here?"

"I'm going to be blunt with you, Glacie, I'm here to catch up with you like old friends should, or would, since we haven't talked for a while. So, go ahead and ask me about my new hobby."

Glacia looks down. "What about it, Axl?"

"If I remember right, I started smoking two cigs a day after their deaths. After their funeral, it went up to five a day. When they found you in that shithole, I started smoking a pack a day," Axl whispers. "My friends, my fake friends, they want me to smoke the electronic sort, but there's a certain thing I hate about electronic cigs. They're too manmade. Not to say regular tobacco isn't. All plants are manmade, technically, but the electronic cigs just aren't authentic, you know? They don't burn the lungs as much."

Glacia's jaw tightens.

"I've tried all sorts of brands. Even tried cigars for a while. But I always went back to this brand. The hardest one to obtain yet the simplest on the market. This one, it's wonderful. Wonderful enough to dull the idea that growing up together means nothing anymore. It helps me get past the thought that the top girl in my class betrayed her country, her company, and murdered two of my other classmates. It helps me cope with the fact that all my real friends are falling around me, leaving me with artificial ones. But you see..." Axl shows his right palm; his tattoo reads *ESXY*3. "...You, Josh, and I are the same. That's the truth. And you're the only ones who can be my real friends."

Glacia meets his gaze. "So, you're here to beat the shit out of me then? Because your cigarettes aren't solving your problems? Because I left you to be with your new friends?"

"No, I just want a conversation with you."

"What?"

"A conversation," Axl murmurs as he reaches into his pocket. "A conversation about Lincoln and Samael. I want closure, you see. It's all I want from you, Glacia. So I can stop smoking these damn things. So I can cut off my artificial friends. So maybe I can forget about what you did."

Glacia's eyes widen.

"'Cause you are—you were—the closest thing I had to a sister growing up." Axl pulls out a lighter from his pocket, showing it to Glacia. "You know that too. I've told you a million times. But now you look at me like I'm some target. Just another person standing in your way, who wants to beat the shit out of you. I don't want to hurt you; I still remember everything you did for me. But now, all I want from you is the truth. I'm not the only one, either. Josh wants it. Jefferson wants it. The surviving classmates want it, too. Hell, Heather wanted it. But she's dead now, killed herself, 'cause of what you did to Lincoln. That's why I want the truth."

"And if I don't provide it?"

Axl stiffens, taking in more smoke. "You won't be my sister anymore."

The smoke billows from his mouth and into her hardened face. Glacia can no longer bear the weight of her stone-cold heart. Her eyes are misty now, but she fights to keep herself frozen.

"I just want to know...why did you kill two kids when they had so much to live for?"

Glacia closes her eyes and turns away from him.

Axl waits for her answer, the cigarette perched between his teeth. When she doesn't respond, he sighs deeply. He stands up, grasping onto the cigarette and hungrily inhaling it. He walks back to the door, grabs the edge of it, and stops. The lighter in his fist is shaking.

"I find it terrifying that you once promised me you'd let nothing bad happen to me. After you promised that, the world seemed less angry at me, and I was less angry at it," Axl whispers as he looks back to Glacia. "But you've broken that promise, Trainee Ivar. Now, sit and rot. Watch me rise without you."

Axl slams the door shut, making Glacia flinch. Glacia buries hers face in her knees. Her ivory fingers tremble.

I hope I never end up like that. The thought of losing my friends shouldn't even be crossing my mind. As intelligent as Glacia has proven herself to be, why did she ruin what she had...or was it even anything to begin with? If she is a murderer, why have they kept her alive? Who the hell is this girl? What the hell has she done?

I shouldn't be questioning her. She's the reason why we're getting out of here. The more I know, the less I'll trust her. My mind can't be occupied with her complexities, only on escaping. But there's something about her that sticks. There's more to her than I realized.

TEN

MOTIVATIONS

JOSH

"There's nothing more frustrating than a man who thinks he's above you," I reply and lean back in the chair. My eyes are still on the blank monitor.

"Amen, brotha. General Sapro really has a stick shoved up his ass by Inman, don't he?" Axl remarks. He presses a button and the monitor rises back into the wooden ceiling.

I crack a grin. "Couldn't have said it better myself."

"But he has a good argument. It'll take a lot to sway Doctor I. now."

"I don't understand his proposal; it doesn't sound like it's effective enough. It's not suited for the four."

"What are you talking about, man? You've seen the damage they can do; his idea is beyond brilliant. The reason why you hate it is 'cause he came up with it."

"I disagree with it. I mean, just engaging them for one task? Why not divide and conquer?"

"You should come up with a proposal then."

"I don't know about that. I haven't written one before."

Axl grins. "One time I read somewhere that in life, we have to be continually jumping off cliffs and developing our wings on the way down," he says. "If you're so worried about it, consult Colonel West or something. She'll give you guidance."

I nod, brushing my fingers against my chin.

"Damn, any advice you could get from your sister would make a difference. That woman is a tactical calculator. The reason she isn't involved in this is 'cause—"

"I know. It's because I'm involved."

He pauses. "How long has it been now, since you saw her last?"

"Four years," I mutter. "I'm hoping I'll see her before I turn fifteen."

"Ah yes, the ol' one five. It only seems like yesterday I was a wee' lad like yourself."

I raise a brow. "You just turned sixteen."

"Yeah, and I just graduated. You still got two years left, bud... How about we get some smokes?"

I lean forward again in the chair. "You can. I don't mind."

Axl places his silver revolver on the desk as he fishes through his pockets for his buzzer. I stare at the bulky, rusted gun. Its muzzle points directly at Axl.

"You need to be careful with that firearm. It could misfire some-day," I say.

Axl pulls out his buzzer. "*Pff,* I never load the damn thing. It's just an accessory. It's the one my granddad used way back when. It's so old and rusty, I doubt it could even fire."

"Still, we're not in a war right now. We're in a base. You don't have to have it on you all the time."

Axl clicks the buzzer on and holds it up to his ear. "Service to the conference room on the eleventh floor. We'll have smokes.... What kind? Just bring up the selection you got. Yeah, all the kinds. We'll have some beer, bourbon, and milk too. I'm eighteen. I don't need to give you any damn identification. I'm in the main conference room for Pete's sake! Bring it up in the next five minutes or I'll come down there myself!" Axl hangs up the buzzer. He tosses it on the table next to the revolver. "The damn service here...they don't know their place."

I nod.

Axl props up his white shoes on the mahogany table, unzips his blue track-jacket, and puts his hands behind his head.

"I've been meaning to tell you something," he says.

"Yeah?"

"About two weeks ago or so, I came by the base. When we were taking a breather from that recon mission. I went and talked to Glacia. Our conversation didn't last long."

"Why didn't you ask me to come?"

"I wanted to know the truth. Stupid of me to think she would give it up. I was hoping she would be more intimidated by just me. I tried to make it look like I meant business, you know?" Axl sighs. "But that girl was stone cold the entire damn time. That's beside the point though. I noticed somethin' about the four. All of them were looking weak and that Twelve was looking especially fragile, like an unfed and sweaty bitch. We were right to wait them all out. I think we were right to keep everything from Doctor Inman today, too. You know she wouldn't let us talk to them, knowing we didn't answer the questions. I think today's the day we're gonna get some answers from all four, besides getting those given names from the others. If not, we could always interrogate that curly-top we arrested again, the one who knows Twelve. Maybe he was just holding out on us last time."

I reach for my necklace. "I doubt he was, but I wasn't planning to leave this base until we get the answers out of them." I rub the locket between my fingertips.

"What's your plan?"

"I'll start with Twelve. I'll get into her head, no matter how long it takes. I'll do it. I have to. Then I'll move to...Thirty-Three. I think she calls herself Hawk. Then to...Viper. After her, Twenty-Seven, Strike. They're the key to all this, like a bridge to the other side. I can feel it."

"Have you ever thought that this bridge may lead right into the river?"

"What do you mean?"

"I mean, what the hell are you gonna do if you hear something you don't like? I'm with you on this. It's obvious they're connected based on all that mumbo-jumbo you told me, but what if—"

"My friend is dead, Axl. She's dead. And it's my job to figure out what the hell happened. I'm the—"

"I know, I know. Don't give me your rehearsed speech that I've been hearing forever. I'm just giving you my opinion."

"Then what do you think I should do?"

"Walk me through your gobbledygook again. I've forgotten half of it."

I stare at the aging locket. It's resting on my tattoo, *ESXY 4*.

"About four years ago, my friend, Ryan, left without any explanation. Colonel West told me she had to move, and I would see her again someday, so I waited. But that never happened. Doctor Castus told me a year ago about the Capital Massacre. He knew about my past friendship and offered to help track her down, but I told him not to. One day he showed me the list of the identified bodies, and her name was on the list. Doctor Castus told me who the perpetrators were. Gave me some footage and reports on the four. Told me he would give me the resources I needed to track them down. He said that if I captured them, he would let me figure out what happened to Ryan. All he could give me was that the four were developed by him and the others. The four abandoned their mission that day, and massacred those people, but I'm not sure how. According to him, that mission was the only thing keeping them in check, but they ended up killing all those innocent people, including Ryan."

"And now we're here. Who do you think did it?"

"There wasn't any footage from Ryan's crime scene, but I managed to map all the footage I had into a timeline of sorts. Twelve was the only one to have even entered the area where her body was reportedly found. The others might know more, or they could be witnesses. Hell, one of them could be the killer instead of Twelve, but at this point, I'm certain Twelve is the killer. I just need a confession."

"Damn. You should show Twelve the footage. Prove to her you know what she did. Then, go from there."

I nod.

"Last time, you started out too broad. Narrow it down to just your friend and get those answers first. Then move on to the bigger questions from there. After that, question the others to get the story straight and fill in any gaps. When we finish, you can map out everything and add it to your case. I can back you up."

"Let's go now—your smokes can wait."

"I'll set up the interrogation room. You can escort her."

I get to my feet; Axl follows. We are already at the door when one of the servers steps into the conference room with the drinks and cigs. Axl splits off from me and I continue down the hallway, my sights on the elevator. Light from each window drowns out the wooden walls and ceiling. Muffled sounds from calls and meetings bounce about the mahogany corridor. Every conversation is hushed, containing the most sensitive information, for the benefit of the company. Those benefits will add to the success of the nation. My conversions will be with mechanical murderers and the information will benefit the souls they stole from this earth.

I press the platinum button and check my watch. It's almost noon. I'm making good time. The metallic doors slide open, revealing one of the guards in charge of the four, standing in the center of the elevator. Her eyes widen.

"Trainee West, I didn't know you were visiting." She steps out of the elevator.

"Yes, I'm here for a follow-up. Shouldn't you be in the surveillance room?"

"I'm getting some lunch for Private Lilith and me. Would you like some too?"

I step past her. "No, Private, but hurry back."

The doors close and I'm left alone under the faint buzzing of the lights. I hit the button and turn to an eye scanner, allowing a blue light to analyze my irises.

"Welcome Trainee Joshua West. Your access has been granted to the cell block."

The elevator creeps to the concrete prison. Once the door opens, I walk to the surveillance room; the steel door is already open. That's not protocol. Only the guards on duty can open and close it with their keys. I peek into the surveillance room; thankfully the loud-mouth private hasn't left. She hunches over the computer screen. The viewing screens for all of the cameras have shut off. I step into the room, leaving the door open, and fold my arms. She's supposed to reboot the system at exactly noon.

"What do you think you're doing?"

Loud-mouth freezes. She turns to me, eyes wide.

"Private, you're not supposed to be rebooting right now. It has to be at exactly noon." I glance at my watch. "It's eleven-fifty-seven."

"I was just gettin' a head start."

"It's not protocol and you left the door open as well, Private."

"Jeez, tough crowd, huh?"

Loud-mouth straightens up and grabs a coffee mug from the desk. She steps in front of the fire alarm.

"Don't speak to me like that. Your superiors will be hearing about this."

"I don't care. Is Montana gettin' my food?"

She brings the mug to her lips, sipping nosily on its contents with her dark eyes focused on it. Loud-mouth pushes back a strand of her red hair to reveal a nick on her right ear. I never noticed that before. She also looks way shorter than what I remember, about five foot five. She was a least my height when we first met.

I glance at the monitors again; they're still black. "Yes, I saw her leaving the elevator. Private, why haven't you rebooted the system?"

Loud-mouth takes a step back and her eyes snap back to mine.

The irises disintegrate from an opaque brown into a glaring green. Her hair gradually darkens to a lighter brown along with her skin tone. The bones underneath her face bubble. Her cheeks hollow away, her jaw dwindles, and her entire frame shrinks in a matter of seconds. All the scars slowly erupt from her skin.

I didn't even guess. How did she escape?

Viper lowers the coffee mug, and her freckles appear on her tan skin. "What a funny question. Trainee West, right? The system ain't what you should be worried about right now," she remarks in a new, overly-confident voice. Viper raises her chin with a grin. A jagged scar streaks across the front of her neck, and an inkling of fangs peek out from underneath her lips. "I am the worry to your safety...Trainee."

She hurls the white mug through the air. I dodge to the side and explode forward, throwing the first punch. Viper takes a step back out of my reach. She grabs onto the fire alarm lever, yanking it down. The bells shriek. Viper shoots her foot into my ribs. I stumble. She twists around and lashes the same foot into my stomach. I fly onto my back, the breath escaping my lungs. Viper bolts for the door. I'm on my feet and hurling myself at her. I lock my arms around her waist just as she reaches the door, and I swing her back to the wall beside us. I grit my teeth and push her squirming frame closer to the wall. Viper rushes forward and plants her foot into the wall, pushing off and flipping out of my grip, causing me to stumble back. Viper whips her foot into my chest. I fall on my back.

Slam. Click.

The door is shut. I throw myself against it, but it's been locked from the outside. I look out the window. Five yellow flashes run across the hallway, from the direction of the cells, toward the fire escape.

"Damnit!" I slam my fist against the metal. My buzzer rings from my pocket. I snatch it. "Hello?"

"Josh! Where are you?" Axl exclaims.

"I'm in the cell block! The four and Glacia have escaped! I bet they're headed for the garage! Hurry and we'll meet there!" I hang up.

Unleashing my top blade, I plunge it through the steel, slash out a rectangle and kick the center of it. The steel clatters into the hallway and I scramble through the hole. The first thing I see is a guard being slammed head-first against the floor by a rabid inmate. Anarchy has taken hold among the formerly imprisoned rebels. Hundreds of them have flooded the hallways. I can't see further than three feet without blood, sweat, and punches spraying. The battle cries wail above the sirens and every guard is too preoccupied with survival to be worried about capturing anyone.

I bolt for the fire escape, pushing through the flying bodies. Bounding up the stairs to the next floor, I burst through the door to the garage and sprint to the vehicles. The garage doors are cranking up and the gate is sliding open. Axl shouts vulgar things from somewhere in the sea of vehicles, and I flank to where his voice is coming from.

I turn a corner to find a blonde bob—Glacia. She's crouching behind a car, trying to break the window with her elbow. I lunge at her from behind and force my forearm underneath her chin. I place my palm on the back of her head and drag her away from the window, my forearm suffocating her. Glacia lurches forward before driving her forearm between my legs. She jabs her fist into my eyes. The nausea takes over and before I know it, Glacia has twisted out of my grasp. She yells as she rotates my shoulder, causing me to fall on my side with my arm caught in her bone-crushing grip. I gasp and unsheathe my bottom blade. Blood from her chest sprays into the air. Glacia lurches backward and releases my forearm. I grab her extended wrist, pulling her to me, and as I stand, I plunge my right blade straight into her shoulder.

Glacia's eyes widen. Her mouth gapes in a silent scream as I slam her into the side of the car. My blade completely slices through her. Glacia's face pales and she's unable to make a single sound. I grit my teeth and twist the blade. The screams finally escape her lips.

I twist the blade counter-clockwise and Glacia writhes underneath my weight. Her eyes glaze over as her adrenaline kicks in, causing her to grab at the blade with her free hand. Blood pools in her palm. I punch her in the face. Blood sprays. I do it again. And again, and again, and again. Just to make sure she feels it. She goes limp sometime between my tenth or fifteenth punch. I sheathe the blade and she crumbles. Blood collects around her figure.

A loud whistle catches my ear. I snap my gaze up. Axl and Twelve stand there. Twelve has Axl on his knees and his rusted revolver aimed for his skull. Axl has his hands behind his head; a smirk spreads across his bleeding lips.

She's about to get an empty surprise.

"You're bluffing," I say as I stride closer. "I bet you don't even know how to use that thing."

Axl winks as Twelve raises the gun at me with a blank gaze. She pulls the trigger.

Click...click-click-click.

Axl jumps to his feet and grabs Twelve's neck. The butt of the revolver whips across Axl's forehead with so much momentum that his body jerks sideways. Twelve breathes in deeply, drops the gun, and casually steps over Axl's unconscious body. She takes a few steps toward me, then stops as her fingers flick. From this distance, I can see every scar on her body, even the one I left her on her cheek. Scars are signs of suffering. She deserves every scar she has.

I clench my fists. "I'll make you pay for that. You'll pay for all of this!"

Twelve narrows her yellow eyes, stiffens, and scans me like a Monstrum would.

"Come at me! Come at me with everything you've got! I'll make sure you never step out of line again! I'll—"

"Shut up."

A chill creeps down my spine. I freeze.

"Focus on my voice. Focus on each syllable because I won't repeat myself," Twelve rasps.

I didn't imagine her voice to sound like that. To sound so...

"I'm asking you to step aside. Before you get yourself killed." Her metallic claws slide out.

"Killed, huh? You're a sociopath, aren't you? I'm just another body to you, aren't I? Like all those people you murdered! You sociopath..."

She remains very still. "I don't know what you're talking about."

"You liar!"

I burst forward at her with a slash of my blade, aiming for her leg. Before I can reach her, an unknown force barrels into my side. Tumbling over I roll back to my feet and square myself with my attacker. Hawk's ferocious gaze meets mine.

"Back off!"

I open my mouth to respond, but another impetus crashes into me and slices apart my hamstring. The wound sizzles and I wince. My attacker launches another blade directly for my shoulder. I block the blow with both blades as a pair of ruthless eyes bore into me. Strike pushes her blade closer to me without resistance, like a well-oiled machine. Instead of pushing back, I roll to the side and struggle to my feet. Sweat drips into my eyes. Twelve stands beside Hawk and Strike. Behind them, Viper holds Glacia's battered body in her arms. Twelve rushes at me, slashing at my stomach. I stagger backwards. As I stumble, Twelve slashes her blade across my thigh. She whirls around and plants her foot against my neck. I'm thrown on my back, the wind knocked out of me.

Twelve takes a step back, analyzing the heaving of my breath. Her comrades stand beside her doing the exact same. They are flawlessly in sync with one another.

I drag my knee toward my chest and my legs tremble. "You won't win Twelve!"

I explode forward, but my blade stops mid-strike as five claws sink deep into my wrist. Blood drips down my arm and I follow the trail of blood to her gaze.

I'll never get used to those damning eyes.

"My name is Storm."

Something powerful smashes into my skull. I'm knocked back, my head bouncing on the concrete, and my world shrinks. Her golden eyes flutter above me, observing me as my world dissolves into a veil of darkness.

Storm... I'll remember that.

ELEVEN

THE GETAWAY

The sputtering of the engine below causes the blood in the seats to ripple and slosh. The thickness and stickiness of Glacia's blood makes me scrunch up my nose, but I stare at her fluttering eyes and keep my hands pressed firmly against the gushing gash in her shoulder. His words hum and buzz deep in my ears: *You're a sociopath, aren't you? I'm just another body, aren't I? Like all those people you murdered!*

He's wrong. I didn't kill them, the damn program did.

"Storm!" Strike yells. "Give her the pills!"

Strike has Glacia's head on her lap to ensure her fragile neck doesn't strain any more than it has to. I reach my dripping hand to Josh's capsule box that I have lodged in my bra strap. I rip it open to reveal two white capsules. The vehicle suddenly lurches sideways, causing me to lose my balance and send the pills soaring through the air. A symphony of shouts and screeching vehicles can be heard from the street as Viper swerves again. I slide across the seat to the wall opposite from Glacia. I yell at Viper to keep the car steady as I scramble to search for the two capsules.

Viper mutters something under her breath. The car lurches again, causing another spurt of pedestrian shouts. I find the pills rolling on the floor, snag them with my bloody fingertips, and hand one over to Strike. Stowing the last capsule back in my bra, I apply pressure to Glacia's gushing wound. There's so much blood that Glacia's pale hairline has been stained maroon, and some of it has seeped into the whites of her eyes. Her flesh has bubbled over where blood pushes out of several purple mounds. The amount of swelling makes it near impossible to know if anything, such as her nose, is broken. Glacia's lucky that Josh, the bastard, didn't kill her.

Strike waves her fingers above Glacia's face, watching for her frosty eyes to follow. Once they do, Strike hovers the pill above her bloody lips.

"Are you able to take it?" Strike asks.

Glacia manages to nod with an agonizing effort and I can't help but dart my eyes away for a moment. Glacia shoves the pill through her cracking lips as the vehicle rattles again. Then she nods off and her breathing stabilizes, but my trembling hands keep pressing down on the putrid wound.

That brute didn't have the damn right, the damn—

"Storm." Strike touches my arm. "She's stopped bleeding. You don't need to—"

"I know." I slowly slip my hands off her chest. "It's all I could do for her; how else could I help?"

I slump back into my seat, rubbing the blood from my palms onto the yellow jumpsuit. It's not enough to get it off. It'll never be enough.

"We're headed southeast, right?" Hawk asks.

"Yeah," Strike says. "All the way to Shawnee. Viper, you know where you're going, right?"

"Sure do."

Hawk turns to us. "Is she doing better?"

"The bleeding is slowing down, the swelling also," Strike replies.

The vehicle swerves but this time I catch myself. Hawk tumbles over and slams into the window. She swears faster than the sputtering of the engine, all while Viper snickers. Hawk shoots Viper a glare and resumes her position.

"Do you think Glacia will have to come home with us if she doesn't heal fast enough?" Hawk asks.

"I don't think it's an if anymore," I say. "A pill can do a lot, but not that much."

"Are you sure? I mean, she really wanted to go her own way. What happens if she can't even walk?"

"Maybe we should give her the second pill," Strike replies.

"If you try..." Glacia suddenly rasps "...I will tan all yall's hides."

Glacia tries to sit up and Strike places her hands on her back for support. The swelling on her face has gone down; it looks as if someone painted over her skin with globs of black, red, blue, and yellow paint that streaks all the way down to her neck. The slice on her chest has scabbed over and dried blood sticks to her jumpsuit.

"I'm not...I'm not taking another pill," Glacia says in a weak, airy voice. "That's too much poison for one day."

"Are you su—"

"I am." Glacia moves to sit in the center of the seat, wincing. "I need...I need a sling or something."

Glacia moves her right hand to hold her injured arm and reveals her tattoo. It reads, ESXX2. I consider asking her about where it came from and what it means, but this is a terrible time. Unsheathing a claw, I tear at the bottom of one of my pant legs. I rip it up to my mid-thigh, and slice it at its base. Reaching over for her trembling arm, I place the cloth underneath her forearm. I ask her if it feels all right. Glacia nods.

I scoot a bit closer, hoping to catch a glimpse of her tattoo again, as I secure the cloth into a sling.

"Are you sure you don't want another pill?" Hawk asks. "You look terrible."

"No pill."

Glacia's skin is as pale as a corpse, one that's had its head bashed with a sledgehammer. I get the chills listening her shallow breathing. I'm not sure if she'll make it through this ride if she doesn't rest.

"At least lie down," I say. "Hawk's right; you sorta look terrible."

Glacia opens her busted lips.

"You deserve a rest," Strike cuts her off.

"Yeah! You kicked some ass today!" Viper adds in.

"Without you, I don't think we would have made it out," Strike says. "If you won't take the pill, do the next best thing."

Glacia leans her head back, refusing. I exchange a glance between Hawk and Strike. She must be off her rocker. It could be due to all the blood loss or the pill hasn't had the chance to heal her brain yet. Either way, Glacia has to save her strength so she doesn't pass out again. We need her right now. She's the only one that can help us get new, free supplies and wheels.

Strike yawns. "I don't know about you, but I'm exhausted. Since we're going to be here for a while, I'm going to catch up on some sleep."

"You know what? I am too," Hawk says. "Wake me up when we get there."

"Glacia, if you don't mind, to make room I'll need you to put your back to the door next to Storm. Is that all right?" Strike asks.

Glacia nods.

I reposition myself and Glacia shifts over with her back pressed against the door. Her legs sprawl onto my lap, leaving room for Strike to comfortably lie down, but Glacia grimaces at every rattle of the door. Strike hesitates before she lies down.

"Are you comfortable?" Strike asks.

"I'll manage."

I open my mouth to tell Glacia to rest already, but I'm interrupted when Strike says, "I can already tell I won't be. Mind switching spots with me?"

I raise my brows a bit. Strike knew Glacia would be uncomfortable leaning against the door because of all the rattling. So, the only option Glacia would have left is to sit in a tempting, open spot with plenty of room.

The two switch spots. Once Strike settles herself with her legs on my lap, there's plenty of room for Glacia to sleep, although she remains sitting up. Hopefully, she'll crack soon.

Strike closes her eyes. "Wake me up when we get there."

"Will do," I say.

Glacia finally gives in and lies down. Quietly sighing with relief, I tilt my head against the window. A quick glance at Glacia's profile shows her jaw is clenched and her hand is wrapped around her injured arm. Her eyes flutter as she struggles, fighting the urge to sleep, but she soon falls into its grip.

"Good work," I whisper.

"Thank you," Strike whispers back.

A small smile graces my lips. Strike has always been the one to be crafty in a low-profile sort of way. Of the four of us, she's the one that could sit and wait for a flower to bloom without any doubts about its beauty or radiance. The benefit of having patience like that is Strike can persuade anyone to do anything without raising her voice or fist. It is effortless for her. I wish that were also the case for myself. I wonder who taught her the ability to be so gentle. It could be that Strike was born with it, just like the other two were born with their unique skills. Were they all just born good people?

Am I a good person? How does someone know if they are or not? I mean, I know if someone else is a good person. Hawk, Strike, and Viper are all good people. But why can't I know that about myself?

I close my eyes, but his words ring in my ears once again: *You're a sociopath, aren't you? I'm just another body, aren't I? Like all those people you murdered!*

He's just a brute. I'm not what that angry, spoiled Brute thinks I am. Josh West knows nothing about me. The program is the thing that gets pleasure from the smell of blood. I scrunch up my nose at the thought of it. But I also can't help but wonder why Josh would get me and the program confused.

I shouldn't worry about what he thinks of me. I'm thankful I'll never have to rot in a prison cell. I can finally spread my wings. No more forced showers or forced meals. No more self-deprecating silence with so much tension surrounding it I can barely breathe. I never thought the sounds of other people's voices would make it easier to breathe.

All that prison was and always will be is a device to crush the strongest of souls. There were many times when I heard the exact moment a person was lost to the concrete depths. It would start with a cry that bristled throughout the halls, followed by the guards rushing over, and then a silence would fall throughout every nook and cranny of the prison. Sometimes the death was caused by another person, or the death was the person's own doing. On those days, the silence drowned everyone because we knew the person who died would only be forgotten. The only remains of them would be an empty cell where they once breathed in the same dense air and shared the same dust that settled around them.

Thankfully, I'll never be forced to breathe that suffocating air ever again. I hope those other prisoners escaped and will live memorable lives. I hope no other souls will have their existence washed away in that prison.

The car rattles as I slowly sink away from Strike's side. The sounds of the engine buzzing and the whistling wind fade when the darkness consumes me. My heartbeat throbs. I settle on something warm, the scent of rust lacing the air.

TWELVE
DEADSVILLE
STORM

Heart-churning cries shake the warm earth sticking to my back. The sky, the earth, and my vision all glare red. When I sit up, I realize that I'm drenched in blood. Surrounding me are motionless bodies, glued to the earth by the sticky blood pooling from their veins. The roar of a thousand beings whistles in my ears. As I turn my head, buildings invade the skyline, blocking out parts of the red sun. Scattered streaks of sunlight dot the red-washed concrete and create a thousand spotlights. In one such spotlight lies a screaming girl on her knees. Looming above her is an armored figure unsheathing a glistening upper blade. The spots of sunlight shimmer off their black armor, creating a purple tint within its darkness. At their back, a pair of black wings spreads and blankets both souls in red shadows.

I'm frozen in place, unable to move forward because of the weight of the blood on my shoulders. All I'm able to do is think, ask, and wish it will stop. The upper blade flashes forward, piercing the little girl's heart. She's unable to cry out, halted by abrupt agony. The armored figure slams their boot into her skull, causing her body to slip off the stained blade.

As the girl's thick blood collects around her, I desperately wish to know why the blood weighs so heavily on me. Why have I never remembered the chaos around me? Am I the person behind that reflective mask? Am I the one with the blood on my hands?

The armored figure then sets their sights on me. Slowly, the figure points their blade toward me. A chill rips down my spine. The figure tilts their head, their motives hidden under the mirror-like helmet, and I see my purple reflection in their armor as they approach. Except, I am unrecognizable. My purple reflection is not glued to the ground by the blood. It is not frozen. It stands proud, with blood seeping from its glimmering purple eyes. My purple reflection has all my scars and my hair and my eyes and my tattoo. It has my eyes with blood oozing from them. My reflection is wearing a vain grin. It breathes in the blood like it's perfume.

It is right in front of me, but I still don't know where it came from and what it once was. It's something I cannot analyze or investigate. It is a monstrosity, one that cannot be stopped with good intentions alone.

The armored figure lowers the blade, breathes deeply, and casually steps over the young girl's body. Their fingers flick. They analyze me like a real monster would, but before they can make another move, I'm sucked away. I fall in no clear direction, but I slam into something cold and uncomfortably nostalgic. My eyes burn from artificial light. Sitting in front of me is the same armored figure, strapped into the electrified seat. They wear a metal crown atop their glinting helmet. The familiar clicks echo from behind me and the humming of anxious electricity vibrates throughout the dense concrete.

"Subject *WDXX12*. Day eleven of respondent conditioning," a voice replies from behind me. "Just tell me when to stop."

I squeeze my eyes shut, waiting for the volts to flood into my bones, but just as the whistling begins, I'm swept away all over again. I wake to the cries of Glacia. I'm now lying on the humming floor of the car and Strike's limbs are tangled with mine. I breathe heavily. There's a deep throbbing in my chest, but I stay motionless until my heart stops pounding. With a groan, I pull myself back into my seat just as Strike does the same.

"What the hell..." I trail off.

I glance beside me to see Glacia wedged between the floor and the seats. I hold out my hand to help her up.

"Damn it, Viper!" Hawk shrieks. "Didn't Strike just tell you to slow the hell down?"

Glacia takes my hand and I ease her out of her spot. She winces but manages to slide back into the seat.

"It was an accident! I pushed the wrong pedal!"

"You almost gave me a heart attack! I swear next ti—"

"Would you two shut up for like two seconds?" I cut them off. "Glacia is hurt!"

"I'm fine." Glacia sits herself up. "Is the car...is the car damaged at all?"

"Only a few scratches," Viper says. "We just plowed through some bushes."

"Good...good." Glacia breathes out. Sweat has begun to form on her forehead. "Keep going on this road. When you reach a place called *Ritz*, turn right into the alleyway. We'll have to get out there."

"Good, because I can't take another minute in this death machine," Hawk mumbles. "Especially with this driver."

"Like you could do better!"

Hawk prods Viper with a finger. "I bet I could do a gazillion times better!"

"Guys," I say. "Just start driving."

Hawk and Viper mutter a few more insults as Viper backs the vehicle up onto its rightful home the road. We drive deeper into the town. Spines of withering brown vegetation strangle every broken window and sandpapered wall of the buildings. Dust, scraps, and leaves stampede between buildings and street corners. All that's left of many of the buildings are their foundations of concrete and brick, while a lucky few still have the luxury of possessing walls. Many sidewalks and doorways are blocked by an abandoned car, seemingly stuck there for the rest of its days. The vehicles have been stripped of everything including wheels, doors, and windows, and have been left to succumb to rust and nature. All previous conceptions of life have left this place. Now only the elements dictate the law here.

"Does anyone live here?" I ask.

"Only a few; the locals here call this place *Deadsville*," Glacia says. "This used to be the center of the black market. The remains of it are still run by a few guys and they aren't the friendliest types, especially to people like you and Viper."

How does she know so much about this place and the men?

"What does that mean?"

She eyes me. "They don't like...different looking people."

I nod slowly. "What do we do then?"

"Hang in the back," Glacia rasps. "Let me do all the talking. Storm and Hawk, make sure your wings are out of sight."

"Storm and I could always shapeshift," Viper says.

"That won't be necessary," I hastily say. "It's fine; we can hang in the back. We can just keep our eyes down and mouths shut."

"Storm, you're gonna have to shapeshift sometime soon," Viper scoffs. "Just get it over with. Get some practice in."

"No thanks."

"C'mon."

"No."

"Then you're training with me next. We'll work on it all day. I'm sick'a always havin' to shift alone. I want a shifting buddy."

I cross my arms. "I told you to let that dream die. I hate shifting."

"Yeah, just 'cause you're such a crybaby about it," Hawk adds.

"Tell me about it," Viper sighs. "She's always like—" Suddenly, her hair lightens and a grey streak forms. "My eyes *burn*, I can't even think 'cause of this terrible *burning*. Oooooh my. Why oh why do I have to change for you?" she says, in my voice.

Viper whips her head toward me, her features now mine, and mocks my current frown. Hawk and Viper laugh. Even Strike giggles with them. I keep my frown. When I glance at Glacia, her lips part. I open my mouth to say something to her along the lines of "You'll get used to it," or "It's okay, I'm still not used to it either," but I stop myself.

Glacia may or may not be staying with us after this car ride. She isn't a part of this group and may never be. There's no point in saying stuff like that when it won't do any good for her later on.

I keep my mouth shut as Viper continues to mock me, in my form, while Glacia sits there in either awe or unease. A red sign reading *Ritz* glistens in the distance. The sign is attached to a grey brick building. There's a cattywampus truck sticking out of its wasted entrance. Viper returns to her original form and swings the car into a small alleyway, leading us to an open space between a few rows of rugged buildings, rustic vehicles, and a pen of rowdy horses.

"Stop here," Glacia orders.

A person appears from behind a row of vehicles and cautiously approaches the car. He's a tall man, with a short mohawk and a long beard. Tattoos cover his arms to the point where there's no distinction between his dark skin and the ink.

"Turn the engine off, get out, and stay behind me," Glacia says. "Locals like him don't enjoy visitors."

"You know him?" Strike whispers.

"Sadly, yes."

Viper shuts the engine off and we all exit the car. Glacia places herself in front of us, clutching her forearm tightly, and stops a short distance away from the tall man. The rough ground is sickly cold on my bare feet; it causes me to shiver. Every step I take is like thousands of icicles forming on my feet. Despite the pain, I position myself behind Hawk, keeping my wings flat and clutching the wooden pill box. Viper stands behind Strike.

Mohawk crosses his arms. "What do you want this time?"

"That favor you owe me," Glacia says.

"Now isn't the best time."

"It's never a good time for you and your roadies, but if I recall, you promised after I helped you out, you would help me anytime I needed it."

"Who are they?"

"They're just my ride."

"You know the others won't like 'em around."

"I couldn't care less what they think. Your boys will just have to deal with 'em."

Mohawk rubs the back of his neck. "You're lucky they out huntin' right now or I would turn you away. You win, Trainee Ivar, but this is the last time."

Glacia thanks Mohawk, and he nods as he beckons for us to follow. He leads us to the back of the Ritz and opens the door. He holds it open for us as we file into the building. I walk fast with my eyes low. A tiny desk greets us with a sign hanging off of it reading *Roadie Trading Post*. Behind the desk, there are a zillion items organized around the space. On the higher level, where the desk is, there are boxes and racks of clothing. At the edge of the platform there's a set of stairs with boxes stacked along the steps. Beneath the stairs, there are various knickknacks and other do-hoppers, all placed in or lying next to labelled boxes throughout the open space. The air smells of past relics and its coldness sticks to the back of my throat. It burns.

As he shuts the door behind us, Mohawk tells us to help ourselves to anything. I scurry across the room right behind Hawk, slipping into the rows of racks, my mouth unhinged. Before me, thousands of clothing options sparkle in the low light. I beeline for the coats first, brushing my fingers across each, and sort through the great variety of fabric. There are denim jackets, and wool jackets, and leather jackets, and even furry jackets.

A black jacket, folded on top of a box, catches my eye. I grab it. It's patterned with red flannel in its interior, the edges are lined with white fur, and the outside is made out of a puffy cloth. It's massive, reaching down to my shins. I fold it over my arm and search for more.

I've always had to steal clothing; picking and choosing wasn't an option. I never thought shopping with consent could be so rewarding.

I locate an assortment of cloth, rubber bands, and things that could be used to pin hair back; I find five hair ties and move on. As I sort through the shirts, I notice that on the other side of the rack Glacia is picking through a pile of hats. Mohawk approaches her, holding a black bag.

"You don't look well," Mohawk remarks. "What kind of trouble did you get yourself into this time?"

I let my gaze drift down and shrink away from the rack.

"What do you think?"

"I have a theory. I'm not sure if you'd like me sayin' it out loud, but I'm assumin' that the plan you had didn't happen."

"You could say that."

"I'm assumin' you got caught. Since you were supposed to pick up these supplies over six months ago with your buddy."

"Yes, you could say that," Glacia mutters.

I find a shirt, a black button-down, and I slice slits into the back for my wings.

"These friends of yours, why is there blood all over a few of them? Are they—"

"Who knows? I just met them, never spoken more than five seconds with them..." She trails off. "Do you still have the truck I wanted?"

"Yep, I'll run out and get it for ya." He walks back out the door, letting in some more cold air.

I wonder how she came upon this place before. How does she know these people? I remember her mentioning that Mohawk owed her a favor. No. It's none of my business. I shouldn't pry. She's not planning to stay with us anyway.

Ripping off the yellow jumpsuit, I throw on my new clothes. I glance back at Glacia, who's heaving as she changes into all black clothes. The straining of her muscles to bend over, her accelerating heart rate, and the grinding of her teeth all indicate a single conclusion: Glacia is too tough for her own good.

If only I could read her mind. It has so much knowledge, I just know it. I haven't heard her story, but I already know it will contain the heaviest of content. Content that could be used as an advantage over Josh and Axl.

After a while, Mohawk returns to her side. Together, they slowly head out of the building toward where I assume he's parked the new car. Glacia can barely manage a few steps without sucking on wind. I slide my jacket on and pull my hair up into a tail before I put the wood box into a pocket. I move down the racks to where Viper sits under hundreds of blue jeans. She's already wearing a camouflage parka, ankle high jeans, an all-black hoodie, and black sunglasses perched atop her messy crown. A green scarf is wrapped around her neck. Viper hands me a pair of jeans, sunglasses, and black boots.

I thank her, unzip the jeans, and pull them on over my grey shorts. Handing her a hair tie, I ask where the socks are. She pushes a box my way. Sifting through the open box of socks, a pair catches my attention. There, in the center, lies a bundle of purple socks. I pick them up and examine the soft cloth in my palms.

"Are you three ready yet?" Hawk shouts.

"Yep!" Viper shoots up.

"I am!" Strike calls out.

I panic. "Um, yeah! Just a second!"

I force my socks on my bare feet and push my feet into the boots without untying them. I jog to Hawk. She has three backpacks at her feet and holds gloves out to Viper and me. Hawk tells us to hurry up. She's wearing a long red coat that reaches her shins, along with jeans and a grey sweater with a deep blue scarf wrapped around her neck. Strike joins us, takes a pair of gloves, then picks up one of the packs and snatches a hair tie from me. She's muttering a few things under her breath as she does so. I give Strike a weird look before I put my gloves on.

"I like the coat," I say to Hawk when we begin walking out of the building.

"Me too," Strike adds. "I never thought red would suit you so well."

Hawk fluffs out the jacket a bit. "I know, right? And you guys don't look too bad yourselves. Except for Viper. You look like a hick."

"You look like *una fresa exagerada*."

Hawk scoffs. "Um, a translation please? You're speaking your gibberish again."

I push open the door, holding it for the two.

"Uh...it translates to something with a berry? What's the red berry again?"

"A strawberry?"

"Yeah, an exaggerated strawberry. That's what you look like."

"Viper!"

Hawk smacks Viper on the back of the head as I close the door to protect the Trading Post from their ensuing insult battle. We walk over to a compact truck with oversized wheels. Mohawk stands next to the door and talks with Glacia, who's already sitting in the back seat. Suddenly, a bright blue flash sprints to the passenger side.

"Wait! Strike! That's my seat!" Hawk yells.

Strike rips open the door. "Too slow!"

Viper runs past us. "I call driving!"

Hawk rolls her eyes as Viper reaches the driver's seat. I grin and approach Mohawk.

"And I told him, well, if you wanna—" Mohawk turns to me. "Oh, sor—"

Mohawk's eyes bulge and his jaw drops. My eyes widen. I slam my palm over my mouth. He saw my eyes and teeth. He raises a trembling finger, but before he can say a word, I flip my sunglasses down and shove him away. I hurl myself over Glacia and into the center seat.

"Drive!" I yell.

The truck lurches forward, tires squealing, and we zip away from the Roadie Trading Post.

I sigh with relief.

"What happened?" Strike asks.

I sit up. "He got too close, saw my eyes and teeth, and it looked like he was about to blow a fuse. Maybe even punch me right in the face."

"He wasn't that shocked," Glacia rasps. "You didn't have to push him over."

I raise a brow. "You're the one who said—" My eyes widen. Glacia looks near death. "Are you okay?" I reach my arm out to her.

Glacia's eyes flutter. "Um..."

"Yeah, you should lie down again," Hawk says.

"I'm..." Glacia trails off as her lips turn white. "I'm fine..."

She collapses, but I catch her and cradle her in my arms. Slowly, I push myself closer to her in order to maneuver her onto my lap.

Hawk swears under her breath. "I warned her, but of course she didn't—"

"Hawk, please, just don't," Strike cuts her off. "You barely even know her."

Hawk mutters something under her breath.

"Hey, a little help please?" I ask.

Hawk reaches out, grabbing Glacia's legs. She carefully pulls them toward her to extend Glacia across our legs and rests Glacia's fragile head on my lap.

"Do you think she'll need the last pill?" Hawk asks. "Like, is she stuck with us now?"

"I doubt we'll be able to shove it down her throat even if she's passed out. It looks like she's with us for now," I say.

"We can always drop her off somewhere. After she wakes up, of course. I bet—"

"No. No let's just wait and see, Hawk," I say. "Who cares if we have her around for another day or so? It won't hurt us."

Hawk crosses her arms and averts her eyes, focusing her gaze on the passing town.

We all sigh, lost in the same thoughts. We're stuck with Glacia and Glacia is stuck with us. Hopefully, she'll wake up soon so we can go our separate ways. I glance at Glacia and examine every bead of sweat, strand of pale hair, and drop of dried blood on her. My eyes stop at her right palm and fixate on her tattoo, $ESXX2$.

I wonder how much use she can be to us. Glacia has connections; she's been behind enemy lines before and knows the ins and outs of where to get information. Glacia is a murderer though, at least according to Josh and Axl. Those two would argue that this truck is filled with murderers and monsters. But the difference between me and Glacia is that it appears she planned the murder. I never asked for it, I think. None of us ever asked for this.

The residue of Glacia's dried blood covers my tattoo; it's on my hands too. I curl my fingers into a weak fist and stare at the scar where my lower blade emerges from my arm.

And maybe murder is just murder, no matter the circumstance. Maybe there isn't a murder for better or for worse. My hands have committed the same act as Glacia's. Monsters are simply monsters, right?

I'm not sure if I can trust her yet, and I'm sure she's nowhere close to trusting me. Despite that, she knows so much about everything and we could use that right now. Desperate times call for desperate measures, even if that means letting a murderer into our home.

THIRTEEN

THE FLAMETHROWER

STORM

The log house looms in the distance under the moon's half-light. I want to run to it like a long-lost relative, to leap for joy and skip all the way up its rickety steps, and fall asleep once I reach its dusty hallways. But with Glacia in my arms and her pack slung over my shoulder, that feat is impossible. She has been unconscious since we left the trading post. There have only been a few instances where I've seen a glimmer of hope that she'll wake, the most recent being when we dented the truck while trying to hide it in the underbrush. But that hope faded. I'm lucky that she's easy to carry.

"Home sweet home," Strike whispers.

"Still looks shitty as usual," Hawk reports.

Viper skips past us. She's up the steps with one powerful leap, reaching for the door, but catches herself. I raise a brow as I climb onto the creaky stairs. Viper whips her head toward us as she places her finger to her lips.

"Do you hear that Storm?" Viper whispers.

Hawk huffs. "What are yo—"

"Shush," I cut her off.

I focus on everyone's heartbeats. Viper's is quick, Hawk's and Strike's are normal, and Glacia's is weary. Then, I hear a fifth heartbeat coming from inside the cabin. It's beating a mile per minute.

"Someone's in the house," I whisper.

Everyone freezes in their spot. We look to the house as if it would give us the answers we need. I beckon the girls over with my head.

"Viper, Strike—you two go through the kitchen window while Hawk distracts them in the front. I'll watch over Glacia. Sound good?"

Viper nods while sliding her sunglasses over her eyes. She bolts away with Strike following. Their footsteps are light and soon vanish. Hawk approaches the door. I tiptoe to the side of the doorframe, where I lean Glacia's pack against the wall. In a crouch, I lay Glacia on the ground and blanket her with my jacket.

I swivel back to Hawk and slide my sunglasses over my eyes. Whoever this is, I don't want any more friction because of me. The rush of the person's heart rate creeps closer, and the wood inside moans underneath the pressure of their footsteps. They must be close to the hallway now. Hawk exchanges a glance with me. I nod to her and unsheathe my claws along with one top blade. Hawk whips the door open.

Blazing flames shoot out at Hawk. She jumps to the side and barely avoids total incineration. A figure hurls themselves from the house with a boot aiming for Hawk. Hawk pivots away from the boot's swing. Viper leaps out from the house and connects her foot with the figure's spine. The figure stumbles forward but squares up to Viper once they regain their balance. Viper rushes them but the figure lurches forward at her. Before Viper can react, the figure has her by the neck and hurls her back toward the door. The figure holds out their hand. A red glow emits from their palm. I plant my feet, ready to join the fight. Then, the next flash appears. Strike grabs their glowing wrist. She plants her free palm into their chest and swings her foot for their ankle. As they tumble, Strike forces their arm into the air and fire erupts from the figure's palm. Its heat radiates a glow that lights up the entire forest. My jaw drops. The flames shimmer and glide so easily in the air in such an unnaturally-controlled manner. It appears to be something entirely new.

Then the flames abruptly vanish. Strike has the figure pinned, with her upper blade hovering over their face. Her forearm pins the figure's neck and her knees keep their shoulders from moving. I stand, sheathing all my weapons, and turn around to pick up Glacia. Viper approaches my side to help.

"Another move and you'll be blind!" Strike shouts.

"Okay! *Okay!* Easy there!" A male voice squeaks. "How the...how the hell is that coming out of your arm?"

Strike pushes her forearm tighter against his neck. "That should be the least of your worries right now."

"Fair...fair..."

"Hawk, what do you think we should do with him?"

"I say we let him off the hook," Hawk says. "He doesn't look like the type to cause us any more trouble."

"Are you sure?" Viper asks while stabilizing Glacia's legs for me.

"What else would we do with him?" Hawk asks. "Might as well let him live."

"Let me what?" he exclaims. "You want to kill—" He's cut off by his own gagging, due to Strike adding pressure to his neck.

I settle Glacia into my arms and turn back to the others, my gaze keen on the squatter. His heart rate is through the roof, nearly deafening. Now that I really look at him, he doesn't seem to be much of a threat, but those flames were something else.

"I'm with Hawk on this. Let's just kick him out. No knocking him out." Viper walks next to Strike. "Maybe ask him a few questions about those flames."

"I don't really want to know how or why he wanted to set us on fire. I just want to eat and go to bed," Hawk replies. "Strike, you think the same, right?"

"I don't. I say we figure out who he is and why he's here. He could be with you know who." From underneath her undone hair, Strike shifts her gaze to me. "What do you think?"

The squatter stares at me with wide eyes.

"Hey! Wait, is your friend hurt there?" he asks.

"That's none of your damn business," Strike snaps.

"Listen! I-I can help her. My ma, she's a doctor. A real good one too! I picked up all of her tricks!"

"Tricks?" Strike asks.

"I mean tech-techniques!"

Strike leans in, nearly nose to nose with him. "And what will you be getting out of this exactly?"

"Um...if I help your friend, I get to stay in the house. We can...we can share it."

Hawk crosses her arms. "Why would you wanna stay in this dump? And how the hell do you expect us to trust you?"

He sighs. "Listen. I don't know. Just work with me here, please?"

It doesn't appear that he's in cahoots with Josh or Axl. He could be useful to us somehow; maybe he'll be able to help Glacia. That's a start for sure. If he isn't helpful later on, we can just kick him out.

Hawk groans. "Let's ju—"

"Sounds like a deal to me," I cut her off. "Let the poor guy up. Let him use his little tricks his ma taught him. There won't be any harm done."

Strike looks back at me. "You think we can trust him?"

"I'm surprised you don't see his heart jumping out of his chest," I say dryly. "If he were a threat, he wouldn't be as afraid of you as he is right now. Besides, if he tries anything, we can all take turns shoving our boots into his throat. It'll be fun."

"Good point," Viper mutters.

"Is that fine with you?"

"Whatever," Hawk says. "I just wanna go sleep."

"Strike?" I ask.

Strike stares him down more, making him go pale. "Fine. He can stay for now, but he's gone by morning."

I narrow my eyes. Why is she acting like this? Maybe she's just exhausted like the rest of us.

The squatter sighs with relief. His bliss is interrupted by Strike hauling him to his feet by his collar. She pushes him away and marches into the house alongside Hawk and Viper. Strike mumbles a few things to herself as she slips past me.

I stay behind, scanning the squatter up and down. He's a bit taller than me, with a stronger build than I expected. Those long legs of his must make him quick compared to an average person.

"Thanks for sticking up for me," the squatter says.

I wonder how the fire comes out of those palms...There must be some attachment under his sleeves that lets him do that. The squatter has wide eyes, they're a strange color in this light and he appears to be around my age. Maybe a bit younger.

"So uh, can I go back inside now?"

Blinking, I reel around on my heels. "C'mon."

I shuffle through the doorway, heading to the bedroom across from the living room. Strike stands in the kitchen door frame with her arms crossed. The sounds of Hawk and Viper hastily rummaging for food echo throughout the halls. The squatter suddenly scoots past, opening the door to the bedroom for me. I ask Strike to grab water for Glacia, and she responds with a small nod before leaving the house.

In the kitchen, Hawk and Viper start a bickering war with each other. It's nearly incoherent due to the speed of their speech. Since they're both exhausted neither is making any sense, and it doesn't help that Viper keeps speaking in her language. I sigh, deciding to leave them be, as I step into the small room. The squatter holds his hands out to take Glacia from me. Ignoring him, I lay Glacia gently on the floor. My hand on her forehead confirms that she's burning up.

The squatter bends down. "Gee, what happened to her?"

"Viper," I call out.

"Qué?"

"Will you please bring in Glacia's bag?"

A few moments later, Hawk and Viper appear in the doorway. Viper kneels next to me, placing Glacia's bag at my side. She puts her hand on Glacia's cheek and winces.

"What happened to her?" The squatter repeats.

"A fight," I say.

"How long ago?"

"Hours."

"It looks like she's already healed a lot though. Some of her bruises are in their final stages."

"We gave her a white pill. Sped up the process, I guess."

The squatter puts his fingers on his chin. "White pill..."

"The healing ones," I say.

"Oh! Whoa...how did you people get your hands on some *Sana Velox?*"

"You don't wanna know," Hawk mutters.

"We wanted to give her some more, but she said no," I say. "Do you think we should give her another?"

"Oh, no-no-no. Your friend—Glacia, right? She made the right call."

"Then why is she still hurt?" Hawk asks. "I mean, it sounds counterintuitive, if you ask me. Why not speed up the healing more with another pill?"

The squatter raises a brow. "You people must live under a rock. Uh, but not in a bad way. This drug, SV, is powerful, very easy to overdose on. The reason she's feverish right now is because the drug is still trying to work its magic. Her body must be super imbalanced, so her brain set in a fever. It's a common symptom if someone is healing from terrible injuries."

"Any more...uh...symptoms we should know about?" Viper asks.

"People pass out, talk nonsense, or sometimes hallucinate."

"Is there anything we can do to help it?" I ask.

"We just need to watch over her for now; keep her hydrated as well." The squatter looks up at me. "I'll keep first watch if you three want to head to bed."

Hawk, Viper, and I exchange looks.

"Strike and I will help him watch over her tonight," I say. "You two need rest...especially you, Viper."

"Are you sure? We could all four take turns," Hawk says.

"If she's like this tomorrow, you two can step in. How does that sound?"

Hawk yawns. "Fine by me. I'm starving though. If I don't eat, I won't sleep."

"Same here." Viper stands. "Hey, fire dude, did you hide the food or somethin'?"

The squatter's face pales. "I ate it all."

"Are you kidding me?"

"I might as well kick you out for that right now!" Hawk shouts.

The squatter puts his hands up. *"Icanhelpyoufindsome!"* He tumbles over his words. "I'm good at finding food. I've been doing it for the past week."

Hawk huffs. "No wonder you look like a twig."

Viper calls him an idiot as the two leave with smoke practically billowing out of their ears. Hawk slams the door, shaking the room, leaving me alone with the squatter. There is a tight silence between us. He exhales before taking off his wool hat, revealing a bundle of short, blond hair underneath. He takes another deep breath, holds it, and I hear him breathe out deeply. I shift my eyes to Glacia as he repeats this over and over and his heart rate steadily lowers as he does so. My eyelids begin to get heavy.

"Thank you again," he says. "For letting me stay."

I take Glacia's backpack and pick up her head as I slide the pack underneath it. When I yawn, I make sure to cover my teeth with my palm.

"I'm not sure what the hell I would do if I couldn't live here," he admits. "It's nice to know there are some nice people out here, people like you."

A twinge hits me in my temple. "If you so much as breathe the wrong way, I won't think twice when I break your jaw. Got it?"

"What the? I thought you were on my side."

"You thought wrong. I just don't want any more work tonight than there needs to be. I don't care if you're able to help Glacia or not," I lie.

He holds his breath.

"A piece of advice, from one squatter to another. Most people out here ain't nice. They just want something outta you. Truly genuine people, those are one in a billion. I doubt you'll ever meet one."

"But have you?"

"Only my friends. They're better than the people around here."

"Oh..."

The squatter lowers his peculiar eyes and wrings his hands. I still want to know how those flames were made from the thin air, but I shouldn't pry. This situation appears to be temporary. A few moments of silence pass between us. I take the opportunity to sit and lean against the wall as I watch Glacia's heaving chest. My eyelids droop. I would hate to be in her position. Fevers seem like the worst, and passing out isn't fun either. It's not going to be pretty when she wakes up. I'm not sure if she wanted to travel all the way here with us.

"I never caught your name; is it as made-up sounding as the other ones?" he asks quietly.

"They aren't made up."

He frowns. "I mean like, they don't sound like your real names."

I don't say a word.

"With names like those, I might as well be named Flamethrower or Flame Punch, maybe even Fire Fist. What do you think?"

I seriously don't care. "I'll just call you Flame, how about that?"

He grins a bit and nods. His heart rate is down. "So what should I call you?"

"Does it matter?"

"I'm just trying to be friendly, you know? Or, maybe you don't know what friendly means...but c'mon, we're going to be under the same roof for the night whether you like it or not, and it was your idea. So, do you want me to call you Sunglasses the whole time?"

"I know what friendly means. I'm just not in the mood."

"Fair, but why are you wearing those anyway? It's the middle of the night."

"Give me a reason to tell you."

"I don't know. Um...because it's weird, but, like, I want to stick around here. I don't wanna leave just yet and I think we should get to know each other."

"What makes you think that you're stayin'? Didn't you hear Strike?"

He pauses. "I thought she was joking."

I resist a laugh by placing my palm over my lips.

"What?"

"Nothin'." I pull myself together. "Well, let's say you do end up sticking around. What can you do, if anything at all, that will actually help us out?"

"I can start fires. That's something. I know how to get food from the woods."

Those are good points. He could do things for us, like the tedious stuff, while we lay low.

"I'm decent company too."

"Okay. I just need to know one thing, if we were to hypothetically live together."

"Yeah?"

"How do you start those flames of yours?"

"That's a long story," Flame says, breaking eye contact. "Basically, I needed an upgrade and got one, but I ended up with fake arms that can shoot fire."

"Fake arms with fire in them?" I narrow my eyes.

"There's a bit more to it, but basically, yeah."

Flame brings his abnormal gaze to me and leans forward. "Anything I should know about you? I already have a feeling you're pretty...uh...peculiar like your friend. Strike, was it? It has something to do with those sunglasses, right?"

He sounds useful, but he sure does like to pry.

"Call me Storm," I reply. "That's all you need to know."

"But—"

The door behind me swings open with Strike towering over us. Flame jumps a little, his heart racing again. He shrinks back, finally sealing his lips. Strike closes the door as I thank her for the water.

"Why's he in here?" Strike asks.

"He offered."

She scowls a bit. Strike places a wet cloth on Glacia's forehead and puts a bowl of water next to her before taking a seat next to me. Flame scoots closer to the opposite wall with his gaze fixed on Strike's arms.

"What was the diagnosis?" Strike asks while adjusting my jacket to blanket Glacia more.

"Flame? Could you explain?" I ask.

"Yeah, uh..." He hesitates. "The pill you guys gave her, it's called Sana Velox, SV for short. One of the side effects can be fevers."

I should write about this.

"Interesting." Strike looks up to Flame. "So, we shouldn't give her another?"

Flame shifts his eyes down. "Exactly."

Strike rubs her temples vigorously, then scrunches up her nose and eyes. "Does it cure headaches?"

"It does, but..." Flame trails off. "Maybe you should save it for something more serious."

I need to take notes on this before I forget.

I stand quickly. "Flame, have you seen a black backpack around here?"

"Yeah, there was one left in the living room. I put all that junk in one of the kitchen drawers."

It's not junk.

Without another word, I wander out into the hallway, speed into the kitchen, and attack the first drawer I see. After opening five dusty drawers, I find it. Snatching the journal and the pen, I turn to use the counter, but Viper has already fallen asleep there. I sigh and walk back to the bedroom. While I flip to an empty page, I stop in the doorway, placing the pen to paper, and draw a blank.

"Do either of you know what the date is?" I ask as I step into the room.

"Uh, pretty sure it's December third," Flame responds.

I sit down, scribbling down the date and then I let the words flow, uncontrolled.

"What are you writing there?" Flame asks.

I draw a few arrows, ignoring him.

"It's none of your business," Strike mutters.

Strike and Flame's voices become a blur to me. Only the words zipping across the thin pages matter. Only the information they hold matters. My eyelids droop over and over as I write furiously. Stopping at another blank, I yawn before asking Flame how to spell "Sana Velox."

Flame reaches his hand out. "Here, I can write it for you." He takes the journal without my permission.

"Wai—" I cut myself off. "—Write the information about it too."

Flame does so with a few flicks of the pen before handing the journal back. I write down a few more details and read through the entry one more time to make sure everything is there.

December 3
Entry #6

TOO MUCH HAS HAPPENED since I last updated this damn thing. To spare these pages the boring details, here's a quick timeline: Got captured (by the way, *do not* trust Miss Joe anymore) → went to prison → met a girl named Glacia → escaped said prison → came home and met another person (Flame) (For more about Glacia and Flame, skip on to Entry #7 for my assessment).

I've learned more in the past three months than I have for the entire year. The girls and I have only scratched the surface. A few new things have come to light that I don't really like. I'll start with the worst of what I learned.

There has been more death by my hands under the program's control than I realized, but there's more to it, and I didn't learn this in the best way. The Brute and the Goon that I wrote about before captured and interrogated us. Their names were revealed: The Brute is Trainee Joshua West (Josh for short) and the Goon is Seeker Axl Emil. Josh West is only good for information; he tends to have a hell of a short fuse around me. His temper caused him to slip up and share his true motivation—he wants to avenge a death he claims was caused by my own blades, and he mentioned "abandoning" some mission I don't remember.

An update on my assessment of Josh and Axl:

Josh: Motivated by hate. Will stop at nothing to get revenge. Clearly needs training with his blades. His lack of filter helps with getting more information. All I need to do to is keep quiet; he'll snap within minutes.

Axl: Motivations are unclear, but he mentioned wanting the truth a few times. Possesses super hearing like Viper and me and was able to detect my heartbeat during the interrogation. Has super speed as well. Carries an unloaded gun with him. Typically remains defensive when he fights.

. . .

BOTH THE MEN have a connection with Glacia. They were classmates (more info in Entry #7).

JOSH'S CLAIM that I'm a murderer could be true, but I'm unsure. He never talked about specific evidence. Usually, I would think guys like him would accuse me of killing someone just to get under my skin, but his words convinced me he wasn't lying.

It's clear that there's more to the memory with the dead bodies everywhere. Hopefully, not too much more. Recently, I did have a dream of an armored figure killing a little girl. I'm not sure if that was my imagination or a memory.

Anyway, my theory is that Josh and Axl are partners dedicated to rounding us up so they can reactive our programs, like past officers have tried to do. What's strange, though, is that they never mentioned activating the program in prison. Maybe they were waiting for their bosses to show up to do the deed. They didn't use the collars at all on us, maybe because they are temporary. So, could they have been waiting for a way to permanently activate the program? There must be more to it.

The two work under people they called "The Doctors." These doctors must be responsible for past attempts to capture us as well. I believe one of them could be the man in the purple tie, the Doctor from my memories. I sure hope he is, because that would be informative. Also, when we were captured, there was an emphasis on not harming the four of us. If we were harmed in any way, we were given white pills with healing abilities. Recently, I've learned the name of these pills and their side effects.

THE WHITE PILLS are called Sana Velox and information on them is as follows:

- *Has the ability to heal a person's wounds quickly.*
- *Only take one at a time; very easy to overdose.*
- *Some bodies may react dramatically to healing process. Side effects include fever, passing out, hallucinations, delusions, wonkiness, and extreme drowsiness.*
- *More than one type. White capsule is most common. Red and blue have different effects.*
- *Only available to certain people in the Safe Zone.*

Our new houseguest, Flame, filled in the additional information above. As I'm writing this, Glacia has been overcome with a fever and passed out. See the next entry for more info on Glacia and Flame and if they will be staying with us.

I'm too tired to keep writing. It's been a long hellish day and thinking about Glacia and Flame sounds awful right now. Speaking of, Flame and Strike are currently talking about taking shifts to watch over Glacia, and how long the shifts should be. I'll be the first shift, but I refuse to go to sleep during the next one, because that's Flame's slot. I already know he can't do much harm, but if I've learned anything from the past few months, it's that I shouldn't trust any new people for a long time, especially if they're friendly with you. I'm reminded of that one saying, "kill em with kindness." It makes sense. It's a way to gain their trust; then when they least expect it, stab them in the back. It's something someone must've told me a long time ago.

And it's still a good strategy for someone to use against us. Hell, it happened to us with Miss Joe. This is something I should keep in mind. No more falling for people's tricks and lies. I promise myself right here in print for anyone to read that I'll be smarter in the future and if I break that promise…well damn. This will be proof that I can't keep any promises.

I SET MY JOURNAL ASIDE. The conversation between Flame and Strike about Strike's blades, has died down. Strike winces and holds her aching head. To try to ease her pain, I rest my head on her shoulder. Strike rests her head atop of mine and, with my support, relaxes. I listen to all the heartbeats thumping in the room for any hint of trouble. Heartbeats from Glacia and Flame have stabilized. Strike's, however, has been increasing by the slightest amount as the moon rises higher and higher. The moon's light showers onto the two of us, turning the matching scars we bear into silvery lines on our arms. The pale light subtly illuminates her features and their true intentions.

Strike is too passive to speak, and I have a feeling of what the real source of her headache is. It could easily be dehydration or hunger, but with us it's never that simple. Maybe Glacia isn't the one I should be keeping watch on. Maybe I should be preparing for Strike's program to make an appearance. I'm afraid if I ask her directly, she won't tell me, or will be upset. She's always worried about being a burden.

FOURTEEN
ICEFALL
STORM

Through a jagged window, I can see the morning light rise weakly. Its fragile rays illuminate each particle of dust on the dulling walls and the decaying floor. The pale streaks reflect off any surface they can find. Rays of sunlight fall into my eyes. Three other heartbeats pulse in the room. Everyone is deep in their dreams, and I await the time for when they stir so I can communicate with another mind, rather than sit in the stagnant void of my own thoughts. The faintest drizzle that's been falling, since the sun first made an appearance, has been my only company.

Outside, a storm is passing through with little effort. The drops lightly ping against the few shards of glass left on the window frame, or deposit themselves against my skin. They come from some misty force in the sky that creates every drop with such precision. Each starts out exactly same, and all wait for their time to fall to the earth. Some move faster than others, some are colder than others, and some are smaller than others, but they are, nonetheless, the same in composition and intent. The only real difference is where they end up falling, where they end up sinking into the ground, and it's always out of their control. What controls these drops is unknown to me. It could possibly be a misty creator or a combination of circumstances. I'll never know the exact answer.

It's strange that all raindrops must shatter to become part of the earth. Why would their creator produce beautiful, precise, and nourishing things that are destined to shatter? Is there something I'm missing from a raindrop's story that would justify their creation in the first place?

They are just pawns that have no say in what they are used for, or where they will ultimately end up shattering. Raindrops never know why they are falling; they only feel it happening out of their control.

A small groan echoes in the room as Glacia sits up, still holding the wet cloth to her forehead. Her eyes flutter and she drops the rag before snatching the bowl. In a matter of seconds, she inhales the water, causing some to pour on her face. Glacia looks around the room in a daze. She wipes the remaining streams of water from her chin, then turns to me, revealing all the dried blood caked onto her face. In a whisper, I ask how she is feeling.

Glacia feels her shoulder, lifting it a little. "Better."

I nod.

"How long was I out?"

"In and out for hours. We managed to get you here, to our home, without any problems," I whisper. I need to know if she'll be staying with us or not. "You're covered in blood right now, but I can take you to get it washed off."

Glacia thanks me with a soft voice. I smile, getting to my feet, and hold my hand out. She hesitates but takes my palm and allows me to haul her to her feet. She winces a bit, holding her head with her free hand. I ask her if she's okay. She nods.

Bending over, I grab my jacket and swing it over my shoulders as I push the door open with my foot. I begin to tiptoe down the hallway. Suddenly something slams in the bedroom, and it's followed by a few shouts. I whip around just as Strike throws Flame into the hallway.

"Oh jeez!" Flame rushes to his feet.

Strike steps into the hall, her sights on Flame, and grabs him by his collar.

"C'mon, Strike, please! I don't wanna leave yet! Just lemme help some more!" Flame rambles on as Strike drags him past me and Glacia.

"You've overstayed your welcome." Strike throws Flame against the front door. "Now get the hell out."

Flame's peculiar eyes widen. "Storm! Please, please help me out here! Don't let her kick me out, please! You said you wouldn't!"

I squint. What color are those eyes of his? I approach the two.

"Listen, I can help you people with whatever you need! I'm useful!"

"I didn't make any promises to you. I thought that was clear," I say.

Flame falls to his knees. "Please, I'm begging you. This is the only place I can stay that's safe for people like me."

"People like you?" Strike asks.

"Those flames you saw. People wanna exploit them, okay? This is the safest place I can be right now. Especially if I stick with you guys. I can pull my weight. Just let me stay. Please!"

I put my hand on Strike's shoulder, leaning forward as I adjust my sunglasses to try to get a clear view of his eyes.

Strike crosses her arms. "What could you do that could help us?"

"I can get you food! I can make you food and heat everything up and....and if you ever get injured, I can heal you!"

His eyes have a red hue to them that's been mixed with a light brown. How strange. I take a step toward him. "I'm all for you staying, pretty sure Glacia is too because you helped heal her, but Strike obviously doesn't want you around. I'm not sure about the other two. If you're gonna stay here, they have to approve of you. So, Strike—" I turn to her. "What can he do to stay?"

Strike raises a brow. "Fine, go on then. Show him what's under your coat, and let's see what happens."

"Show me what?"

She's right. If he handles that surprise well, he can handle the rest. I take a step closer to him as I slip my jacket off, squatting to his level.

I sigh. "You wanted to know more about me? Here you go." I spread my wings so that my black feathers wrap around my shoulders.

Flame's reddish eyes bulge and his mouth gapes. He's tense and ready to bolt, but after a second, he takes in a few deep breaths and closes his eyes.

"I'm not afraid," Flame mutters, opening his eyes. "I've seen stranger."

"Doubtful," Strike says.

"I have. You people could have tails and I wouldn't care. Listen, from what I've gathered, we may be in the same situation—on the run and nowhere to go. So, we might as well stick together, right?"

"Right..." Strike trails off.

"And okay, yeah, I'm a stranger. I get that you people won't trust me in the beginning, but—"

"Fine," Strike cuts him off. "I'll let you stay, but it's going to take a lot more to prove yourself to Hawk and Viper. Don't get comfortable."

I fold my wings. "I'm surprised we didn't wake 'em up. Good thing those two could sleep through a gunfight." I zip up my jacket. "Might as well get some supplies while they are asleep. How about you and Hot Shot go find some food in the forest? You can see how helpful he really is."

"What will you be doing?" Strike asks.

"Glacia and I are heading for the spring. We'll bring y'all water. The containers are still up there, right?"

Strike nods and orders Flame to get going. Flame jumps up with a small grin on his face and opens the door for her. Strike ignores him, walks out the door, and heads down the steps before he can blink. He jogs after her, rambling on about tree bark, leaving Glacia and me in the dusty hallway. Glacia slips past me and we make our way down the steps.

We move to the right of the house, into a swamp of frozen grass that crunches under my boots. Above the swamp, the barren branches have iced over by the rain, causing all of them to painfully sag. Glacia stares at them as they capture her with their distorting lights that darken the frigid swamp. A coldness stings the back of my throat.

"I've been meaning to ask you..." I say. "Will you be staying with us for a while?"

Glacia puts her hands into her leather pockets and tilts her head downward in thought.

"It's fine if you don't, but I think you could really help us out. You know so much; you know so many more people than we do."

"What do you mean?"

"Those Doctors, and Josh, and Axl. We need intel on them, a way to get 'em off our asses. I bet you want the same, right?"

Should I tell her the whole truth, including the program part? The memory loss? No, of course not. That can wait. That should be kept under the rug for now.

"Yeah," Glacia replies. "I do."

"Then I think it's best for us to stick together, since you know more than we do."

Glacia finally locks her frozen eyes with mine. "Ok, but I gotta know somethin'."

"Yeah?"

"Why were y'all imprisoned? And put with me...an enemy of the state?"

I hesitate. "Honestly, I'm not too sure. Before I could even get a punch in, Axl and Josh showed up and shot us with those tranquilizers."

"You hesitated."

I stop in my tracks. "Yeah?"

"Did you just lie to me?" Glacia stops a few feet in front of me.

Her eyes quickly scan me up and down, watching for the next wrong move, trying to find the next lie. The scattered light illuminates the side of her face and despite the protection of the trees, it's almost as if a freezing whirlwind has taken hold of me, all from a simple glance.

I take a breath. "It wasn't a lie. I hesitated 'cause I don't know the reason why. We have been chased by others in the past, but nobody like those two have ever gone after us."

"And that's where I come in, because I know them," Glacia says quietly. "Because I know the Doctors, too. I know stuff that could help you get them off your back."

I nod and point to a dim trail that leads deeper into the tangled mess of icy raindrops. The fading path is shrouded in masses of patchy shadows. After I explain that this is the direction of the spring, we begin walking again.

"You know, y'all were what I needed back in that prison," Glacia murmurs.

I stop walking. I'm standing at the edge of the tangled shadows now.

"I don't know what would have happened if you'd abandoned me after I hurt my shoulder. I'll help you out and tell you anything you need. I'll stick around if you want. I don't have anywhere to go or anything to do, anyway."

I raise a brow. "I didn't expect you to say that. Why do you want to stay?"

Glacia keeps her eyes on me. "I need to get the Doctors off my back too. And...let's just say that I have a score to settle with them."

"Good," I say. "We can talk about the details when we eat with everyone, to see if they are cool with you staying."

"Do you think they'll say no?"

"Probably not. Now, let's get you washed up."

I reel away from her and bend over to avoid the chilled branches. I slide my hands in my pockets, having to move side to side to avoid the drooping branches. Dried dirt, cold bark, and withering grass lace the air. There is minimal illumination along the forgotten trail. The sole source is from the light that manages to reflect off the frozen drops. Every ray of light is scattered and unpredictable.

"How did you find this trail?" Glacia asks.

"Dumb luck. Viper was tryin' to hide from Hawk over some stolen food, and she ran down this path to hide. I'm glad she did. We wouldn't have stayed long in this place if she hadn't found it."

We've nearly reached the end, where the shadows have begun to crack.

"How did you find the cabin?"

I push a branch out of my path. "We were passing through, resting after flying, and came across it."

"With those wings of yours, right...?"

"Yeah, with our wings. Before that, we were jumping around city to city, across the state."

We reach the end of the trail at a new forgotten place: the spring. It's frozen over, surrounded by dead grass and leaves, begging to be freed from its icy prison. I walk over to the spring, testing it with my heel.

"How did you get captured?" I ask.

"It's a long story. Maybe I'll tell you about it some other time."

"I was just wondering, since Josh and Axl were so..."

"Aggressive? Yeah, that's normal for those two. They were aggressive to y'all as well. Especially you."

"You heard him screaming at me in the garage, didn't you?" I ask as I turn to her.

"Yeah."

Sighing, I turn to the water. I raise my boot and shove the heel deep into the ice, causing it to shatter instantaneously.

"What can you tell me about them? Anything we should know?" I ask. "Since you grew up with them and all."

"Oh, so you picked up on that," Glacia says faintly. She comes up alongside me, bending down and cupping her hands to scoop up the water before she buries her face into her palms.

"Why didn't you want me to know?"

Glacia cups more water. "I used to be a part of their company, their cause, and it's not something I want to advertise nowadays."

I can relate. I think.

Glacia brings the water to her face once again. The dried blood gradually flows off her skin until she's clean of all the red stains.

I wonder if she willingly joined them? Did she willingly leave them?

"Where I come from, their cause is everything, you know? In the Safe Zone, it's all people talk about. It's strange, but I used to believe in it." Her eyes twitch between me and the spring. "Storm, I know why you wanted to get me alone. You wanted to see if I'm staying, to see if I'm trustworthy or not, right?" Glacia rises.

"How did you figure that?"

"I know how to read people, and it's something someone like you would do."

"Someone like me?"

"You're protective of people. You protect anyone who you think deserves it. I'm pretty sure since you met me, you've been trying to figure out if I'm a threat or not, if I'm worth your time or not. You've already decided I'm worth your time. Now, all you gotta do is figure out if I'm a threat."

Damn.

"I guess we both have the same goal. We're trying to figure each other out."

"Then I'm telling you, I'm not a threat to you," she urges. "We both want the same things."

I tune into her heartbeat. "Tell me something then. The reason you were in there, for murder, why did you do it?"

Glacia hesitates, but her heartbeat remains steady. "There was never a why. It was a misunderstanding. I was trying to do something else, but people got hurt in the process. It all was unintentional; I was just the closest *scapegoat* they could find."

Her heartbeat hasn't spiked.

"You won't have to worry about being a scapegoat with us around," I say gently.

She nods and her eyes have a new warmth to them that I never thought I'd see. I walk over to a log next to the edge of the spring. Inside lay the containers for water. Grabbing two, I hand one to Glacia and we fill the containers to the brim. I carefully walk toward the entrance to the forgotten trail.

"I hope everyone is awake by now," I say. "I hate havin' to wake up Hawk and Viper at the same time. They hate the morning. Especially Hawk."

"Yeah, I could see that." Glacia joins my side. "How long have y'all known each other?"

I smile. "As long as I can remember."

"One big happy family, huh?"

"Pretty much. I don't know how I would function without them. I'd be so bored and well-rested."

Glacia gives me a small smile as we reach the end of the trail.

"How about you? Any family worth mentioning?"

Glacia shakes her head. "They aren't as interesting as yours."

"Figures. Nobody ever could be."

We both break eye contact and silence follows. My eyes drift over Glacia, catching hints of her tattoo that glare in the misty light.

"I was wondering something the other day," I blurt out. "Back when we were in the truck, I saw your tattoo. I was wondering what it means. Who gave it to you?"

Glacia shifts her gaze further away. "My superior, Doctor Bristol Inman, had an older seeker put it there. It's simply an identification number. You're asking because you have a similar one, right?"

"Yeah, right." I pull my sleeve up. "Do you know what it means?"

"I know the X.X means female, but that's all I can give you."

"I have another one too, on my neck." I move my hair up "Do you know anything about this?"

Glacia pauses. "I'm not sure. I've never seen that before. It looks old though. I can't make it out too well."

"It says K_192. Viper has one that says K_90."

Glacia nods as we make it to the cabin. I stop at the steps, staring at the looming door as the rumblings of voices vibrate within the walls. There's a heavy debate storming inside. I take a seat on the steps.

"We should wait here for a second. They're deciding whether Flame should stay or not."

Glacia raises her brows. "How'd you know that?"

"I'm a good listener."

"You have enhanced hearing, like Axl, don't you?" she asks. "Do you have night vision as well?"

"Yeah, how did you guess?"

"Back in the prison, you and Viper seemed more alert. Axl has the same thing, you know. That's why his eyes are so strange; the night vision makes them glow."

"Oh..."

"You didn't know that before?"

I shake my head and tune back in to the debate to find out where it has finally settled. Flame will be staying with us after all. Now we'll have someone to run all our errands—what a relief.

"Interesting," Glacia says. "I thought it was something else when I first met y'all. What other enhancements do you have?"

"You'll see soon. They've settled down—it's safe to go inside."

I get to my feet, trudge up the old steps, and swing the door open. Walking into the kitchen, I find all four munching on a pile of opened acorns. Strike, Viper, and Hawk are sitting on top of the counter while Flame is stuck standing next to the center table.

"Thanks for waiting to eat with us," I say.

"No problemo," Hawk replies. "Thanks for the drinks. Appreciate it."

I take a sip before I set the container down next to the stack of acorns. Glacia does the same.

"Hey, Glacia! How you feelin'?" Viper asks.

"Better."

"Yeah, you look a lot better," Hawk remarks. "I see Storm had you wash off the blood, too."

"Yep."

There's a brief silence between everyone.

I lean against the table. "So, did you two decide if Flame could stay or not?"

"Sure did," Viper says. "Hawk sure was a pain in the ass about it."

"Not really," Hawk mutters. "I was skeptical 'cause the boy just brought in some lousy fucking acorns for breakfast. I bet the water Storm brought has more flavor than these things." She pops an acorn into her mouth. "But he can stay, I guess."

Flame thanks them a few times. Another unsure silence follows.

"Glacia has decided to stay with us," I say. "She wants to help out, if y'all are cool with it. It sounds like she has an idea of what to do next." I give Glacia a nod.

Glacia hesitates. "It sounds like y'all want to know about the Doctors. The best way to do that is by targeting the bases. They typically have intel that would be useful to y'all."

Of course! Why didn't I think of that?

"Great! Then I guess we can start with the Oklahoma City base," Hawk replies. "That should be a walk in the park."

"Not so fast. Since we caused a mass prison riot, I'm assuming the majority of those prisoners escaped, and the higher-ups are probably scrambling. They'll be on high alert for a while. We're high profile right now," Glacia explains. "I think the best thing is to get outta this state for a while. Go incognito while we plan the first raid."

"Where should we go?" Viper asks.

"Nashville, Tennessee."

"Wait, but that's in the Safe Zone," Hawk says. "We've seen that wall. How would we get in? Isn't it too risky if we try to sneak around it?"

"Not if we go right through the front door," Glacia replies. "It's December fourth, right? In about a week, they will open a section of the gate for a day, on the border between Tennessee and Arkansas.

We'll be able to slip past easily, if we act like migrants. It'll be our only chance to get in. They only open it up every three months, so we'll have to leave soon. From there, we can travel up to Nashville. I know a place we can camp out while planning the raid. We can target the Aurex Facilities where they keep all the intel about manufacturing and resources, but there's bound to be something related to y'all as well. Those tattoos came from ink found somewhere in the Safe Zone, I bet, and those Doctors had to order it to give it to y'all. Maybe we could get their mailing addresses and go from there?"

"Aurex...why does that sound so familiar?" Hawk asks.

"The Aurex family is a huge benefactor for the organization that runs the bases. I bet you've seen their name around Oklahoma City," Glacia says. "They mainly provide the machinery for both the military and the company."

Viper nods. "I think this is a good plan. Everyone else cool with it?"

We all nod except for Flame.

"And how do I fit into all this?" he asks.

"I was thinkin' you could stay here and protect the house from other squatters," I say. "I mean, you managed to hold us off for a little bit, which is impressive. You can handle anything that makes their way in here."

"I like how that sounds, but I sorta wanna come with you guys."

I shrug. "Maybe. For now, let's figure out the supply situation. Who's going into town and what will we need?"

"Why don't you and Viper just shapeshift so nobody will know who you are? Not even that bitch, Miss Joe," Strike replies.

"Shapeshift?" Flame mumbles to himself.

I frown.

Viper grins. "Yeah, Storm! You and me, the shapeshifting trio!"

"Do you mean duo?" Hawk sneers.

"Whatever, you know what I mean."

I put my hands on my hips. "I don't wanna. Why can't you and Hawk just go? Hawk can stay by the entrance while you get all the supplies, or I could stand by the entrance." I can see my audience is unimpressed. "Please, V! Please don't make me."

"Fine, but we train tomorrow. You need to practice. It's a gift you can't lose."

"Deal," I sigh.

Viper beams and I can't help but smile in return.

"Can I take a nap now?" Strike asks as she rubs the back of her neck. "I mean, are we done?"

"It's a wrap," I say.

The others scatter from the kitchen into their own realms of conversations about what will happen next or how things will work out from here. I gaze out of the window, up to the rays of light escaping the thick cloak of clouds. They reach my fingertips, travel up, and something suddenly embeds itself in my chest. It's a hot sensation. Its energy spreads across my body and all the way up to my lips, causing a smile to form. The sensation provides a reminder that as those poor raindrops fall, they can always look up at the radiant sky.

FIFTEEN
UNREALISTIC REFLECTIONS
STORM

December 5

Entry #7

Honestly, I never realized that information could
come to me by accident. I stumbled upon someone
who knows more than I could have ever imagined.
Two people, actually. They are out of the house
right now, so I thought this would be the best
time to write about them. Here are my assessments
of Glacia and Flame as of right now.

Glacia Ivar: She's fourteen like the rest of us
and mentioned to me, when I asked about any fun
facts about her, that she speaks Spanish like
Viper. Personality wise, she's cold and quiet.
Very analytical. She picks up on things quickly.
Hell, she's better at it than me. I'm sure I
could learn a thing or two from her. Glacia will
ask tons of questions to get the information she
needs. I guess one could say she's curious and

intuitive. She's already taught me the meaning of the XX part of my tattoo, because she has a similar tattoo. The XX apparently means female.

Glacia's tattoo is similar to the ones Josh and Axl have; it reads, ESXX2. Also, she used to work with Josh, Axl, and the Doctors. Another piece of important info is that she was put into prison for murder. She claims it was unintentional, a crossfire sort of situation, and I believe her. It sounds like she had no control over where she would end up because everyone wanted to blame her for it. From what I've noticed, she had a plan. Glacia wanted to do something that involved going to Roadie Trading Post first, then running for the hills with someone else. I know there's more to it, but her past won't unravel easily.

Her motivations aren't completely clear yet. She tells me she wants to help us because it's in her best interest to get the Doctors off her ass. She wants payback too, for what they did to her. But I'm not sure. We did save her life and help her escape the prison, so she must feel like she's in debt to us. She may want to redeem herself for killing someone, or she may have become invested in the four of us. Based on our talks, she wants to learn everything she can about us. True or not, I guess we all gotta have some type of hobby. I just get the feeling that I'm missing something about her.

She said to me that she doesn't want to be a threat. Now that I think about it, it's like she wants a new start. She doesn't like to talk about the past; she gets very guarded, something I understand, but I'm annoyed that she tries to figure me out without letting me do the same to her. It puts me on edge. Hopefully in the future, I'll be able to get to know her and find out what actually happened, but I can't help but try to figure her out right now. She's one of the most interesting people I've met. She's not just three-dimensional; she's like ten-dimensional.

Flame: My first encounter with him was when he ran out of the house, either on a suicide mission or due to pure stupidity, shooting flames from his hands. It was very strange. Afterwards, when Strike had him pinned, I figured out that he's not much of a threat. It just so happens he's able to shoot fire out of his arms. Nothing else shows that he can hurt us much.

Flame told me he just turned fourteen. He's friendly, outgoing, and a bit confident. He's also the most talkative person ever, more so than Hawk, and rambles often, which can get very irritating. He may turn out to be a smartass, hopefully not though. So far, he is very willing to help out. He volunteered his help in exchange for living in the house with us. We all accepted the offer, of course. He has knowledge of gathering food in the forest, as well as first aid. Flame is surprisingly useful for someone who fights like a chicken running on acid. I may teach him a thing or two in the future; the kid has potential.

As for his fire-control abilities, he said he has fake arms that can shoot fire, but I'll need to do more investigating.

What I know of his life before us is that his mother is a doctor, and it doesn't seem like he's had much other experience with people. He's almost too trustworthy; he thought we were friends after I saved him from Strike's wrath. I had to explain to him I was just too tired to deal with him at the time. Hopefully he grows out of that.

On a scale of one to ten, Flame is a solid five and a half for trustworthiness. Since I haven't had a solid conversation with him yet, I'm unsure if he is 100% trustworthy, but I'm hopeful. His reaction to my wings was frightened at first, but he eventually became comfortable around them. This tells me two things: one is that he's never seen wings before and two is that he wouldn't have any connection to Josh or Axl—unless they are more people out there like us, which I highly doubt—because of this lack of knowledge. I don't think he works for anyone but himself. Plus, he passed all the girls' tests. If they think he's trustworthy, I do too.

On another note, he'll be a great asset to us. Not because of his knowledge of medical things and forest things, but because he'll be able to protect the house while we're away. He could possibly be the one to go into town for supplies so that rat bitch, Miss Joe, doesn't know we're here.

Now for the most exciting news. The first raid. Of course, Glacia came up with most of the ideas because she's our new starting point. As of right now, we've decided to hit a base in Nashville, Tennessee called the Aurex Facilities. The Aurex family is a benefactor for the bases. I used to see their name on all the military cars in Oklahoma City. Maybe if we were to ever encounter this family, they would have some useful information.

Glacia says that a section of the Safe Zone is opened between Tennessee and Arkansas. This section will be opening in about a week's time, so we're frantically gathering supplies to make it there. We'll be staying in Nashville for a total of three months, mainly for planning, and we'll leave after the raid, then go from there. We need to figure the next step soon. I'll keep the status of the raid updated. I hope we don't have any setbacks.

As of right now too, Glacia and Flame haven't picked up on our programs or our memory loss. Most likely, I'll tell them about the memory loss. I'm not sure about the program part yet.

I PUT my pen into the spine of the notebook, tapping my index finger on the page and staring at the neat handwriting.

Should I add anything? I could talk more about the Safe Zone, but I've only heard the stories. I remember Curly telling me the streets are paved with gold. At the time, I wanted to go there so badly, but now, I'm not sure. What will we do if we run into Josh or Axl? We don't know the place at all, and it's their home field. And what happens if another program attacks, or worse? What if all of our programs attack at the same time? Who's going to snap us out of it? Glacia? She doesn't know anything about it, and we shouldn't expect her to know what to do. Hell, none of us know what to do. So, what will happen if we all lose control?

The door swings open. Viper stands there and steps inside, grinning ear to ear, with her hands behind her back. I raise a brow as I set my journal down.

"I thought I told you to give me until midday," I say.

"It is."

Great.

"We'll do some sparring first." She smiles. "I can tell you're so excited to shapeshift."

"Totally am."

I get to my feet, take off my jacket, and slip off my boots.

"I saw a move Josh tried to pull on Glacia," Viper says. "I thought that maybe you would remember a move of Axl's so we could use that too."

I start to unbutton my shirt because I don't want to mess it up. "Yeah, I picked up on how he dodges people. It seems pretty simple and looked familiar too. It's this circular motion, mainly. I think the goal was to stay behind the attacker's back where they can't touch you."

"Let's hope the muscle memory kicks in. I hate it when it doesn't."

I peel the shirt off, leaving the handmade bra, and fold my wings. Viper throws off her boots and grey shirt, while I tie my hair up. I turn to Viper as she jumps side to side on the balls of her feet, practicing the motion she wants to show me, before she beckons me over. Before I know it, she whirls around to my back. She snakes her forearm under my chin and plants her palm on the back of my head. She drags me back, forcing me to balance on my heels. My airway constricts.

"Okay, so I think what he was trying to do was knock her out." Viper puts more pressure on my neck.

The air stops coming. The dizziness sets in. I tap on Viper's forearm frantically. She releases me and I cough up a storm.

"What happened?"

"You nearly knocked me out there," I say as I rub my neck. "And you said Glacia got out of that? That's nuts. Here, let me try it on you."

Stepping behind Viper, I loop my forearm underneath her chin and put pressure on the back of her head with my palm. I drag her back, until she's putting weight on her heels, and apply more pressure. Her breathing changes as mine did, then she taps out and I release her.

"Does it feel familiar to you too?" She asks.

I nod. "Let's practice it a few more times, though, just so we have it down."

Viper and I trade places, nearly choking each other to death about five more times. I give in when we start for the fifth time, because my neck has been throbbing since the second one.

"So, you said Glacia was able to get out of this hold?" I ask.

"Yeah, I didn't see it, though. I was too busy tryin' to break the car window for her. We should have her show us when she gets back."

"Good plan," I say. "Now it's my turn."

I get into position, but before I can apply pressure Viper gags and she rips away. Her fist flies into my cheek, knocking my head to the side.

"Ow!"

Viper gasps and takes a step back. She leans over, hands on her knees, and breathes rapidly.

I hold my throbbing jaw. "Viper?"

"I'm...I'm fine."

"Did you just have a—"

"I'm fine." Viper straightens up, still breathing hard, and crosses her arms. "It's not a big deal. Sorry...it was the memory where they give me that tattoo on my neck. Not a big deal...let's keep training. Didn't you want to show me Axl's moves?"

My gaze softens. "Honestly, I'm worn out on learning moves," I lie. "Wanna work on shapeshifting?"

"Are you sure?"

"Yeah. Yeah, let's shapeshift. I have to learn from the master sometime soon, right?"

Viper smiles. "I don't know about master, but I'm good enough to train you."

I sit. "Well, I guess I don't need shapeshifting. If you can't master it, I can't either."

She scoffs. "Don't need shapeshifting? Don't need *shapeshifting*? You need to stop being a idiot." She punches my knee as she sits. "Shapeshifting is a art, a gift, and it can be fun. I thought you loved havin' fun."

I shrug. "It's not that I hate it; it's just painful and uncomfortable for me."

"Those blades of yours hurt when you use 'em, right?"

"Right."

"Then you don't got no excuses. C'mon, don't be a *mocosa*. We'll do some easy stuff, all right?"

I sigh.

"I don't get how you don't like it. I get to control what I look like and looks are the first thing people see, so it's a leg up that we have control over how people see us."

I look down. "I dunno. I don't like it."

"Well, I promise you'll fall in love with it by the end of the day."

Highly unlikely. "We'll see about that," I say. "What do you want to me to do first?"

She's unable to contain her bright smile as scoots closer to me, almost nose to nose.

"Let's just try changing that grey streak of yours into brown," Viper says. "And to help, I'll give you something to base it off of."

In an instant, the freckles dotting Viper's cheeks and nose gradually sink back into her lightening skin. Bones in her face boil underneath her skin, making it look paper thin. I flinch at every pop and crack. Viper's scars on her neck fade and are replaced with two familiar ones that carve themselves through the side of her left cheek and across her right eye. Her dark hair lightens into a pure brunette. Viper's eyebrows grow and thicken, one single strand at a time. Finally, her green irises melt away to reveal a gleaming gold. My reflection sits in front of me; she's breathing actual air that lightly brushes across my cheeks, but there is no grey streak in sight. She is not my complete reflection.

"All right," my reflection replies in Viper's voice. "Focus on my hair."

I close my eyes.

"Now, take in a few deep breaths. Let all your worries go away," Viper says softly. "Picture yourself without the streak. Picture yourself looking just like me."

I keep breathing deeply, imagining the streak vanishing from my hair. My scalp starts to prickle. When I tense up, I lose my train of thought.

"Keep going. You're almost there."

I breathe in again, trying to accept the prickly sensation. It vanishes.

"Perfect! Now bring it back to normal; you remember how to do that right?'

"It's my favorite part; how could I forget?"

Allowing every muscle to relax, I picture myself as I am, and the prickling returns but with less tension. It stops before I can take another breath. I let out a sigh and open my eyes. Viper claps, grinning ear to ear with my smile.

"Such a natural!"

"What can I say? I've got a killer mentor."

"How about we try eye color now? Oh, oh! And then I can teach you voices! What color eyes do you want?"

"Hmm..." I trail off. "Maybe like a hazel blue?"

"You wanna challenge yourself, don't ya?"

Viper's golden eyes dissolve into a deep blue with highlights of green interwoven within it. I'm so drawn to its color that I immediately begin to picture myself with the same eyes. My eyes dry to the point where I'm sure they will roll out of my head. I close them. The sockets burn, forcing me to squeeze them shut even further. I scrunch up my nose and clench my jaw.

"Keep going. Keep going."

A tiny tear drips down my cheek, extinguishing the burning in my eye. Viper wipes the tiny tear away with a finger. When I open my eyes, the first thing I see is my smile beaming once again.

"Nice," Viper replies. "See, it wasn't so bad."

"My eyes were on fire." I allow for my original eye color to return.

"You get used to it. For me, it's just like a little sore spot. You'll get there one day." Viper's freckles splatter across her cheeks.

Her skin and bones alter more rapidly this time, more desperate to return to their natural state. Less than a second later, she's back to normal. I hold her gaze.

"For voice copying, you'll do my voice and I'll do yours," Viper says. "The trick to it is to keep repeating what I say, trying to match it. It still takes me a few tries for someone new but—" She clears her throat. "—for you, it's pretty easy since I'm around you all the time," Viper replies in my deeper voice.

I cringe. "Ooh, that's so weird."

"C'mon, you try," Viper replies normally "Repeat after me—my name is Viper."

I clear my throat. "My name—" I try to say in a higher and smoother pitch, with a twang. "—is Viper."

Viper points to the center of her throat. "Say it from here, but that was good, you made it higher. My name is Viper."

"My name is Viper." I push my fingers on my vocal cords. "My name is Viper." My voice is altering slowly.

"Almost there. Open your throat more. Try it one more time. My name is Viper."

"My name—" I cover my mouth. I sound just like her. "—is Viper."

"I knew it! I knew it! I knew you could do it! You must've learned it before, right? You did it so quick!"

"My name is Viper," I say in her voice, my eyes wide. "My name is Viper."

Viper grabs me by the shoulders and shakes me violently. I laugh and drop my hands from my mouth. She stops shaking me, keeping her hands firmly on my shoulders.

"Try saying a whole made-up sentence in my voice. That's the tricky part."

I clear my throat. "My name is Viper...I have...green eyes and freckles."

"Keep going, you're still on it."

"I love to shift and—"

The door flies open, and there stands Strike. Immediately, my heart ties into a knot. Strike's more pale than any full moon. The whites of her eyes look like a red pen exploded in them. Her entire body shakes with each slight breath. I rush to my feet. Viper mimics my actions and we cautiously approach her. Strike's blades shoot out. She flinches as her blood splatters on her legs. I freeze. Strike looks at me with wide eyes, her jaw completely glued shut. She tries to speak but can only manage to make a strangled cry in between heavy breaths.

"Strike..." I trail off, taking a step closer to her. "It's going to be okay. Stay with us."

Strike shakes her head before her knees turn into trembling weak branches and her legs give out. I burst forward, barely preventing her skull from ricocheting off the wood floor. Strike's back arches. Her entire body tenses to the point where she's unable to move. It's as if her bones have turned to concrete. Viper rushes to my side.

"Hawk!" Viper screams. "The program!"

Cradling Strike's head, I lean over to examine her eyes. I go numb when I look into her irregular pupils; it's like staring at a demon. She's now frozen under its influence. Suddenly her arm shoots above her head, past my arms, stiffening into an unnatural position. The limb inches toward dislocation, but Viper grabs it with all her strength.

"Hawk!"

Strike's head jolts to the side, every vein pops out of her neck, and a low moan escapes her lips. I try to hold her head steady.

"*Hawk!* Where are you?"

Strike's free arm lurches down, the blade aiming for her own thigh. Hawk grabs it as she dives down next to us. Strike's bloodshot eyes roll back.

"We're right here, Strike. We're here," Hawk whispers. "Keep it out. Keep it out."

Strike breathes in painfully. We watch as her legs and arms relax. "That's it."

Her back straightens and her body slowly melts from a stiff posture. Her jaw relaxes and her eyes flutter. The blades shoot back into her arms. Viper rises to her feet, stepping away from us. I push back one of Strike's eyelids, checking the pupils.

"She's back to normal," I murmur.

Hawk hangs her head, sighs with relief, and squeezes Strike's arm more. I look to Viper, who's turned toward the door. She's clenching her fists.

"We have to leave by tomorrow. Who knows when it will attack me?" Viper whispers.

"Hold on a second," Hawk replies. "We barely have enough supplies and we still have to go into town."

"Then let's go right now. Any longer could mean that we get slowed by my attack," Viper's voice quivers. "I can't let that happen. Y'all know what happened last time. It's only gonna get worse." She walks out of the room.

"I'll go talk to her," Hawk says. "I'll talk some sense into her."

"I think she's right," I say.

Hawk narrows her eyes. "But the supplies—"

"If I have to, I'll stay up all night to get them. I'll stay up all night waiting for Strike to come around, but Viper has a point. We need to leave tomorrow."

Hawk sighs as she stands.

"Just think about it," I reply. "We're running out of time. Pretty soon the programs will have more power. This attack on Strike was longer than last time. We're running out of time."

"Like I don't know that."

"Then you know we can't wait anymore. Like Viper said, it's only gonna get worse."

"What do you know..." Hawk murmurs. "Fine, I'll think it over. Just let me calm Viper down first."

Hawk leaves the room, and I hear her tell Viper to wait up before their footsteps exit the house. When I look down at Strike, her complexion is still pale. I bring my forehead down to hers. Her heartbeat pounds in my ears. My eyes close and I grit my teeth.

When will Viper's program attack? What will happen when it finally attacks me for the first time?

"What are we going to do, Strike?" I whisper.

Will anyone catch us when we all fall victim to our programs? Or will we be left to helplessly watch ourselves shatter...

SIXTEEN

A NATURAL DEPARTURE

STORM

"Why are you leaving so soon?" Flame asks. "Why get all that stuff in one night and then leave the next day?"

I glare at him.

"Ok, none of my business. I get it. You want to make it there early in the morning, but I was hoping I could convince you guys today to let me tag along. Like I've been saying, I can be useful."

"I already told you that staying here and protecting the house is the best thing you can do for us." I sling my pack over my shoulders. "You'll slow us down by coming along anyway."

"I won't be a drag at all. Just please let me come."

I take a step toward him, making him take a step back.

"I already told you no. And even if I said yes, the others wouldn't. I'm not gonna go against something they wouldn't want."

"I completely understand that, but maybe they don't know what's best for them."

I scan him up and down. Why is he so pushy? I don't understand why he can't just stay back. What is wrong with him? Why is he so desperate?

"Listen, I know Tennessee pretty well. Maybe even better than

Glacia. When G and I were talking yesterday while getting supplies, we figured out we both know the area pretty well. I even knew some places she didn't 'cause I lived there for a long time, and like I—"

"A no is a no," I say. "You staying here is the best bet."

"And if I abandon it?"

"More room for us when we get back." I start to walk away from him.

Flame grabs my shoulder and tightens his grip. I whirl around to him and flick his hand off. His shaking palm lingers, then drops.

"Storm, I can't be on my own. I can't do it for three months. I'm like you guys, you know. I'm running and I need someone backing me up. I can't be alone. Just let me come, please! Please! I'll do anything. You're the only one I can make understand. You're the only one that I can convince."

"You can talk to Miss Joe if you get lonely. Like I said, you coming along could ruin our whole mission, and I'm trusting you to keep this place safe. Besides, the others don't want you around. I'm not goin' against them."

Flame nods sluggishly, and my chest tightens as a result.

"Goodbye. I'll hopefully see you after three months," I say. I take a step but hesitate at the sight of the door.

"Before you go," Flame says. "I gotta know something."

I nod.

"I saw your tattoo yesterday when all of you guys were freaking out." Flame holds up his trembling left hand to reveal a tattoo which reads, *ECXY 1 3*. "Yours is in the same print as mine. The others have it too. Even Glacia. I just gotta know who gave it to you and why..."

I don't know. I'm asking myself the same questions. I give him a long, silent stare. His hand is still shaking.

"You asked me about my sunglasses before, right?" I ask. "And why I bothered to wear 'em at night."

"Yeah?"

I place my fingers on the lenses, holding my breath, then turn my eyes downward.

"What's...what's wrong?" Flame asks.

I hesitate but slide my sunglasses off to meet his red gaze. Flame's face pales as he pushes himself against the wall and freezes. He trembles at the sight of my eyes. I sigh, head hanging, and place the sunglasses back on.

"Goodbye, Flame."

I turn away from him and walk out the door. The freezing air hits me, serving as a cruel reminder of the grueling days to come. It will be nothing but trudging along the landscape, avoiding all possible signs of civilization in order to reach our goal. Clambering down the steps, I stop next to the circle the others have formed. With my eyes low and a lump in the back of throat, I glance over my shoulder. There is no sight of him. I sigh again. I knew it wouldn't work out.

Glacia mutters a few words to Strike before she slips past Hawk and Viper. She looks up to the rising sun behind the cabin and motions for us to follow her lead. She walks toward the dawning light.

I file in next to Viper, while Hawk and Strike take the back. We follow Glacia in silence, listening to the frigid air whisper through the forest. It beckons us to return to shelter. We resist, and pass the rotting cabin, leaving Flame to keep it from falling too quickly to the elements. It doesn't matter how much resistance there is, nature always wins.

I thought Flame had a different nature. He seemed so much more than just a lonely, selfish squatter. Maybe he didn't have any bad intentions, but I'd rather not find out. His face said it all. He was afraid of me. And I assumed that—

A pair of footsteps stomps through the underbrush toward us. I turn to see a blond figure running at us from the cabin.

"Wait up!" Flame yells.

My jaw drops.

"I'm coming with you guys!" Flame declares, swinging his pack over his shoulders. "Whether you all like it or not!"

Hawk steps forward. "Like hell you are! You better get ba—"

I cut Hawk off by grabbing her shoulder and pulling her away. Hawk whips around to me with her teeth grinding.

"What are you doing?" Hawk spits. "Are you seriously gonna say we should let this bum come with us?"

"I am."

"That's not your call to make; we all have to agree on it. Just let me knock him out so he can't follow us."

"No."

"Why not?"

I glance up at Flame. "I think he can help."

"You've known him for two days."

"He knows things that could help."

"So does Glacia," Hawk replies. "You can't seriously let a stranger come with us. He hasn't seen what—"

"That doesn't matter. He doesn't care. Besides, he could blab somehow to Miss Joe. He could tell her where we're going and set those two boys after us."

"As if, don't be—"

"Just stop," Viper cuts her off. "If he wants to risk his life by followin' us, it's his problem, not ours. We've had enough trouble in the last few days," she mutters. "Hawk, just leave him be."

Hawk turns to Strike. "Do you want him to come too?"

Strike nods.

"You're the one who wanted him gone the most. Why the hell are you letting him tag along now?"

Strike looks right at Flame. "I'm just thinking it would be nice to have a little warmth in the winter, you know?" She looks back at Hawk. "And he told me all about the Safe Zone the other day. He knows a lot. How about we give him a chance?"

Hawk looks at Glacia. "What do you think?"

"He does know a lot about Nashville. He suggested about twenty different hiding spots. I had to cut him off after naming that many. I only knew of one and I used to live there, but it's up to y'all."

Hawk turns to Flame and crosses her arms. "Like what I already told you, one misstep or anything suspicious and I'll break your damn legs."

"I get it," Flame says. "I won't do anything wrong. I swear."

"If you are actually useful, maybe one day I'll be fine with you being here, but not right now, and there's no way that you get to be a part of the raid. That's a girl only thing," Hawk says. "Understood?"

"Understood."

"Then what are you doing standing around? We're losing daylight!" Hawk spins around and marches off.

Glacia leads again and we follow behind her with Flame. The sun barely makes it past the bare, frozen trees. It's almost as if it's clawing its way up the sky and out of the twisted branches' snares. It stands alone in its struggle. Despite all its wounds from the snares it must adhere to nature's law—provide warmth to all who need it.

I slip off my backpack and grab my journal. The weak yellow rays settle along the blank pages.

December 8

Entry #8

CHANGE. The action is on a spectrum that causes the feeling of fear or gratitude. Change can come from the smallest of things. It doesn't matter if it's how the wind feels that day or if someone breaks their leg, it's all change. I've found that change can only be temporary in the real world. For example, my bruised cheek from Viper's punch, is only temporary. But right now, it hurts like a bitch. My scars are thick now but will fade with time.

Mankind can chop down trees and build homes on top of their burial grounds, but nature always reclaims itself when man disappears. Just like with our cabin, Roadie Trading Post, the town nearby, or all the wreckage from the war; everything is taken back by nature in one way or another. This sort of change is so gradual, it takes months upon months with no disturbances before any signs can be seen. Sometimes it takes so long people don't live long enough to see nature take back its land.

Our stay at the cabin delayed nature's course. Eventually, when we're gone, nature will change the cabin again, and it will be defeated once more when we return and rebuild. But is it actually change if it will be brought back to its original state? In that case, does change even exist if everything is balanced back and forth between two extremes? Hell, maybe even three?

Is my program my natural state? When will the program reclaim me? Am I a balancing act that I can't see? Am I like those ruined cities, roads, and homes? If so, who will be the one to rebuild me to keep me from nature's grip?

SEVENTEEN

BENEATH THE FALLING TREE

STORM

The imposing wall blocks the rising sun from clawing its way to the sky. It blocks all possible rays of light from hitting us, ensuring that nothing can provide warmth to the other side. Behind that wall are thousands of wondrous cities. I've heard rumors that the streets are paved with gold and there are platinum sewer drains. Every street corner has streaming bucketloads of free food open for consumption twenty-four hours. My stomach growls at the thought. There's even talk of free places to sleep. Free medical care too. I've never known what to believe but seeing the glowing light from behind the wall might as well be proof.

And yet I'm stuck here on the other side. Stuck in the manmade wasteland with dying vegetation and eroding roads. The wall stretches on forever at a height that matches the buildings of Oklahoma City. It has stainless steel rods lining the outside like prison bars. Another layer of them stretches horizontally. Behind those is dense concrete. The wall looms as we approach it. At the top, tiny grey figures mill about with weapons in hand. Some are pacing the wall, but others are planted in place with their weapons aimed at the wasteland's inhabitants. On the earth, a line of migrants has begun to form on the crumbling road.

I doubt anything living could slip past the wall. I already know flying over isn't an option, but I wonder if anyone has ever tried to go underneath the wall. Or maybe someone could try to climb the bars when the guards aren't looking? I wonder if there's a way to take out the guards before that climb. Not that I want to, but if I ever need to.

Our group approaches the line of migrants. All of them are filthy, hungry, and exhausted looking.

"Finally," Viper mutters from behind me. "We're finally here."

Viper sprawls on the road, face down, her pack thrown beside her. Strike falls on top of her. The two are dusted with thousands of dirt particles, making their skin a shade darker. Flame drops to his knees next to them, holding his stomach. All the while, Glacia and Hawk show no signs of weakness as they chat at the head of the pack.

"Can I please have some food already?" Flame begs. "I haven't eaten since yesterday."

"None of us have," I say. "You'll survive."

"But I'm starving!" Flame falls onto his side.

I shake my head, turning away from the scene even as Flame continues to complain. My own stomach complains too. It twists and howls, and my throat cracks from the lack of water. I cradle my midsection and close my heavy eyes. We've been walking for days with little time for rest and little time to eat or drink. When we do eat or drink, there are few rations. I sway a bit, trying to get as much rest as I can before our next journey: Memphis. Luckily, Glacia says that it's only a day away, but I'm sure that it'll feel like a year.

Sighing, I open my eyes as my stomach churns once again. I stare out to the grimy landscape, where mud conceals the debris that scars the earth. The two combined undoubtedly hold thousands of untold tales buried deep within the relentless land. Each buried story is like a tree that fell when no person was there to see it. Nobody knows if it made a sound or if it fell violently.

I shiver. Every single bone in my body splinters at their seams, making me feel like I'm about to collapse. Every instinct begs me to lie and rest, but I refuse. That grimy mud will swallow me if I do. I could easily fall at the hands of Axl or Josh if I do. They could appear from the thin air and drag me back to that prison. If any of us fought them here, we could become one more buried story in the debris that surrounds us. Even after we pass through the wall, we won't be safe. There's no way that Flame can get the funds for our supplies by himself. We'll likely have to pitch in and expose ourselves. I won't be able to put my guard down, even in the Safe Zone, because we don't have the manpower to... No. No. I shouldn't be doubting any of this now. I'll be fine. I have to be.

I'll be smart about everything. These other migrants are fools if they cause a scene or try to force their way in. If another person falls here from a bullet, I won't get stuck under their fall.

Suddenly a trio of shouts emerge from the line and a tussle unfolds. The heart-churning cries of a young girl echo out as a cloaked figure rushes toward her. They struggle over some object. The cloaked figure throws the girl on top of a third, fallen figure. I plant my feet and prepare myself to spring into the fray, but I stop. It's best to keep my head down, especially here.

A red flash sprints to the scene. Hawk connects her fist into the cloak's jaw, causing them to stumble back. The cloaked figure releases the object they stole—a wad of money—and howl as they hold their jaw. My mouth gapes but I snap out of it, rushing to Hawk's side by pushing past the other migrants. They swear my ear off.

Hawk picks up the wad of cash, tossing it between her palms. She stares the massive figure down with a scowl. I glance between the two and put my hand on Hawk's shoulder to help her keep some restraint. The cloak removes their hood, revealing an elongated female face. The rest of our group weaves through the crowd to join us.

"How 'bout you mind your damn business, you little shit, and give me the cash? It's mine," the woman replies.

Hawk looks to the little girl, who's now standing over the fallen person, and then back to the woman. The massive woman casts a shadow on Hawk's petite frame. Hawk slips the wad into her pocket.

"How about you come take it from me?" Hawk replies.

The woman's lip curls. "It's my money. Give it to me, you twat!"

"Make me bi—"

"I doubt that it's your money," I cut in. "Now, if you'll just—"

"It's mine! That brat there stole it! Now give it, or I'm callin' the guards when they come out here!"

"Stop lying! I saw you take it from her, Horse-face!" Hawk screams.

The Horse-woman turns bright red, something glints in her hand, and she lunges at Hawk with a blade slashing straight for her neck. Hawk pushes me to the side and dodges the blade by jabbing toward the Horse-woman. As she rushes past Hawk, Hawk hooks her foot onto Horse-woman's ankle and allows gravity to take hold. Horse-woman falls on her teeth and drops her knife. Glacia swoops in and grabs it. The woman stands slowly, whipping her gaze around to the eyes all around her.

Glacia inspects the knife. "It would be a shame if the guards found an unlicensed weapon on a migrant. I doubt you would make it a single breath without a bullet in your brain."

Glacia tosses the small knife into the deep grime. Hawk tries to rush past me, but I grab her again.

"Go back to the damn barn where you came from bitch!"

Viper joins our side and steps between Hawk and Horse-woman.

"Hawk," I say.

"I hope all people like you die alone!"

"Hawk," Viper replies.

"I swear! I swear! I'll—"

"Hawk, she isn't worth it," Viper says. "You already kicked her ass."

Hawk shuts her mouth and nods. The woman brushes herself off again, swearing at us, and retreats to the very back of the line with her head hanging. Dawn has broken, but there are still shadows looming over us from the wall. Every migrant remains cold. I shift my eyes over to the small girl and her companion; both are stuck in those shadows.

We approach the child with Viper not far behind. Strike and Flame are already at the figure's side to examine him. Glacia joins, attempting to help them. The girl is holding the fallen figure's hand with tears streaking through the caked dirt on her cheeks. She looks up at Hawk with hazel-blue eyes filled with tears.

Hawk bends down to her knees. "Are you all right?" She wipes a stray tear from the girl's cheek. "My friends and I, we're gonna help you out. Do you mind if I ask your name?"

"Sage. This is Alo."

"It's nice to meet you, Sage. You can call me Hawk."

Hawk reaches into her pocket. She pulls out the wad of cash and holds it out to Sage. Sage's lip quivers.

"What's wrong?"

"I can't take it."

"Why not? It's yours, fair and square."

"I stole it!" She puts her head in her hands. "I wanted to help... to help my brother! Please...please don't get angry."

Hawk sighs. "I'm not. I only yelled before because that woman kicked you. I couldn't stand for that, even if you did steal some measly cash."

"Really?"

"Yes." Hawk takes Sage's small hands. "Now, my friends and I are going to help you and Alo. We're even going to help you guys get all the way to Memphis."

"We are?" I blurt out.

Hawk turns to me. "Yes, we are."

I open my mouth to object, but I meet Sage's gaze. Underneath all the dust and grime, her cheeks are hollow and her skin is pale. Her dark brown hair is matted and riddled with more dirt. There are scrapes on her cheeks, old bandages wrapped around her hands, and patches dotting her clothing. I sigh.

"Perfect," I mutter.

Hawk scoots closer to Alo's side, studying him with a gentle gaze. He's wearing a cloth over his eyes and a black beanie over his hair. The only feature visible is the sweat trickling down his freckled, tan skin. Glacia pulls the green sleeve back on the arm he's cradling.

"What's the issue?" Hawk asks.

Glacia continues moving the dark fabric. Sage looks away at the sight of it and buries herself into Hawk's jacket. Hawk holds her close. I wince and put my hand over my mouth. There's a small but deep gash going across the side, all filled to the brim with yellow pus and blood; his entire forearm is a red-purple mixture. The back of my throat burns with bile.

How the hell did that happen?

"Infection," Flame replies. "A deep one at that."

"It looks like we have two options," Glacia says. "We either try to get him to Memphis and hope they can fix him or—" she looks at me "—we could give him the last SV."

"I highly doubt they'll help him in Memphis. They'll just—" Flame cuts himself off, glancing at Sage. "They won't do his arm any justice."

Glacia nods.

"Will the pill fix...that?" Viper asks. "All of it?"

"It'll get rid of the infection." Flame says. "The pill sounds like the best option."

"Storm? Don't you have the SV?" Hawk asks.

I hesitate. My hand hovers over the strap to my pack. Will this be a waste? I mean, I only just met these people. Why not save it for us? I glance between Sage and Alo.

"What is it?" Hawk asks.

But I'm not heartless. At least, I'd like to think I have a heart.

"Nothing," I say

Slinging my pack off, I hastily zip it open and rummage through its contents. Despite the fact that I don't know these people, it's the right thing to do, isn't it? They're in need, but we're in need too. These two will only drag us down. Wait, is that a bad thing to say?

I find the box and pluck out the last white pill. I get on my knees right next to Alo. I set the box back into my bag and hover the pill above his lips.

"He's out of it," Flame says. "You'll have to snap the pill open and pour the powder inside."

I coax his mouth open and snap the capsule. White sparkling powder cascades into Alo's mouth, causing him to cough. Once it stops, I throw the empty pieces to the side, zipping my pack back up.

"How long until it kicks in?" Strike asks.

"A few minutes tops," Flame says. "It should take a few hours for the infection to completely go away. As for the cut, I'm not sure. I may need to give him stitches."

Alo groans. "Sage..." He rasps. "Where...?"

I put my hand on his back to help him sit up. "Slow down. We don't need you to pass out again."

Alo looks toward me wildly, his eyes hidden underneath his red cloth.

"Do you mind if I untie that cloth around your eyes? I think we should use it to wrap around your arm," I reply.

"Yes... where is—"

Sage throws herself onto him. She wraps her arms around his neck.

"Ah...There you are"

I pull off his black hat to reveal a head of coiled red hair before I untie the cloth from his closed eyes. Across each eye lie three jagged scars. Alo opens his cloudy eyes, with no discernible pupil, and they flutter at the sudden light. I hand the cloth over to Glacia; she briskly covers the wound with it.

Suddenly, the sound of a million bells rings through the dust-filled air. The sun has finally reached us. A portion of the wall begins to rise at the pace of icicles melting. There is a glimpse of the Safe Zone, a dense forest with a tar road cutting through it.

"Quickly, get him up," Glacia says. "Make sure to hide the wound."

Flame and I help Alo to his feet. He's staggeringly tall, and I barely reach his ribs, especially for someone who looks around our age.

"What did you people give me?" Alo coughs a bit. "It tastes... potent."

"Sana Velox," I say. "Pull his sleeve down, Flame."

Alo sways a bit. "How did you—Why are you—?"

"If the guards see that your injured, they won't let you in," Glacia explains. "Since you're considered a migrant, injuries could get you rejected."

The wall stops moving, a square-gash lies in the center and the bells stop ringing. The line of migrants shuffles forward.

"Will they care if I'm blind?" Alo asks.

"Hopefully not," Glacia answers and turns to Hawk and Strike. "Y'all go on ahead and take Sage while we stabilize him."

"Why?" Hawk asks.

"If there's too many in a group, they get suspicious. Now hurry. Act like y'all are a family or somethin'. You'll have a higher chance of getting in."

"I won't leave my brother!"

"You have to," Glacia snaps. "It's the best chance you have at getting in."

Hawk takes Sage's hand. "We'll see you guys on the other side then," she says. "Good luck."

Hawk gives Sage an encouraging nod, leading her away from Alo's side. Strike puts her hand on Sage's shoulder. Sage looks back as they disappear into the shuffling crowd.

"Alo, can you walk on your own?" Glacia asks.

"I think so."

Glacia darts her pale eyes among the four of us and runs her fingers through her hair.

"What's the problem?" I ask.

"Our group is still too big. How about you and Flame go on ahead? Viper and I will stay with Alo," Glacia explains quickly. "And you and Viper need to change your eyes and take off your sunglasses."

This girl knows more than I expected...

"Change your eyes?" Flame trails off.

Screw it. "Stay safe, V. Don't do anything stupid."

Viper slides off her sunglasses as her green eyes morph into a pale blue, identical to Glacia's. I hear Flame choke as I leave Alo's side.

"Do the same," Viper says. "Good luck."

"How did—"

I cut Flame off by grabbing his forearm, ripping him away from Alo's side, dragging him into the surge of migrants moving forward. Unluckily, we're close to the entrance. I won't have much time to change my eyes.

"Are you going to do...whatever the hell that was too?" Flame sputters.

"Shut up for a second. I need to focus."

I close my eyes, letting Flame guide me through the crowd. I imagine Glacia's eyes. I picture every highlight, every scale of blue, and visualize those tones replacing my own. My eyes start to burn; I embed my nails into his arm.

"Hey! Ow-OW!"

I scrunch up my nose as the dryness replaces the burning. Unlatching my hand from Flame's arm, I slip off my sunglasses with it.

'Sorry," I say. "It's a reflex."

Flame's jaw drops to the ground when he looks at my face. "You can do it too! But how—"

"Keep your voice down. I'll explain later."

"How the hell could I?" Flame whispers. "You just changed your damn eye color in like two seconds!"

How can I get him to shut up? "Yeah, I did."

"Does it hurt? I bet it does! That's why you nearly chopped my wrist off, right? Why do they look like Glacia's? Is that the only color you can turn them into besides gold?"

He keeps rambling on and on, but I tune him out. We're getting closer to the gaping entrance. I elbow Flame in the side.

"Listen. Now's not the time to question me. You can do that to Viper or me literally any other time," I hiss. "Don't screw this up. I'm not gettin' thrown into prison again by Josh and Axl because of you."

Flame rubs his ribs. "Thrown in prison, again?"

I ignore him and look up at the looming wall, straining my neck to see the very top. We're only three people away from entering. The guards are stopping each person and examining their face with a metallic object that makes a tiny beep. After that, the guards ask a few questions and the person is let through. What would happen if they get rejected? Glacia mentioned something about being attacked.

"Next!" the guard shouts.

I snap out of my thoughts, pushing Flame forward. He glares at me but walks up to the edge of the entrance. The guard has an open-faced helmet and wears grey armor just like the officers who were with Josh and Axl. Just like the ones in the bases. The woman looks like she just rolled out of bed. The guard narrows her sagging eyes as she studies Flame, and she holds up the strange rectangular object. It lets off a small beep.

"Why are your eyes like that, boy?" She asks.

"They're tattoos."

"Oh, so you're one of those people. What's your reason for entering the A.F.A.?"

"The outside sucks. Real money is inside."

"And are you traveling with anyone?"

"Her."

"Your relation to her?"

"She's my sister."

"Go ahead. Next!"

Flame slips past her. I step up to the edge where I can finally see the other side completely. There are miles of barren trees and finely cut grass with a single road, leading to hints of a town in the distance. The guard holds the metallic object in front of my face, blocking my view.

Beeep. Beeep. Beeep. Shreeeeee.

I jump.

"Error? That's never happened before..." The guard mumbles and holds the object up to my eyes again.

Beeeeep. Beeeep. Beeeeep. Shreeeeee.

The guard shrugs. "You look human to me. I mean, your brother was. Have you had your eyes tattooed like his?"

I nod slowly. Sweat forms across my brow.

The guard glances at the machine. "I highly doubt your parents were into bestiality or anything. This thing must be sensitive to your ink. Are you coming in for the same reason as him?"

I nod.

She sighs. "Usually I would ask for your papers, but I don't want to deal with that this early. Go ahead. I can't deal with this. Next!"

I slip past her, heading to Flame, while wiping away the sweat. We walk along the smooth road. Flame slides his hands into his pockets, his demeanor now quiet. Taking in a deep breath, I allow the dryness in my eyes to slowly flood away. I slide my sunglasses over them.

"Are you going to change your eyes?" Flame asks. "Does it hurt?"

"I already changed them and yes, it hurts."

Flame frowns. "How do you know how to make your eyes normal again?"

"Not sure."

"Seriously, how do you shapeshift? Have you always been able to do it?"

"For as long as I can remember."

"Since you were born?"

"Sure."

Flame studies me for a moment. "Sure, huh?"

His heartbeat suddenly increases. I gaze at him and meet a pair of narrowed eyes.

"Is this why you want to go all the way to Nashville? Away from that little house on the prairie?"

"What do you mean?" I ask.

"I mean, for the past six days I've traveled with the four of you, with all your crazy abilities. After talking to you and the other three about those crazy abilities, I've noticed something weird..." Flame trails off for a brief moment. "All you give me is this '*for as long as I can remember*' response. And it got me thinking, why do they all say that?"

It's like I've been thrown a curveball straight into my stomach.

"I think you've given me the answer, or part of it. It has something to do with those two guys, Josh and Axl, that you mentioned. It has something to do with you being imprisoned. But why were you thrown into a prison? And how did you escape? I see why you say the phrase; I think you don't want to get into how you guys met and what happened before I met you. You're running from someone or something. It's why all of you have been desperately trying to get here. Like time's running out."

My fingers flick.

"If I were to guess, you got put behind bars because of your abilities for some reason, but I'm confused by one thing. Why are you trying to break into the Aurex Facilities when you just escaped a prison in Oklahoma City?"

"Why do you care?"

"I just wanna know what I'm getting into, and I'm only hypothesizing here. I could sound completely crazy right now. But I'm pretty sure I'm right, based on the conversations you have with your friends."

"Maybe you should have thought of this before you came with us," I reply. "You should have asked sooner."

"You wouldn't have told me."

"Exactly. You know I wouldn't talk then or now, so will you stop hypothesizing about—" I cut myself off as a new thought hits me. "Why did you come with us?"

Flame takes a few paces. "I already told you. I'm on the run too and need backup."

"Yeah, and you don't see me questioning you about it, about your flames, about who exactly is trying to exploit you and why you're running. How would you honestly feel if I did that?"

He shrugs. "Uncomfortable, I guess."

I walk again. "So how do you think I feel?"

"Oh."

"Stop asking me about things." I cross my arms. "Try to get to know me first. Don't try to get to know my past."

"Sorry," Flame mutters. "I came on too strong, didn't I?"

"Yeah, you did."

"I didn't mean to. Sometimes I'm too curious, you know? If I do it again... Well, I won't do it again. It's just that I've never met someone like you before."

"Someone like me?"

"Yeah, someone who's more out of the ordinary than me." Flame stares at me in silence. His red eyes are begging for something, but I'm unclear as to what.

I lower my gaze. "I get that."

"Hey, Storm..."

"Yeah?"

"I never thanked you... And I'd like to now."

"For what?" I ask.

"Letting me come along, even after I freaked when...you know."

"When I took off my sunglasses?"

"Yeah, I shouldn't have done that," he says. "And I'm still embarrassed about it. I know now that you aren't a...you know."

In the distance, I see Hawk, Strike, and Sage sitting on the side of the road. Hawk waves at me.

"I've already forgotten about it," I say. "Now, c'mon. Let's pick up the pace."

I lengthen my strides, adding distance between us and the massive wall. The sun blooms across my skin now, but the wind that slips between the barren trees overcomes me. My hair stands on end and even when I'm in the sun's brilliant wake, I can't find the warmth it promises. But at least I'm not stuck on the other side. At least there is life, and tales to be told here.

EIGHTEEN

A NUMB PAIN

STORM

Drip.

My vision blurs, and a harsh light fires upon me. I grit my teeth. A heated throbbing caresses both of my arms up to my nails. I sluggishly roll my head over to see pristine, white bandages covering my arms.

Drip.

I try to sit up, but my chest doesn't budge. When I try my moving my arms—nothing. Leather straps hold me down to a cold surface. Needles attached to long tubes leading up to bags of syrupy blood stick out of the tops of my feet. One bag is running low from an invisible puncture that allows only a drop at a time to freefall to the earth.

Drip.

Someone's breath whispers before a pair of footsteps approach me. The air smells of withered grass now, as if the footsteps had just come from outside. Then he blocks the blinding light. My chest caves at the sight of him. The Doctor adjusts his glasses where my reflection momentarily shimmers across the lenses.

"Ah, Twelve, you're awake. Good. You've been wonderful so far."

Drip.

"As I promised." He reaches into his coat pocket. "You get to have a higher dose of your favorite."

Drip.

The Doctor holds out a purple capsule. "I've named this strand *Angelus Oscula*. It's quite a new development from Doctor Aquinas, just like you. It's only fitting that you get to be the first to have it after it has been cleared."

Drip.

"It will work very quickly, more so than its parent, SV. The pain you feel now will vanish just as if it were a bad dream." The Doctor examines the capsule.

He glances at me before lowering the pill just above my mouth. He snaps it open. The purple powder showers down my throat, and the taste of fresh fruit flows through my senses.

Drip.

A coolness spreads from the back of my throat, down my chest, and out to my sizzling limbs. My veins chill and my arms float into nothingness, a numb sensation. All feeling dulls. My vision doubles.

The Doctor's heels click as he makes his way further down my side. He carefully unstraps my arm, holds it by the wrist and unravels the bandages from my fingertips to my forearm. My eyes widen as the bruises fade, the stitches pop out one by one, and the incision on my arm forms into a long, thick scar that's right underneath the black letters: *WDXX12*.

Drip.

The Doctor turns my hand to examine the dense scars tracing my fingers, the top of my hand, and the top of my forearm. A smile glints when he turns to me. It brings me comfort from a distance.

"How interesting... This is beyond excellent. I think you're ready." The Doctor turns my forearm up. "I need you to focus. Even if you can't feel your arm yet, I need you to focus. Part of it should come naturally to you, but the other half will not. With time and practice, it will. Your focus now will determine how long that process is. I'm sure you understand." He changes his grip, holding his hand at my elbow and props my forearm up.

Drip.

"Take a breath, flick your wrist side to side and flex your fingertips. Focus on those muscles. You may get it on the first try."

Letting in a breath, I flex my fingertips. The metal claws appear with a snap. I grit my teeth from the pain underneath my fingertips and hand, but it soon vanishes. I let in a hesitant breath and flick my wrist side to side.

Shink.

I gasp as blood drizzles out of my arm. The snapping pain sears from underneath my skin, all because of two thin blades protruding out of both sides of my forearm close to the center. My arm trembles. My breathing changes. The pain fades but my heart pulses in my throat.

"Excellent," the Doctor says. "Let's try the other arm, shall we?"

He disappears from my sight and moves on to unwinding the bandages on my remaining arm. I'm entranced by the blood as it trickles out from under the metal and falls to the floor. The metallic scent burns the back of my throat.

Drip.

I close my eyes. Something in a distant world beckons me to open my eyes after the last patter of blood. I'm met with the gruff sound of my blade scraping the concrete. It beams in the low-light, as if it were mocking me. The scars surrounding it throb relentlessly at my fingertips, where my claws have revealed themselves without permission. I keep my head against the rough ground of the alleyway. My mind goes numb from the constant pulsing. My body and my soul all shake without reason. The two weapons glare at me. My blood drips out of my forearm, just like the memory. My numb eyes water. I hold my breath, trying to dim it all.

Will I ever be able to stop this? Any of it? My program? The other programs...can I stop them? All of them? The only thing I can think of is to find the truth and only the truth, but what happens if

Josh and Axl get to us? They could easily see us one day when we're in the open. We're all on their radar. Even if the place we're staying is safe, and I'm not sure if any place is safe, Josh and Axl can still find us. If they find us, they'll take us straight to the Doctors, straight to the Doctor with the purple tie. From there, we're doomed. I'll have a collar on my neck. My program would control me and hurt people. It's already happened before and history repeats itself, right? Every single ounce of effort I've made will be for nothing. I'll never know the truth about the girl before me, or why this all happened. How the hell can I stop history from repeating?

I blink the tears away, sheathing the blades, and notice a fidgeting figure sitting across from me. My sight pierces through the darkness and reveals the figure to be Alo. He's leaning against the brick wall with his chin up, staring at the blank night sky above. Next to him, in a bundle of jackets, is Sage. He towers over her and guards every inch of her. Alo lightly rubs his fingers across his stitched-up arm as if he's making sure that it's actually fixed. Alo's scarred eyes search the sky for those invisible stars, concealed by the grainy city lights and stained alleyway walls, but there are none. Not a single ray of light finds him. He doesn't seem fazed at all. In fact, I think he's in awe of it. He must be imagining it for himself. My view swings to the invisible stars, where I try to also imagine the light.

When I can't, I bring my gaze back to Alo. He would never know if I was watching him or not with his lack of sight. Usually people would have noticed my presence by now. I wonder if—

"I know you're awake," Alo whispers and tilts his head to me. "Your breathing changed."

I raise my brows.

"It's okay if you don't want to acknowledge it. I know it's strange that I can hear your breath, but I guess it's a perk that comes with being blind."

I slowly sit up. "I didn't think there were perks, to be honest."

Alo grins a bit. "Most people agree with that, but blind is such a slur to them that they don't even have the guts to acknowledge it."

"That sounds awful."

Alo chuckles.

"What?"

"I'm not sure. It's just the way you said it. People don't typically say things like that. It's refreshing."

"Good. We all that need that sometimes."

"You're right, Miss...?"

"Storm."

"Storm. Yes, I remember now. You're the one who gave me the SV, correct?"

He didn't question my name...

"Yeah, that was all me," I say.

"Thank you. Without your kindness, I don't think Sage and I would have made it any further than the wall," Alo whispers. "Seriously, thank you. You didn't have to do that."

"No worries."

"So, Storm, where were you and your party coming from, if you don't mind me asking?"

He's so polite, so nice.

"Oklahoma City. How about you?" I ask.

"Sage and I have been hopping around the place for a while looking for work and such. We originally came from the Floridian Isles together. Before then...I lived alone."

I wonder what work he's done. Maybe he can help us out with finding easy jobs around here.

I blink. "Oh, I thought you two were siblings. Sage kept calling you her brother."

"Really? We don't look alike at all. We are siblings, but not by blood. I like to think that our souls are related in some way. We have a strange connection, a bond. I guess in a way we became siblings when I first met her," Alo says.

"I understand that. How did you two meet?"

"I came across her, not in the best of places, but when I first heard her voice, I knew that I had to do something for her," Alo whispers.

"So I did everything I could, and managed to leave the Isles with her by my side."

"That must have been difficult."

"Yeah, especially with Sage's age, but it was worth it. It still is worth it. Heck, that infection I had, I got it from a mugger who was going after Sage. She's my family though. I would take a bullet for her if it ever came to it. The people you're with, are they the same way? Family?"

"Yeah."

"You're pretty lucky. There are so many of them," Alo remarks.

I smile. "There's never a dull moment with them."

"How long have you known them?"

"For as long as I can remember," I reply. "We've lived together for a long time."

"I bet Oklahoma was wonderful," Alo says softly. "I've always wanted to see it. I've heard so many good things about it."

"Really?"

"Yeah, I hear it's really easy to find work and housing. Not to mention there's so much land for farming and stuff. I've always wanted to work in the country, just to be with nature, you know? Far away from all the bad stuff in the cities."

I nod. I wonder if he could help us somehow. It sounds like they need work.

"I hate cities. Too much going on at once. And..." He trails off. "Having Sage around in them can be difficult."

With him and Sage around, we could keep a low profile easier.

"I get that. The noise is terrible," I whisper.

But I have nothing to pay him. I can barely make a dollar for myself.

"The crime is too...It's hard to protect her when I can't see it coming," Alo murmurs. "Sorry, that got personal. I don't want to make you uncomfortable."

Bingo.

"No, it's okay," I say. "You're really easy to talk to, and I think that protecting people should always be something to worry about, especially when it's your family."

"You have some good virtues then. Most migrants aren't like that."

"I'm not most migrants."

"I've noticed," Alo remarks. "I heard Glacia and... Viper, is it? I heard them talking when we were walking through."

"What did you hear?"

"Something about altering your and Viper's appearances, something about wings and breaking into a base in Nashville? Was I just hallucinating?"

"You'll find out for yourself if you stick around long enough."

"What do you mean?"

"I mean, since you and Sage are already with us, and you need a job and protection, I was wondering if you would like to stay with us."

Alo gawks a bit. "What kind of job?"

"You won't do any breaking in, if that's what you're thinkin'. Y'all will just get us supplies with Flame, while we keep a low profile. We'll pay you with our protection."

Alo hesitates before he says, "Why do you have to keep a low profile?"

"My family isn't exactly welcome here right now. Being in public is risky, and I can't rely on just one guy to get all the food and other things we need. This way, you'll also be protecting us in return."

Alo puts his fingers on his chin.

"I understand if you don't want to, but I felt like, you know, why not ask?"

"Will your family be okay with this?"

"I can tell that they already like you and Sage. I think the only issue would be y'all slowing us down. Adding two more is a big deal, but also sorta an honor."

Alo smiles. "I'd gladly accept that honor, Miss Storm."

I smile. The numb throbbing vanishes. I'm finally able to breathe again. Alo and I continue on with our conversation. He tells me where he grew up and about the ocean and its wonders. The way he describes the vastness and mystery of it makes me want to end up there one day when this is all over. Alo also explains the dangers of the ocean and all the crime and factions living on the islands. Although the subject matter is dark, as he goes on, my nerves feel less tightly strung. I find myself looking up to the invisible stars, finding hints of their radiant light.

NINETEEN
OLD STUPID DREAMS
STORM

December 17
Entry #9

Currently, we're on our way to Nashville. It's been three days since we passed through the wall where Hawk nearly got killed by someone. We had to give the last Sana Velox to a blind guy with an infection, and I almost got caught. The blind guy, Alo, and his sister, Sage, will be helping Flame get supplies for us now.

Hawk got into another fight yet again but standing up for Sage and Alo was the right thing; they will be a good addition to our group. When the girls and I were cleaning off the filth from Sage, I could tell everyone liked her. Flame even helped Alo with fresh stitches.

Alo is blind, extremely tall, and he told me that he's sixteen. He has curly red hair and freckles. Sage is very small with hazel-blue eyes. I think she's around seven or eight. Alo admitted to me that they're not related by blood; they're more like "soul-siblings." I'll probably do an assessment on the two of them in the next entry. I need to learn more about them. So far, though, I really like them.

Something has been nagging at me since I passed through the wall. Glacia had Viper and me change our eyes because of an eye-scanner the guard used before we entered. I was with Flame and when she scanned him, it was normal, but whenever she scanned my eyes, the machine freaked out. The guard said that I looked human to her, so she let me pass. I asked Glacia about it in Memphis and apparently the eye-scanner is used to find the monsters. Whenever it finds one, it doesn't beep. This system helps to keep the monsters out of the Safe Zone. I'm not complaining about that part, but I wonder why my eyes said error? Viper mentioned the same happened to her. I get mistaken for those monsters all the time, Curly thought I was one of them, and I think Flame did too when he first saw my eyes. Glacia might have thought so too, but she never said anything to me.

I've thought that maybe I am related to them, but from what I've heard, those things are completely rabid. Nuts, actually. Viper and I aren't crazy or foaming at the mouth, so we can't be one of those things, right? I've only seen them in dreams, my memories, when the program was fighting them off. Other than that, I've never seen one before.

Anyway, I have two explanations on why my eyes caused an error:

1. My eyes could be gold ink, just like the tattoo on my arm. They could be like Flame's eyes. I don't know what the purpose of that would be, but it's still a possibility. The only issue with that is, how do they change color when they shift?

2. Glacia mentioned before we left that Axl has "enhanced" eyes like Viper and me. His blue eyes, color-wise, look normal, but I did notice that they have a glow. I've seen it in Viper's eyes too. So, I guess the error could be caused by enhancements for night vision.

What the hell am I missing? Even if one of my theories is right, it doesn't explain the teeth, my streaked hair, or all the super senses. Plus, I know Axl isn't completely like me, even if he has two of my traits. And he's not one of the monsters. So the question is, am I more like Axl or am I more like a rabid beast?

I should ask Glacia about all this. She knows more than I anticipated. Maybe she has additional insight or an explanation.

I was lucky the guard let me through. Josh or Axl could have swooped in and gotten all of us if she hadn't. I do give Flame some credit for that. His good cover is the reason why the guard was coaxed into letting me in. Also, I finally got to

talk to Flame more one on one. He's very observant. Flame should be considered just as observant
as Glacia. He's figured out that my whole "for as
long as I can remember" line is a cop-out. I think
he thinks that everyone met in the prison. He
picked up that the whole reason we went to prison
was because of our abilities. He even mentioned
that we act like our time is running out, but he
hasn't figured out the program part…or the killing
part…or the lost memories—I think. He's still
trying to piece together why we are breaking into
a base. I hope he doesn't figure everything out
too soon. It's much safer for him, and for us, if
he doesn't know.

I'm worried about the program. I know there's a
pattern to the order of attacks: Hawk, Strike,
then Viper. I've noticed a trend in symptoms
before an attack. It seems to happen right after
signs of aggression or a "short fuse." For example, Hawk became angry with me for not allowing
her to help someone in the town and Strike was
extremely aggressive toward Flame at first. With
Hawk, I dismissed it because it's her personality
to be brash, loud, and violent. Her temper has
gotten all four of us in trouble in the past. But
Strike is much more passive. Strike is more
likely to kill someone, even an enemy, with kindness. I think the signs repeat between the three
of them. I can't confirm yet, but it's something
I should watch for more often.

If the pattern holds, the attack cycle lands on
Viper next, and her attacks are the worst of
them. Physically, all of them are terrible, but
for Viper, it's different. She's the only one who

has had a collar around her neck. I don't know what happened while it had control of her that day. I'm not sure what the program said or did to Viper. All I know is that the program is now one of her greatest fears. For her sake, I'll watch for every single sign. I'll make sure she's safe. I already know how to help them during an attack and what choices to make, but I'm useless when it comes to trying to prevent it because I have no idea what it feels like to have an attack. I don't know how the program truly operates either. For now, it's all a waiting game and Viper is a sitting duck.

Is it bad that I hope it never happens to me? I know how painful it is. Hawk described it to me as "feeling the weight of the air, but you can't breathe it." Viper said it's like "smoke in your veins that can't escape." Strike has never told me her experience; I'm not sure if she ever will.

I wonder if I were to lose control, complete control, would I die? Or would I just be trapped? I shouldn't be asking myself that. I should be hopeful for what the future holds for me. Maybe I can control my program. Maybe it'll never attack me. But it's not my fault that I'm afraid of the possibility. I can't help but fear an unknown.

Speaking of the unknown, I had a dream with the Doctor in it. I saw myself unsheathing both my blades and claws, possibly the first time. It was painful and I saw how powerful Sana Velox can be, except the pill in my dream was purple rather than white. Flame mentioned to me that there are different colored pills, with different effects, but I wonder what is so different about a purple

```
pill compared to a white pill. I'm planning on
asking Flame and Glacia more about it.
```

I TAKE A DEEP BREATH, my exhale visible in the crisp air, and close the journal. I didn't expect the sudden weight coursing through my veins, pumping through my heart, making each step I take a thousand miles long.

Slipping my journal back in my pack, I put my palms on top of my head and stare at the approaching ridges of a massive bridge. The skyline behind the bridge twinkles as the afternoon sun edges toward the horizon. In front of me, Hawk and Viper talk among themselves while Flame and Strike make conversation behind me. Glacia has taken the front, alone. Alo and Sage walk beside me. The road we follow has lacked vehicles. I can't figure out why. It's not a good sign though. It could mean this new place is stricter, which will be a culture shock coming from Oklahoma City.

That type of control could be an obstacle for our potential escape plan. If we were attacked by Josh or Axl, a different type of getaway would have to be put into place, rather than a car. I can't figure out what the best option would be. Flying is out with this group. Running could work if we could make it to the forest, although Alo and Sage would make that difficult.

I glance at Alo. Sage is fast sleep on his back. He's panting from exhaustion; it's incredible he hasn't keeled over from walking all day. Sage is sound asleep. I doubt anything could wake her.

We walk underneath the arches of the bridge and I look at the body of water below us. A hodgepodge of ships bobs about on the murky river, weaving through its reflective shadows. Each boat sails away from the horizon, where the river leads to unknown bodies of water. The invisible ocean pushes its prattling current inland. Every ship, every being, is subject to that vast ocean's invisible will.

My fingers reach for my journal. I turn back to entry nine.

· · ·

I'VE NEVER SEEN the ocean. I've heard so much about it from Alo recently, and Strike and I once found a book about it. I read it to everyone to help Viper understand our language better. We learned how many rivers are connected to the ocean and it made me dream that, one day, I could sail along a river, never returning to land. All of us could live on the ocean's salty waves where we could all sail how we pleased and fly in the warm sea air. I found it fascinating how many people disappeared in the waves, that they sailed away and were never found by civilization again. The book I read aloud made it seem like a terrible fate, but I disagreed. All I ever wanted then was to leave Kansas and see it for myself. Sometimes all I ever want is to disappear and find new things.

I can't disappear though. I shouldn't even be thinking about that old and stupid dream. The ocean sounds like a wonderful place, but I could never live on it without a past. I used to be so stupid. I'll probably never see it, but I'm fine with that. As long as I get what I want, I'm fine with letting an old dream die.

I PUT my journal away a second time as we approach a set of vertical roadblocks at the end of the bridge. They have red lights glaring at the cars, bikes, and motorcycles ripping across the street. I walk past the metallic cylinders, entering the city of Nashville at long last.

Airy gas, crusty sweat, and fresh trash lie on asphalt. Their scents swell through my senses. There's ringing and yelling, and honking, and laughing and probably crying. Everyone and everything are running or walking. It all makes me cringe. Every piece of machinery and every window reflect the glaring winter sun into my eyes, past the protection of my sunglasses. The city takes a hold of me, drowning me in its wake.

Taking in a breath with my hands on my ears, I keep my pace with the group. Glacia weaves us through the swirling sidewalks. There are more skyscrapers than I imagined. The manmade structures shine in the sun's low rays as if all of them were dipped into a vat of liquid silver. There isn't a broken window, fractured wall, or crumbling brick to be seen. Every tower has been polished vigorously, like an officer's grey armor. Sidewalks, alleyways, and streets have no blemishes, cracks, or holes to haunt the cityscape. The majority of people rely on artificial transportation. Even that transportation is wiped clean of all stains. The walls have no graffiti. The trash cans are shiny and the air is bitter, but open. The city isn't closely knit together like a woven cloth; it has space for me to breathe. This space means less cover for us, which means a chance that we'll be seen by prying eyes.

My fingers slide from my head, allowing every sound to funnel its way into my eardrums and allowing me to keep a careful ear out for those three voices: Josh, Axl, and the Doctor. I check over my shoulders. For all I know, they could come out of the open air.

Flame, Alo, and Sage will lessen the chance that they'll see us coming, and we're lucky to have that. I should find a way to keep my face hidden though.

"Storm?" Strike cuts into my thoughts.

I stop, turning to her. There's nobody around me anymore; only Flame and Strike remain.

"C'mon, you missed the turn." Strike points to her side.

"You seriously zone out hardcore, don't you?" Flame teases.

I walk back toward them, peeking into a cramped alleyway that's almost invisible to the naked eye. The others are nowhere to be found.

"Pretty much," I say.

We head into the alleyway where the concrete is caked in dust.

At the end of it, there's a sliver of the river. Despite my small frame, my shoulders graze the two walls. As I walk, the bustling sounds condense into blurs, as if I were underwater, and are replaced by the creaking wood of hulls, the hums of apartment heaters, and the distant voices of those inhabiting the surrounding buildings.

We reach the end of the cramped alleyway and find ourselves on a narrow wooden dock. It leads to a cockeyed brick building that hangs slightly off the dock where Glacia is holding open a metal door. She beckons us over. I walk hastily across the moaning dock and slip past the rusty door. My mouth gapes.

Fragments of light from a smudged skylight above fall onto a wooden floor. There are four brick walls with a mishmash of decaying decor, three stained metal doors, and an elongated wooden table. Behind this table, there's a mirror that reflects blurry light across the room. It's so quiet I can hear the tiny heartbeats of the fish in the river. As I walk, dust spirals into the murky space. I take off my sunglasses, attempting to process it all.

Glacia walks to the center of the space, hands on her hips; she admires the brick walls as if they were old friends. Strike and Flame disperse to investigate the long table and other tables plus chairs skewed around the room. Both of them have wide eyes. Hawk, Alo, Viper, and Sage are exploring the other regions of the shack. The door behind the long table whips open to reveal a grinning Viper.

"This is incredible! This place is incredible Glacia!" Viper exclaims.

"I mean, it's not that—"

"How did you find this place?"

Glacia hesitates. "I used to come here when I was younger and go fishing off the side dock over there." She points to the metal door on the side wall. "This was like my hideout. Nobody knew about it but me."

That's good. No chances of strangers coming in, then.

"Man! I can't believe this place was ever abandoned," Flame adds in. "When do you think this place was built, G?"

"Don't call me that, but I don't have a clue." She approaches the long table, swiping some dust from it on her finger. "It hasn't changed much since I last saw it, but it's a little dustier than I remember."

"I guess we'll have to clean it up," Viper replies. "Strike and I have cleaned up worse things. It'll be a...run in the park."

"Yeah, this will be a piece of cake," Strike says.

"Actually, I was thinking Flame, Sage, and Alo could stay behind and clean up while the rest of us check out the base," I reply. "So we can start planning today."

Flame groans.

"That sounds good to me," Strike says.

Viper and Glacia nod their agreement.

"Hey, where's Hawk?" I ask. "She'll kill us if we leave her behind."

"Hawk!" Viper yells.

"What?" The door swings open.

"Time to go! We're goin' to the base!"

"Okay! Sounds good!"

"Don't you like this place?"

"It's amazing!"

"Why are you two yelling?" Flame yells.

"I'm not yellin'; you're yellin'!" Viper yells back.

I laugh. "C'mon, let's go already."

Viper and Hawk drop their bags on the table and file out the door while cracking jokes. Glacia follows behind. I walk to the table to set my pack down as Strike leaves me behind with Flame. I ask him if I can borrow his hat and scarf.

"Sure thing." Flame takes his red hat off. "Be careful out there today. That base is pretty uptight." He slings his red scarf over my neck and holds out the knitted hat.

"Don't worry about us." I take his hat. "We'll be back before sunset."

Flame nods. I walk toward the door, taking out my ponytail to fit the hat on my head. Flame wishes me good luck. Thanking him, I stride out into the biting air.

* * *

I GRIP the bars of the iron ladder. Glacia trudges on above me and disappears after she hoists herself onto the roof. I mimic her actions. When I straighten up, I get a glimpse of the Aurex Facilities. I stand tall to get a better view, but Glacia pulls me down by my wrist. She scolds me, telling me to keep out of sight.

I nod. Hawk pops up and joins us. Strike and Viper follow. I cautiously make my way to the other end of the roof, keeping lower than the cement wall outlining it. Once I reach the other side, I allow only the tip of my nose above the wall. The others gather around, and we watch the base in silence.

The base has massive barbed-wire fences and guards marching at every corner. It has a slanted roof with spikes running along it. The spikes cast deep shadows across the whole city. There are countless red and blue flags flowing through the winter wind that ward off every crime they deem wrong. The army vehicles roar in and out of its gates. Sparse rays of light gleam off the base's polished silver windows, doors, and walls as if it had been built just last night. Massive engraved letters above the front doors read *Aurex*. I shrink back and pull Flame's red scarf further over my face.

"Damn..." Viper trails off.

"Agreed," Hawk replies.

"How the hell are we gonna do this?" Strike asks.

"We'll have to time this just right. Just like the prison," Glacia says. "Everything will have to be timed perfectly if we want to get out of the city and to the wall before Axl and Josh, or worse, show up." She pauses and turns to us. "Are y'all really up for this?"

I exchange a few glances with the small group.

Hawk opens her mouth to answer, but I cut her off. "We've seen tougher things. I think we'll do just fine"

"Nobody has ever broken into this place before," Glacia says. "Just so you know."

"What we pulled off in Oklahoma City was a first," I retort. "If you're having doubts, Glacia..."

"I'm not. Trust me."

"We can do this," Hawk replies. "We've faced a lot worse before."

"We'll have to be secretive so we don't get into too much trouble," Strike says. "I'm sure we can work out something that's less intense than last time."

"No fun," Viper remarks.

"Strike's right," Glacia says.

The four of them fall deep into conversations about when and where we should scout. I remove myself for just a moment to gaze back at the base and its polished finish. I will not let something as mysterious as the ocean stop me from my next dream. I'll find the truth. If I have to, I will dive into the essence of it and pick it apart from the inside out. I'll do anything and everything, even if I have to break all my promises and admit every lie I've told. I'll do anything for this. Nothing will stop me.

TWENTY

FOGGY MINDS

"Come out, come out, wherever you are!" I call out.

I extend my senses, looking for Sage's heartbeat and creep beside the long table in search of her. Giggling echoes from the door that leads outside to the second dock, and I smile. I make my way over to the metal door.

"I wonder where she could be?"

The wind hits me when I open the door, causing me to shiver as I glance around the dock for her. The water surrounding the walkway reflects the early dawn. The city still sleeps blissfully under its light. Morning mist accumulates on the dock and above the restless river.

Another giggle emerges from the cold air. Its source is a small, abandoned boat bobbing at the end of the dock. I approach the tiny dinghy, where a moving sack is giggling inside, and lean over.

"Doesn't look like Sage is here! But I should take this sack of potatoes inside for dinner tonight!"

Sage laughs as I grab her legs and dangle her upside down. I sling her over my shoulder. Sage's laughter echoes along the waves, and it's almost as if the fog clears to make way for her.

"Storm!" Sage laughs. "You found me! You found me!"

"Sage?"

I swing her off my shoulder, holding the bag in front of me. Sage bursts out from the top of the material.

"My goodness! I nearly boiled you alive, kiddie!" I embrace her in my arms.

Sage giggles. "You wouldn't do that!"

"I don't know. Whenever I get hungry, nothing else matters!"

Sage leans back into my arms and places her fingers on my cheeks.

"I don't believe you!"

I bare my teeth at her. "You should!"

"Alo told me you would never hurt me. Flame did too! They both said that you would never hurt a fly, so I don't believe you."

I sigh. "Did they now?"

"Yeah, and Viper's the same! Both of you wouldn't hurt a damn thing!"

"Doesn't Alo not want you to say that word?"

"Alo isn't here right now! He's asleep; he'll never hear me." Sage takes my sunglasses. "It's our secret now, Storm! Until we die!" She slides on my sunglasses.

I laugh and set her back down on the dock while taking back my sunglasses. "C'mon, let's get you inside. I don't want you catchin' a cold."

We walk back and I open the door. Sage scurries inside and heads for Viper, who's now lying on top of the table. Viper stares up at the ceiling with puffy eyes, but her peace is broken when Sage scrambles to her side.

Viper lifts her head up. "Good morning, mija. Where did you come from?"

"I lost in hide and seek. Storm found me."

"Storm? Found you? I bet that bitch was cheatin'. She was using those super-ears of hers."

"I figured."

Viper chuckles.

"Sage, how about you go see how Glacia's doing? I'm sure she'll want to say good morning to you," I say.

Sage nods and hops down from the table. She skips over to the door, leading into the makeshift bedroom, and disappears. I turn back to Viper, her gaze distant again, and I place my hand on her knee.

"Ready for today?"

Viper moves her knee away. "I don't wanna go, actually."

"What's up? Are you getting sick?"

Viper slowly sits up, bringing her knees to her chest, and refuses to look me in the eyes. Her complexion is pale, flushed too, and parts of her green eyes are bloodshot. There are dark circles under her eyes, and bruises along her lips from biting down too hard.

"I'm havin'...symptoms. You know, the sort we've seen before with Hawk and Strike," Viper whispers. "I have it under control right now. I should be good for a few weeks, but it's been wearin' me down lately."

"What sort of symptoms?"

Viper ignores me. "I'm gonna act sick for the other ones. Please don't worry too much."

"I'm glad you told me. If you need anything while we're gone, I'm sure Flame will get it for you."

"He'll ask too many questions. You know that," Viper whispers. "You're the one who warned me about him, remember?"

I shrug. "Yeah, but maybe it's time they knew. We've waited long enough. We can't hide it forever."

"Why tell them now?"

Because when you have an attack, how the hell will I be able to lie in front of them? How will I be able to lie to any of them much longer? I want this raid to be successful, even if that means that they have to learn the truth about us.

"I just think it's time," I say. "We've known them for a while, really gotten to know them. They could help us somehow. They could be like a safety net, you know? What happens if all of us get a collar stuck on our necks one day? Who's gonna be the one to pull it off?"

Viper rubs her temples. "Maybe..."

"And we don't have to tell 'em about the bad stuff yet. Just tell 'em about the program part and the memories part," I mutter. "It doesn't have to happen now."

Just after you have an attack...

Viper nods and the bedroom door opens again. Hawk and Strike stand there. Hawk's brows furrow as she rushes to Viper's side to ask if she's ok. Strike follows.

"I'm havin' symptoms... Me and Storm were talking about it. We think maybe that, you know, it's time the others knew," Viper explains with a low voice.

A vein pulses out of Hawk's forehead, but she takes in a breath to defuse it.

"Don't get all angry with me. I know you don't wanna talk about it but—"

"Let's talk about it later, okay? After we scout or maybe before bed or something like that. Just get some rest. Get more than what you actually need."

Viper nods. Hawk turns to me and opens her mouth but holds her tongue. She shoulders past me, beelining for the door, and leaves to scout without another word.

I glance between Strike and Viper.

"Did I do somethin' wrong?" Viper asks.

"I think she's annoyed with me. We'll work it out," I say and walk toward the door.

"Yeah, we'll work it out, V. Focus on getting some rest," Strike replies and follows me.

I bundle myself up with a new grey hat, purple scarf, and grab my jacket. Rushing out the door after Hawk, I throw the jacket on as I approach her. She's not even looking at me. Hawk crosses her arms.

"Hey," I say. "What's goin' on?"

"What's goin' on?" Hawk sneers. "What's going on?" She mutters something incoherent. Hawk starts walking again.

"Hawk, seriously." I grab her arm. "Talk to me. I don't know why you're so irritated."

Hawk rips her arm away. "You should know why."

"I don't though. I can't read minds."

"You always act like you can," Hawk mutters. "Just why the hell would you say that we should tell the others about the program?"

"To be honest with them...for the raid and stuff."

Hawk breathes in. "Are you kidding me? For the raid? You honestly think it's a good idea to tell them before the raid?"

"Yeah, so we can all trust each other better."

"If anything, telling them before the raid will make them not trust us at all. And it's not your decision to make either."

I blink.

"Right, Strike? We shouldn't tell them yet, and Storm shouldn't be the one to make the decision."

"Don't ask me," Strike mutters.

"Why not?"

"I'm not taking sides."

"Whatever." Hawk sighs. "The point is that you shouldn't act like you know everything when you don't, Storm. You always do this. Acting like you know everything about everyone."

"And how does this apply?" I ask. "Why do you really not want to tell them?"

"I want the raid to work, and it's our decision, not yours."

"Why isn't it my decision too? I'm a part of this."

"Cause we don't actually know if you have an active program or not, okay?" Hawk snaps. "You barely know anything about the attacks, so you don't have any say in this, got it?"

A small twinge hits my chest. I open my mouth to respond.

"See, exactly. You know I'm right."

"Sorry for tryin' to help." I shoulder past her. "Whatever. We're wasting time."

Hawk mutters something to Strike before they follow me. As we enter the small alleyway, I slide my sunglasses on. I flick my index finger feverishly against my pant leg. When we step out into the open street, the fog floods into my vision. It's the heaviest of fogs, dragging me down, making it impossible to see clearly. It pulses and festers. It swirls and hums. It burns and freezes. It cannot be shaken by anything but the fleeting distractions of the city, but today, that remedy is not working.

The streets, the buildings, the vehicles, and the people along with each noise like a shout, honk, or even the screeching of brakes—all of it is muted in the dense fog. Stopping at an intersection, I stare up at the flaring red light. I tap my foot and shiver at the fog drifting along the back of my neck. Hawk and Strike catch up to me.

"Did we decide to scout the east or west entrance?" Strike asks.

East.

"West," Hawk answers.

"It's the east," I say. "Glacia said it at dinner last night."

"You sure about that?" Hawk asks.

"Yeah. I wouldn't forget. We're checking the morning rotation and seeing if there are any more blind spots over there."

The light goes green. Hawk slips past me to take the front. The gleaming peaks of the base hide between the lines of buildings and the haze. Hawk leads us toward the rising sun—at least she actually listened to me. I clench my fists. A twinge sparks in my chest and begs to ignite.

I don't understand it. Trust is built by being honest. She doesn't get it. Hawk never gets it. All she sees is her side, never the other, and I don't know how I've put up with her this long. Hawk needs the wakeup call, not me. I have every right to help make the decision of telling the group. I'm being helpful. Everyone will benefit from telling Alo, Flame, and Glacia. Why can't she see that? More importantly, why did she get all annoyed with me? It doesn't make any sense for her. Could her program be acting up? Or is she just being difficult, like usual?

We pass by the base's entrance, walking to the closest apartment building. Hawk stops us at the alleyway with a ladder hidden inside and slinks into the cramped space. Upon closer inspection, the ladder is too high for us to reach by jumping. Hawk puts her hands on her hips.

"How about you lift me up Strike?" Hawk says.

Strike nods and squats down in front of her with cupped hands. Hawk steps on her palms before Strike throws her up just enough to grab the ladder. Hawk dangles by one hand for a moment, looking down at us. She tells me to help Strike up, which I do by allowing Strike to stomp all over my fingers and crush my shoulders. With all my strength, I shoot her up as high as possible. She grabs the bottom bar and hauls herself up just as Hawk climbs the ladder.

"What about me?" I ask.

Hawk doesn't even look down. "You can keep watch. We'll fill you in afterwards."

Hawk climbs up. Strike and I exchange a glance, but Strike sighs and continues climbing. They disappear, leaving me alone to lose my way in the hazy alleyway.

* * *

January 23
Entry #11

IT'S BEEN about a month since I last updated this. In Entry #10, I made my assessment about Alo and Sage, then went on my way. I've decided that it's best if I keep a monthly entry now. Everything that we're planning has made me a very busy gal; it's been hard to write lately.

I just came back from a scouting routine with Hawk and Strike. I'm actually very annoyed at

Hawk, but I'm not going to go into what exactly happened because there isn't much to say.

Anyway, I've helped the girls and Glacia plan and gather everything necessary for the raid. It's been difficult. The raid will be difficult, but our plan is coming together well. Here it is so far:

Task #1: Find the weakest entrance point. So far, our best bet is on the east side of the base. Enter through that point by any means.

Task #2: Locate the information room. Glacia is trying to get ahold of a map right now, but she mentioned that she's seen it before. It's filled with computers and files just begging to be stolen.

Task #3: Get Glacia the information from the computers and steal the files. Glacia is currently building a computer and printer in the house we're at. Once we get her the information, she'll print it out for us.

Task #4: Escape. We'll immediately leave after the raid. Our set date for the raid is March 8, which should give us plenty of time to slip out of the Safe Zone undetected. We're still figuring out where to go afterwards.

Things we still need:

- Specifics about where the information is kept.
- A safe entrance point.
- A fully built computer and printer.

Until March 8, we'll be working around the clock to get everything done. Luckily, we've had no run-ins with Josh or Axl. In fact, there hasn't been any sign of anyone searching for us here. We have to be careful, though. More careful than before.

Between all the work, I'd say a lot has happened. I'm not sure where exactly to start. Usually, it's best though to start with the bad things and end with the good. At least that'll boost my spirits.

I've had another dream about my blades. This time I was training with them alone against a mechanical target. It was awful. My lungs were on fire and every time I tried to take a break, a band on my foot would zap me. What I learned, though, is that this Doctor with the purple tie was highly involved with my training. He coached me the entire time, telling me to move faster and stronger.

I hope I'll never have to dream about training with blades again. I had a second dream that was awful but familiar, so I looked back at these entries and found that I'd already had the dream back in October, entry #4. I mentioned something about the Doctor electrocuting me while blowing a whistle. This was the same dream and the same amount of pain with it. I still don't know why the Doctor was doing this. Electrocuting me when training with blades makes sense: he wanted me to build up endurance and strength or something. But using a whistle and electrocuting someone in a chair? It doesn't add up to anything. I hope I'll figure out why soon. Part of me hopes that this is the last time I have that dream. At the same time, I want it to come back; I could learn more from it a third time around.

Speaking of things I learned and moving on to the good, Glacia told me why she hates Sana Velox so much, why she thinks it's "poison." It's interesting. It could be an explanation about why I have a streak in my hair.

Apparently, Glacia was not born with white hair, blue eyes, or pale skin. She told me that she used to look similar to Viper with dark hair, tan skin, and brown eyes, but she changed because of the Sana Velox. She required a lot of SV doses growing up. She didn't tell me why she needed be healed all the time, and when I tried to pry she pushed me away, but that's beside the point. Glacia said that since she used it too frequently, it started to change the levels of melanin in her.

When she went to an expert for the symptoms, they told her that it might be irreversible, but they could still try to treat it. That visit was just before she went to prison, so she never got any treatment for it. I mean, she looks fine now. I can't imagine her looking the complete opposite. Glacia said that the long-term effects of Sana Velox, including her symptoms, are:

- Eye, skin, hair color change.
- Voice change from smooth to rough usually, but sometimes deepens.
- Sometimes a docile person can become more aggressive or the reverse.
- Extra body hair, thicker hair, or a change in hair texture.

- Early puberty.

I never thought that those tiny pills could change so much in a person. It makes me wonder if any of those effects have affected Flame in some way. He's mentioned that he's had Sana Velox many times. I could have been affected too, with the hair change and my unusual eye color. I guess it's another theory to add to my list.

That's pretty much all that has happened. There haven't been many signs of Viper's program. She's only complained about having symptoms today, which led me to debate over telling Glacia, Flame, and Alo about our programs. This also led to that previously-mentioned disagreement with Hawk and me.

But I can honestly say the past month hasn't been depressing or terrifying, compared to everything else, and I've had actual fun. For example, Sage demanded that we celebrate New Year's on January 1, which I didn't even realize was a thing, and we all had such a good time. During the day, Flame and Alo went out and bought a fresh loaf of bread with butter and sugar from our leftover funds from Flame and Alo's odd jobs (and a few pickpockets from me). When we all came back to the house, we celebrated by having buttered bread with a sprinkle of sugar on top. I never imagined something could taste so good! I've been changed for life. I'll now demand buttered and sugared bread forever.

That same day, we did a little gift exchange as well. The person giving us the gift was kept a secret. Sage wanted to do it because she wanted us all to celebrate our birthdays together. So, I guess I'm 15 now. I was assigned to Glacia, which was very stressful, but I managed to steal her a pen and a journal just before our celebration. She didn't have much of a reaction, but I've noticed her keeping notes in it. As for myself, Flame was my gift-giver. He did a great job by gifting me a grey hat and purple scarf. He said, "For you, so you won't have a chance of giving me lice anymore," and I actually laughed at his joke, partially because he was laughing at his own joke with his ridiculous laugh.

Over the past weeks, I've gotten used to the idea of having a bigger family. Flame and I always exchange laughs together. He still rambles often, but I've gotten used to it. He's turned into somewhat of a relief after a long day or a long night. Flame has stopped prying to an extent, too, and has opened up to me more. He's still suspicious of me, and I think he can tell when I hold things back. He doesn't tell me much about his feelings or his past either.

Glacia and I still need some work. I understand why she's so guarded. I empathize with that, but I wish Glacia didn't act like I'm some ticking time bomb or a wild animal around her. Every sentence she says comes with hesitation, even the simplest of commands. I have faith that time will make her walls crumble, but Glacia needs to start trusting us before March 8. If she doesn't have faith in the girls and me, why the hell should I have faith in her? But I don't tell her much about my worries. I may need to change that.

As for Alo, he's my talking buddy. I get to

chat as long as I want with him. We talk about the stars and about nature. We talk about simple things like the weather, our day, and our hobbies. I love talking to him. I call it a hobby now, but it's more than that. It's addictive, like writing in this journal can be. If I don't have a conversation with him every so often, the withdrawals hit me.

Alo sees things so differently, not in a way someone would usually imagine, because of his blindness. I used to think his blindness would stop him from doing many things, but he's more efficient than most. He's a killer cleaner, fisherman, and shopper. Alo makes Flame near obsolete, except for the flames he provides for cooking. What I like about hanging out with Alo the most is that he never questions me. He never pries. We never have to talk about the dark details of each other's lives. He's never told me how he went blind, if it was an accident or not. Or why he left the Isles with Sage. It causes a strange distance between us, though, and I really want to change that.

And Alo's sister, Sage, has become a little sister to me too. There's something about Sage; I can't put my finger on it, but I would take a bullet for her. Hell, I would jump off a building or leap in front of traffic for her. She has something about her that's really comforting.

I could see Sage doing so many things when she's older. Sage told me that she's always wanted to be a doctor. It'll let her heal people and help everyone. My usual thoughts about doctors are so negative. I hate the sound of the word, but Sage's dreams have made me think differently.

Sage has given me another outlook on why the Doctor with the purple tie has done all this. It could be that he was trying to help me in some weird way. I'm not sure. I mean, he didn't heal anyone. In my dreams, the Doctor only did damage. I don't think he's a true doctor in that sense then.

Mostly, things have been good, except for some parts of today. I'm sure I'll forget about it soon though.

LIFTING THE PEN, I blankly stare at the page. I try to find the words, but it's almost impossible to describe. I glance at the mirror and my blurry reflection ponders the same thoughts. The room is quiet because Flame is reading a book and everyone else is in the back room, giving me plenty of quiet to let my loud thoughts come to paper, but they won't.

The silence is broken by the innocent scream of a little girl from the back room.

"What the hell?" Flame blurts out.

I rush to my feet and throw myself past the metal door with Flame right behind me. My heart stops.

TWENTY-ONE

THE THREE DEMONS

STORM

Hawk and Strike stand over Viper, creating a barrier that neither Glacia nor Alo can pass. They shout as Viper shakes and shakes and shakes. Her eyes roll back to the point where they bulge out of her skull. Viper's bones have transformed into stiff metal rods that quake from the force of thousands of electric volts. Alo yells at Strike to let him help Viper.

"Put her on her side! Put her on her side!" Glacia shouts while struggling to get past Hawk.

"Storm! Pin her down!" Hawk grabs onto Glacia's shirt and pushes her further away.

Before I can rush to Viper's side, the shaking stops. Viper lies still and her eyes roll forward, but they have no pupils. The program is there now. It rises to its feet.

"Get the others outta here Strike!" I scream.

Viper's claws sprout and I slam into her before they inflict any damage. I pin the program to the ground by its wrists. The program slips a hand out and strikes me across my head. I slam onto my back. The program appears above me with a heel aiming for my skull.

But Hawk barrels into the program, tumbling over me. The two struggle to keep the other pinned for more than a second. The program gets to its feet and Hawk does the same before rushing the program again. But the program throws its foot straight into Hawk's face. Blood flies into the air. Hawk flies onto her back and the program flies toward me.

A flash appears when Strike pummels her fist into the program's neck. The program grabs Strike's arm, pivots away from me, and throws Strike over its head, slamming her back onto the ground. I scramble to my feet and launch myself onto the program's back. My forearm loops under its chin. Planting my palm on the back of its head, I drag it to its heels. Its airway strains. It digs its claws into my forearm, but slowly begins to strain less in my arms. The clawing weakens.

"I'm sorry," I whisper.

Viper's body goes limp. I gently lay her down and wrap my fingers around her palm. Blood drips from my forehead into my right eye. I don't bother to wipe it away. Glacia and Flame yell and pound against the door, the noise thundering through the room. We ignore them.

"Are you guys okay?" Strike asks, crawling over to Viper's side.

"Yeah," Hawk says and kneels next to me.

I just nod. I've gone numb.

There's a quietness between us. We can't find the words that can help. All we do is listen to the shouts and pounding. I take my gaze from Viper to the pounding door.

"What should we do now?" Hawk asks. "How long will she be out?"

"Do you think we should tie her up?" Strike asks.

What will we do when Viper wakes up? Will the program be back? I doubt rope would stop her. Damnit. What are we supposed to do now? We have—

"Storm." Hawk waves her hand in front of my face. "What do you think?"

I keep my eyes on the door. "We have to tell them."

"No. I didn't mean that, but..."

I turn to her. Hawk's holding a bloody nose, blood streaming down her face. Her blue eyes ignite.

"That's all you care about...isn't it?"

"No, I—"

"Shut up!" Hawk jumps to her feet. "You don't get to talk right now! Don't even try! Cause you never listen anyway!"

I stand but Hawk gets nose to nose with me. More blood streams down her chin and lips.

Strike stands with us. "Hawk, wai—"

"You don't get to say anything! I thought we already talked about this!" Hawk shoves me.

"We never talked about it!" I push her back. "All you did was run your mouth at me as always and didn't even let me speak!"

"Guys—" Strike starts.

"And as always, you looked down on me!" Hawk shoves me onto the ground, towering above me. "I don't get you! I don't! Why do you always think you're right all the time? Why do you always stop me from doing what has to be done? Why are you always making decisions for other people? I never asked for Flame to come or Glacia or Alo or Sage! That was...that was all you! Now we have strangers sleeping right next to us every night! Now we have strangers knowing every damn move we make! I thought you always said not to trust people and never give them your name. But you never keep your word!"

Hawk breathes heavily, tears and blood rushing down her face. "Why? Why would you ever let strangers know about something terrible like this? Something that doesn't even apply to you?"

A growl rises in my throat and I rush to my feet. "Shut up! I'm just trying to help!"

"I'm right! You know it! *Your program is gone!* I swear by my life, I know it! You don't understand what this is like. Having to wait day in and day out to be tortured! It's fucking terrifying! And you don't get it! They won't either. So why the hell would Strike, Viper, or I would want to ever tell anyone?" Hawk grabs my shoulders with her bloody hands. "You've never helped! You're not one of us! You're just wrong! *You're a monster!*"

I push her away. My nails dig so deep into my palms that I draw blood. I open my mouth, but nothing escapes. I grind my teeth together, and the numbness ties me down. Hawk stares at me, gasping a bit. She puts her hand over her bleeding mouth.

I want to cry, to scream, to run, to punch her. I can't do it, though. I don't know what to do. I'm helpless.

"Storm..." Hawk breathes out. "I..."

I itch to punch her, but I choose to run. Sprinting to the door, I blow past it to the next room. I rush past Glacia, Flame, Alo, and Sage to the outside door. Once outside, I trip over my feet and slam into the dock. But instead of getting up, I grind my teeth together and clench my fists more. Blood pours out of my forehead, my heartbeat shrieks in my ears, and my breathing has gone off the rails. I can't find the strength to cry.

"Storm!" Glacia cuts in. She grabs my shoulder and turns me toward her. Flame, and Alo. Her eyes widen. "What happened?"

I stare at them, trying to get my breathing under control. Alo puts a hand on my shoulder when I get back to my feet. I unclasp my nails from my red palms.

"There's something we've been keeping from y'all," I say quietly. "It's one of the real reasons why we're here."

"What is it?" Flame asks.

I put my hands on top of my head as I take in a heavy breath. Alo slips his hand from my shoulder and I meet his cloudy gaze for a moment.

They don't have to know everything.

"The program," I say. "It was the program that caused all of this. It causes everything, I guess."

"Program?" Glacia asks.

"It's this thing in our heads that tries to control us. It makes us do terrible things."

"What do you mean?" Flame asks.

"I mean that someone put something in all of our minds, we think, and that thing tries to control us. To do bad things with our abilities. There was a point where it had control of us all the time, and it's those days we don't remember. We don't remember much of anything anymore, most likely because of the program, but somehow, we all managed to snap out of its grasp. We woke up in the middle of nowhere together with no memories, no past, and picked ourselves up to survive. All that we had was a note in Strike's pocket telling us to go north and to keep moving so we wouldn't get caught. To trust no one but each other," I whisper. "So that's what we did. Not even having a name or clue where I was or who I was, I took off with the girls."

Through it all, we stuck together.

"Since then, we've been running from the officers. The program has been attacking Hawk, Strike, and Viper. That's what you saw: an attack. That's why we're running from Josh and Axl. Every time we see them or other officers, they try to reactivate the program with these collars that force it on us. They already collared Viper once, but we snapped her out of it. The attack you guys saw, the ones we always see, are the ones where the program reactivates on its own. They've gotten worse."

I grind my teeth and my cheeks get hot. My brain feels like it's about to explode.

"We are...we're running outta time. We don't know anything about this or how to stop it. Right now, we have no idea when our programs will take full control again. I don't know if they'll be able to snap out of it again..." I trail off. "That's why we're here...for the truth to help us stop it."

"What happens when this program takes control?" Alo finally asks.

"Terrible things happen to us and everyone around us. It's dangerous, okay? I mean, just look at the damage Viper's program was able to do in a few seconds." I tremble.

"Is this why you guys were in the prison?" Flame asks.

"Yeah, there are these Doctors. We think they're the ones who did this to us. We think they're the ones sending people to hunt us down to reactivate it. If we get enough information, maybe we can beat our programs and the doctors, but our time is running out. Nothing like this has happened before," my voice cracks. "I don't even know if we're getting Viper back. I just managed to knock the program out, but I don't know if it'll be her when her eyes open."

"What can we do to help?" Glacia asks.

My lips part.

"Yeah, we'll do anything. Just give us the word," Alo says.

Flame nods with him.

Tears come to the rims of my eyes. "There's a cycle that the attacks follow. It goes Hawk, Strike, then Viper. I need all of you to watch for the signs. It's usually a headache, mumbling, aggression, and when it happens, they'll shake or go stiff. Their pupils will disappear. And if an attack starts, get the hell out of the room. Keep Sage far away from it. It's too dangerous for any of you. Stay safe; that's all I need you to do."

"What about you? You're not in the cycle?" Glacia asks.

"I've never had an attack. Hell, I don't even know if I have a program anymore. I have only one memory with it there, but that's it."

I'm either a ticking time bomb or...

"Storm, are you okay?" Alo asks.

...or I could be a distraction. I shake my head.

"Do you need anything?" Flame asks.

"I just want Viper to be okay," I whisper. "I want all of them to be okay again. That's all I ever wanted. I need...I need to be alone right now. Just, please leave me alone."

They do so with much hesitation. Eventually though, I'm left to stand alone and listen to the swishing of the shadowy waves below the fog. I close my eyes, resting my face in my trembling palms and silently scream to myself.

I'm helpless.

TWENTY-TWO
DUSTY WORDS
STORM

January 24
Entry #12

In the last twenty-four hours, Viper's program took full control. We had to fight it off and I had to knock Viper out. Hawk and I fought after-wards. I can't get what Hawk told me out of my head:

"You're not one of us! You're just wrong! You're a monster!"

I wanted to tell the others about the program after the attack, but Hawk wasn't happy about it. Pre-attack, yesterday, we had debated it briefly because Viper was having symptoms. I didn't think it would come to shouting at each other. Yeah, Hawk and I have fought before, but last time we had a fight this big was when we got the collar off Viper.

Hawk told me I'm nothing like them, that I'm

not really a part of the family because we don't know if my program is still around or not. All based on the fact that I haven't had an attack. So, when I mentioned telling the others, Hawk said it wasn't my decision to make. I sort of understand why she was upset. I've never had an attack before, so I don't know exactly what they're going through. I can see where it would be hard to admit that to people who don't have a program.

And yes, I see now that I can jump to conclusions faster than other people tend to. Things do sometimes go through one ear and out the other when people talk to me. I don't know why I do these things, but I do and I want to fix that, but how? I don't know if it's possible to "fix." The decisions I make are based on if something is good or bad, and I try to stick to the good parts. Maybe I have a hard time seeing the other good paths I can take? I'm not sure. When I stick to my morals, does that make me wrong? A monster?

What's bullshit about her argument is that I've been just as scared as she is. I'm always afraid, just like they are. I have bad memories, just like they do. I've been around Hawk, Strike, and Viper long enough to know what they need help with. This makes my opinion valid, right?

Hawk doesn't get it. I didn't want to tell the others at first because I was afraid of them knowing what we did and what I did to other people. Glacia, Flame, and Alo don't have to know that yet, but with time they will. They have to know what the program is and how to help because somebody has to save us when we run out of time.

Somebody has to save us when the program comes back completely.

None of us can rely on ourselves. If someone does, they're already gone. Life isn't fair that way, but it's the truth. As people we are forced to make connections, right? It's a survival tactic. Simple as that. That's all I want, to survive and keep my friends safe.

I learned yesterday that I may not be able to keep the girls safe forever. I could be a bomb that no one knows the countdown for, but that ticking clock still continues. It may never go off or it could go off at any second. The point is, I'm the thing that everyone should be careful around. I am an unknown variable.

I'm scared that if anyone sticks around me long enough, they'll get caught in the explosion. I'm already messed up as it is. I'm wrong anyway, and they may be better off without me.

I SLUMP my forehead on the table.

What am I trying to say? Am I really just a liability to them? Am I holding them back from getting answers? Without me around, would all of this have happened?

Turning my head on my cheek, I face the mirror on the wall. I focus on my dirty reflection staring back at me. She's bruised, wrapped up, and unrecognizable due to of all the dust and grime that has gathered on the mirror's surface over the years. It would take decades to clean her of every black spot or scratch. Only more dust will collect on her, so why bother wiping the dust away now? It might be better to accept the dirtiness, but that wouldn't be pleasant to look at. Everyone would want to cover it up.

I bury my face into my arms on the table. The quietness vibrates between the walls. It's like I'm living in a brick coffin that's eleven feet under concrete. Only the silence can get to it. The bricks don't allow in the whispers of the wind or the prattling of the river. This home doesn't allow any relief from the tension dusting its walls. The only relief I can get from the dust and the quiet is if I were to fall into the river and let it carry me to the bottom. Even then, there would still be a murky silence.

"Storm?" Hawk's quiet voice echoes. "Are you awake?"

I lift my head to find Hawk standing at the far end of the table. She's staring at my bandages.

"I was just writing," I say.

"Are you feeling any better?"

"Yeah, are you?"

Hawk nods and looks at her hands, fidgeting. She doesn't say a word. A dense hesitation spirals in the air between us. I distract myself from it by staring at my journal.

"Viper still hasn't said a word," Hawk replies. "I can't get her to say anything. Maybe you could give it a shot? Tell her a stupid joke to cheer her up or something?"

"Flame would be better for that."

"Yeah, you're right. He would be..."

I drum my fingers on the table. My eyes avoid Hawk's.

"Storm, I... What happened yesterday, I...I thought you handled it well. You were the one to knock her out with only a few bruises to leave behind. It was really smart."

"Thanks. Good job keeping Glacia and Alo safe and punching the program before it could hurt me."

"Oh, uh, no problem."

Another silence hums between us.

"So uh... How's your writing going?" she asks.

"It's okay."

"Pretty difficult, I bet, with those bandages and all. Flame was really determined about wrapping you up tight," Hawk says. "What were you writing about?"

"It's not that important, just meaningless stuff scribbled on paper."

"Your stuff, or words, aren't meaningless. They're important. You shouldn't put them down like that."

I look up at Hawk. She doesn't meet my gaze. Instead, she stares at my damaged arms. Hawk has two black bruises on her eyes that make me wince.

"All words have meaning anyway," Hawk whispers. "That's what makes them so powerful, you know? Words can be so uplifting or so hurtful...even if the person didn't mean it."

"Yeah," I mutter. "You have a point."

Hawk's glassy gaze meets mine. "You did too, yesterday. Didn't you? And I didn't let you make it."

I don't answer.

"I thought it out last night, and what you were saying about telling the others. You were trying to be honest with them, right?"

"Yeah. I think that if push comes to shove and we're all controlled, they're the only ones who can help us then, but you were right that I shouldn't always try to make decisions that I'm not a part of."

"No, you are a part of this. You've gone through the same stuff we have. At least, I think you have."

"The things you said are true, though. I do jump to conclusions. I don't listen either and I make things worse sometimes. It's stupid of me to do those things because we're supposed to be a team, right?" I ask.

"Yeah, and I do the same things. It's something we'll work on, together."

I nod. Hawk smiles softly and inches closer to me.

"You're my sister; you know that, right?"

I can't help but smile a bit.

Hawk sighs and leans in next to me. "I guess what I'm trying to say is for the other sisters' sakes and our own, let's just forget yesterday happened at all."

"Let's."

For Strike and Viper's sake...

Hawk rests her head on my shoulder. I close my eyes and cradle her palm in my own. We sit there for so long that the dust settles around us, but Hawk's heartbeat drowns out the silence.

TWENTY-THREE

AN APPLE A DAY

STORM

"You promised me!" Flame throws his hands up. "You have been for the past few weeks!"

"Promises are meant to be broken," Hawk fires back. "Besides, you're far from ready!"

"I literally did everything you psychos told me to do last week. I nearly died during Viper's task!"

"Hey, hey, you didn't almost die; you just fell on your face," Viper says.

Flame whips his head toward her. "I fell out a window face first!"

"And you safely landed in the garbage face first. It was only out of the second floor. Don't be such a pansy."

Flame pinches the bridge of his nose before he goes off on another tangent with Hawk and Viper. I sigh, tuning them out, and rest my chin on my palm. Leaning up against the table, I glance over at Strike, who's doing the same. We give each other the look.

"You still haven't done a task for Glacia, so you can't come scout with us," Hawk says.

"Are you kidding me? What would I even do for her?" Flame yells. "All she does is work on that stupid computer all day long!"

"Then give Glacia some company today," Viper replies.

"C'mon, you guys!"

"If you don't want to do that, you can always run errands with Alo and Sage." Hawk throws her jacket over her wings. "Those are your two options today."

Flame's mouth hangs open.

"We still don't think that you're ready yet," Hawk says. "It's for our well-being."

"What is there to do? All you guys do is stare at a base all day long, talk about it all night, and then have Storm write it all down! I can do that! Hell, I bet even Sage could do it and she's like nine!"

"Sage would be better at it than you," Viper sneers. "And will you lower your voice? I bet Glacia is about to come in here and whip your ass."

"Just. Let. Me. Come. I will do whatever you say. I won't even talk. Just let me come and help, please."

"N—"

"How about you just trade places with me today?" I cut Hawk off. "There, problem solved."

Hawk crosses her arms. "It's not that I think we have too many people. I just don't want him to come."

"Hey!"

I sigh. "I get that, but I honestly don't want to go today. I'm glad that Flame's willing to take my spot."

"What's the matter?" Viper asks.

"I haven't been sleeping," I say. "I don't want to slow y'all down. So how about I stay back today? Is everyone ok with that?"

"I mean, I'm cool with that," Strike replies.

Viper nods and looks to Hawk for the final answer.

Hawk stares me down. "You should have told me this morning. I wouldn't have made you make breakfast."

"I thought it was obvious. I can barely keep my eyes open."

Hawk sighs. "We'll talk about this when we get back...with Flame."

"*Finally!*" Flame shouts. "Finally! Finally! Finally!" He grabs his backpack. "C'mon you guys! We gotta get a good spot!"

Flame bolts out of the room. After some hesitation, Strike and Viper follow him. Hawk strides to the door but stops in the doorway. "Rest up," she says. "We'll need you tomorrow."

"Yes, ma'am."

"I'm being serious. When I get back, you better have gotten some sleep. Promise me?"

"You're the boss."

Hawk swings the door shut and the room settles back into a silence. Rubbing my eyes, I walk into the bedroom to check up on Glacia. I make my way across the room, avoiding all the sleeping mats sprawled about, to Glacia's setup.

A table has been pulled up to hold the massive amounts of metal and wires that interweave into Glacia's prized project. It radiates an inorganic heat. Wires drape off the table and slither toward the back of the room where Glacia found and fixed a generator. There are random pieces of metal, wire, and plastic scattered around. On top of the table piles of tools, metal, and a rickety computer with a complementary printer lie. Both pieces of machinery have been built by scraps held together with glue, tape, and a few pieces of gum. A green light highlights bits and pieces of the bricks behind her.

Glacia's messy blonde head is barely visible from where she's hunched over. Her expert fingers are soaring across the keyboard. The constant typing is so loud that I can't hear myself think. Beside Glacia is a plate of sliced strawberries from this morning, completely untouched. Glacia has been typing since dawn. Not a word has escaped her mouth and not a single movement has betrayed her work.

"Glacia," I say.

Tip. Tap. Tip. Tap.

"Glacia."

The typing stops and a pair of frosty eyes appear at the rim of the screen. They have dark circles underneath them but are twitching between the computer and me. I put my hands on my hips.

"Do you want me to fix you somethin' else to eat?"

Glacia's eyes zip beside her. "Oh."

"Do me a favor and eat, maybe even move today."

"Sure. I'll do it later."

Tap. Tip. Tap. Tip.

If she hasn't moved by lunch time, I'll make her.

"Did Alo and Sage go out on the dock?" I ask.

Tip. Tap. "Yeah."

"Okay. I'll be out with them if you need me."

Tap. Tip. Tap. Tip. Tap. Tip. "Uh-huh."

I roll my eyes. "And I'll be meeting up with Josh and Axl for tea afterwards. Josh and I are planning on living together soon. Do you think we should live in the mountains or the woods? Maybe we could live in a van? Axl's pretty interested in living with you too, in a tree-house, of course."

"Uh huh."

I shake my head and walk away to leave Glacia to be consumed by her craft. I know better than to try to talk to a pile of circuits. Strolling past the doors, I go out to the rickety dock. I walk toward Alo and Sage. They're sitting in the abandoned boat. They have their backs to me; Alo has a pole in his hand and Sage sits on her knees, holding a makeshift net. She stares at the rippling water in anticipation of a possible fish at the end of Alo's hook.

"Anything yet?" Sage whispers.

"Not yet. Keep even more quiet. Fish can hear everything."

"But they're in the water."

"Yes, but it's easier to hear things in the water than on land," Alo explains softly. "The water lets everything shine through, even whispers."

"Good morning, you two," I say.

Sage reels around. "Storm! Don't talk so loud!"

"Good morning," I whisper and sit behind them. "What are you up to?"

"We're fishing for lunch today," Sage says. "Alo is going to make his fishy-surprise for us."

"Fishy-surprise?" I ask.

"Yeah, it's a treat I used to make for Sage," Alo replies. "It's a secret family recipe."

"It's great!" Sage beams. "But we still haven't caught any fish yet. It's taking forever."

"We've only been fishing for ten minutes," Alo says. "So, a definite eternity."

I smile. "Well, I'll be hanging around with you two and Glacia today. Flame is finally gettin' to go out with the girls. Do you want me to get the ingredients in the market while you two hang back here?"

"Why didn't you go with them?" Alo asks.

"I haven't been sleeping well lately. I told the girls to go on without me. I didn't want to slow them down, you know?"

"How about I stay here to fish, and Sage will go to the market with you?" he says. "She knows the recipe by heart. Just make sure she doesn't go over budget. Sage, go on and get your shoes and jacket on. Storm will meet you out in the front."

"But I wanted to put the fish in my net," Sage replies.

"After your date with Storm, you will. When you get back, you'll catch all the fish in the river with that thing. Now, get a move on or Storm will leave you behind."

Sage smiles, leaps from the boat, and bolts down the dock, leaving Alo and me in her dust.

I stand. "I've never seen her this hyper over food before."

"She's been raving about it since last night. She spent all morning making that net of hers." Alo smiles. "And good luck. Wrangling Sage in a marketplace can be a workout."

I grin. "Oh, I see what you're doing. You're just passin' the buck to me."

"I prefer to call it dividing and conquering."

Chuckling, I say goodbye. I walk back down the dock to the first room. I slide my jacket from the table and over my shoulders while

Sage gathers her things. I bundle myself up, with my sunglasses, and help zip up Sage's puffy yellow jacket. We head out of the house. Sage skips down the walkway, making me jog after her through the alleyway, and bounces on her toes at the end. I catch up with her, but just as I do, her two braids zip away into the street. Calling out to her to wait, I squeeze out of the alleyway and head toward the market. Sage zigzags back and forth on the sidewalk, twirling and skipping as I follow her bright jacket through a sparse crowd. The sun has barely crawled out, its light still groggy.

Sage basks in a warm light, one that hasn't touched my skin in many weeks, and the city gradually wakens as we get closer to our destination. The sparse crowds thicken, vehicles turn into ear-splintering herds, and the buzzing of the city intensifies. As a patch of people shuffle past me, I close my heavy eyes and take in a deep breath. I rip my eyes open, keeping a close eye on Sage, but my focus tends to falter when the glaring lights, rummaging sounds, and biting smells drown my mind in a monsoon.

I catch up with Sage when an intersection stops her. She bobs up and down at my side as she waits for traffic to stop. I look around the intersection and find a man wearing a reflective orange vest shepherding the herds of cars, buses, and bikes with a wave of his hand and a whistle in his mouth. Suddenly, his hand whips in our direction.

An uncomfortably nostalgic pitch emerges, shackling my feet. I await the anxious hum of electricity to pierce my bones. My heart bangs against my lungs, making my breath strain. My jaw and fists clench, causing my lips and palms to go numb. The warm light turns into a buzzing, artificial one that reflects off a pair of glasses with the eyes of an abyss underneath. I have to run, but I can't. There's nothing I can do, but wait for—

"Storm?"

The whistle stops. I'm brought back to the shuffling strangers walking past Sage and me. My heart permits me to breathe in again, and I do so loudly.

"Storm?"

"Sorry, kiddie... I just zoned out there. What did you need?"

I unclench my shaking fists and a few drops of blood pool on my palm. I wipe the evidence away on my shirt. Sage grabs my pant leg.

"Are you okay?" she asks. "You look like you saw a ghost."

I plaster on a smile. "I'm all right. Go on ahead, I'll catch up with you at the entrance."

"Alo said I have to hold someone's hand when I cross the street."

Pull it together.

"Of course." I hold her hand.

Sage side-eyes me for another moment until we eventually walk past the street and down the sidewalk toward the marketplace.

"So Sage, I never asked Alo when you first tried this famous fishy-surprise?" I ask.

Sage beams. "Back in the Isles. He cooked me the fishy-surprise when we first met down by the beach. That's when he asked me if I liked living there, and I said no. Then he asked me to be his sister and helped me leave to get to the Safe Zone."

"How long did you live there before meeting him?"

"Zayvion told me I'd been there since I was born. He called me his Seafoam Sister 'cause he said he helped my pa out by raising me for him. But Alo told me if I wasn't happy living with Zayvion, I should live with him instead."

I hesitate. "Why didn't you like Zayvion?"

"Zayvion told me what to do too much. Told me I couldn't be a doctor because he wanted me to be in his family business. It was annoying, and I didn't like Zayvion's friend Donnie. Donnie was mean. Alo really didn't like him either; he even punched him one time!"

"Oh wow..." I trail off. "I hope Alo gave him a run for his money."

What happened to make Alo punch someone? He's not the type to be violent...

"But Alo told me to forget that stuff. He said I have a new family now and Zayvion wasn't really family anyway."

"Yeah, just forget about those Zayvion and Donnie guys. You have us now." I squeeze her hand.

Sage squeezes mine. "So, you're my sis now? Even though we aren't related?"

"Hawk, Strike, and Viper are your sisters. I'm the cool aunt."

Sage giggles. "What are Glacia and Flame?"

"Hmm... Flame is your kooky uncle and Glacia is more like your grandma."

"Yeah! What's our last name? I haven't had one of those before!"

"How about you come up with one?"

Sage looks down in deep thought. "Um... How about the Star Family? 'Cause I love the stars!"

"I like it, Miss Star."

We finally make it to the entrance. Sage jitters from impatience. I jitter from the waves of people surrounding us. I check over my shoulders for anyone too familiar. Sage and I enter the marketplace through sliding doors and the heaters hit me with a satisfying gust. My eyes widen. I'll never get used to this sight. Miles and miles of food, sitting on top a pristine glistening floor; all beckon me to ravage the area. There are signs pointing to different sections dedicated to a certain type of food, giving us a choice of what we will eat. It's breathtaking—a work of art, the peak of innovation.

What I hate about this place are the prices. We only get to come here every few weeks, and we have to make the food last as long as possible. The alternative is to scrape by for food. I don't know if I can go back to that life completely again. I remind Sage to buy only what we need. She leaves my side and inspects a chalkboard positioned a little way from the entrance. It reads:

February 8th Specials
Smoked Salmon and Rice
Mac n Cheese Bacon Delight
Shrimp n Grits
Granny's Apple Pie

"Can we get mac and cheese?" Sage asks. "Apple pie?"

"What did I just say?"

"We have the money, don't we?"

"I want it just as much as you do." I laugh. "How about for your next birthday we have it?"

"That's a year away," Sage groans. "We could steal the pie right now."

"Waiting will make it sweeter. Stealing won't." I take her hand. "Now, help me get these ingredients, please."

Sage guides me through the store. Along the way, though, she tells me about all the other things apples are put into, like apple crisp or applesauce and other delights.

"Are caramel apples actually good?" I ask. "I've never heard of such a thing!"

"They're great! Alo and I had some when we were back in New Orleans."

"Man, that sounds amazing."

"Why do you like apples so much?"

I laugh. "An apple a day keeps the doctor away, right? So, I try to eat as much as I can."

"You know that's just a saying."

"Who cares! I live by it!"

Sage and I crack up as we make it to the vegetable section. Sage picks them all out for me. After we fill a few bags and grab a few limes and garlic, Sage takes me to where they distribute the spices.

"Time to spice things up!" Sage exclaims.

Shaking my head, I place my hand over my smile. I follow Sage to the spice section. She grins at my giggling.

"Are you *in-salting* me? *In-salting me*! I'll have you know that I take my spices seriously."

I nudge her. "You're not punny."

"You don't have a punny bone."

I smirk. "I'm not trying to be... I'm not trying to be..." I groan. "You got me. I can't think of anything else."

We laugh and continue our shopping journey while Sage continues with even more witty remarks. I find myself laughing at every turn between the towering rows of food. My tensions dwindle with each breath I'm unable to take from Sage's dry humor.

* * *

I OPEN the door leading into Glacia's permanent lair and zip toward the source of the expert typing. She still hasn't touched her breakfast. The aroma of Alo's fishy-surprise fills the room, causing my mouth to water. Glacia, however, shows no signs of interest.

Tip. Tap. Tip. Tap. Tip. Tap. Tip. Tap.

"Glacia."

The robotic sounds of crunching plastic squares answer me. I scoff and place my hands firmly on my hips.

"Glacia. You haven't moved, have you?"

"Hm?"

"Have you moved at all since I left?"

Her eyes briefly appear over the peak of the lit screen. They constantly twitch between me and their task. The typing continues.

"Um. Sure."

Glacia's heartbeat snitches. She's such a liar. I rush behind her, grab her by the waist, and pull her out of her chair while she's still typing out computer gibberish.

"Wait! I just gotta finish this phrase."

"Yeah. Then another one and another one and another." I drag her away from the mountain of machinery. "You're gonna have lunch with us whether you like it or not. Alo has slaved over this. He wants everyone to enjoy it together."

I set Glacia on her feet at the exit. She raises a brow at me.

"C'mon, it'll be fun. You need a break anyway. He's grilled up some fish with some vegetables. You're gonna love it."

"I hate fish."

"Okay, now you're just being difficult." I grab her shoulders and push her backwards into the room. "Everyone wants to see you, even if you do mope around the whole time."

Everyone cheers when Glacia passes the doorframe.

"You actually did it!" Viper exclaims.

"Y'all underestimate me," I say.

Glacia drags her feet and sets herself next to Flame at the head of the long table. Flame smirks at her. Alo passes us small bowls of his dish. All cooked by Flame and cut by my blades. Hawk sets two bowls of water in the center and takes her place next to Strike on the other side. I stand next to Viper, Alo at her side, and Sage sits on top of the table.

"Before we eat, I just wanna say, it's been a great few months spending time with you guys," Alo says. "I can't imagine life without being around all of you."

"Me too!" Flame replies. "Thanks for everything and thanks for letting me tag along today."

"You did good," Strike says. "Better than any of us expected."

Flame tries to hide his grin as she says this but fails. We chatter amongst ourselves. A humming laughter bursts throughout the room and builds as the food cools. The brick walls protect its growth from the ravenous sounds of the outside world. There's nothing that could suppress it.

"Could we eat already?" Sage asks.

We grow silent and return to our efforts consuming Alo's food. The chattering finally ceases, but the warm hums continue to swell among us.

TWENTY-FOUR

BUT A DREAM

STORM

I heave painfully while Strike towers above me. Sweat cloaks every inch of my skin. I try to get up off my back, but Strike pins me with her heel. I go limp on the cold earth beneath me.

How did I get myself into this?

Viper snorts. "Ha! You only lasted like three seconds against her!"

Strike holds out her hand. I grab it and she hauls me to my feet. Bending over, I use my knees for support.

"Hey...like...you could—" I cut myself off as bile sizzles in my throat. I swallow it. "—Could do... any better."

"I don't know. I probably could last ten seconds against her," Viper replies. "I bet Hawk would only last one."

Hawk raises a brow. "I would kick her ass."

"I'd like to see you try." Strike wipes some sweat from her forehead. "And I think Storm put up a decent fight."

I put my hand over my mouth to keep more bile from attempting escape. I walk over and lean against the long table next to where Viper sits. She snickers at me.

"I guess you've learned your lesson," Hawk says. "You can't fight on only an hour of sleep."

"I slept two."

"Two, one, there's not much of a difference," Viper says. "You better plan on gettin' more than that tonight."

"Give her some credit," Strike replies. "She was doing good for a while there. It's only been this week."

I close my eyes and lay my cheek on the table. Its coolness subdues the burn and chills the sweat.

"I guess we'll have to tire you out today," Hawk says. "Just to make sure that you go to sleep."

I open one eye. "I told you. I'll sleep fine tonight."

"You've been sayin' that for the past few days," Viper says. "I'm not believing it anymore."

I sigh and close my eyes again.

"Are you even gonna tell us why you haven't been sleeping?" Viper asks.

I shrug.

"What? You don't know?" Hawk asks.

I nod.

"How do you not know why you can't sleep?"

"How could I? Sometimes I just can't, you know. Most of the time I want to, but still can't."

"What do you mean?" Strike asks.

I open my eyes. "It's like wanting to eat your favorite food. Like, it's the only thing you wanna do at the end of the day, but for some reason, every time you try to eat it, your stomach hurts or you feel sick. You wanna eat it, but your body won't let you," I say. "There's no clear reason why; it could be a million things. You just can't eat your favorite food that day."

"Let's make sure you do then," Viper says. "It's our day off. Why not spend it putting you to sleep?"

"No."

"What else are we gonna do today?" Hawk asks.

"We could go swimmin'," Viper says.

"It's literally the middle of winter," I reply. "If we went swimmin', our hair would freeze."

Viper points a finger at me. "Hey, at least I'm tryin' ta help. All you're doin' is having one of your hissy fits, and it's making us feel shitty."

I roll my eyes.

"Golly, you're so grumpy today! C'mon— " Viper hops off the table and wraps her arms around my waist. "We are goin' out for a walk."

Viper pulls me off the table, dragging me on my heels toward the door. I cross my arms and lie limp, determined not to help her cause. Hawk and Strike watch the two of us, both snickering.

"What are you planning on doin' when we get outside with no sunglasses, shoes, or coats?" I ask. "You just gonna tough it out?"

"I'm plenty tough. You're the one who ain't."

"Says the girl who refused to bait Alo's hook with a little worm."

Viper stops. "If you keep givin' us this attitude, I'll make you do shift training. That'll make you tougher, won't it?"

My eyes widen. I spring to my feet and march over to the door where I slip on my boots, coat, hat, and scarf.

"I know the perfect place. It's not too far; we'll be back by dinner to see everyone," I say quickly as I slide on my sunglasses and open the door. "Y'all coming or what?"

When I step out, the rush of the frigid air hits me; I jolt awake as if I'd gotten a full night's rest. However, the alertness coursing through my skin is swept away in a matter of seconds. It's taken into the grey sky where fragments of white light flow between the marble clouds. The dark horizon draws in every shard of warmth from my blood and provides the reminder that winter will prevail. No one will be able to predict its end quite yet.

I take a few steps in an attempt to warm myself up. The shuffling of feet, gathering of things, and a muffled conversation seeps through the walls.

"I guess that worked," Hawk says. "Good job, Viper."

"I try...Where do you think she'll take us?"

"I doubt we go a block. I don't think she can walk that far," Hawk says.

"Have some faith," Strike laughs. "Maybe she's been planning this the whole time. You never know with her."

I don't have any clue where I'm going.

Hawk and Viper bounce around a few more sly remarks about me; Strike gives up on countering any of them. They join me and I lead them off the walkway, through the quaint alleyway, out to the streets. I scan the block with heavy eyes for something to do, hoping something will turn up soon. I yawn and my eyelids keep falling like my eyelashes weigh a ton each. The droning on of the city isn't even enough to keep me awake. My ears refuse to tune, my nose resists calibration, and my joints rust in place every time I attempt a step. It's like my body is shutting down to save energy.

"Hey, Storm." Hawk joins my side. "Where are you taking us?"

Viper jumps in at my other side. "Yeah, anywhere fun?"

"It's a surprise."

Viper slides a hand onto my shoulder. "I hate surprises—" She's totally baiting me. "—so tell us, or just me. You know, just whisper it in my ear or something. How about that?"

A pit forms in the back of my throat as Viper cups her hand around her ear. My eye twitches.

I lean in. "It's a surprise!" I yell.

Viper yelps. "Geez! You coulda said it! Not sprayed it!"

"Yeah, well—"

"Storm! Were you taking us to that bookstore up ahead?" Strike cuts me off. "That's such a good surprise! Are we getting a book for you to read aloud to us?"

Bless you, Strike.

"Yup," I say. "I thought we could do some light reading. Like the good old days. Ha! And y'all didn't think I had a plan, did you?"

"How are we going to read a book if we're broke?" Hawk asks.

"We'll cross that bridge later," I say.

"What? That doesn't make any sense," Viper says.

"You don't make any sense," I reply.

Hawk and Viper's banter blooms as we approach a white build-ing. I reach for the door and push it, but it doesn't budge. I roll my eyes before pulling the door open. A weak bell chimes above us as we walk onto a mahogany floor.

Rows of books swirl throughout a rectangular space, down a cramped hallway, and up a set of mahogany stairs into another room of books. Grey light cascades from a skylight. Green plants line the masses of books and thrive in the dense light. It's almost as if I've stepped into a forest of words that provides fruit for new minds.

"How may I help you folks today?" a voice asks.

Off to the side, there's a counter with a tall man behind it. The man comes from behind the counter and adjusts his wooden glasses. Strike asks him if he has any reading suggestions.

He points to the hallway. "For your age, I suggest browsing through there."

"Would you mind showing me what you recommend?" Strike asks. "I'm not too well-read. None of us are, so we don't really know what's good and what isn't."

The man beams and agrees. Strike and the man wander to the hallway where their conversation softens bit by bit. Hawk and Viper spread out to different shelves with gleaming eyes.

I approach the massive wall that's overflowing with a rainbow of spines and crane my neck to take it all in. A chill runs down my spine from the smell. It's a sweet and airy scent that people crave. If no one ever craved it, then there would be no books. Without books, there would be no words and without words, everything might as well be meaningless. People wouldn't be able to communicate and pass knowledge along to each other. Communication and knowledge combined create the books and those words create depths of power. As the smell lingers and travels to the tip of my tongue, a craving forms in my chest. A hunger.

I skim my fingertips across the covers, and one tiny book catches my eye. A black spine bears golden letters spelling out *Rusty Lockets*. It is wedged between two dull, white books. I hook my finger in the notch to slide it out before I gently open the book to a random page with two poems.

Modern Remonstrative Rasps

Rhetoric is serious.
I am not serious.
Debate is pointless to me.
Why not forgive those who have had their vocal cords cut?
It is much easier.

If Cad Freethinkers Soak War

The freethinkers see war.
They see it from a window.
They see it on the horizon line.
I see it on my doorstep.
But,
Freethinkers know how to fight from a leather chair.
I do not know how to fight on a throne.
I watch atop an iron wall to the red horizon line
where a caddish war ruins red land.
But,
I do not see war.
I soak in it.

I WANT IT.

I glance over my shoulder. Strike and the man are out of sight. I extend my hearing. They're far down the hall, and they are far enough away for me to do it. I run my fingers across the smooth cover, stroking it.

I need it.

Opening up my jacket, I slip the book into the inner pocket and zip it up. I grab the two dull books from the shelf. One is titled *A Complete History of the A.F.A* and the other is *The Early Monstrum Seekers*. I position the books back so there's no gap between them and briskly walk to the stairs.

My feet drag across each wooden step. Once I reach the top, I lean against the wall. Strike and the man cross the space to the counter. I sigh and trudge back down the stairs.

"Thank you very much," Strike replies. "Maybe next time we stop by, there will be something more interesting."

"It's all right," the man says. "I hope y'all come by another time."

I join Strike's side, Hawk and Viper do as well. Another book catches my eye: *My Life and Struggle* by Dr. T.G Castus.

"I never caught your name," the man replies. "Same with you three."

"Uh...I'm Scarlet. This is—uh—Zoe." Strike points to Viper.

I snap out of my trance. "And I'm Sue."

"I'm Columbine," Hawk says.

The man compliments Hawk's fake name. We all say our thank yous and goodbyes. I rush out of the store before the man can notice anything, although I doubt he'll miss one book. The girls thank me for taking them, saying they want to go back when we have extra money.

I unzip my coat. "Oh, we can never go back there."

All of them turn their heads to me, brows scrunching up. I pull out *Rusty Lockets*.

"I stole this to read."

Strike sighs and puts her face into her palm. Hawk shakes her head at me. Viper shoots a wide-eyed, tight-lipped face in my direction.

"What?" I ask. "C'mon, don't give me that. It's a good book—I swear. There's a bunch of cool poems in it and everything. Y'all will love it. Trust me."

"You could have said something before you stole it," Hawk replies. "So we would have had the chance to stop you."

"It's just one book. I'm sure the man will get along just fine without it."

Strike sighs. "He was so nice though, and now I can't ever talk to him again."

"I'll prove it to y'all. It's worth it. Trust me. Just...Just listen," I insist and open the book to the first poem.

Wait

He couldn't stop on the rooftop.
He could castigate.
But,
he said wait as his blue eyes bled.
Sorry was left unsaid.
I pushed him down in an ambush.
He was left to bifurcate.
But,
I was left to lament.

TWENTY-FIVE
RUDE AWAKENINGS
STORM

My chest tightens at the sharp footsteps approaching my side. I jerk the cuffs back and forth until my wrists are raw. The strap across my forehead contracts and slams my head against the cold chair, making me wince.

A purple tie drifts over my nose, then retreats back to a man in a glossy suit. Anxious hums vibrate around us. The Doctor takes off his glasses and rubs his temples. Artificial light illuminates him, and he morphs into what I can only describe as a wolf in sheep's clothing. My breathing quickens. I tug at the straps and cuffs pinning me down.

"WDXX12," the Doctor snaps. "I hear that when your chaperone here tried to revise an action, you didn't respond to the stimulus. Your chaperone claims that your conditioning has become extinct."

I shrink back into the chair and tug my body every direction humanly possible. My wrists bleed. The Doctor's bottomless eyes flick up to me. He leans forward, so close that his hot breath burns my skin.

"Have you been resisting your inclinations, Twelve? We have

discussed this. The first thing that appears in your mind is what I want you to do, always. That is your instinct." He places a hand on my shoulder to stop my movements. "A refusal of the inherent proclivity that you have toward your mission would be...Let's say that things will become far more difficult if you keep resisting in this way."

I hold my breath and my fingers flick as the Doctor pulls out a silver whistle. Its glimmer sears my eyes.

"We aren't going to leave here until I know that you're properly trained, so I suggest that you stop. But if you do decide to resist more...Enough pain will convince you otherwise."

The Doctor bites down on the whistle and nods to the chaperone behind me. I tear at the chair, causing every inch of my strapped skin to rip apart and bleed.

The whistle screeches. I scream as the anxious hums inject into every pore. Thousands upon thousands of needles ricochet through my veins. My jaw locks up. Convulsions ripple against every muscle. I can no longer scream. I can no longer think. I can only go numb.

The whistle and the electricity stop. I go limp, my breathing heavy. The whistle starts again, and the agony worsens, then stops. It starts and stops, starts and stops and starts and stops, and with each passing wave the whistle's power consumes me. The Doctor looms above, dictating every second of relief I can get. I'm filled with only a whistle that bursts my eardrums and electricity that melts my skull. I cannot struggle to escape, nor can I even think about it.

Then a miracle drifts through me. My vision alters and I'm pulled away from the pain. I float. I've become an outsider peering through stained glass. I'm not breathing. Something else is doing the work for me. Through the foggy vision, I see the Doctor smile ear to ear, as if he's greeting an old friend. He shouts for the chaperone to stop. The hums dwindle away, but I remain in the depths. He puts the whistle away.

"Finally," the Doctor says.

The Doctor uncuffs my hands. Another being takes over, moving my fingers for me. It examines my palms and flexes my metal claws out. I float further back and as I go, my hearing fades.

"You're what I've been looking for," the Doctor says, in the distance.

I watch as he unbuckles the straps and unlatches the restraints from the rest of my body. In my place, something else stands without any resistance. The Doctor places his hand on my shoulder and leads my body toward the door. I attempt to stop, but something else pushes my feet forward.

"How about we see how you handle your instincts now? I have a feeling there won't be any issues," the Doctor replies.

I am no longer in control.

The Doctor and my body stop at the reflective door, and a new reflection stares back at me. It has a silver streak, sharp canines, and golden eyes. It's unrecognizable. It's something new. It is, it must be, the program. The vision disintegrates into black waves that drown me. I fall. I fall through the blackness with nothing to catch me, nothing to save me. I'm completely out of control, unable to determine where I'll end up shattering.

In the distance, the roars of a thousand beings shake my bones. My vision returns to an unholy awakening, the silver and gold eyes of a monster in a red-soaked alleyway. A force shatters on the right side of my helmet. I'm thrown back into a freefall.

I smash into a new surface and thrust myself to my feet with a scream. My arms sting and my breath struggles as I swivel my head back and forth. A crack of light casts on one side of my face from the open door. I'm standing on my sleeping mat, surrounded by messy bundles of empty beds in a dusty room.

I stare at my arms. My blades and claws have all sprung out without my command. Closing my eyes, I force the weapons to sink back into my skin and the nails to shrink. Slumping down, I bury my face in my palms. I try to stop my heart from rupturing my lungs. Wiping the sweat from my brow, I lay on my bed with my arms sprawled out.

Why do I even let myself sleep anymore?

Yellow light fragments on the ceiling and creates torn and grainy lines. There's no reasoning to its pattern. Light always bounces off the darkest of objects and reappears in the strangest of places. The afternoon rays reflect off my scarred eye, but do not provide the slightest amount of warmth; all they do is irritate my eye and force me to sit up.

His words whisper to me: *Enough pain will convince you otherwise.* The vision, the reflection, has imprinted on the backs of my eyelids. My eyes water when I close them. My hands shake from the hums echoing in the back of my mind. I stare at my tattoo. My vision becomes misty and I graze my fingertips over the scars and black letters.

Maybe this tattoo doesn't mean anything. Rational thought says that the Doctor who helped create the program might as well be a maniac. He is probably a murderer, by association. No, the Doctor is definitely a murderer. He has not healed anyone. He has only broken people down. There are four I know of that he's done this to.

I roll over on my stomach and allow my wings to stretch out. No matter how tight I close my eyes and no matter how much I shield myself with my wings, the buzzing of artificial light tightens my throat. The anxious hums cause my heart to pound against the floor. His voice whispers over and over along with that whistle. Along with the roars of a thousand and the cry of a monster with uneven eyes. I grit my teeth to hold in the tears.

Getting to my feet, I grab my discarded shirt. I throw it over my shoulders and don't bother to button it. I drag my bare feet toward the cracked door and open it. The newfound light forces me to shield my eyes so they don't burn. I blindly trudge to where my pack is, and I snatch my journal and pen.

The words fly out of me.

February 27

Entry #13

It's been a long time since I last wrote. Everything has been moving so quickly. Finding a moment to breathe has been difficult. I've focused so much of my energy on this mission and staying hidden that I almost forgot why we are actually doing all of this.

As of right now, we've planned out the entire raid from start to finish including a timeline. We are raiding on March 8, which will give us plenty of time to train, get supplies, and perfect our plan. We've decided to head back to the old cabin afterwards. Then to Oklahoma City to hit the base there, no matter what we find here. It's almost perfect. Since we figured out where the information room is located and made the computer, things have slowed down, but the anxiety of completing the raid is still there, very much so. Even Glacia is nervous. Maybe I should be too.

Viper has recovered from her attack, and I'm on the lookout for Hawk. I've been trying to keep their spirits up the best I can. The only issue is that I haven't been sleeping well for the past few weeks. I'm not sure why. Strike told me she thinks that I may just be "jittery" because Josh and Axl are still after us. Since there hasn't been any sign of them, she thinks that I'm trying to anticipate them somehow. Viper thinks that I'm thinking too much about things that don't matter, like money or keeping everyone happy all the time. Hawk just thinks that I'm afraid to sleep. It could be one thing, a combination of all

three, or something else entirely. Whatever it
is, I want it to stop.

Another issue is that falling asleep makes me
susceptible to all sorts of things, like getting
attacked or kidnapped. I am exposed while asleep,
and the worst part is the dreams. I keep having
the same ones over and over again. It's either
the one where the program is running around
killing those monsters, fragments of training
with my blades against a mechanical dummy, me
recovering from surgery to install my blades, or
the one where I'm shocked with electricity. And
those aren't even the worst ones.

The one I just had has been the worst so far.
It was new, sort of. It was new in that I've had
a dream like it before, but it was different this
time around. It was the dream with the Doctor and
someone else I never saw that the Doctor called
my "chaperone." The Doctor was talking to me and
seemed frustrated as he spoke. I wasn't doing
what he wanted me to do, which was to follow my
instincts. Then he blew a whistle and electrocuted me, per usual, and I knew from the past
dreams that there was no way out. There was never
a way out. But something strange happened. I was
pushed back. I had no control over my body. When
that happened, the electrocution stopped, and he
smiled before he let me out of the chair and led
me to the door. It wasn't me walking or breathing
or feeling. Something else was there and I have
no doubt what that something was: the program.

The memory was the program taking control over
me. I was so helpless. I'm not sure if it was
when it first took control or not. I used to

think it was safer to say it still lives in me, but it's weaker or stabilized. If it's actually "alive," when will it come back? Could it come back? How much control could it have over me? I hope it never comes back. I hope I never have to see that memory again. Sometimes I wish I could forget everything entirely. I wouldn't have to worry so much about the truth. I could just live a life without the worries and the dark details.

Would I be living, if I didn't know my past, though? I'm not sure. What happens when I find the truth and I end up not liking it? I'm not sure. I'm so afraid of this. Of all of this.

I have to keep reminding myself that I'm doing this because I don't want anyone else to get hurt. I'm tired of having to second-guess every-thing about myself, having to fight and run, and seeing my friends hurting. The truth will stop all that pain, right? But…when I find truth, the light, will I want to cover my eyes?

TWENTY-SIX
CARPE NOCTEM
STORM

My stomach twists into the tightest of knots as I lean over, holding my head in my palms. I drum my fingers along my scalp and wipe the sweat away from my brow. My knee bounces as I lean back in the chair to stare up at the dark ceiling. Thankfully, daylight has not broken. Although I'm sure it's about eleven o'clock at night, I can't help but anticipate dawn, even if it is hours from now.

"Storm?" Strike whispers. "You ready to go?"

I nod.

"Hawk will be another minute."

"Oh, okay. Just hurry."

"Yeah, please do," Glacia replies.

Strike disappears back into the room.

With her arms crossed, Glacia props herself against the long table. She hasn't said a word this whole day. I can't remember any of us having a decent conversation recently; the only thing we've talked about is the plan for the raid. Glacia runs her fingers through her white hair, which reaches her neck, and glances at me. As she studies me, her gaze thaws a bit.

"Take a breath for me," Glacia orders. "I can't have you gettin' jittery or the others will too."

"How could I not be?" I whisper. "How are you not?"

"If it helps, I visualize what I gotta do over and over again. I do it until it's like a memory. If that doesn't work for you, just remind yourself why you're doing this."

My throat catches my response. There's a deep silence between the two of us.

Glacia takes her eyes from me and sighs. "And just so you know, I'm nervous too, but I can't show it and neither can you. You need to pull yourself together for them."

I nod, but before I can say another word, Hawk, Strike, and Viper come bumbling into the room. Flame and Alo lag behind them. Sage is at Flame's side. The three girls shuffle about, each of them checking and double-checking their supplies. Flame and Alo fidget. The room drifts into a tense void, empty of conversation.

"Let's go over the plan one more time," Viper says. "Just so everyone has it straight."

"Hijack car. Sneak into base. Steal information. Escape through roof. Fly here. Have Glacia print documents. Meet Flame, Alo, and Sage at the edge of the city. There, that's the plan," Hawk says. "It's only the millionth time we've gone over this."

"We have to make sure we're on the same page," Viper says. "You know that."

"Yeah, sorry." Hawk rubs her neck. "I just wanna get this over with."

"We all do," Strike mumbles.

Another still silence.

"Should we head out now?" Hawk asks.

Everyone stiffens.

"We probably should," Glacia says before she grabs her bag.

The others follow suit and walk toward the door while Flame, Alo, and Sage watch. I clench my fists and take a deep breath before standing.

"Before we go, just remember that we've worked too hard for any of this to go to shit. Don't be afraid to do your job. I know I'm not," I lie. "All of you are ready; there's nothing to be afraid of."

"Yeah." Flame says. "You guys will kick some ass!"

Hawk smiles. "We sure will!"

I sling my backpack over my shoulder as we make our way to the door. Something tugs at the tail end of my jacket, and I turn to see Sage pulling me away from my mission.

"I'm coming too!" Sage says. "I'm going to help you guys!"

Alo steps forward. "Hold on a second."

Sage whips around to him. "I wanna help them!"

I open my mouth, reaching out to Sage to explain to her why she can't come, but Glacia slips past me, getting down on one knee to Sage's level.

"You know that you can't come with us," Glacia says quietly. "And do you know why?"

"Because I'm a kid." Sage crosses her arms "And kids can't go with you guys because they're not strong enough."

Glacia puts her hand on Sage's shoulder. "No, you can't come along because you're like our commander, and a commander has to stay back to lead her soldiers from a safe distance. Do know why that is?"

Sage shakes her head.

"Commanders are the most crucial part of any operation like this. They can't be doin' the dirty work; that's a soldier's job and we're your soldiers. You gotta stay back for our sake. You gotta stay back and make sure we keep our heads clear. Is that all right with you, Commander?"

Sage nods, a small smile on her face. With a smile, Glacia pats Sage on the shoulder and swivels back to the door. With her back to Sage, Glacia's brow furrows and her smile fades as she opens the door for us. Alo and Flame wish us good luck. Glacia side-eyes me, sharing a small nod of approval. She takes the lead once in the alleyway. I follow behind her with my fists bunched, but my chin held high.

Hawk, Strike, and Viper catch up to us. We walk in silence before we slip through the alleyway out to the street. I sprint across the pavement with light footsteps. The others do the same, moving with the breeze that sweeps across the barren streets. The moon illuminates us, and it's as if we're running away from the light in fear that it will give us away.

I let the shadows shroud me when I dart into an alleyway, jump on a dumpster, and leap up to a windowsill. Burrowing my claws in the skinny ledge, I carefully haul myself to my feet. My heels dangle off the edge but I'm thankfully right next to my position—a small porch that extends over the sidewalk out to the street. It's a difficult leap, but I don't have time to hesitate. Hawk is waiting to join me on lookout.

I throw myself at the edge of the porch. My ribs slam into the railing, knocking the air out of me, but I manage to keep my grip. Climbing to the porch, I get my bearings. Hawk follows my lead and joins my side as we creep to our position.

It's a near-perfect watch point. It allows us to see the military van from a distance and provides a vantage point if backup is needed. Glacia is something else when it comes to planning. I don't think the rest of us would have gone into this much detail.

Hawk and I watch Strike, Viper, and Glacia get into position. Strike lies down in the street, in front of Hawk and me, and Glacia stands next to her. Viper moves to an alleyway, hidden from the passenger's sight.

"Are you ready for this?" Hawk breaks the silence.

I don't look at her. "I've been ready for a long time."

"What do you think we'll find?"

"Glacia told you we'd probably find manufacturing stuff since that's what the base handles," I whisper.

"No. I mean..."

"Now's not the time to talk about this."

"I just wanna know one thing. How do you think this will connect?"

I pause. "It's obvious we weren't born this way; we're manmade. There has to be a record of us there. It may be only a hint, but it'll lead us to where we need to go next. I'm not expecting it to reveal everything." I turn to her. "But it'll speed up the process."

Hawk nods.

"Who knows? Maybe we'll run into those Doctors there or find out where they hang out. Then we can get all the answers we want outta them."

A glimmer of headlights falls between the buildings. I whistle to Glacia and Strike, allowing them to prepare themselves. The van rolls up to the dark street and my heart skips a few beats. Glacia has her back turned to the van as she shakes Strike vigorously. The van rolls to a stop almost directly underneath Hawk and me, before the driver's door opens. The officer slams the door shut with so much force that the entire car shakes.

"Civilian! State your business! It's past curfew!"

Glacia whips around. "Please, sir! My friend, she needs a hospital!"

The officer mutters something and approaches the two. Glacia wipes fake tears from her cheeks as he stops a few feet away and asks what happened.

"I'm not...I'm not sure. She passed out. It's bad sir. Very, very bad. I can't carry her for long. Would you please help us?"

The officer sighs as he walks to Glacia's side and bends down. I hold my breath.

"Of cour—"

He's cut off by Glacia wrapping her forearm around his neck, forcing him to his knees before cutting off his air. The officer reaches down to grab her shoulder, but Strike jolts up and punches him across the face. He slumps to the cement. The passenger door opens, and the second officer prepares to charge the two. Before she can take a step, Viper rushes the officer and grabs her shirt. She bangs the officer's head against her own. The officer collapses. But the back-door whips open, revealing a third officer with a shaking taser drawn on Viper. I grip the railing. This wasn't a part of the plan.

"Hands in the air!"

I catapult myself over the ledge. I freefall and land directly on the target's shoulders, causing both of us to fall over. Rolling toward Viper, I spring to my feet and hurl myself back at the officer—who's on his hands and knees. I drive my boot into the bottom of his chin. The officer lands on his back, knocked out cold with blood falling from his lips. Viper turns to me, eyes wide, and thanks me.

"Don't mention it," I say.

"Storm? Viper? Are you okay?" Hawk calls out.

"Yeah, we're fine," I say. "Go on ahead. We'll see you soon."

Hawk gives us a thumbs-up, perches on the railing, and uncurls her wings. She leaps, then soars, and eventually vanishes above the city's skyline. I get to work by hauling the officers to the dumpsters. Strike joins me while Glacia and Viper change into the officers' uniforms. We quickly dispose of each guard in the dumpster. Hopefully they won't wake up soon.

Strike and I jog to the van as Viper situates herself at the wheel, with Glacia taking shotgun. I jump into the van after Strike and slam the door shut. Viper speeds off. Glacia whips out an I.D. card from the first officer and holds it up for Viper to study as she drives. Viper lets in a deep breath and her hair shrinks into her skull. She winces as her skin ripples and forms a masculine jawline, hairline, and scruffy beard. Viper turns the van, and Glacia slides the I.D. into Viper's front pocket.

"Let's hear your voice," Glacia whispers.

"Hello. I'm delivering the packages," Viper says in a deeper voice.

"Good. Remember that less talk is more." Glacia sinks into her seat.

"Got it."

"And when you get inside, you study the next person perfectly. You have to look perfect to get past the security."

"Yes, I know. I've practiced. You made me practice. I got it."

Viper turns, and my stomach drops as we face the gates of the base. Shrinking behind Glacia's seat, I curl up to stay out of sight of dangerous eyes. My hands are shaking. The brakes squeal as Viper rolls the car up to the entrance and cranks her window down. My heart is hammering in my ears.

"Hey, Chuck! Bringin' in the deliveries?" a voice asks.

"Sure am," Viper says.

"Hey? Is that the new trainee sitting next to you? I heard you got cleared to mentor."

There's a pause.

"Sure is," Viper says. "She's pretty lucky, ain't she? She's learnin' from the best!"

"Hey, but where's Dani? I thought she was working tonight?"

Another hesitant pause.

"She called in sick, but we all know she's probably taking a vacation."

The voice chuckles a bit. "I bet! All right, man, I'll see you tomorrow night."

"See you." Viper rolls the window up.

The machinery cranking open the gates shakes the earth. We lurch forward, closer to the heart of the base. I peek my head over the seat and drum my fingers on the padding. Viper steers the van into the delivery area, with the other vans, and inches toward a loading station.

A mounted steel door climbs up into the building. Viper swings the car around and backs the rear into it. Strike and I scramble to the back portion of the van, where we hide behind stacks of packages. Viper stops the car, gets out, and walks through the side doors. All the while, Glacia is changing out of the uniform and into her original clothes.

Viper's masculine voice and another person's voice echo when the doors swing open, letting in a blinding amount of light.

"Hey, do you mind grabbing that back one?" Viper asks. "I threw out my back the other day."

"Will do, as long as you don't make me do all the lifting," the female voice says.

She approaches the box that Strike is hiding behind. Before she can lift the box a flash hurdles it, punching her straight in the nose. Strike roundhouse-kicks the woman's side and swings her boot into the woman's jaw. The woman crumbles over. Viper immediately shuts the doors and strips the female officer of her clothing. She gives the uniform to me, and Glacia throws her stolen uniform to Strike. While Strike changes, Viper morphs from a bearded man into a woman with long hair. Viper wipes the sweat from her brow. The aches must be getting to her, but she has to fight through it. She knows that.

Viper hands me the I.D. for the bearded officer. Now it's my turn to walk in his shoes. While Strike and Viper hide the female officer in one of the boxes, I change into the uniform. I stare down at the I.D. picture.

"You only gotta do it for a few minutes," Viper says. "You got this."

Taking in a breath, I picture his hairline, beard, skin color, and eyes. My skin burns as I imagine his lips, nose, ears, and brows. My jaw tightens. I grunt from the popping of my bones and the searing across my face. Viper's hand finds my shoulder, urging me on, while I finish the deed.

"Let me hear the voice," Viper replies.

I clear my throat. "Hello." There's no change. "Hello."

I repeat *hello* about ten or twelve more times before I nail a masculine voice. I can't help but cringe every time I hear it.

"I'll see y'all on the other side," I say. "Be careful in there."

"Don't worry about us," Strike says. "We've got this."

I hope so. I wish them good luck as I retreat to the driver's seat. Strike and Viper open the doors, working to take all the boxes out of the trunk, including the one they hid the woman in.

The rear doors slam and I start the van, leaving them behind. Glacia slips out of the passenger seat and hides behind mine. I creep the van back to the gate. Glacia instructs me when to stop as we impatiently wait for the gate to open. My skin has gone tight, my breath heavy, and my head is light. The officer in the security booth waves to me; I wave with a fake smile and the gate opens slower than molasses in a blizzard. Finally, when it opens enough for the van to squeeze through, I take off back to the streets. With a sigh of relief, I return to my original state. Steering the car to the next block, I whip it into the first alleyway I see before jumping out, allowing Glacia to take the wheel. In the alley, I hastily change into my original clothes. I hand the officer's clothing to Glacia through the window and turn to climb on the van to reach the fire escape.

"Storm," Glacia says.

I stop.

"Be careful. The roof is totally unknown territory for me. Just be focused. Don't hesitate. And don't do anything stupid."

I nod and leap on the hood of the van. Jumping over the windshield onto the roof, I bound across the gap and land on the fire escape. The van roars to life and backs out of the alleyway as I rush up the stairs. I reach the top, spread my wings, and sprint off the edge of the building.

Soaring, I find myself back at the immense base. Artificial light combines with the moonlight on the metal spikes of the roof. My hair stands on end. But I shake it off. I aim where Hawk is waving me down, dodging a few spikes as I land on uneven metal. Tiptoeing after Hawk, I zigzag and slide between the jungle of spikes. We approach the vent protruding in the center. I examine it briefly, identify where the screws are, before I unsheathe my claws. One by one, I twist the four screws out with a claw. Hawk and I tear off the vent. I lean in, listening for any signs of the signal.

"It all went okay, right?" Hawk asks.

"Mm-hmm."

"Are you feeling okay? I know shifting can b—"

"Please be quiet."

Hawk peers into the vent with me. Together we listen for signs of our friends, or signs of danger in case we have to shoot ourselves down the vent to their aid. I hate that I can't see if they need the help. I'd much rather not be a sitting duck.

A low whisper echoes through the vent. My eyes widen. Hawk and I spring into action with Hawk holding my legs as I lower myself into the vent headfirst. She wishes me good luck before letting go of my ankles.

Gravity takes hold, pushing me down the metal shoot. I slow my momentum by digging my toes into the sides. Once I stop, I crawl toward my position. I have to find my way through a maze of cramped air ducts and ventilators. Each move I make has to be precise. I could either fall through the vent or gain someone's attention by making too much noise. Focusing becomes difficult when the tube shrinks with each turn I make. It feels like I'm running out of air. With one last turn, I see my target at the end of the tunnel: the exit to the information room.

"I'm here," I say.

The vent disappears, replaced by Viper's claws. I grab her wrists and hoist her through the opening before she does the same for Strike. Shuffling around, I lead the two back toward the exit. After millions of turns, we reach the incline that leads to the exit. The moonlight streams onto Hawk's outstretched hand and beckons us up the slope.

We did it. We actually did it.

I grasp Hawk's hand, allowing her to haul me up with a grin on her face. Once up, I prepare for flight while trying to hide my smile. I can't help it. None of us can. We stand together with smiles brighter than the moon. I clutch Viper's hand as we dodge the endless jungle of spikes to the edge of the roof. We soar above it all. Above every spike, officer, and secret within that base. As we glide above the overwhelming city that's cloaked in moonlight, something brilliant swells in my chest and strengthens every flutter my feathers make. I can't help but feel warm.

As fast as humanly possible, we fly back to the street and land.

Viper's in the lead with the flash drive proudly held between her fingertips. We sprint through the alleyway to the doors of the house. Viper kicks down the door with a yell and in an instant, she's in the back room where Glacia waits for us. I make it the door to see Glacia snag the flash drive and force it in the side of the computer. I rush to her side, the screen blinding me with light, as Glacia mumbles and types nonsense.

The screen flashes a new image while titles stream down it. Glacia sorts through it all and hits a few buttons before tearing the flash drive from the computer. The printer cranks out what seems like a never-ending number of documents, information in the form of pictures, reports, and logs. It's too much for me to process.

While everything is printing, the five of us scramble around the house. We gather up the last of our items. I shove everything into my pack, not even bothering to double-check, and I rush over to the fresh prints. Placing the papers into my bag, I carefully zip it up. I swing my pack over my shoulders, order everyone that it's time to go, and we speed out the front door. As we run across the walkway, I look back on the cockeyed house where so many of my memories will be left behind in silent rooms.

The house vanishes like an apparition when I reach the alleyway. I run to the street so wildly even a dog chasing his own tail would laugh. We head toward the bridge that takes us far away from this place. We hurl ourselves closer to the next mission: Oklahoma City.

TWENTY-SEVEN

A BRIGHT FUTURE

JOSH

"A connection...There's gotta be one," I mumble as I rub my temples.

"Dude, you've been sorting through that footage this whole time. That tape was filmed like in December and it's March eighth," Axl replies. "How 'bout you take a break and have a decent conversation with me."

"But—"

"That footage is near worthless. You know that. Our targets don't speak a word the whole time. Well, besides them saying their new names. If you really wanna find a connection with that film, try to focus on the mission at hand. Think of something new. Don't dwell on old news."

I nod. "You're right."

Powering the screen down, I slip it into my leather briefcase before setting the case onto the seat beside me. The transport van shakes a bit, probably going through a patch of potholes. Neither of us is fazed. Axl sits next to me with an ankle resting on his knee as he leans back into his seat.

"If you wanna get something out of it, how 'bout you talk to me about my account of it, instead of shoving your nose up stuff you've already seen twenty-three million times? After all, I was knocked out by one of those bitches. I still get headaches to this day."

"That one. She calls herself Storm," I say.

"The girl sure hits hard as hell." Axl rubs the back of his head. "Her and Twenty-Seven, both. She called herself Strike; I think. Nearly did me in with those blades of theirs."

"How do you think those two hold up in a fight?"

"Well. Twelve, Storm, right? She's sloppy as hell. Almost feral when she fights. It'd be pretty easy to maneuver around her moves if she wasn't as fast as she is. She's not too clever in a fight either, but decent with those blades. I bet you she trains with the other one, Strike. And then Strike, she's pretty fuckin' hard to dodge. I swear that one is the most dangerous outta all them. Most athletic chick I've seen in a while. She just doesn't attack enough though. You fought the shape-shifty one, right? Number... Forty-Five?'"

"Yeah, Viper. She talked smack a bit," I say. "She barely managed to fool me with her shapeshifting, but she completely fooled the guards. She also barely managed to get away. She was calculating and smart enough to buy time while she shut down the cams and pulled the alarm. If she had played by the rules though, like not throwing stuff at me, I would have been able to stop her."

"Sure. If she played by the rules, huh?" Axl remarks. "I know Glacia didn't put up much of a fight, but the one with the wings did. Damn, that chick was a powerhouse. You fought her too, right?"

"Yeah."

"We'll for sure get those rats next time, since we know how sloppy they are. It's only a matter of time 'til we corner them. So, don't get down on yourself for getting knocked out by one of them."

"I wasn't."

Axl raises a brow. "Sure, but it really is only a matter of time. Then we'll get the answers that you're looking for about your long-lost friend and all. And you'll be one step closer to graduating. Don't worry too much about it."

I nod. I hope so.

"Enough of that talk. With all these meetings we've had in the past few days, months... I'm sick of it. I wanna talk about something else."

"Like what?"

Axl shifts his blue eyes to mine as he reaches down to grab a cig. Putting it between his teeth, he holds her lighter up to its tip. I can see the letters *G.I.* engraved into it, from her. I'm not sure why he's kept that gift for so long.

"Maybe what we're gonna do when our service is over. Nobody ever talks about that and it's hella irritating. Like, how am I supposed to keep the Emil name going when I don't know how I'm gonna keep it going, you know?"

I open my mouth to answer.

"You don't know. Well, you sorta do. Being the only son in the family, I mean. You're not an only child, so you get less pressure."

"So, how are you going to keep the family name afloat?" I ask. "Are you going to be a lawyer like your father on the side?"

Axl flicks his lighter on. "You know...I've thought about it for a while. I think I'm gonna open up a flower shop after this service, and maybe my next service will be on the side of my flower shop."

I blink. "A flower shop? Why that?"

"It'll never fail."

I raise a brow.

Axl lowers the lighter. "Everyone likes to stare at the things, take care of them, or gift them. Those are three things that all suckers and hard-asses fall for on any given day. As long as there's a demand, there's profit." Axl takes the cigarette from his teeth. "And man... flowers are such a test, especially taking care of them. If you don't do everything right, they die. If you take them for granted, they die. Hell, if you even give them the wrong water...they die. It's bonkers how dependent a flower is, and if I open a flower shop...It'll be a mutual dependence."

"What would you sell then?"

"I would put a shit ton of chrysanthemums at the front of the store. Only those. Only those so I can lure the money in. Then, right when they walk in the door," he says with a grin, "I'll have pink carnations there to sucker punch those walkin' dollar bills, just to seal the deal."

"No roses?"

Axl smacks my shoulder. "Don't be a mook, man. Of course I'll have roses! You think I'm a mook or something? I'll have so many damn different colors of roses that my customers won't be able to see straight for weeks!"

I chuckle.

"What about you? What do you wanna do after this service?"

I shrug. "I'll probably try to shadow my sister, then graduate."

"C'mon. You gotta have something better than that. Don't get me wrong, Colonel West is great and all, but have you ever thought about doing something outside of the company when you're off? You could still serve year-round if your little heart desires it, but maybe do something on the side so that you don't go nuts and get service fever."

I shrug again.

Axl's smile spreads. "I could see you owning an antique store or something along those lines. You're such a sucker for old stuff. You could travel outside of the wall, looking for all the old stuff that survived through it all. Man, that would totally be your thing, with you reading all those dusty books and all."

"Yeah, but how would I still serve?"

"We can figure that out later. All you gotta figure out right now is where you're gonna get and sell those antiques of yours. Wasn't there a place in O.K.C.? I'll help you. I'll help you get it all started after I open my flower shop."

I smile. It's a nice thought.

"Thanks," I say. "I'll make sure to buy all my roses from you."

Zzzzzz Zzzzzzzzzzz Zzzzzzzzzzzz Zz

The seat vibrates, its source coming from inside my briefcase. I open it up and grab my buzzer. The screen reads *Doctor Bristol Inman* as it vibrates furiously.

"Is that Doctor Inman?" Axl asks. "What is she doing calling at this time? She knows we're on the clock." Axl leans in to eavesdrop and help me through the conversation.

I accept the call. "Hello?"

"Trainee, is the car ride treating Seeker Emil and you nicely?" Dr. Inman's monotone, light voice says through the phone.

The vehicle shakes. "Yes, it's gone smoothly so far. Is there a reason for your call? Have there been any developments we should know of?"

"Negative. Doctor Castus asked me to speak to you before Seeker Emil and you returned to the A.F.A. We both want a status report. Right now."

Axl scoffs. "Seriously? Right now? This lady has been in the bourbon early or some shit."

I take a breath. "We picked up a lead on the four in Nashville. A camera picked up Trainee Glacia Ivar on our facial recognition search in a marketplace, and Twenty-Seven was with her. I figure they are all travelling together now and must be staying on the outskirts of town, since Trainee Ivar knows the area well, given her family's occupation. I'm not sure why they decided to travel and stay together though. Trainee Ivar could be...lashing out at the company by helping them. Seeker Emil and I will be taking her into consideration during our search. We'll be much more careful with her on the prowl. There's no telling what she has planned when we find them. Also, I still can't believe they managed to slip past the wall. We'll investigate and ask the locals, and then we'll pick up some more supplies from Aurex for when we have to go back to the Processing Territories."

It's silent on her end, except for incoherent mumbles from her and someone else who I assume is Doctor Castus.

"Yes, that is very good news. That is all we need from you. Do you have any questions for Doctor Castus or me that could help with your search?"

"Quite a few, if you and the Doctor have the time."

"Go on."

"I've been reviewing the interrogation footage of the four, and I was wondering about something that came up during their interrogations. Were they trained to stay quiet in that sort of setting? Axl and I were only able to get a few words out of them."

"Yes, they were trained in that manner. How were you able to answer the questions we sent?"

I exchange a look with Axl. "Axl was able to read their body language. The answers were clear."

"Nice save," Axl whispers.

"Very good of you two. That training has proved to be more effective than I recently thought."

"About that..." I trail off. "I think after this mission has been completed, I should have further training, especially with the weaponry of my arms, because of my previous encounters with the four. I believe that training against and seeking the Monstrums hasn't been enough for me to master the skill."

"Yes. It is always difficult with enhancements like yours, since the techniques haven't matured yet. I think that is a very good thought. Doctor Castus and I believe that with time, you will master the art of using the weaponry." Dr. Inman pauses to speak to Dr. Castus. "Doctor Castus has just informed me that you're more than capable of outsmarting the four, and that you do not require your weaponry, but if you wish...after your current mission, we can arrange a training schedule for you."

"That would be great. Thank you. Do either of you have any suggestions on how we should approach this next attempt to catch the four? Any weaknesses you can think of to exploit?"

There's another conversation between the Doctors.

"Number Twelve has a lack of training, less than the others. Forty-Five cannot hold a separate appearance for an extended amount of time and cannot conceal the nick on its right ear. Thirty-Three has a weak spot on the middle of its back where its wings are attached; make sure to attack there. Number Twenty-Seven has few weaknesses; tiring it out may be the best option."

I'll keep note of that. "Also, there's a new development about the four. It appears they have given themselves new names."

A pause. "What are they?"

"Thirty-Three calls herself Hawk, Twenty-Seven is Strike, Forty-Five is Viper, and Twelve is Storm."

There's a louder conversation on the other end.

"Interesting development, but not surprising. We expected them to rebel in some way since they...mysteriously abandoned their missions, but new names...very strange. Thankfully, their reign will soon end. Doctor Aquinas and I are currently finalizing the revisions to the M.R.A. devices. Their new names won't matter soon."

"Affirmative."

"Thank you for letting us know. Any other questions?"

"Yes, I've been thinking a lot about this since my failure to stop them. I think an answer may help me because things aren't adding up. It's about the appearances of Viper and Storm. You see, Viper has those canines, strange green eyes, and claws. And Storm has golden eyes, sharp canines, the claws, and a marking in her hair. I was wondering, are they descendants of Monstrums? Are they some sort of experimental hybrid? If so, how are they not rabid?"

"Good question," Axl mutters, while the Doctors whisper on the other end.

"Doctor Castus applauds you for that intuitive question. Your seeking skills have improved. It is a very simple explanation; they are not hybrids nor descendants of those monsters. Those specimens were given hearing and sight enhancements like Seeker Emil. The canines and claws were also enhancements that were being tested at the time, but Doctor Castus decided to terminate their usage on others."

"And her marking?"

"Twelve has always had it. Doctor Castus assumed it was a birthmark."

That doesn't explain their shapeshifting abilities. If they have the same enhancement as Axl, then he would be able to change his eye color, right? Maybe they are keeping the technology classified right now. There must be a decent reason.

"And I ask that you don't refer to the weapons as their false names or as 'she' or 'her' anymore. It doesn't fit their natures. Remember that, Trainee West," Dr. Inman says. "Is there anything else I can help you with?"

I clear my throat. "Yes, I'd like to request that if another failure occurs, we have Colonel West come out to provide guidance."

Dr. Inman sighs. "Doctor Castus and I will consider it, but I wouldn't count on another failure as an excuse to see a relative, Trainee West. Nonetheless, Colonel West's guidance may prove effective if you two should fail again. We will discuss it today."

"Bitch," Axl mutters. "Does she even know how long you two have been separated? Four years. That's fuckin' child abuse."

"Doctor Castus will be in Oklahoma City tomorrow and for the next six months. I'll be staying in New York. He wants to know if you would like to schedule a meeting with him?" Dr. Inman asks.

"Yes. Thank you."

The van suddenly stops, and I look out the front window to see the wall's entrance towering above the vehicle. We've finally made it.

"He also asks if you have an answer for him regarding the flight enhancement surgery."

My stomach drops.

"If you do not have an answer yet, he has ordered that you have one by your meeting. Doctor Castus says that you will meet with him the day you return to Oklahoma City with the four and Trainee Ivar in your possession."

"I will answer him then. Thank you for your time. We have arrived at the wall."

"Good wishes to you and Seeker Emil. And I wish you a pleasant late birthday. Fifteen suits you."

She hangs up and I slowly lower the buzzer, placing it back into my briefcase.

"So, Samael's wings, huh?" Axl says. "Are you going to go through with it?"

"I'm not sure yet."

"I know the surgery is risky. The recovery is decent. I understand why you wouldn't want to do it but..." Axl trails off. "Samael would have wanted you to have those wings. I mean, being able to fly wherever the hell you want...That sounds like a miracle."

"We'll see what happens. I just don't see myself ever needing them on a mission."

"I mean, you never know; it could come in handy."

I nod, but I doubt that.

TWENTY-EIGHT

RED LIGHTS

STORM

A dim flame seeps through the sides of a tin can; it twists from the slightest breath passing over it. Its anemic light sends red rays across the countertop and onto the features of Hawk, Strike, Viper, and Glacia. Far away from the rays is Flame, sitting on the counter. Surrounding the little fire is a smear of documents, ranging from letters to blueprints, each barely shows any light skittering across. What little light there is can't reach the far corners of the old cabin because the shadows from the Oklahoma wilderness consume it.

Hawk slides the letter to me. The wrinkles that I created a week ago from my first reading of it remain.

You have been assigned to subject WDXX12. Report to the Aurex Facilities immediately. Pick up the following items from the supply center:

    New Uniform

    Cattle Prod

    Identification Card

    Train Ticket

Everything you need will be provided for you once you reach Montana. The train will leave at 11:00 a.m. today.

Please give this order to the manager of the supply center as proof of our request. I don't want any setbacks for your journey to us. I am very pleased with your new position as chaperone. We will make marvelous things happen together.

With great esteem,

Dr. T.G. Castus

I slide the paper back into the pile as I pinch the bridge of my nose. Along the thin pages of my journal, I tap with a frantic finger before I write the date, March 18. I don't want to forget.

"And you said that these letters are sort of like...telegraphs, an order?" Hawk asks.

"Yeah," Glacia replies. "They are typically direct messages for instantaneous orders. Based on the documents, it appears that each one of you had a chaperone, all summoned at different times; that's not protocol. Transporting officers at the same time is preferred in order to make the best use of time and resources for the train, especially in a place like Montana. The timeline doesn't make much sense. Some orders are separated by years."

"I've never heard of a chaperone before in any of my memories," Hawk says. "I don't think any of us have."

Viper nods; I do not.

"You said you didn't know of any bases in Montana either, right?" Strike asks.

"It looks like it may be classified," Glacia says. "Something that only higher-ups like the Doctors and the Colonel know about."

That could be where our answers lie, somewhere nobody even knows about. I jot down the possibility of a base in Montana.

"But our tattoos were mentioned," Viper replies. "That could mean we were there too."

"So, this place does exist then," I say.

Glacia rubs her temples. "It could. It for sure could. It may not be a base at all. It could have been a location where they put the armor together or a gathering place for the chaperones to be taken somewhere else that's classified. Maybe even where y'all were staying."

I scribble a few more notes down.

"What's strange is the blueprints. The orders for the materials for the armor came at the same time after the chaperones were sent, but the designs appear to be slightly different." Glacia snags the four blueprints. "We can safely assume these were made for y'all since they are labeled with your tattoos, but there's still one question. This armor is very high-tech. Things I've never seen before. So, what was it used for?"

For murder.

"What do y'all think? Is this making any memories bubble up?"

I look up, exchanging glances with Hawk, Strike, and Viper, before quickly looking back down. I finish my thoughts on paper as slowly as possible.

"We know what the armor was used for," Hawk says quietly. "We've had memories of us...well...using it."

Glacia's expression changes, waiting for more information. Flame leans forward, his attention grabbed.

"It's not pretty," Hawk continues. "It has to do with the program and what it did. What all of our programs did."

"What happened?" Flame asks.

Another look between the four of us falls within those red rays cascading through the room.

"Death," Strike whispers. "Our programs killed a lot of people against our will. But—"

"We don't know how much killing, what happened before or after, what day it was, where it was, or even why we were there in the first place," Viper says. "All we know is the fighting."

Strike looks down, fumbling with her fingers. Glacia scans her eyes over the blueprint, leaning both hands on the countertop. She bites the inside corner of her cheek.

"And you remember yourselves wearing the armor, while...the program killed people?" Glacia asks.

"Sadly..." I say.

Glacia hesitates, keeping her blue eyes away from the rays. She stares at the blueprint, index finger tapping. Her heart skips a beat. Flame's does as well, and he keeps his gaze low.

Glacia clears her throat. "It does appear that the armor was meant for things like that, like heavy trauma. The ones that match up with Hawk and Storm have slits in the back of them. Strike and Storm's also have slits in the arms, and it looks like Viper and Storm's had slits in the fingers. It all matches up with your abilities."

Flame jumps off the counter, approaching the blueprint. His brows furrow. "What is the armor made of?"

"It's called RM Metal." Glacia scratches her head. "I've never heard of it before."

Flame holds up his arm. "I'm pretty sure I have some of that in my fake arms. I remember my mom talking about that stuff a lot, going on and on about how great it is and how it can be used for anything. I'm pretty sure my eyes have some too."

"What does it stand for?" Glacia asks. "And how many prosthetics do you have?"

"Something with a Ross, I think, then memory metal. And it's only my eyes and arms, so not too many."

"Can we please get back on track?" Hawk asks. "So, the armor. You've never seen anything like it, but we know the metal it's made of. How can that help us?"

"We could track down the person who designed it," Strike replies. "Maybe the girl, or guy, who made it."

"I think we should track down the chaperones," Viper says.

"But we don't know anything about them," Hawk replies. "Not much anyway. Only that they worked for this Castus guy."

I bite my lip.

"I'm sure we can find things at another base," Glacia says. "For now, we can use what we have."

"Actually..." I trail off. "I've had a memory about my chaperone."

The room goes silent. Eyes all on me.

"And you didn't think to tell us?" Viper asks.

"I know. I know. I just...It wasn't the most promising memory, and it's something I didn't want y'all to stress over."

"What do you mean?" Strike asks.

I sigh. "The Doctor with the purple tie was angry about something and mentioned my chaperone. I think they were flipping the switch."

"Flipping the switch to what?" Hawk asks.

"To electrocute me while the Doctor blew a whistle. They did it over and over again until I lost all control. Until my program took over."

The room goes silent again.

"That would have been good to know," Hawk says. "Storm, that's a memory with your program. What would happen if—"

"It's one of two I've had. It's not the same as you guys."

"That doesn't matter. It's the program. Promise to tell us next time, okay?" Viper says.

"Yeah, please," Strike replies.

"Okay, I promise."

"You mentioned the Doctor with the purple tie, the one that gave the orders," Glacia says. "That must be Doctor Castus. He used to give orders to my superior, Miss Bristol. I mean, Doctor Inman. This makes more sense. They did help make y'all after all then, right? I think it adds up."

"But what do you know about them?" Viper asks.

"I don't know much about Doctor Castus, I've only had a few conversations with him, but I know some stuff about Inman. She oversaw my training and gave enhancements to other Trainees. Josh got his blades and Axl got his eyes, ears, and legs from her. Inman probably is still giving orders to those two, and others, to this day."

"So, Doctor Castus could have done the same to us?" I ask.

Glacia nods. "Or they both could have."

I carve more notes into my journal.

"Are there any more doctors we should know about?" Strike asks.

"Not that I know of," Glacia says.

Strike narrows her eyes.

"Flame, do you know anyone? Like who gave you the prosthetics?" Glacia asks.

Flame lets his eyes drift away. "I'm not sure. I was young. I don't remember it well."

I jot that into the journal as well.

"So, what's our next step?" Hawk asks. "Are we still gonna hit Oklahoma City?"

"I say that's our best bet," I reply. "Since we already know some of the details of the base, we'll be able to plan faster."

"Yeah! And I'm totally up for sneaking in and posing as a worker there!" Viper beams. "It'll speed up the process more!"

Glacia leans forward, the light glimmering across her pale eyes and a smirk growing on her lips.

"Oklahoma City will be a big one. It's a recon and intelligence-based center for the A.F.A. and the company Castus runs, of course."

"Company?" I ask.

"Yeah. Doctor Castus is the head of it; it's a private organization. The government commissions them for defense against those monsters, among other things. But anyway, I bet there is a shit ton of stuff on y'all, and this time we'll search for even more keywords on their network since Viper will hopefully be an inside man."

"Strike, Flame?" I ask. "What do y'all think?"

Flame blinks. "I'm down for whatever. I'll help in any way I can."

"I'm worried that we're jumping the gun here," Strike says. "Shouldn't we wait a bit before going back to Oklahoma City? We have no idea if it's still on high alert since last time. Maybe we should—"

"My dear friends, would you kindly keep it down or go to sleep already?" Alo cuts Strike off. "Sage and I are trying to get some shut-eye. We aren't really night owls like you people."

"Sorry, Al," Hawk says. "We'll go on to sleep and plan all this tomorrow. Sorry!"

Alo waves us off with a yawn and retreats back to his and Sage's room.

"I'm gonna summarize this real quick for the journal," I say. "So, we remember that based off my memory and the letter, Doctor Castus ordered the chaperones to help oversee us. We know that the chaperones and our armor were sent to Montana, but we don't know if there is a base there or if we were there. The chaperones were sent at random with big gaps of time in between, but the armor was sent all at once. And the armor made of RM Metal that matches our dreams was customized for each of us. So, they are for combat...Is that all?"

"Inman gave Josh, Axl, and a few others their enhancements," Glacia says, "so they could have done the same for y'all."

"Others? Who are they?" I ask.

"Don't worry about them."

My eyes narrow but I write everything down. Everyone agrees to hit the hay before heading to their sleeping mats, but I stay back with my pen at the ready. It rips across each page, question marks nearly overtaking the words. I question the existence of a base in Montana, the meaning of my tattoos, the others that Glacia mentioned, why Castus did this, who the chaperones are, and my true purpose besides killing.

I know that I can't be here just to end life.

The red light that casts onto my journal dims the words. I blow out the flame. The smoke spirals, and I'm left alone in the dark with my pen still poised. I wait for something to illuminate my mind, but nothing rises. There are embers there that burn my mind and refuse to allow my eyes to rest. I doubt the embers will go out tonight.

TWENTY-NINE

RUMBLE AND RAMBLE

STORM

My fingertips burn from the velocity of the pen. Glacia, Strike, Hawk, and Viper throw out ideas for a new plan into the air; they leave me speechless as I smear the ink to keep up.

"So, until then we'll train and gather more supplies," Strike says. "But how long until we move to Oklahoma City?"

"Two weeks?" I ask.

"How about we wait until May? It'll give us plenty of time to think this through and to get the company off our scent. The base has certainly realized that there was a breach by now," Glacia says. "They'll expect us to strike Oklahoma City quickly, because our confidence is high."

"So, we just train until then?" Hawk asks.

Glacia nods. "I have a feeling we'll have to force our way into this base, unless we go through with Viper posing in a different form within their ranks. I'm not sure if we should take that risk, though. If Viper were to get caught..."

"I'll practice," Viper says. "It'll be fine."

"I don't know, V," Strike replies. "It's a huge risk."

"If you got caught, the chances of getting you back would be slim," Glacia says.

"I say we go for it," I reply. "Viper held her form last time. And if she trains well, why not put her power to use? They wouldn't expect us to put someone on the inside."

Hawk hesitates. "I don't know, Storm. How about we think on it more today? Can we get to fixing this place up for now? Get organized with our supplies?"

"Good idea." Viper beams. "You wanna go into town now? I can get some shiftin' practice in."

"Yeah, and we should get some fries and some tools to fix that damn door."

"Be easy on the money," Glacia says. "We don't have much left."

"And don't get into any bar fights," I remark. "At least not without me."

Hawk grins as Viper shifts her hair into a sleek black. The scars on her neck vanish and her green eyes distill to a deep brown. Grabbing the money, they walk out the door to the forest.

"I'm going to go fill Flame in," I say. "Will y'all fill Alo in?"

Strike nods.

"And I'm fixin' to take a look at the roof," Glacia replies. "Since it's spring, I'm sure the showers will come soon. Are there any supplies left?"

"I stored some in the back. I'll show you and help you out with the roof," Strike says. "Let me fill Alo in first."

Strike leads Glacia away, their voices lingering as they walk to meet Alo. Leaving my journal on the table, I walk out to the front porch, stopping right behind Flame. He's sitting hunched over on the steps. Mundanely, he sparks a flame, only to put it out with a clench of his fist. His gaze appears to linger on the tops of the green, white, and purple budding trees, and he listens to the murmuring of birds and crickets. Dawn has fully broken above the tree line, but it's clear light has been consumed by the grogginess of a dark horizon.

"Hey," I say. "Turns out we'll be hanging here for a while, and we'll be going to Oklahoma City in May. So, in the meantime, there's gonna be trainin' and workin'."

Flame springs to his feet. "Perfect! We should train right now! C'mon!"

"Hold o—"

Flame snatches my arm and hauls me down the stairs. After a few steps, my protest stops. I roll up my sleeves and take the lead, heading for the clearing.

"What are we going to work on? I was hoping you could show me how to do that flipping someone over your head bit. I bet it's hard, but if I could do it, I'd be unstoppable," Flame replies. "Or maybe I could work on using my flames?"

"You'll see. I have a few ideas."

"Like? Are you going to swing your claws or blades at me? Are you going to flip me over your shoulder!?"

I smile. "If you test me, I will."

A low rumble echoes in the distance, providing a fair warning of the brewing storm. I push a delicate branch aside for Flame and me. The branches obscure the incoming weather but hold the bountiful life of emerging buds. It's one for another.

"What does that tattoo say?"

"Huh?"

"Your tattoo here." Flame pokes the back of my neck "What does it say? I've seen it before, but never really bothered to ask. I figured you were embarrassed to talk about it, you know? I'm embarrassed 'bout my eyes all the time. I shouldn't have chosen red," he rambles on. "But anyway, what does it say?"

"It says K192," I reply. "And uh, thanks for thinking of me."

"Always. Do you know what it means?"

I shake my head.

We step into the open air of the clearing, the grass dotted with same purple and white buds, with a groggy sky to illuminate it. I turn to Flame and he beams. The forest behind him sparkles with little dewdrops falling into the weak light. Returning his smile, I slip off my boots to feel the mud between my toes. I pull up my jeans to keep them from the muck below my feet.

"Take off your jacket." I swing my hair into a ponytail. "And your shoes."

"Why? It's cold."

I raise a brow. Flame slips off his leather jacket and a red hoodie. All that is left is a white tank top. He flips off his sneakers, tucks in his silver necklace, and puts his hands on his hips.

"Swing at me," I say.

"What?"

"Punch me." I point to my cheek. "Here."

I slip my hands behind my back and give Flame a small nod as I get into a ready stance. He hesitates as he raises his fists. Eventually, he cocks his elbow back and takes the swing. I duck, step forward, and grab his forearm. Using his power to trip him, I sling him on his back. Flame stares at me with wide eyes as he lets out a huff. I help him to his feet.

"People will think you're weak. So, you gotta use that. Put them off balance by dodging, you know?" I say. "You're good at the attacking part, using your flames, but sometimes you gotta rely on the other parts of you. You gotta rely on gravity."

Flame nods as he wipes the mud from his shirt.

"If you're gonna help us, then I gotta know how good you are at dodging."

"Why?"

"When you're in the base, we can't afford you gettin' hurt. Fighting like this helps us, at least me, avoid that. You won't be able to use your flames inside too much, obviously, unless you want the place to burn down. You gotta learn how to not rely on them."

Flame nods. He raises his fists again before giving me another grin.

"Don't hold back."

"Trust me. I won't," I lie.

Rushing him, I plant a heel into his chest. He staggers back. I hurl myself at him again, but Flame throws a punch. I pivot my foot and slip past his blow. My shoulders are now square to his back. I slam my foot into his spine. Instead of falling, Flame regains his balance by spinning his shoulders to me, but I leap at him. I punch his shoulder before throwing an uppercut in his direction.

But I'm stopped by his rock-solid arm. A blunt force smashes into my temple and I stumble sideways. He flashes toward me with a kick. I dodge to the side and regain my balance. He cocks back an open palm, his hand glowing red, and throws another punch. I dodge. Then another. I dodge again. He uppercuts, but I arch my spine back. I throw myself at him and jab his throat with no restraint. Flame gags and keels over, holding his neck, while he sputters violently. I try to collect my own breath and rub the side of my head.

"You got cocky," I say. "I mean literally. You cocked back your punches there. It made it easy for me to see it coming."

Flame rubs his neck, still trying to get his breath. Wind hits the clearing, and with it, comes a much louder rumble from the ill-tempered sky.

"It's almost like you're thinking about what you're gonna do next, instead of what I'm gonna do," I say. "For this next one, try to figure out what I'm about to do, then make your move. That's what Strike always tells me to do."

Flame coughs. "Watch you. Got it."

"And sorry about that last jab. I didn't mean for it to hit that hard."

"Yeah, sure. You just wanted to show off, didn't ya?"

Flame raises his guard, grits his teeth together, and squeezes his brow. I grin a bit. I dig my toes into the ground, but Flame charges forward and throws a right hook. I weave away. He hooks left. I step to the other side. He attempts an uppercut, but I swivel away. Flame grunts and throws another left hook with all his might. I dodge and slam a right hook into his jaw. My foot rockets into his chest. Flame staggers back. He yells and struggles to get his footing. I step toward him, a punch to the face in mind, but I hold myself back. Flame finally gets his footing and raises his fists. He's ready to—

Boom!

I pause, my bones shaking, and gaze to the sky. My breath is hot. My veins buzz, making my fingers twitch. Flame puts his hands on his blond head as he stares up to the sky. We sit in impatient silence for a moment, but nothing happens.

"You didn't do much dodging. Dodge, then attack. Not attack, then attack," I reply.

"Why can't I just punch until they get knocked out?" Flame sighs. "It's worked for me before. It works pretty well for you. If it works, why are you trying to fix it?"

"What are you saying?"

"I'm saying that I've seen you fight before and you don't always fight like this, so teach me how to fight like you."

"You need to know the simple—"

"I don't care about the simple things. I want to know the big things that'll end a fight," Flame says between his teeth. "It doesn't matter how much I get hit or how many bruises I get; ending a fight myself is winning a fight."

I narrow my eyes.

"What? Is that wrong? I wanna be like you guys fighting. I wanna—"

"I get it. You're frustrated and you wanna help out, but if you get hurt...if you take on too much before you're ready..."

Flame looks down. "I know, but I can't stand watching everyone fight it out while I'm left to wait around, you know? And when I watched you spar back in Nashville, you always threw the first punch. I figured I should do the same if I wanna be able to fight like you."

I sigh. "You shouldn't wanna be like me."

Flame doesn't look up.

"And you stick up for your friends even if you're outgunned. You already fight like we do."

"I know. But I—I'm not capable of backing it up. I can't put my words behind my actions. It makes me feel almost like...I don't know really...like..."

"Helpless?"

"Yeah, I feel helpless and I'm sick of it."

I nod slowly. A lump forms in my throat. I never realized that he felt helpless.

I sigh. "Sometimes I don't even realize I do things. It just explodes outta me. And I shouldn't be like that. You shouldn't want that. It doesn't protect people how you hope. Yeah, being strong helps, but being smart about fighting, that's what everyone needs. The things that I'm showing you will let you think in a fight so you can end it the right way," I explain.

"What's the right way?"

I stare at his red eyes for a moment. "The right way..." There is a long pause. "... people just get hurt but not taken away. You win a fight by taking control. The right way to do that is by knocking someone out or by dodging enough to tire them out. Sometimes it's even better to run away."

"If you run, doesn't that mean you've lost?"

"It depends. Sometimes it's the only thing you can do to win the right way. Sometimes dodging things makes you smart, not weak or a loser, because it gives you more time to react with a better punch." I take in a deep breath. "And if it makes you feel any better, I need practice dodging, so you training with me is helping me a lot."

"Really?"

"Yeah, and if you don't want to practice dodging for the rest of today, we can do it tomorrow morning. I'll train with you, everyone will, whenever you want. So, what do you want to work on with me today?"

Flame pauses and glances at his palms. Thunder rumbles on once again above us, a warning. Red flames emit from his palms.

"I want to work on control and how I put my fire into a fight more easily." Flame clenches his fists and the fire goes out. "But I'm not sure now."

"Why?"

"You're right," Flame says. "I can't rely on the flames completely. Maybe I can make them my defense...I just need to be smarter with them."

"Don't worry about—"

A drop of water falls onto my cheek, following by another and another and another. Soon, Flame and I find ourselves in a downpour. We are forced to retreat to the trees against the sting of a cold spring shower. Once we settle ourselves on a damp log to wait for the rain to stop, Flame starts laughing between his chattering teeth.

"What?" I ask.

"I dunno. The rain just came so fast! I didn't expect it to come that quick!"

I smile between my own shivering lips, and I blanket Flame with my wings. We sit together and watch the raindrops shattering on the earth as the mist of each drop's soul encompasses the budding branches. I close my eyes and focus on the drops hitting the leaves, branches, buds, and the grass. The aroma of newly born mud and the grumbles of the sky glide through the mist. A chill runs down my spine.

"Is this why you made your name Storm?" Flame asks. "Because you like rainstorms?"

I open my eyes, meeting his dazzling, red irises. He pushes back his wet hair and waits for an answer.

"Not exactly. I do like the rain a lot, though."

"Why?"

"It relaxes me and makes me feel warmer inside."

Flame raises his brows.

I look to the rain. "I mean, it's like I'm experiencing something warm that I haven't felt for a long time. I'm remembering something actually good..."

"Like nostalgia?"

I nod. "But I guess I could say that's why I chose the name Storm, if I'm fixin' to have less explaining to do."

"It's really that complicated?"

"It's a long story, a really long story, and I would ask you about your name but—"

"You're the one who gave it to me! To get me to shut up, right?"

"Pretty much, but what's your real name anyway?"

"You seriously haven't asked me before?"

"Why would I? I already gave you a name."

Flame laughs a bit.

"What?"

"How do you expect me to tell you my real name when you won't tell me why yours is Storm?" Flame smirks. "I thought it was obvious that I wanna know the reason. I have since the day I met you!"

"You really want to know?"

"Yes."

I lean in close, the thunder booms, and I whisper to him the short version: that I like the rain. Flame then gives me a false name, something along the lines of Buckminster, and we end up rambling on about new false names. We laugh about how we would introduce ourselves to people we want to mess with, and talk about the small things to let the sky have its grumbling fit.

The raindrops, as they shatter, don't just hear the rumblings of thunder. They hear the feverish laugher of two souls in the midst of a light conversation. The entire forest listens and feeds off the warmth emitting from our smiles. All life within the forest, the birds, the bees, the rabbits, pause to bask in it. Any remaining ice thaws from the vibrations of our voices and creates a void for something to be born into. Buds burst at the seams of many branches in colors of violet, white, and red, shielding the raindrops from muddy graves and producing a pattering echo. Those saved drops drip onto the sturdy branches and soft grass. They create a dense song about not only a storm, but about the life one finds where they fall. I drift into the harmony without hesitation. I'm falling for it. I'm falling for its warmth.

I don't want the rain to stop. I'd rather live in it for the rest of my life. There's nothing that would make me forget the warmth and the coldness. Absolutely nothing. At least, I hope not.

THIRTY
THE BEST MEDICINE
STORM

My eyes close but my mind refuses to slip into slumber. They burn for sleep, but the light rain diffuses all chances of it. Usually the rain helps. Usually the rain is comforting like a blanket. I'm on the porch to be closer to the raindrops. Although my body is bruised and battered from training with Flame, it fails to relax or recover from the sparring. It's like my body, my shell, refuses to believe that the fight is over. The shell is my permanent armor, but it doesn't protect my burning eyes and muscles. All it protects is the girl who used to live in it. Maybe if I were to remember my old self, that girl, I would finally get the sleep I long for when my eyes close.

The laugh of a young girl follows a deeper one. The footsteps attached to the two laughs emerge from the underbrush and walk up the steps. I open my eyes. Alo and Sage walk beside me to the cover of the remaining roof. I'm leaning against the wall beside the door. Sage sees me through the darkness and smiles. I smile back. She releases her grip from Alo's hand and jumps into my lap where she wraps her arms around my neck. I hug her back.

"Isn't it past your bedtime?" Sage asks.

"I could say the same to you. And why are you out in the rain? Y'all could get a cold."

Alo smiles. "Sorry. Sage was just helping me look at the stars."

"Yeah! And Alo told me all the constellations too! I remember them all. Big Dipper, Little Dipper, Leo...and Polaris, Regulus...um..."

"Remember now, Polaris and Regulus are stars that make up the Little Dipper and Leo," Alo says. "But we better get off to bed now, ma'am. Storm needs to as well."

I push back a few strands of Sage's hair. "Aw, come on, let us stick together a little longer."

"Please, Al?" Sage asks.

Alo sighs and I stop hugging Sage.

"I guess you should get going," I whisper. "Or Al will be grumpy tomorrow."

Sage frowns and crosses her arms. She sits back in my legs.

"I'll make a deal with you. If you go to bed right now, I'll take you on a flight after I do my training and writing."

Sage doesn't budge. "Make it a flight and a shapeshift, then I'll go to bed."

I laugh. "Whatever you want. Now get to bed. You'll need all your energy tomorrow."

Sage shoots to the door and Alo lets her by. Her bare footsteps fade deeper into the house, but Alo lingers. There are dewdrops in his coarse red hair and stubble on his jaw. Water soaks his black shirt and camo pants. The aroma of grass sits on his skin. He looks my direction and leans against the wall.

"You should come inside too," Alo replies. "You're bound to catch a cold staying out here too long."

"Please. Me? Get a cold?"

"You're bound to get sleep deprivation at this rate too."

"Way ahead of you."

Alo smiles briefly. There's a break in our words. It's almost as if we are both listening to the rain for too long and basking in its lovely hums.

"What's going on with you?" Alo asks. "Is...Are you having symptoms?"

"No," I whisper.

"Your memories are bubbling up?"

"No..."

"Is it...I don't want to pry, but you don't sound good. Is it anxiety or any stress of some kind?"

I look away. "It's not that. Sometimes I just can't go to sleep."

"That's not uncommon. I used to have trouble sleeping too. Granted, I was in a different situation, but I found one trick that might help you out."

"What is it?"

"Stargazing. It's the best medicine. I hope it helps you." He opens the door. "And thanks for getting Sage to sleep. I appreciate it."

I say goodnight. Alo leaves me behind; his soft footsteps glide down the hall and into his room. The cabin doesn't make a sound. The rain drowns out any hints of life, and I'm left alone with my own agenda in mind. I rise, walk out from the shelter, and trudge my bare feet onto the muddy grass. I'm drenched within seconds. I don't want to stay awake long enough to see the sun anymore, so I scrape my bare feet along the underbrush and allow the dripping branches to claw at me. I don't bother to move any obstacles from my path. Shadows crawl at my toes and enclose me. They turn the forest into silhouettes. Despite my night vision, my burning eyes cannot see the shadow's fine details. I'm forced to wander and rely on my memory to guide me to the light.

I stop at the edge of the clearing. The moonlight bounces off the individual strings of long grass. It's like a bucket of silver is spilling into the clearing. In the center there's indented grass that hints at Alo and Sage's presence here. Slinking through that grass, I lower myself in the larger indent. With my hair thrown back, I spread my arms and stare at the dotted night sky. A silver moon is its centerpiece, causing the stars around it to blend into the background. My eyes are heavy. The wet grass provides a lovely bed as I sink deeper toward the roots. Rain hits me hard, but I'm no longer fazed by it. It's more like a blanket at this point.

Stargazing is the best medicine, huh? I wonder why Alo likes it. It's not like he can see it. Sage tells him the little white dots she sees, that's all. But maybe using his imagination is better than actually looking at the stars.

I take a mental picture of the night sky and close my eyes. Minute dots flash across my eyelids, the moon now nonexistent, and I can't help but smile as I sink deeper and deeper. The white dots swirl together. I'm completely consumed by the grass. One dim light seeps past my eyelids, a light that doesn't come from the moon. I open my eyes, and I'm greeted with a dawning light that weakly shines through fog and thick branches. My body still rests in a bed of drenched grass that has been frozen in time. I sluggishly sit up. I find the remains of brick walls surrounding me, each wall cemented by crimson roses and a massive tree that provides a flimsy roof.

My teeth chatter. I shiver violently. My fingertips have turned purple. A misty hum bounces between the dying bricks and warmly brushes over my skin. I turn to its source, hungry for more, and rise to my feet. The humming becomes a monsoon of warmth. It brings tears to my eyes. I walk past the last crumbling bricks to find a woman in a black dress. She stands in the last fading rays of skylight, a limbo between night and day. With her back turned to me, I can see her brunette hair strung in a single braid that's untouched by the rain. Her warm hums beckon my hand outward to her. Tears drench my cheeks as I reach. My hand finds her shoulder, turning her to me.

The humming stops. Everything turns black. Suddenly, I'm standing in swaying gold. Before me, a shimmering field of golden strands wave in the crisp breeze. The fog has lifted. Dawn has broken at the edge of the glimmering field. The light is blood orange and royal yellow with no clouds to block its radiance. There are blue and purple contrasts along the golden horizon that remind dawn of where it once was. The mixture of rays reflects across the shining plants and onto a massive oak tree in the center of the living gold. The breeze smells of cracking, frozen underbrush.

Resting on a low branch is a black owl. Its yellow eyes watch me with too much interest. The owl coos softly, beckoning me, and a light melody appears from the thin air. The melody is slow and warm. As I approach the tree, listening more closely, I realize that it's the fluid hymns of a piano. Its invisible player conjures an identical tone to the misty hums. I reach the roots where I find two items: a ukulele and a yellow, old-fashioned radio. The radio is rusted over, but it plays the comforting tune perfectly. The owl coos loudly and I look up. With wide eyes, I hold my breath. A chill runs through me.

Resting on the low branch is a young girl. Her hazel blue eyes watch me with too much interest. Her head is shaved to dark stubs and she's wearing a yellow jumpsuit stained with blood. She has three thick scars on her right forearm and a fresh one on her neck by her collarbone—hints at a deep scar on her chest. She has hollow cheeks, no expression, and pale skin.

The girl tilts her head, fidgeting with a small silver item between her fingertips. The radio cuts off. A buzzing overwhelms the air. I cannot hear my breath, the wind, or my thoughts. The little girl mouths something, but the buzzing washes away her voice. Everything turns black again.

In the distance, there are sounds of unknown birds. My eyes flutter open and I'm greeted with a pastel sky, no moon or stars to be found. Sluggishly rolling my eyes side to side, I realize I'm still laying in the bed of wet grass. I sit up with a groan as I hold my head. Rubbing my swollen eyes, I listen to the morning songs of those thousands of unknown birds for a little longer. I stagger to my feet and shake my tousled hair dry while I walk to the cabin. My skin is cold and drenched. I can't stop sneezing or coughing as I trudge up the steps and tug the door open. My toes drag as I slip into the kitchen. Strike is sitting on top of the table as she finishes cutting Alo's hair with her blades. They are laughing about something.

Strike turns to me. "Good morning, sleeping beauty."

"Good...good morning."

"Did you fall asleep stargazing?" Alo beams.

"Yeah."

"I'm guessing you slept well?" Strike asks.

I nod, but I fall into a sneezing fit.

"I prescribed you the right thing," Alo replies. "And since I'm the resident doctor now, I think you've caught a cold."

I cough. "That's a stretch."

"Oh really? You sound congested," Alo says. "I mean, it only makes sense. You fell asleep outside while it was raining."

"Yeah. Did you fall asleep in the field or something? There's grass in your hair," Strike says.

I nod and run my fingers through my hair, taking out a few bits of grass.

Strike sheathes her blade. "Since you slept well and feel perfectly fine, do you wanna train with me today?"

"Sure," I say. "What's everyone else up to right now?"

"Sage and Flame are still asleep. Glacia is trying to figure out where all the leaks are in the roof. Hawk and Viper are off training somewhere, I hope," Alo replies.

"Are you good here by yourself?" Strike asks.

Alo nods. "I'll make breakfast for the two children still asleep and maybe coax Glacia off the roof. Storm, make sure to take Sage on a fly. You promised her."

"Will do."

"Okay. We'll be in the back if you need us," Strike says.

Strike grabs my wrist. I let her drag me past the kitchen counter to where our sleeping mats are. We weave through little puddles from last night's leakage, but eventually walk out of the back door. There's a small, sunny strip of untamed grass and weeds between the tree line and the cabin. Vines grow on the back of the house and provide a daring ladder up to the roof.

Strike releases my hand, rolls up her black pants, and tucks in her shirt. As she does so, I roll up my muddy jeans and unbutton my black shirt, throwing it off to the side to let it dry in the sun. I embrace the sunlight.

I yawn as I pull my hair up into a tail.

"Do you actually want to unsheathe today?" Strike asks. "And work on maneuvering things?"

I shrug. "Why not? Since we have the Brute to worry about, we might as well practice with the real thing."

Shink.

Strike's upper blades shoot out of her arms, and blood drips off her hands. I follow her lead, flinching at the temporary pain.

"What did we work on last time?" Strike asks.

"Block, then attack," I reply.

"Hmm...Let's do that move we had trouble with. That one whenever you get stuck blade to blade, and then try responding to that."

"Sounds good."

Strike and I approach each other, carefully crossing our blades against one another. I force all my weight into the hold.

"I'm going to force your arms up, then slash down on your thigh. I'll kick your chest, pin you by your shoulders, and hold the blade there," Strike explains. "Let's do it slow at first. Ready?"

I nod. Strike slowly shoves one blade up, pushing me away, and lightly taps my thigh with the free blade. She mimics a kick to my chest, forcing me down. She rests her knees on my shoulders to prevent my arms from moving and hovers her blade near my neck.

She lets me get to my feet and we repeat the same motions again, except she's being pinned this time. We switch back and forth as we practice, speeding up the process as we go, but take care not to cut the other.

"Okay. Last time for me," I say. "Let's do it full speed."

"I'm ready."

We slam our crossed blades together, causing them to clang loudly. I push Strike's blades up, tap a blade to her thigh, and kick her chest. She falls on her back. I rush at her, pin her, and hold my blade to her neck.

"You good?" I ask.

Strike smiles. "It feels like you're about to cave in my lungs, but other than that..."

"Yeah, yeah, whatever." I let Strike up. "Stop being dramatic."

"I don't know. I think you're gaining a bit of weight from stealing my food all the time. Maybe we should go on a run to lighten your load."

"Pfff. Shut up."

Strike and I share a smile and suddenly hear a loud cough. I lift my gaze up, where Glacia sits on the edge of the roof.

"Glacia? What are you doing?" I ask. "I thought you were fixin' the leaks?"

"Well, you see, I was, but I heard a bunch of clanging so I was makin' sure nothing fishy was going on. Just ignore me. Get back to y'all's practice."

Strike and I exchange a glance.

Strike raises a full brow. "It's all right if you wanna watch, G. We don't mind."

"Yeah? I'm just gonna watch then. Since you said I could and I'm already here, you know," Glacia says.

"Let us know if you have any tips," I reply. "We don't get a bird's-eye view very often."

Glacia gives a thumbs-up.

"Sounds good to me," Strike says. "How about we practice blocks?"

I nod. "I'll attack first."

Strike and I get into position. I slowly swing my left blade at her. She parries with her right and steps to the side. I jab and swing right, but she blocks each blow with ease.

"Más rápido! Más rápido!" Glacia shouts lightly.

A chill runs down my spine. I throw the blade upward—hard.

Strike blocks it and takes a step back from me. The words echo and transform into something uncomfortably nostalgic.

"*Más rápido!*" A new, deep voice whispers to me.

It's like Strike is a mirage; she morphs into a large figure with a careless blade and shadows surrounding him. Those callous hands batter me with a knife. I violently swing left at them.

"*Más rápido!*"

My leg sizzles from electric shocks. The figure with the blade says no words, but the one behind him speaks. It's the man with the purple tie, Doctor Castus. The dark figure throws another blow, and I'm forced to jab at him with all my might. I miss. Something in the distance screams at me from what sounds like under the water. Doctor Castus continues to yell. I slash at the stomach of the figure to make it stop. My blade gets caught, pushed into the air, and I'm kicked in the chest. Right when my back hits the ground, the images dissolve into nothing. They are replaced with a blue sky, golden rays of sunlight, and frantic grey eyes hovering above me.

"Storm!" Strike screams. "Storm! Stop!"

I let a breath out and quickly shift my eyes side to side. Strike has her knees on my shoulders. Her blade is pressing on my throat.

"Where..." I trail off. "What...what happened...."

I feel the long grass brushing on my wings and Strike's hot breath on my cheeks. My eyes flutter as his voice rings in my ears.

"You...you just like, I don't know. You started attacking me," Strike says. "Are you okay?"

I hear footsteps running toward us. I glance up to find Glacia.

"What the hell!" Glacia shouts. "Are you two okay?"

"We're fine," Strike replies. "No...physical wounds."

"I..." I whisper. "I saw him."

"Saw who?" Glacia asks.

I slump head back on the grass, just to make sure it's actually there.

"He was there. Behind him..."

"Storm..." Strike replies. "You're not making any sense." She presses harder on my neck. "Are you with us right now? Do you feel like you're slipping away?"

"I saw him."

"We don't know who him is. Could you tell us?"

I close my eyes, taking in a few more deep breaths, and try to relax myself. I can't.

"Storm?" Strike's voice breaks. "Don't close your eyes right now. Not right now."

"I'm here," I say. "I'm fine. I need...I need to get up. I need to write it down. I need to remember it."

"Hold on a second."

"Glacia get my journal. I need my journal now."

I try to move from underneath Strike. I feel a hand on my forehead and see a dark expression hit Strike's face. She narrows her eyes, studying mine. They dart over to where my hands are and then back to me.

"You don't need it yet. Just take a second, Storm. I need you to relax. You're shaking too much," Strike says.

Looking down my arm, I see that my fists are clenching with blood pooling out between my fingers. I uncurl them and all my fingers drum the air.

"Is your program...?" Strike trails off.

"I'm here. I'm okay now...I think...I think I had a memory, a flashback."

Strike and Glacia sigh with relief.

"I saw him. I saw Castus. Castus and some other person were training me with blades, I think. He was saying...*más rápido* over and over again. I was being shocked. And the other one...he..."

"He was slashing at you, wasn't he?" Strike asks.

I nod.

"I remember one like that. Is this the first time you've seen it?"

I shake my head. "I've seen parts of it. I should have told all of you. I'm sorry. I've seen the training and electrocuting part. And I've heard the Doctor yell, but that's when I was asleep. I thought it only came when I sleep. I–I'm awake Strike. I'm wide awake."

Strike's expression softens.

"I've seen things while awake but not like this..." I whisper. "I need to write it down."

Strike gets off me, sheaths her blades, and helps me stand. I break away from them, rushing to the door and into the house. I throw myself on my mat, grabbing my backpack, and rummage through it.

I find the journal, whip it open, and scribble my pen across the clean page.

March 21

Entry #14

I'VE HAD my first memory that controlled me while awake. It was awful. It was the training memory. Doctor Castus was screaming at me, and this time a large man beat me with a knife as I swung my blades around wildly while being electrocuted. I'm sure it was for training, but the incident nearly made me hurt Strike. I almost hurt her and didn't know it. She said she has a memory like that. I remember Viper mentioning the same. I'm sure Hawk has too.

Since Viper was the last to be attacked by the program and since I've now started having memories while I'm awake, does this mean that I'm next? Staying awake doesn't guarantee me anything anymore. I could hurt them anytime.

I DROP the pen and close the journal as Strike kneels down next to me. She places a light hand on my shoulder and drapes my shirt over my lap.

"Promise me that you'll watch me," I whisper. "That you'll make sure that the program doesn't—"

"I was already planning on it." Strike sits next to me.

"Make sure that I don't hurt anyone."

"I can do that. You've done it for us. It's our turn to help you stay in control. Okay?"

I nod.

"The best thing you can do for yourself now though is to stop thinking about it and..." Strike leans her head on my shoulder. "Calm yourself down. Listen to your own heartbeat."

"How will that help?"

I turn to Strike as she lifts her cheek from my shoulder. She stares down at me with her light, grey eyes. A strand of golden hair sweeps over them, concealing their intentions.

"Because in all of those memories, well, it's almost like we're tools being built to do horrendous things, you know? It hints that nobody ever saw us as a she or her, but an it. Seeing those things over and over, you start to believe that you're not a human being," Strike whispers. "You have to remember that we're still people. Your heartbeat will remind you that everyone, including yourself, has one too. And that no matter what you are called or how people see you, nobody can take that heartbeat away from you. Nobody can make you less of a person, Storm. Not a single person can."

THIRTY-ONE

KEEP AWAY

STORM

May 28
Entry #15

In the last entry, I couldn't really put into words what I was feeling. Nothing bad happened since then. There hasn't been a single hint that my program is building up. I overreacted. But there is a lot going on, and keeping up with this journal can be tedious, almost annoying at times. Writing everything down has been hard, but this is important, so I should stop taking this for granted.

I've been feeling glad lately, mostly because of the raid. Somehow, I'm also feeing anxious because of the raid. I may just need to toughen up. I can't let things rattle me as much anymore, not with the raid just around the corner.

Since my last entry, we've mainly gathered supplies and trained. Glacia and Flame both train regularly and well. Flame has made incredible strides. Glacia has taught us a shit ton, while me and the girls have done the same for her. She even taught Alo a few things he could use to defend himself, and he's gotten pretty damn good at it too.

We've arrived at Oklahoma City and set up camp, in spite of my hesitations, in the brick building where Josh and Axl almost caught us. Since we know the area so well from that spot, the others thought it would be best to stay there. I'd still like to move. There's rubble here from last time and who knows what low-life or officer knows about this place. It's too risky, but it's a roof over our heads.

It's strange being back here. I'm where I first started this journal…I knew that I would eventually set foot in this city again, but everything is different now. Now I know how to get the truth.

I was hoping that I would see Curly again. I stopped by the square yesterday, but the old booth is gone. I don't think I'll ever know what went down after I left. Maybe the Boss and him decided to find a bigger audience or Curly could have finally become his own boss. I don't know. I just hope that Curly is okay; that's all I can ask for. I owe Curly, more than I like, and I hope to repay him someday.

Today, the plan is to go scout the base with Glacia for a bit and then meet up with everyone after they job hunt. Glacia wants to check on a few things and needs a set of enhanced ears. To cover more ground, we're all splitting up for the day. Right now, I'm waiting on Glacia to get ready; she tends to move in slow motion in the morning. I think I'll have a good time today. Glacia and I don't get much one-on-one opportunities. She's been so helpful these past few months. I owe her so much, and I can definitely say that I trust her now. Honestly, after we get all the answers we need, I want Glacia to stick around when it's all over.

I never think much about when this is over. I've always thought it would all fall in place for me, I think. It would be nice to find a place somewhere in the woods next to a lake that opens up to a field. It'll be big enough for everyone to have their own room and there will be a fireplace for the winter days. Flame can grow food while Alo and Sage can fish in the lake. There will be a working kitchen, running water, and thick blankets. There will be a porch that lets us sit outside and watch the rain. Hawk will be able to plant any flower she desires and put them along the polished window sills. Strike will have all the paint she needs and can paint the walls whatever shade she desires. Of course, Viper will have all the books in the world so she can finally learn what each word on the pages mean. We'll be able to train, run, and fly all we want in the field. Glacia will get to sing along to the morning chirps of every bird, and I'll take naps all day on the porch. It'll be a sanctuary.

I'll find it. I swear I'll find it after we figure all this out. We all can stay there for the rest of our days and rest easy.

. . .

"Storm? Are you ready?"

Glacia is standing on top of the rubble. The early sun peers through the cracks on the boarded windows and sends bright stripes onto her skin. I'm sitting at the base of the rubble. I nod and slip the journal into my backpack. Glacia throws on her black hood as she tiptoes to me and slides on a pair of sunglasses. She stops next to me, scanning me as I kick the board out into the alley.

"Maybe you should change your hair," Glacia replies. "That streak is a sure-fire sign of who you are."

"What do you mean?"

"I mean, we're goin' back to a place where we broke out of. You need to disguise yourself."

I scoot down, my legs hanging out of the slit, and I pull my hat from my coat pocket before placing it over my hair.

"Better?"

"Don't forget your sunglasses."

I put them on and jump out fully into the alleyway. Glacia follows my lead. I meticulously slot the board back onto the open window. A chilling wind tunnels through the narrow walkway as I do so. It's so powerful that I nearly lose my hat. Its whistling is comparable to when I go flying. It's relentless.

Glacia and I trudge against the wind to the open streets. Once there, the wind is less concentrated, but that doesn't stop it from blowing away the buds of the unprotected bushes along the sidewalk. We walk together in silence.

I stare up at the torn tower clawing at the skyline. It has always been the tallest building here—the highest point in the city. I bet I could see everything from up there. I could find out anything I want or see any terrible things coming from miles away.

We stop at an intersection. A stream of traffic rumbles inches away. Both carriages and cars compete to gain space in the street. Their noise makes the concrete shake. The dense vibrations rattle my bones. The pound of each hoof, creak of each wheel, and rev of each engine churn in my eardrums. With a red light, the intensity diminishes. We make our way across the street in a growing pack of people.

"Hey, Storm?" Glacia asks.

"Yeah?"

"So, when y'all lived in this area, what exactly did you do for work?"

"Well, Hawk and Viper sorta floated around doing odd jobs like washin' horses. Strike would sell her paintings or float too."

"Yeah, but what did you do?"

I beam. "I was a magician's helper. I got stuff for the show, ran errands, or pickpocketed the crowd. It was a pretty good job. I'll show you where the tent was."

Glacia nods. Her lip twitches back in thought and she scans the street.

"Why did you want to know?" I ask.

She keeps her gaze off me. "This city isn't known for its high employment rate. Usually migrants seek out jobs in the rural areas 'cause Oklahoma is more agriculturally equipped to feed the Safe Zone."

"And that has to do with me?"

Glacia shrugs. "I was curious what the low-income workers do here. That's all."

"Why?"

Glacia pauses. "No real reason. Curiosity, you know?"

"Sure."

"And I've read about this place, the history. I was wondering if anything had changed since it had a base established here. That base was made in a hurry, by the way. It'll work to our advantage."

"It seems well made to me."

"I mean, it's old. Before it was a base, it was a hotel called the Skirvin. It was converted into a base in a hurry during the war. Officially, it was supposed to be a temporary place of service, but it became permanent after a few years," Glacia says. "So, it's old. There will be plenty points of entry other than the garage we escaped from."

"Makes sense...How do you know all this?"

"I learned it out of a textbook. It was a requirement to read. My teacher thought that learning about cities like this would 'encourage our insight on improving the world beyond our borders,'" Glacia scoffs. "If you can't tell, I hated history class."

"Um, sure."

"Oh, but I learned about that tower over there too. When it was first built, it was the tallest in the city, still is today. It used to be called the—" Glacia glances over to me "Sorry...um, you probably don't care."

"No. No, it's okay. This is just the first time I've heard all this."

Our conversation dies down and the quaking sounds rush back into my ears. We reach the edge of the market and the bustling square. The market still thrives with vendors busily selling themselves and their products. Instead of the swirling colorful smoke in the center, it's barren. There is nothing left of the Boss and Curly. It's almost as if they were a mirage. I tell Glacia about the show in full detail, and hope my words will make it as if she was there with me so at least two people remember them.

Glacia and I walk beside the old tower. Its base is lined with new sets of barren trees, not yet bloomed. The trees look so fragile that even the birds avoid sitting on their branches. With time, I'm sure they'll blossom into pink groves. Hopefully their branches will be sturdy enough to catch any falling hatchlings. The tower will finally have some brightness to it, if they do.

We navigate to the base. A small chill runs down my spine at the sight of it. It reminds me of a castle on a hill. It's an old, but massive, brick structure with darkened windows and barbed wire fencing enclosing its perimeter. The tops of it are spiked with polished granite and steel. Guards prowl along the top and bottom. Vehicles roar in and out its gate at the end of a closed-off street. Each vehicle is stopped in its tracks and searched by guards with their weapons ready.

Glacia leads me to a bench away from the barbed wire, but in direct view of the entrance. Packs of people walk in front of us, concealing our presence, but Glacia grabs a newspaper and acts as if we're reading it; she says we need to do it to be on the safe side. I read along with her, to catch up on the news.

"What do you think about that?" I ask. "Crazy that there was another prison break in Topeka."

Glacia keeps her eyes on the base.

"I hate it," she says. "It'll only make things harder for us later on."

"The article talks about some rebels doing it. Sounds like we could get some more friends in the future."

"You don't need to concern yourself with the rebels. I hear they shelter those monsters from the A.F.A., and anyone who does that is a fool."

"Why?"

"You've never seen one, have you? Only heard about them?"

"People think I'm one of those things, which I'm clearly not. That's about all, though..."

Glacia turns to me. "You don't ever wanna see a *Monstrum*. Trust me. They're dangerous, savage, can't be reasoned with. If you ever see one of those monsters, I don't recommend trying to fight it. They have no mercy. I recommend runnin' for your life, or in your case, flying for your life."

"So, you've seen one? And what did you do about it?"

Glacia looks back to the entrance and opens her mouth to respond but freezes. I follow her gaze. My stomach drops. Josh West is opening a black car's door, greeting the person inside with a handshake. The person steps from the car. My throat tightens when a purple tie flashes as the vehicle's door is shut. His glasses glint. He pats Josh's shoulder. Sweat breaks out over my skin.

"That...that's him," I whisper. "Him..."

Josh and Doctor Castus walk toward the castle. Castus's hand is firmly on Josh's shoulder. As their footsteps echo into my mind, the sound of anxious buzzing throbs in my ears. The vibrations strangle my throat and prevent me from breathing. My heart pounds so hard, it'll soon break my ribs.

"Storm?"

"I-I don't know—"

The whistle strikes.

My heads spins. I run my fingers through my hair and concave into myself. I try to keep my heart from tearing out of my chest, but the whistle shrills and shoves thousands of needles into my throat. It spreads like an infection through my bones all the way down to my toes. I drown in the needles. My lungs collapse. The artificial light buzzes on my skin. I have to run but my bones crack at the seams. His eyes flash before my own. His dark blue gaze is filled to the brim with an abyss of strange curiosity; its power pins me to that cold and elec-trified chair.

I have to run. I have to—

Someone grabs me. I shrink away and the shaking starts from all the needles transforming into spinning bullets.

I have to run. I have to run but I can't breathe.

The tears won't stop. He whispers to me: *Enough pain will convince you otherwise.* Castus owns my breath now. I'm drowning in his electric gaze. It forces me to go numb.

I am helpless to his will.

THIRTY-TWO
PROMISED INSURANCE
STORM

May 30
Entry #16

My life as of right now has been dedicated to raiding the base. We've set the raid date for June 11, and we'll go to Louisiana afterward to prepare for the next one. We're unsure where the next raid will be after that. Viper has set out to get a job at the base so we can use her as an entry point and an inside source. We're hoping she'll be a janitor, so she'll have a master key for us. Currently, we're thinking of dividing and conquering during the raid. Glacia says the base has tons of information, but not all in one room like the Aurex Facilities. When Viper gets inside, we'll have a clear idea of where everything is. The plan is far from being final.

Naturally, I'm worried that Axl and Josh may interfere. I'm going to push for us to live somewhere else rather than this destroyed home. It's an unsafe location for people like us. The girls need to listen to me on this one. We're not getting found by them like last time, no matter what. If push comes to shove and we encounter Josh or Axl, I may have to do something that will take those two out of the picture. I won't kill them, but I'll have no hesitation paralyzing them by breaking a few legs. Somehow, I'll keep a lookout for them while I'm stuck here. There's nothing else for me to do anyway, except hanging out with Sage and Alo.

Lately I've noticed Hawk has been on edge, but it's not enough for me to suspect the program. It may be that she's feeling the same feeling as I am—worry. Actually, Strike and Viper have been on edge too, but they try not to show it. I don't think it's anything to worry about. We're all stressed. They would tell me if it was something that's program related.

I've tried to write more lately, but until today no train of thought has stuck around for long. I'm not sure what changed for me to write again, to think again. I've been sitting here too long not doing anything, I guess.

I don't want to be the one who drags everyone down with her. The best way to avoid that is by staying busy. Being stagnant won't get me anywhere, but I haven't left the house in two days. The thought of being stuck here, while all the others are out there, while Viper is risking her life for us…It makes me want to scream.

They're worried about me. They said I should

lay low for a while. I was forced to promise that I'll tell the others if I have another terrible feeling or flashbacks, even though I already promised that, but I can't. I shouldn't be complaining about those bad feelings. The others have had worse happen to them. I just had a moment of weakness. Glacia thinks I had a *panic attack*. It started when I saw Doctor Castus while Glacia and I were scouting. It was like I was in the middle of one of my memories. I don't know what came over me to break me down like that.

I don't want to talk about it, but I have to for the sake of figuring things out. This journal is the only insurance I'll ever have. I'll never leave out a single detail, no matter how difficult it will be to think about. I promised myself I wouldn't lie. When I first wrote that, I didn't realize keeping my promise would be so painful. That some of my thoughts would be like smoke in my lungs.

Now I'm more than ready to break into this damn base and steal everything I can. I'll give up a leg or an ear if I have to. I won't let this Doctor Castus guy get to me again. Never again. I have to focus on the raid.

I just hope that one day, when everything has worked out, I won't be a burden.

I want to be stronger than that, than this.

THIRTY-THREE

FROZEN IN TIME

STORM

I smile as Sage copies *Rusty Lockets'* lines into my journal. She tunes me out completely, in the trance of her own work, learning to write. Today is the third lesson, and she's learning dozens of new words. I'm considering getting her a journal of her own soon. Hopefully she'll write her own journal entries one day.

Light footsteps head in our direction. I glance up and Viper appears in the small doorway. She leans her head against the wall.

"Sage? Are you almost done? I need to head out with Viper soon," I say. "We don't have much time to get food."

Sage nods and writes quicker.

"Have Strike and Hawk left already?" Viper asks.

"Yeah. Hawk mentioned something about gettin' a job all the way in Automobile Alley. Strike is with Glacia scouting the base. Is something up?"

"Alo still hasn't stopped throwing up. Flame said he wants to watch Alo's fever so he asked me if you would go out and get the supplies for today."

I hesitate.

"And Alo asked me to tell you to take Sage with you. He

promised her that she would get to see the market for herself today. That cool with you?"

"Yeah, totally." I get to my feet. "Will you be okay getting the food by yourself?"

"I'll manage without you."

I gaze at her for a moment. Viper has dark circles underneath her eyes, and her hair is tousled in every which way. Her face is pale, lips bruised. I walk to my mat in front of Viper, slipping my coat over my wings.

"Are you sure? Or do I need to worry about you falling asleep while walking there?" I ask.

Viper weakly smiles.

"What? Should I?"

"No... No." Viper yawns. "I'll manage. I'm gonna get plenty of rest today. Now I know why there's a rest day on Sunday. People would go nuts if there wasn't."

"Are you tired from shifting? Is it getting to you now, or are you having symptoms?"

Viper flicks her eyes down. "I'll be real with you. The shifting is gettin' tough. It hurts, especially at the end of the day, even when I shift back. But—" Her hair suddenly blooms into a dirty blonde and her eyes a deep brown. "— I'm getting the hang of it." Viper's freckles have vanished, her scars as well, but the dark circles remain.

"Honestly, I don't know how you do it," I reply. "You're incredible really."

Viper shrugs. "Yeah, yeah. I know."

I pick up Hawk's backpack, sliding the money out of it. Grabbing my own pack, I sling it over my back as I look over to Sage.

"Commander? You ready to go?"

"Yeah..." She moves her hand faster.

"C'mon Sage. I'll leave without you if you don't hurry." Sage doesn't move. "I mean, I guess you wanna be stuck here all day with Alo's upchuck."

Sage rushes to her feet and closes the journal. She returns it to my mat, pushing past Viper into her and Alo's room.

"Crazy kid..." Viper trails off.

I slide on my sunglasses and my hat.

"But jeez, she's still the best," Viper goes on.

Viper pauses with her fake eyes on me and removes her head from the wall. Her features return to normal. Her real eyes continue to watch me closely.

"Hey, Storm."

"Yeah?"

"How have you been feelin' lately? Are you sure you're all right to go out today?"

"It's been a week. I'm fine."

Viper crosses her arms. "Are you sure?"

I nod.

"I'm askin' 'cause you still haven't told me what happened. I think you would feel better if you talked about it. So far, the only thing you've said is, 'I don't know what came over me,' and brushed it off."

"You don't need to worry about me. I doubt it'll ever happen again. I promise, if it does, I'll come straight to you."

Viper blinks, but nods very slowly. Sage appears at my side and tugs at my sleeve.

"I better get a move on before Sage has my head. Good luck with getting food today," I say.

"Don't get into much trouble," Viper mutters.

I wave her off, walk up the dusty steps, and slip out of the cellar door with a quiet sigh. I shut the wooden door and face Sage, who's bobbing on her toes. Placing my hand on her back, we walk past mountains of trash cans and dirt bunnies onto the streets. I steer Sage toward the old tower, looming closer to us than ever before. There are no crowds to hide in. The air is thick with a strange humidity. It cloaks my skin to the point where I want to lay down after every step I take, but Sage keeps me moving closer and closer to the marketplace. I clear my throat and turn to Sage. We stop at the first and only intersection of our journey.

"How do you like the new place?" I ask. "It's pretty cool living in a cellar, right?"

Sage beams. "I like it. Alo told me he thinks it used to be for illegal things, though."

"Like what?"

"He said it's not appropriate for me to know, but something about older women and older men. He said, *'You ought to never know that kiddo. Unless we move back to the Isles; then I'll tell you.'"* Sage pauses, her gears grinding, and she turns to me. "Storm, what do you want to be when you're older?"

I blink. "Hm?"

"What do you wanna be when you grow up?" she repeats.

The green light blares in the corner of my vision. I slowly swim past the heat across the rumbling intersection.

"Well, that's not important," I say. "How about you? What kind of doctor do you wanna be?"

"I don't know. Whatever Alo thinks is better."

"You wanna make Alo proud, huh?"

"I sure do."

"Well, I think you already have. You're a smart kid. Real smart. I don't know many people your age, but I think you're pretty mature. Alo sees that too, I bet."

"You think so?"

"I know so. In fact, I think you're ready for a mission."

Sage's eyes widen and her smile grows; it makes the shadows thaw away from us.

I hand over a few dollars. "Let's divide and conquer today. You go find me a super thick cloth for Flame and Glacia." I hand her the rest of the money. "And as a reward, get something extra for yourself after you find the cloth."

"Are you sure? This is a lot of money. Don't you have to buy something too?"

"No. Don't worry about it. I always find a way to get what I want. Now, make sure to meet me by the old tower underneath that line of trees when you're done. Got it?"

"I won't let you down."

I smile as we enter the borders of the marketplace. Life swarms the area. Laughter becomes fragrant in the summer breeze and every beaming face radiates, especially Sage's. I've never seen an expression like hers as we stroll past the rainbows of vendors and crowds. Sage skips away into the glittering crowd. I walk along the edge of the center square. I can't help but smile.

Whenever I close my eyes, I remember exactly where she stood and what words my Boss said. I remember the wondrous smoke that swirled around Curly. Curly's nicknames for me float through my mind and make me laugh to myself. He always made me smile back then. Leaving the open area, I head for the outer edges of the marketplace. I walk past piles of old antiques stacked high, glimmering in the sun. That area beckons me. I freeze to the cement as I stare at the maze, tracing a finger along the thick scar on my cheek.

I look away, wondering if Bub still runs it, and continue on for my search for a free rope. The one that catches my attention is attached to a vendor's black horse. The vendor is a man in old sweatpants selling seashells. He's asleep with shells lined up in front of him. A sign reads, *Authentic See Shells* in dribbling black ink on faded cardboard. The horse has been tied off to the lamppost. I study the rope and decide that it's long enough for Glacia to use.

I check my surroundings for any officers, finding none. Then I check for any witnesses, finding only a few. Since the man is asleep, I doubt there will be much resistance. He's leaning against the lamppost, right underneath the rope, and he's surrounded by his personal items, mainly cans. I'll have to sneak behind the lamppost to get to the rope.

I creep to his side, stepping over the plastic bags full of cans. The horse huffs at my sudden appearance. I brush my hand over her snout to keep her quiet. The horse calms down. I untie the rope from her bridle and wrap my new rope into a loop. The horse moves away from the lamppost, walking right through a patch of cans next to her owner. The man's head jolts up.

"Hey!"

I take off straight through the cans. The man screams while chasing after me. I push past pedestrians as his screams get further away. My heart pulls away from my chest as I zip toward the meeting spot. With the adrenaline still fueling my legs, I rush up to Sage, who's holding a new sack of goodies. The man's screams are still audible in the distance.

"Storm?"

"Jump on my back!"

Sage hurls herself onto my back. I sprint past the grove of trees into the crowds. And once the furious cries of the vendor fade; Sage's contagious laughter replaces it. It overcomes the humidity. It's as if every blurry face of this city listens to her. Every cold splotch soaks her up to have color for a fleeting moment.

I will always love having her laughter in my life, and I can feel the jealousy of every stranger we rush past. We share the laughter together. I run all the way home. When we reach the cellar door, Sage asks me to run around the block again. Although my lungs are straining, I do it. I run as fast as I can. I run faster and faster. I leap, twirl, and skip just to fuel her laughter more. I'll never get tired of it.

Sage and I finally reach the cellar doors at the end of the alley. She jumps off my back and I open the door to our home.

"Glad we got away, huh?" I ask. Sage and I step past the wooden frame.

"You coulda taken him. He was scary, but I know you coulda. I'm glad he didn't catch up with us. I didn't want him to steal this camera."

Sage pulls out the camera like a trophy. My eyes widen as the smell of roasting beans fills the air. I glance over and see Flame heating up a can of beans in his glowing palm. Alo is at his side, wrapped in a blanket with a pale complexion. Everyone sits at the makeshift table, a blanket on the floor with empty cans ready to be filled.

"Are y'all eating without us?" I ask.

"We were hungry," Hawk replies and looks at me. "Why are you all sweaty?"

Sage and I exchange a glance. "We just got into a bit of a rush, but look what Sage found!"

Sage holds up the camera with a triumphant grin, and everyone flocks toward her. Glacia is the first to examine the camera.

"How much did this cost? Did you use all the money?" Glacia asks. "'Cause we're on a budget here."

"C'mon G," Hawk says. "It's cool. I booked me and Strike a job today. No harm in an impulse buy."

"Yeah! We might as well take a picture now," Flame says. "I'll set it up." He snatches the camera from Glacia, setting packs against the wall to hold it.

We huddle around each other behind the table, and I make sure to take off my sunglasses. Glacia tells me to let my hair down. I stand in the sandwich of Hawk, Strike, Viper, and Glacia. Alo sits in the front with Sage in his lap. Flame clicks a button, runs to us, and sits next to Alo as he pushes his blond hair back.

There's a moment of stillness, a waiting. A light flashes, blinding me for a second. It fades as the camera cranks out a glossy slip.

"Can I stop smiling?" Alo asks.

"Yup," Strike says. "Now, let's eat! I'm starving!"

We disperse. I volunteer to keep the picture safe while Strike offers to hold onto the camera. Taking the picture, I pull out my journal from my pack. I gaze at the developing picture of everyone. Viper's eyes and mine are bright, more so than everyone else's. Everyone's scars are there, but it isn't the focus. The picture has dim lighting, but we all have beaming smiles. Not a care in the world. The picture is an everlasting but fleeting moment.

I write the date on the back of the picture and slide it between the pages of the journal. My eyes linger there a second longer. I smile and flip the wonderful page to a blank one before placing my pen to the paper. I write: *Things do get better*.

THIRTY-FOUR
WHITE LIES
STORM

June 11
Entry #18

Operation Oklahoma City has officially started. Well, it started this morning. Right now, I'm waiting to head out, waiting for the sun to set. Instead of letting myself pace around the cellar, I thought it would be a good idea to write out the plan and review it. We could use the details of it for future raids. I have a feeling there are many more to come.

Operation Oklahoma City
Phase #1:

- Viper will unlock one of the windows during her shift, steal the keys to all the informational rooms, and destroy all records of herself at the base.

- These informational rooms hold computers with databases, according to Glacia and Viper. To be time-efficient, we'll spread out to the three rooms and look up keywords in certain sections of the database, then print them all off. Someone doing it all at once with one printer would take way too much time. We will comb through the documents after the raid and see if there is anything valuable.
- The Keywords: Everyone's tattoos, including Flame and Glacia, Castus, Inman, Chaperone, Montana, and RM Metal.

Phase #2:

- Once it's night, Hawk will fly Viper to the unlocked window where they'll head inside and shut off all alarms and cameras. Hawk will take the first key into the first informational room while Viper goes back to the window and signals to Strike and me. Hawk will search the archive section.

Phase #3:

- Strike and I will fly to the roof to get inside. I'll head for the second informational room and meet Viper there to let me in the room, where I'll type in the keywords into the recent section.
- While I'm doing this, Strike will take

the third key and go to the third room.
She'll search in the history section.

Phase #4:

- Viper will run to the garage to open the
  doors for Flame and Glacia, who'll have
  the car ready. Hawk, Strike, and I will
  head to the garage and we'll head home to
  pick up Alo and Sage. From there, we'll
  drive for Roadie's Trading Post in
  Shawnee, get everything we need, and head
  for Louisiana on new wheels.

The Side-Phase:

- While Phases #1-4 are happening and after
  Viper's signal, Glacia and Flame will
  climb the barbed wire fence using
  Glacia's fancy rope and cloth trick, to
  avoid injury before taking out the guards
  at the gate and hot-wiring the car. Those
  two have a lot cut out for them. But I
  trust them.

Note: Avoid the night guards at all costs and
stay focused.

I'll make sure to write out everything we find
in the documents. Hopefully we'll get something
groundbreaking. Hopefully.

"STORM? ARE YOU READY?" Hawk asks.

"Yeah, I am."

I shut my journal, shoving it in my backpack. Getting to my feet, I strap the backpack around my shoulders and slip my hair into a tail. I wrap my purple scarf around my neck.

Glacia and Flame have already left. The four of us remain and form an interlocking huddle. We bring our heads so close that our heartbeats sync. There's a deep silence among us as we listen to our own breathing.

"We can do this," I whisper. "After this...After we get this information, we'll be one step closer to beating the program. Promise me we all come back from this. We stick to the plan."

"I promise," Hawk says. "Nobody gets left behind. Okay? Nobody. We've got this."

"I promise," Strike replies. "And nobody gets hurt. I'll make sure to protect all of you; I'll give you all I got."

"I promise too," Viper says. "Nobody doubt themselves either. We're capable people. Don't forget that."

"And I promise to always fight for all of you, no matter what," I say. "Now, let's go."

We disperse to the rickety steps leading up to the cellar door. I throw it open and shoot out of it, down the alleyway, to the sidewalk. The night air is humid, the streets sparse with life, and the moonlight is a spotlight on each of us. Our hurried steps echo between the grimy skyscrapers and murky alleyways. All is silent, like the stillness before a storm.

Strike and I break away from Hawk and Viper, running to a small building across from the unlocked window. Its highest point is a few floors above the base's roof. We scramble into the alleyway and I leap onto a garbage bin. I rocket up, grasping the fire escape, and hoist myself up onto the ladder. As I climb up, Strike follows my lead.

Once on the roof, we kneel behind a small concrete wall. A few minutes later, Hawk and Viper glide through the air and stop at the window. Hawk suspends in the air as Viper opens the window for her. They disappear into the darkness, leaving us to wait. Strike leans her head closer to me. She hesitates.

"Something up?" I whisper.

"You should know something before we go in there. It's about Hawk, Viper, and me."

I don't say anything.

"Our programs have been more active ever since your flashback with Glacia, and it's gotten worse since we finalized the plan. Hawk asked me and Viper not to tell you, but I can't do that anymore."

Are you kidding me?

I sigh. "How bad is it?"

"Just more whispers saying that this is a mistake, a betrayal of some sort. A betrayal to maybe the Doctors? But Hawk and Viper had a few new memories about that day, about all the bodies."

Why wouldn't they tell me? They promised. A heat rises in my throat, a yell, but I breathe out to stop it.

"Why not tell me, then?"

"We were worried about you. We didn't want anything to bubble up in you. But just know, there's more to that day, Storm. Way more to it." Her voice trembles. "And I wish I told you everything that happened...recently, but I'm telling you now in case something happens when we're in there."

Why are they so worried about me? I'm fine! What if something happened, and I didn't know about this?

"In the car ride to Shawnee, I'll talk to Hawk about it. I'll write everything down for y'all," I say. "Thank you for telling me."

They broke the promise. We were supposed to be honest, but why?

"Are you angry?" Strike asks.

"I don't have time to be angry right now. Focus. Right now—" I take the scarf and put it up to my nose. "—we have bigger things to do. Do me a favor and stop thinking about it."

"Yeah...Of course," Strike murmurs. "Sorry. It's just that I re—"

She cuts herself off when a small light glints rapidly from the window—the signal. Strike brings her red bandana to her nose and pulls her blue hood nearly over her eyes. Exchanging a nod, we step up on the ledge and I hand my pack over to Strike as I spread my wings. I grasp her wrist; she does the same to mine. The night wind makes us sway along the edge. Strike's palms tremble.

"Do you trust me?" I ask.

Strike nods.

We leap off the ledge. My wings catch the wind and carry us downward to the spiked roof. Strike hits the ground first, rolling on impact. I land a few feet in front of her. She throws me the pack as we sprint to the metal door. I get to the handle first, but it doesn't budge. I try again by shaking it. Nothing. Strike ushers me away. She takes a step back.

Shink.

Strike's upper blade flashes and the handle flies off the door. She kicks the door open.

"What the hell!" A voice booms from the inside.

A massive night guard appears in the doorway. Strike bolts forward. As he reaches for his gun, Strike slides between his legs to get behind him. She jumps up and connects her foot with the back of his head. The night guard stumbles forward, his head down. I spring at him, pressing my elbows into his shoulder blades as I drive my knee into his face. The night guard collapses. His nose is now a bloody mess. I walk to Strike, breathing heavily, and close the door.

I bound down the stairs, stopping at a door labeled *Floor 11.* Cracking it open, I peer into a hallway smeared with moonlight. Its wooden walls shine in a ghostly manner. There's no one in sight. I lead Strike down the lengthy corridor with an elevator at the end.

Bing.

The elevator doors open, and a flood of white light trumps the moonlight. Viper stands in the open doorway. The light disappears as she runs to us. She beckons me over and stops at the only metal door, where she slides a small card into the door handle. The door swings open. Viper and Strike run back to the elevator, wishing me good luck along the way. The doors briefly provide another spout of light, but it vanishes with Strike and Viper. I'm left alone to fulfill my work.

The information room is empty except for a thin screen jutting out of the ceiling. On either side of the room there are cameras eyeing me, but they have been turned off. The screen is transparent. When I approach it, a thick, white light illuminates the stainless room. On the screen, the words *Database Search* appear. As instructed by Glacia, I press my finger to the screen and an array of blue letters unfold below the Database Search. I type in the keywords from the recent section. A slew of titles zap onto the screen and I briefly scan them over. There are around ten documents. Hopefully all of them will be valuable. With a few taps of my fingertips, a box pops up with the word *Printing* in it. I hear the sliding of paper, cranking, and blotting of ink in another room. Leaving the room, I prowl toward the printing sounds.

Moonlight cascades past the spotless windows and lights up the hallway. No shadows are there to conceal my presence. Suddenly the thuds of footsteps rush down the staircase. The door flies open in a blur. The night guard's face is bloody, eyes rabid. He holds a gun pointing directly at me.

"Hey!"

Shit.

I slam into the nearest door and take cover in the room. There's a row of windows with piercing moonlight and a long table in the center. No place to hide. I wedge myself between the open door and wall. The night guard thunders down the hall before stopping at the door. I hold my breath and press my hands against the door. The night guard inches into the doorway; his heavy breath fills my ears and I watch the edge of the door...Waiting...The barrel of the pistol appears. I ram the door into him. He stumbles sideways. I flash forward, aiming a fist at—

Wham!

Something collides with my forehead. I fly onto the table. My vision blurs. Blood pools into my left eye. Someone grabs my neck and rips me away from the table to my knees. I look up. The end of a pistol greets me.

"Put your hands up!"

I do so. My vision slowly focuses as the night guard holsters his gun and reaches for a pair of cuffs. The tips of my nails beg to be unsheathed.

"You are under arrest for trespassing and assault. Now, slowly hold out your wrists."

The cuffs dangle from his palms as I carefully lower my wrists. My claws shoot out. I dart my head to the side and jolt forward. I slash at his face. Another to his shoulder. As the night guard stumbles back, he attempts to draw his gun. Ducking, I grab the gun. I strike my boot between his legs, then rip the gun away from his stomach. Stepping back from him, I place my finger on the trigger. He stares up at me, wincing, barely able to catch his breath.

"Who the hell are you!?" The night guard raises his hands.

"Cuff yourself to the table. Now!"

The night guard cuffs himself to the table leg and remains on his knees. He keeps his eyes on me the entire time. I swear he doesn't blink.

"You won't get away with thi—"

Wham!

I cut him off with a whip of the pistol straight to his temple. He slumps to the ground. I'm sure this time he'll stay knocked out.

I leave the room and shut the door. The sounds of printing have ceased, and I stumble to where the source came from. I enter the room and leave the pistol on top of the printer as I take all ten documents. Packing the papers away, I rush out the door down the hall. I press the button to the elevator and tap my foot as the blue numbers, on its frame, count upwards.

Bing.

A flood of white light reappears and I enter it. The room buzzes with the foggy light, increasing the throbbing in my head. I press the button to the garage, and the elevator descends. I hold my head in my hands, wiping away as much blood as possible, but it smears more. The wound is tender. Bile rises in my throat from touching it. My head spins at the thought of it. I lean my back against the wall, trying to regain my balance, but the doors slide open before I can ground myself. I stumble out into the hallway and find Hawk and Strike watching a closed door. Hawk looks over at me. Her eyes widen. She takes her blue cloth from her lips.

"What the hell happened?" Hawk whispers.

"Yeah, are you okay?" Strike adds.

I nod as I walk to them and settle my shoulder against the wall. Before I can catch my breath, the door whips open. Viper appears and rips the green cloth from her face. Her cheeks are flushed red, breath heaving, and she beckons us with her hand. We run straight for a humming truck in the center of hundreds of cars. Hawk rips open the door. The four of us pile in. Glacia is at the wheel with Flame in the passenger's seat. The wheels screech, and we zoom out of the garage past the open gate.

My head churns as Glacia speeds through the empty streets. Viper is still breathing excessively. Hawk is meticulously wrapping my head with her blue cloth. Strike stares out the back window. All the while, Flame is holding a bruising cheek from a squabble with a night guard. Despite the consequences of the raid on my body, I find myself smiling. The weight of the pack makes me feel lighter than air. We did it again.

My smile fades, however. A heat simmers in my stomach when the car stops. Flame volunteers to run inside to grab Alo and Sage.

"Are you sure you're okay?" Hawk asks. "You look pale." She pulls a few strands of loose hair away from my wound.

The heat rises up to my chest. I could ask her the same thing. I could ask how managing her symptoms is going, how she managed to do it during the raid. I could ask Viper too. I could ask why they think it's okay to break promises.

"I think she's concussed," Strike says.

"No, I'm just a bit confused."

"Dizzy?" Hawk asks.

I breathe the heat away. "Confused."

"What do you mea—"

"Get in here right now!" Flame screams.

Stumbling out of the car, I sprint for the cellar doors. I leap past the stairs, past Flame, and I'm met with the wreckage that used to be our home. Alo is leaning against the far wall. Blood coats his entire face. His head is buried in his shaking palms. I run to him and kneel, placing my hand on his shoulder. Alo shifts his head to me, and tears stream past the blood on his cheeks. I look away from him, around the room, as everyone comes to Alo's aid. The torn walls, upside-down chairs, and scuffed floor are empty. Lifeless.

"Alo! What happened?" Viper exclaims

Alo's lips tremble as he raises his head. He clenches his teeth while running his sticky fingers through his hair.

"They took her. They took Sage," Alo whispers. "I couldn't... couldn't do anything. They, Josh and Axl, came out of nowhere. I don't know how they found us. I couldn't stop...I couldn't stop them."

My heart plummets to my now boiling stomach.

Alo tries to wipe the tears away. "If we want her back, Hawk, Strike, Viper, and Storm have to turn themselves in peacefully, at dawn, on top of the old tower."

My fists clench, my throat burns, and I close my eyes. The heat spreads from my chest all the way up to my ears. I keep my fist on Alo's shoulder as the silence vibrates throughout the tattered room.

"What the hell are we going to do...?" Glacia trails off.

"Not we," Hawk says. "Me, Strike, Viper, and Storm. We're what they want. We'll...We'll...I don't know what we'll do."

"Turn ourselves in?" Strike asks.

"We can't. I'm not doin' that," Viper says. "I'm not letting the program win that easy."

"Then what are we supposed to do?" Strike snaps. "This is Sage we're talking about! We don't know what they'll do to her if we don't turn ourselves in!"

"I know! I know!" Viper growls. "I don't know what to do either!"

All of us sit in thought. My fists shake as the heat travels down my spine.

"We fight," I say through clenched teeth. "I say we fight for her."

"We can help you," Flame whispers. "Let us help you. Let's figure this out together."

Glacia stands. "Yeah, I'm not leaving y'all behind. It's our fight now too."

"I don't want any of you getting hurt because of us," Hawk says. "None of you are coming up there with us. It's our fault they're here."

"Yeah," I reply. "Y'all will wait for us with the car. We'll get Sage and fly down to you. Then we'll get the hell outta here." I get to my feet, facing Hawk, Strike, and Viper. "Be ready to fight at dawn."

I'll be ready.

THIRTY-FIVE

SILENCE

STORM

It's currently twilight. I'm the only one awake. I'm always the only one awake. But this time I have a reason…a good reason. The raid didn't go as planned. At least not until the very end. We got everything we need, but we haven't even touched the documents. All we've done since is plan how to get Sage back. They only went to sleep when we finished the plan. I still can't.

I don't know about this at all. It's a plan. But I'm worried that Axl or Josh will go after Alo, Flame, or Glacia. The thing I know for sure is that Sage isn't in any danger. They want us, not her. And if I've learned anything, it's that I'm sure I have those two figured out. I even looked back at old entries about them. Josh is out for revenge, but he doesn't want to kill anyone. Axl carries an unloaded gun, doesn't engage in hand-to-hand combat often, and never laid a finger on Glacia in the prison, even though he seemed furious at her. The only time I've seen Josh and Axl violent is toward the four of us, and I'm sure if we're there, their violent trend toward us will continue.

It has to; that's what we're betting on. Our plan is good because nobody gets hurt in it. We'll be fighting the right way. What we're going to do is act like we're going to surrender, wait for Josh and Axl to lower their guard, and then attack. Give it all we've got to get Sage back. Once we get Sage, we'll fly down to the old house where Glacia, Flame, and Alo will be waiting with the car. We'll drive to the Trading Post, then to Louisiana. It'll work. It has to. I promised that...

THE INK FAILS ME. I stare at the shaking pen. I slowly set it and the journal down, only to focus on my shaking palms. The weak moon-light peers past the cellar doors. Its rays crawl on my tattoo, on all my scars, and provide no warmth. All it provides is the illumination of another life, another person entirely. Possibly a person without a heart or a mind of her own. I slip my forearm underneath my legs to conceal the scars and press my head to my knees.

I won't be that person. I'll never be that person.

Someone sits by my side, resting their palm on the back of my head. Their fingers swirl in my hair. I move my head and look up at Hawk. I doubt she's slept either.

"What are you thinking about?" Hawk murmurs as she slips her hand away.

"Nothing," I whisper.

We are silent. I keep my eyes on hers; she looks away at her fingers.

"Hawk," I mutter. "You know, I'm so lucky I have all of you and that we've stuck together like we have."

"Yeah, I feel the same way."

"And we're honest with each other." I pause. "I've been thinking about everything. The raids, the attacks, the Doctors, the Brute, the Goon, and now Sage. We've gotten through it by talking to each other."

Hawk runs her fingers through her hair. "Strike mentioned that she told you about us keeping things from you. Are you mad at me?"

I don't answer.

"I can explain. I swear I can. I just..." Hawk whispers. "Viper didn't want you to know because she was afraid you would treat her different. Strike didn't want you to know because she was worried you would watch her all the time. We were going to tell you. We really were. After the raid."

"Why didn't you want me to know?"

"I didn't because I wanted you to be focused on the raid. I didn't want your mind to get too crowded. We needed you to have a clear mind for this; that's when you do your best. Don't be mad at the others, please. It was my idea."

"How long has this been going on?" I ask.

I already know that it's been a few weeks.

"For a few weeks. When we finalized the plans, it got worse. Are you mad?"

"My first thought was to yell at Strike when she told me, because what if it took control of one of you during the raid? I would be caught off guard."

"I get that."

"I would read minds if I could, but I can't Hawk. No matter how long I spend time with all of you, especially you, I'll never be able to read your minds. So next time, tell me. I can help. I'm not that helpless."

"Okay, I can do that. But if you ever feel panicked again, you'll tell me, right?"

"That was almost two weeks ago."

"Time doesn't age things like that," Hawk whispers. "We were all scared. I've never seen you so...so..."

"Helpless?"

"I guess you could say that. And I never want to see you like that again. I guess it's like how you feel about us..." Her lips part slightly. "Oh."

"I feel helpless when I don't know."

We are silent again. I have been overly concerned, but I have to be. Hawk has a point though; they all do. I treat them differently when they act out. I bet it makes them feel like wild animals, like people are just waiting for them to lash out.

I sigh. "Let's forget this happened and be more honest in the future." I get to my feet and hold my hand out for her. "Now, help me get the others up?"

Hawk takes it.

I try to slip my hand away, but Hawk grips it. She brings me in and wraps both arms around me. I do the same. Her heart pounds against my chest. Her breath is shaky. Once we finish, I walk over to nudge Viper awake while Hawk does the same for Strike. Viper springs up and immediately packs her bag. We all follow her lead. Our shuffling causes the others to wake as well. I hand my bag off to Alo, who embraces it tightly. Hawk leaves her bag with Flame. Strike and Viper leave theirs with Glacia. And after a few looks among the four of us, Hawk, Strike, Viper, and I walk toward the cellar doors.

"All of you be careful," Glacia says. "I'm not breaking the four of you out of prison again."

There's a tiny bit of laughter, the kind that only comes after guarded silence. We say our goodbyes to Glacia, Flame, and Alo. I promise them I'll see them soon, with Sage, as I push past the cellar doors into the cold night.

We take off to the street and split into pairs. I stop in the center of the dead street. Since the streetlights are all off, it's up to Viper and me to guide Hawk and Strike through the night. Strike joins my side and grabs my hand. I squeeze her fingers as I flip out my wings. Hawk and Viper sprint down the street and eventually catch wind, becoming airborne. We spring forward down the tough tar. As I gain speed, my wings flow away from my back. I leap into the air and grasp her waist. I glide through the rushing of buildings, following Hawk's lead by beating my wings frantically to gain elevation. As I do, the old tower grows and grows, like I'll never reach the top of it.

The tower partially conceals the weakening moonlight. The only light able to come through is between the tower's jagged gash at the top. It's dripping in cold shadows like a stain on the skyline. No matter how hard nature tries, it will never disappear.

I rise to the torn edges of the tower. The sun replaces the moon, but the sunlight is only a thin yellow line. The rest of the sky contains the darkest hues of blue, red, green, and purple; they overpower the yellow light as if it were water being diluted by an oily poison. Those few rays illuminate the cracked windows of the tower, the twisted copper and torn iron, and three figures sitting on the very edge of the dismantled side.

Hawk swoops down to the stable side of the tower. Wind screeches in my ears as I angle my wings down. Hawk and Viper land before me, and just as they do, I flip my wings back and Strike and I land. I rise up with my fists already clenching. My teeth grit to near the breaking point.

Sage's eyes flood with tears. She's trembling violently on her knees with a yellow cloth over her mouth and cuffs forcing her wrists together. A rusted revolver presses against her temple; its carrier is the man in the blue tracksuit, the Goon, Axl Emil. Beside Axl is Joshua West, and he's holding four silver collars. He's itching to clamp them around our necks.

"I'm glad you guys can tell the time," Axl replies. "I was worried we would, well, take good care of this one. Her name is Sage, right?"

Axl grabs the back of Sage's neck and forces her to her feet. I tense up but hold myself back. The wind picks up and whips against our bodies, making everyone off-balanced.

"It would be a tragedy to let someone so young...well...you know...don't you all think? So, here's what's gonna go down. Trainee West will put those collars in the center, leave, and all of you will put them on at the same time. Is that clear? If you don't—" Axl presses the gun harder against Sage's skull. "—things will get messy."

I narrow my eyes. When I try to listen to Axl's heartbeat, the rushing wind blocks me. I know the revolver isn't loaded. The revolver isn't loaded. It's not like Axl would do that. He's bluffing. She's fine.

I take a deep breath as Josh creeps forward with his hollow eyes fixed on us. He sets the collars down one by one, then steps back to Axl's side. Cold wind settles on the tower. In the distance, a dark horizon begins to form among the last golden rays.

"We don't have all day," Josh snaps. "Get on with it."

Hawk is the first to step forward, then Strike, Viper, and myself. I pick up the metal collar and stare it down as if I'm at gunpoint.

We'll get Sage back. I'll get her back.

I flick my eyes between the girls and back to Sage's misty ones. Giving her a slight nod, my hands tighten on the collar.

"Get on with it!" Josh yells.

I hurl my collar at Josh and throw myself forward. My sights set on saving Sage and—

Bang!

Blood cascades into the remaining golden rays before everything is consumed by the dark horizon. Sage lays in her own blood with her eyes fogging over and mouth gaping in a silent cry for help. Axl and Josh lurch back. Axl drops the rusted revolver. They are frozen with mouths wide open.

I go numb.

My ears ring, hands shake, and a scream gurgles in my throat. The blades shoot out of me. I bolt forward, blades extending, and ram them into Axl's shoulders. Gravity takes ahold of us as Axl loses his footing. We plummet off the tower toward the grove of pink trees.

Axl cries out. We lock eyes as the world slows into a blur around us. Axl's blue eyes bleed with a sudden realization. His eyes bleed out his entire life for him. Tears bleed into the air.

Axl screams louder as our speed picks up. I flip out my wings. "Wait!" Axl screams.

A tear splatters across my cheek. I'm unsure if it's mine or his. "*Wait!*"

I sheathe my blades from Axl's shoulders, leaving his blood on my hands. I let go, fly away, and Axl vanishes in a cloud of pink buds. The petals shoot into the air. They weren't sturdy enough to catch him.

I cover my eyes from the sight of broken branches. I beat my wings furiously to return to the top of the crumbling tower. Once I reach it, I find Josh's unconscious body underneath Strike's powerful boot. I find Sage still bleeding. Hawk is pale, standing where I left her, and Viper is at Sage's side. Everyone is silent.

"We have to go!" I yell. "We have to go now!"

I run to the center, past Sage, and grab one of the collars, looping it onto my belt. I grab Strike's wrist, but she doesn't budge.

"You...you didn't keep your promise." Strike rips her hand away from mine. "Why wouldn't you keep your promise?" She trembles. "You promised nobody would get hurt again."

"We have to go," I say. "C'mon, we don't know what's coming next. We have to go."

"What about Sage...?" Viper trails off.

I look back at the pool of blood; she's still bleeding. Axl is gone.

"We're not leaving her here Storm," Viper says through her teeth.

"Then take her. Take her with us."

I pull Strike along with me as I grab Hawk by the shoulder. I shake Hawk enough to get her to flip her wings out, but no words leave her lips. Instead, Hawk walks to Viper, who now holds Sage's limp body and they lock hands. I do the same with Strike. We leap from the torn edges of the tower, sailing past the broken pink buds.

Axl is still gone. I can't see him. Sage is still bleeding. I'm still numb. Everything is silent. Warm blood drips from my hands onto Strike's arm. Cold wind whispers in my ears. Dark horizons encase the city as our shadows drape on the streets below. We reach where the others await Sage's arrival, but Sage's skull continues leaking blood.

Hawk swoops and lands. I do the same. The truck is parked outside of our old home. Glacia, Flame, and Alo jump out of the car. Alo cries out and runs to Viper and Sage. Glacia and Flame yell, asking what happened, but only Strike can provide the answers. Hawk, Viper, and I sit in silence. Everyone crowds around Sage's body. I stand behind as a chill hits me in the back. I flick my fingers.

Axl is dead. I killed him. Sage is dead and it's my fault. I was wrong all along; things don't get any better.

Everyone turns into blurs. I hope they leave me to shatter in the dust and blood on my hands. Someone tugs at my sleeve. My ears ring with his final screams, with a gunshot, and with the roars of a thousand beings. The numbness consumes me. I don't dare move.

I am helpless. There is nothing left for me but the silence.

ACKNOWLEDGMENTS

First, I'd like to thank my parents for supporting me in this project. They allowed me to fill my summers with it, rather than getting a typical summer job.

I'd also like to thank my editors, proofreaders, and formatters at Three Point Author Services for helping me improve my story and for giving me, a first time author, advice on the publishing business and how to navigate it. Without Breann, Michele, and Andrea's help, I would have been very overwhelmed.

A big thank you to Evan Cakamurenssen for creating a wonderful and beautiful cover, I'll cherish it for a long time.

Thanks to all my friends: Mal, Josie M, Michael, Megan, Josie C, Viv, Elliot, Katie, Gracie, Ellie, Meg, and Julia (my dear twin sister) for putting up with me being a hermit for the past two years. I appreciate your patience.

Also, thank you to my family as well. You've all supported and encouraged me in this endeavor.

Last but not least, I want to thank the woman this book is dedicated to. Grandma, you have been with this story since day one and have always pushed me to keep writing. Without you this story wouldn't exist, and I'm so excited for you to finally get a hard copy. There's so many more stories I want to write because of you. And I promise I will write all of them.

ABOUT THE AUTHOR

Emma Love is a college student studying English at the University of St. Andrews. She's an Oklahoma native that has been writing longer than she remembers. The Chronicles: Dark Horizons is her debut novel, and she plans to write many more stories.

To learn about new projects and updates, visit Emma on the following social media channels:

Facebook
Instagram
Twitter
VSCO
Tumblr

Made in the USA
Coppell, TX
06 November 2019